Where This Road Ends

Rebekah Colburn

Books by Rebekah Colburn

<u>Of Wind and Sky</u>
Through Every Valley
The Whisper of Dawn
As Eagles Soar

<u>My Brother's Flag</u>
On Grounds of Honor
For the Cause of Freedom

From Fields of Promise

<u>Ridgely Rails Legacy</u>
Where This Road Ends
Along the Way
A Passing Mist

Where This Road Ends

by

REBEKAH COLBURN

Where This Road Ends
Copyright © 2018
Rebekah Colburn

Cover Design by Jody Christian, Christian Graphic Solutions

Scripture quotations are taken from the NKJV, New King James Version of the Bible. Copyright © 1982 by Thomas Nelson.

This is a work of historical fiction; the appearances of certain historical figures are therefore inevitable. All other characters, however, are products of the author's imagination, and any resemblance to actual persons, living or dead, is coincidental.

Dedicated to Leroy & Mary
for everything

In their hearts humans plan their course,
but the LORD establishes their steps.

Proverbs 16:9

Prologue

*I*f she fixed her gaze on the view immediately beyond the window, the speed of the train distorted the details of green shrubs and wooden fences turning them into an indistinguishable blur. But when Ella Mae stared farther out into the distance, acres of peach orchards and fields of berries came into focus. Above them a golden sun situated in a swathe of blue, broken only by occasional tufts of white, completed the vista.

As the train carried Ella Mae eastward, the rolling hills had leveled out and fields of yellow corn and wheat had given way to a sprawling panorama of ripening produce. The distance between towns and hamlets grew longer and the city faded into hazy memory. She was almost home.

Like a heavy woolen shawl, the weight of melancholy lay across her shoulders. The sun-soaked fields shimmered as tears glazed her eyes and the view once again slipped out of focus.

The miles raced by, one much like the other, until the landscape was suddenly broken by a jagged line of factory buildings. Announcing its intentions with the hiss of brakes and the screech of wheel on rail, the train slowed to a crawl before finally heaving a sigh as it stopped in front of the Ridgely Train Station.

On the platform stood those waiting for the passengers to disembark, either to welcome them or to take their place on the railcar. Ella Mae scanned the row of faces through the grimy window in search of her father, finally spotting him standing off to the right of the station.

Clutching her reticule in one hand, Ella Mae lifted her skirt with the other as she stepped down. Her father's leathery skin creased into a smile as he covered the distance to her side, the action not quite reaching his eyes. He squeezed her arm gently in greeting as he requested her luggage ticket.

A lump grew in her throat as he sought out the porter to claim her trunks. Apart from a new wardrobe and a soiled name, Ella Mae was returning home as empty-handed as she had left ten years before.

How had all her hopes and dreams come to this?

Part One

"We all have our own life to pursue
Our own kind of dream to be weaving ...
And we all have the power
To make wishes come true
As long as we keep believing."
-- Louisa May Alcott

Chapter One

New Year's Eve, 1886
Ridgely, Maryland

"Where do you see your life in five years, Ella Mae?" Daniel asked, his dark eyebrows raised as he challenged her to peer into the shifting shadows of the future.

She blushed, unable to answer with the truth. In her imaginings she was married to him, and instead of being seated in front of her father's fireplace, they sat hand in hand in front of their own with a child on each of their knees.

She was only sixteen. Five years seemed such a long way off.

The greenery of pine boughs still decorated the mantle, brightened by a sprig of holly berries. The colors matched the plaid of the bustled dress she wore. Ella Mae watched as the flames danced within the brick fireplace, the logs crackling and popping as they were consumed. "I hope I'll be married by then," was all she dared to verbalize. "What about you?"

Daniel's even white teeth flashed in a grin that never failed to make her heart skip a beat. "I'll be rich and famous with a beautiful European wife, living in a mansion in a faraway city."

He loved to make jokes, but the jest had a sharp edge to it. Daniel didn't think she was suitable to be his wife, to fit into the life he had planned for himself. She was a farmer's daughter and he was the son of a merchant with great aspirations. Two years her senior, he was handsome enough to charm any woman he desired.

Ella Mae pushed down the rising fear of losing him and instead took hold of the moment. He was with her tonight.

"You'll be married to that swine farmer," Daniel continued his prognostication. "You know the one who lives on the edge of town, the one with the pockmarked skin and greasy hair?" He chuckled at the horror that crept into her expression at the idea.

"Oh! You're incorrigible!" Ella Mae swatted him playfully, feeling the solid muscle beneath his black coat. He chortled in satisfaction at her response, and Ella Mae donned a scowl. "You really are a scoundrel, Daniel Evans—a black-hearted villain."

"Ah, but it's one of the things you love about me," he retorted flippantly.

"You'd like to think," she replied.

He grinned. "Among many," he added, winking roguishly. Ella Mae felt her insides weaken, even though she knew he was only teasing.

"You are both arrogant and tiresome," she informed him, smothering a yawn. "We have half an hour until midnight. What shall we do to pass the time?"

"Sing with me," he answered. Then he promptly burst out: *"God rest ye merry gentleman, let nothing you dismay..."*

Smiling, Ella Mae joined in, her contralto voice mingling with his bass in a pleasing sound.

"What was in that punch?" her mother demanded as she entered the room, making a show of sniffing the contents of their empty glasses. She was quite used to their antics and smiled indulgently.

"Mr. Evans, as soon as the clock strikes the hour I'm afraid I must send you on your way. An old woman needs her sleep."

A regular visitor at the Hutchins house, Daniel was accustomed to being treated more like a member of the family than a guest. "Yes ma'am," he answered dutifully. "I shouldn't want to keep Ella Mae from her beauty rest, either. She's in dire need of it."

"Oh, get out right this minute!" Ella Mae swatted him again, and his robust laughter filled the room.

"Not much of a gentleman, is he?" Mrs. Hutchins teased, collecting the glasses and empty cookie platter before taking her leave.

"No, he certainly isn't."

Ignoring her, Daniel linked his arm through hers and launched once again into song. "*We three kings of orient are...*"

Ella Mae couldn't stifle the smile that came to her lips. Leaning her shoulder into his, she felt the warmth of him through his coat jacket and her woolen dress. She surrendered to the moment, belting out the next line of the hymn: "*bearing gifts we've traveled so far...*"

They were struggling to recall the lines of the third verse when the bell gonged the midnight hour and ushered in the new year: 1887.

"Happy New Year, Ella Mae," Daniel pronounced. A large bell rested on the whatnot table nearby, and he took it in his hand, ringing it vigorously to symbolize the victory of good over evil in the coming year.

"Happy New Year," she echoed, wincing at the clatter.

Daniel grabbed her hand and drew Ella Mae to her feet, placing one hand on her waist and spinning her around the room in a dizzying jig. He sang as he twirled her, in a wild and boisterous fashion: "*Should old acquaintance be forgot, and never brought to mind? Should old acquaintance be forgot, and old lang syne?*"

From the other room, Mrs. Hutchins called, "I've never quite heard it that way before, Mr. Evans. Now go on home with you!"

He grinned and, bowing at the waist, kissing Ella Mae's hand. "I bid you goodnight, my lady, before your mother throws me out on my ear."

"Good night, Daniel," Ella Mae replied, laughing at his foolishness.

Without further ado he let himself out the front door and disappeared into the darkness.

May 1887

"Are you free on Wednesday?" Daniel queried, crossing his ankles as he drank a glass of lemonade on the front porch of the Hutchins farmhouse.

"Yes. What did you have in mind?" Ella Mae replied, folding her hands and letting them rest languidly in the lap of her white cotton dress. A humid summer breeze stirred the flounces of her blouse and flirted with the stray tendrils of brown hair that had slipped from her braid.

"I'm going to Chestertown to register at Washington College. I'll be starting there in the fall. I'd like some company."

"Ah," Ella Mae said, a sinking sensation growing in the pit of her stomach.

The breeze stirred the tall stalks of corn growing in the fields. Ella Mae was reminded of the ebb and flow of the seasons, of planting and harvest, of meetings and partings. Fear squeezed her heart as she considered what this new season would bring—change, irreparable and complete.

"You can't get Morris or Penelope to go with you?"

"No. It has to be you, Ella."

She sighed. He was so arrogant to assume that just because he asked, she would say yes.

14

"Very well," she said, affirming his assumption. She wasn't going to waste an opportunity to spend time with him. All too soon such opportunities would disappear.

As the railroad had yet to reach Chestertown, the only way to travel there from Ridgely was via horse and buggy. Her acquiescence guaranteed an entire day in his company, walking the streets with her hand on his elbow as if they were a real couple, and dining out at a restaurant for supper. Although she knew in her heart that this was the beginning of the end, Ella Mae would take his insistence that she be the one to accompany him as a gift and hope that it foreshadowed a declaration of his affections and perhaps even the promise of a future together.

Washington College was named after the first president of the United States, who had contributed to and invested in its founding. The tall brick buildings dedicated to educating men to be responsible citizens of this great democracy left Ella Mae feeling very young and provincial as she walked alongside Daniel.

The day passed with the same easy banter usually exchanged between them. Ella Mae might as well have been his little sister. She looked at herself through his eyes and saw a slip of a woman, with freckles across her nose and the look of the farm clinging to her. If she was ever going to be worthy of him she would need more than a mere diploma of graduation from a small-town country school. Then and there Ella Mae made up her mind that she would find a way to continue her education.

The following evening at supper she presented her case to her parents. "After touring the college campus and meeting the students and professors, seeing the grand library full of books and the buildings dedicated to different fields of learning, I realized how small my education is, and by extension how small my opportunities. I would love to be able to attend an institution of higher learning. More women are attending college now than ever," her carefully rehearsed speech concluded.

Her parents exchanged a glance which Ella Mae read to mean they suspected her true motivation, but also that what she asked was too great a financial burden for a humble farmer. Washington College only accepted male students, but there were female seminaries dedicated to the education of women. There was one as close as Centreville.

"We'll consider it," her father said quietly, never one to deny his daughter if there were any way he could grant her request.

Sunday afternoon, Daniel picked Ella Mae up in his buggy. They had planned a picnic on the bank of the Choptank River with Morris and Penelope. The four friends had spent many hours together over the years and now that adulthood loomed before them, their separation was imminent. Ella Mae fervently wished she knew a spell that could make time stand still and hold them all together here in their hometown.

Why was life so complicated when it appeared so simple? That Morris cared for Penelope was plain to see, although she was insistent that they remain only friends. While the conversation had yet to be addressed between Ella Mae and Daniel, she feared that he felt the same for her. Whenever she was tempted to pose the question, fear silenced her. The last thing she wanted was to push him away, to taint the camaraderie and closeness they shared.

The day passed like a dream. The weather was ideal, with a gentle breeze blowing in from the river to cool them as they sat beneath the summer sun. A picnic basket filled with sandwiches and pie quickly disappeared, accompanied by laughter and lemonade. Penelope had contributed the food, and Ella Mae had brought the beverage and desserts. Daniel provided the transportation, while Morris had been responsible for the quilt upon which they reclined.

Penelope shaded her eyes, pointing out a sailboat in the distance on the glittering surface of the river. Tall and angular, her appearance was softened by blond hair and blue eyes framed in dark lashes. Beside her, Ella Mae appeared even more delicate.

16

Morris and Daniel were as opposite in their appearance as Penelope and Ella Mae. While Daniel was tall and lean with hair as dark as molasses, Morris's face was as round as his belly, though he hid the curves of his jaw beneath a beard of reddish brown. With their shirtsleeves rolled up, the pair leaned upon their elbows, exchanging jokes and reminding Ella Mae more of little boys than of grown men.

The hours slipped away all too quickly, the sun marking a path above them in the sky. Daniel drove Penelope and Morris home, then proceeded out of town to return Ella Mae to the farm. As the carriage turned down the dirt lane, the sunset painted the clouds with hues of crimson and lavender, and the golden light spilled across the fields and forests. The air smelled sweet as an evening breeze blew its breath over them like a lover's sigh.

"How can you wish to leave this?" Ella Mae spoke in a voice barely above a whisper.

There was no where on earth she would rather be. She'd gone into Baltimore twice for shopping expeditions, and into Annapolis occasionally to visit her grandparents. The cities were crowded with strangers, the streets paved with brick and lined with buildings that crowded out the skyline and blocked any sense of communion with nature. While she enjoyed a brief excursion to the city she always felt as if the farm welcomed her home with open arms and she sank into them with relief and contentment.

When she voiced these thoughts, Daniel snorted. "You've spent too much of your life reading novels. The city is full of opportunity, excitement, and adventure. There's no room for upward mobility in a town this small. You're content to be a little mouse here on the farm. I'm like a big hound on the prowl for greater things."

The truth sank into her chest like the sharp blade of a dagger. They had no future together.

Two weeks later, Ella Mae's father announced at the supper table that she could attend the Female Seminary in Centreville. "Your grandparents have agreed to help us finance your education, and since it isn't very far away, we can visit often. We've contacted the seminary and made arrangements for you to live with a family in town. The Turners have a daughter attending the school and have hosted other young women in the past. They live on a farm too, so you should feel at home there."

Rather than elation, Ella Mae only felt an overwhelming sense of loss. She would have been happy to follow in her older sister's footsteps and married early, having two children by the time she was twenty.

"Thank you," she said quietly, understanding the sacrifice that was being made for her benefit. "I'm very grateful."

Her mother twisted the napkin in her lap. "I wouldn't have agreed if there wasn't a train direct to Centreville, so we can be sure you are well fed and staying out of trouble."

Ella Mae came to her feet and walked around the table to her mother's side. She wrapped her arms around her mother's neck and pressed her cheek against the familiar face of the woman who had nurtured her since birth. "I promise to visit often and stay out of trouble."

Going to the seminary would mean leaving home, but she couldn't bear the thought of staying in Ridgely without Daniel. If there was any hope of him one day finding her worthy, she would have to step away from the farm and expand her education. She would have to become more than a mere field mouse.

Chapter Two

December 1887
Centreville, Maryland

thin blanket of snow covered the ground. The stubbled fields, which had been yellow with corn and wheat in the fall, now lay fallow and frozen. From the window of her second story bedroom at Laurel Hill Ella Mae could watch the deer and geese as they foraged. As its name indicated, the white Federal style house was perched atop a hill, flanked on both sides by laurel trees.

The farm was situated on the edge of town, not far from the Female Seminary on Commerce Street. Shops and stores lined the street but the heart of the town was the big, whitewashed brick courthouse with an iron porch adorning its center edifice along with the seal of a golden eagle. A spacious green lawn in front of the building was known by the townspeople as the Courthouse Green and was often used as a gathering place.

Unlike Ridgely, whose streets were dirt and easily turned to mud with rain or melting snow, Centreville's streets boasted crushed oyster shells. The train station on Maryland Avenue remained busy and the Corsica River wharf continued to be a port of trade. It wasn't quite a city but it was still quite different from the life Ella Mae knew in Ridgely, which was little more than a stop on the way to somewhere more developed.

For this reason she was surprised by how quickly she adapted to her new life in Centreville. The Turners and their daughter Ruth were kind and gracious. Their farm was a respite from the bustling vity of the town, without which she might not have been so content. Like Ella Mae, Ruth was of a contemplative nature and they enjoyed discussing literature and life as they relaxed together in the evening by the fire.

Mr. and Mrs. Turner didn't seem the slightest annoyed by their chatter. In fact, Ruth assured her that they enjoyed it. Their two older children had moved away, and they were happy to have the sounds of youth and laughter in their home for as long as they could.

Jeremiah Turner had fought in the War Between the States, giving his left hand for the preservation of the Union. He was outfitted with a prosthesis with interchangeable tools: he could attach a fork for meals, a rubber hand for special occasions, and a hook for the sake of utility. Ruth confided that, according to whispered stories, it was Uncle Charlie who had shot him, having sided with the rebels during the war. To see the brothers together now one would find it nearly impossible to believe such an outrageous claim.

When Charlie came to visit, Clara Turner treated her brother-in-law with as much love and kindness as she treated everyone else. Ella Mae suspected it was just a legend fabricated by the children when they were young to add an element of mystery and excitement to their father's injury. She couldn't imagine that they should all live together in such harmony if it were true.

The first four months at the seminary passed quickly and Ella Mae discovered a curiosity for learning that she had not previously known. Surrounded by women who were eager to study, grateful for the privilege, and desirous of proving their intelligence, it was difficult not to be inspired with a thirst for knowledge.

The Female Seminary was a two-story brick building with every look of being an institution despite the Victorian elements of architecture. Inside there were four classrooms, two downstairs and two up, with a staircase at the far end of the building. What it lacked in warmth it made up for in utility. There were four teachers, dividing the studies by math, science, literature, and Latin.

Literature was by far her favorite class, while algebra was undoubtedly her least, although Latin could be tedious at times. Science, botany specifically, she found fascinating and she was startled to realize how much information she could store in her brain. Her days were busy, though pleasantly so. She developed friendships with most of the women who attended the seminary and held her teachers in great respect.

It wasn't until she was lying in bed and the quiet darkness began to press in on her that thoughts of home and Daniel troubled her. She corresponded with her parents regularly and visited the farm every few weeks. Daniel wasn't as frequent with his letters as she might hope, but he did write to her faithfully.

He was as enthusiastic about his education as she was hers, sharing quotes from the founding fathers and regaling her with details about the life and history of George Washington. He told her about the friends he was making, mentioning a few persons by name. Though she had no claim to him, Ella Mae was jealous of every moment he spent with another woman.

As she packed her suitcase to take home for the Christmas holiday, Ella Mae wondered if she might get to see Daniel or if his family would hold him hostage throughout the break. She certainly hoped he would make time to pay her a visit. She'd invited Penelope and Morris to the farm for a gathering the day after Christmas, and she prayed that Daniel would be able to join them.

The railroad connected Centreville to Ridgely, and although she'd made the trip several times, it still felt strange to arrive in her hometown as a visitor. Her father always met her at the station with the buggy, listening to her incessant gossip as he drove her home. Without fail, her mother welcomed her with a hug and a cake every time. Ella Mae realized that what she had always felt upon returning to the farm, what she'd tried to explain to Daniel about the warmth which embraced her, was much more than just the place itself: it was the people who resided there.

Her older brother Randall was unable to leave his work in New Jersey, but her sister, along with her husband and sons, would spend Christmas Day gathered around the table with Ella Mae and her parents. It was a treasure that she had once taken for granted, this place called home and the people she called family.

Ella Mae could hardly believe how her nephews had grown in the short time she'd been away. James Jr. was three and little Mark had only just turned one. They were chubby, boisterous, and adorable. She took turns hugging one and then the other, delighted by the sweet smiles that lit their faces.

"Nora," she said when the sisters had a moment alone together. "You truly don't mind that I was able to attend the seminary?" She worried that her elder sister might harbor resentment that a privilege had been given to one of them and not both.

"I have no right to mind," Nora answered. "I chose marriage," she said, her tone indicating that she had chosen ill-advisedly.

Taking a closer look at her sister, Ella Mae noticed the dark circles under her eyes and lines of fatigue around her mouth. "You look tired," she observed gently.

Nora sighed. "I *am* tired. I feel like I could lie down and sleep for a week," she confessed.

"Would you like me to come watch the boys while you rest? The day after tomorrow, I'm available."

Embracing her gratefully, Nora said, "That would be wonderful. Thank you."

"It would be my pleasure," Ella Mae replied.

While Grandma entertained the boys, the sisters indulged in a brief conversation about the evolution of the bustle, comparing the cut of their dresses and laughing as they had when they were girls— when they weren't fighting, which had been often. Ella reflected that it was nice to be on the other side of adulthood, an equal and a friend, rather than merely the annoying younger sister.

December twenty-sixth Ella Mae awoke with a flutter in her stomach. She had invited Penelope, Morris, and Daniel to arrive at two o'clock. She still was unsure if Daniel would be coming, but just in case she donned a new dress made with festive red fabric and a generous bustle and put extra effort into styling her hair in the fashion Ruth had shown her from the Godey's Lady's Book.

The appreciation on Daniel's face as he came through the door gave her hope that he might see the lady she was becoming instead of the mouse she had been. Penelope and Morris were generous with their praise while he hung back, allowing his eyes to speak for him.

Penelope and Morris, having been left behind in Ridgely, wanted to know all about their experiences away and Daniel and Ella Mae entertained them with stories of their adventures. The afternoon passed with much laughter, cookies and pies, and a ridiculous game of charades.

Morris, rotund and bearded, drew a card requiring him to act out a feline. His attempts at walking gracefully and licking his paws left the group laughing so hard they had tears in their eyes. Daniel on the other hand, who considered himself too sophisticated for the game, made a very half-hearted attempt to perform. He fanned his face and patted his back but no one had any idea what he was supposed to be.

"I'm a camel," he huffed. "It's hot in the desert and I have a hump on my back. You are all sorely lacking in imagination," he stated.

Penelope's chuckle came out more like a snort. "You take yourself far too seriously, my friend."

For the remainder of the evening, whenever there was a lull in conversation someone patted their back or fanned their face, and they all erupted into fresh laughter.

Ella Mae had the good fortune of drawing a ballerina, which was easily enough conveyed by standing on her toes and holding her arms over her head. She was relieved that she need not humiliate herself in front of Daniel. He looked more dashing than ever, his chiseled chin more pronounced than before, his dark hair tumbling over his broad forehead. And his smile... It still made Ella Mae go weak in the knees.

Having no such reservations, Penelope energetically acted out a gorilla, beating on her chest and puckering her lips to epic proportions. Ella Mae laughed so hard she feared she might faint, and wished she'd laced her corset more loosely despite the flattering figure it gave her.

The party was a great success, and Ella Mae was even more pleased to discover that Daniel intended to stay when Morris and Penelope took their leave. She found herself feeling suddenly shy, hoping against that hope that this would be the time he would declare his affection for her and make some gesture of commitment.

Without Morris' imposing presence and Penelope's energetic personality, the parlor seemed suddenly quiet and intimate. Daniel pulled two chairs before the fire, as was his habit, and Ella Mae settled into one while he knelt to prod at the embers and add another log. Her heart raced as he brushed off his hands and sank down into the plush armchair beside her. His reserved demeanor often disappeared when they were alone together, something Ella Mae took as an indication of the bond they shared.

He chuckled. "Penelope is the strangest girl I've ever met. No one else I know would have put so much enthusiasm into the gorilla!"

Ella Mae had to agree, giggling at the memory of her friend's antics. "At least we knew what she was," she teased, fanning her face in mockery.

"You lucked out, that's all," he grinned in reply.

An easy silence fell between them. "So, you are enjoying the seminary?" Daniel asked.

"More than I expected, truth be told. I was afraid I wouldn't be able to keep up, but not only am I making good marks, I'm enjoying it. Especially the literature class."

"Well, that's no surprise. You were always a book worm. Me, on the other hand, I'm struggling through my literature class. I just finished reading Shakespeare's play, *Macbeth*, and I have no idea why they couldn't just speak normal English. It would make it so much easier to figure out what they're actually trying to say."

Ella Mae laughed. "You do know the play was written in the seventeenth century, don't you?"

"Shakespeare still should have consulted me," Daniel retorted, tossing her that lopsided grin which made her insides melt.

Trying to hide her reaction, Ella Mae quickly posed a question to distract him. "What is your favorite subject then, Mr. Evans?"

"Political Science. We've been studying the Federalist Papers, written by some of the founding fathers promoting the ratification of the Constitution. It sets out '*to decide the important question, whether societies of men are really capable or not, of establishing good government from reflection and choice.*' The answer, I believe, lies in the individual good of the man at the helm. Which is why I believe I should run for President."

"I'm not sure that you possess the 'goodness' required. You're a mite more arrogant than I would recommend," Ella Mae replied, only partly teasing.

"Not arrogant. It's self-confidence and natural leadership skills," he corrected with a wink.

"Oh, is that what you like to call it?" she arched an eyebrow. "I'm still unconvinced that you're qualified for such a position."

He grinned. "Do not fear. I'll be more mature by the time I climb the political ladder to the very top rung. By then I'll have won over all my critics, including you."

"I suppose that's just more confidence? And who shall you appoint as your Vice President?"

"Morris, of course."

"You could be a radical and appoint a woman," Ella Mae challenged, only to get a rise out of him.

"You?" he snorted. "I'm sure the White House will need a housekeeper."

"On second thought, I think I'd rather not. In fact, if women could vote, I most certainly *wouldn't* vote for you."

"Since you can't, I'm not too worried about it," Daniel assured her.

"You are an insufferable—"

"All right, I'll tell you what. In my first term, I'll pass a law allowing women the vote. But only on the condition that you promise to vote for me to have a second term."

Ella Mae sighed dramatically. "Very well. Agreed."

His even, white teeth flashed in a victorious grin. She couldn't help but laugh. He *was* insufferable…

"All joking aside, the future of the nation depends on the quality of its leaders. I would like to make a positive contribution to our great country, to steer it in the right direction. I have a lot to learn, and a lot of growing up to do," Daniel admitted in a rare moment of humility, "but I love the United States of America and I want to follow in the footsteps of these great men who made it possible for us to enjoy the freedom and comforts we have today."

Embarrassment crept into his expression as he continued, "True leadership begins with service. Don't tell anyone, but I've been volunteering at the almshouse. I know reform has been made, but more is needed. The idea of providing a place for those in need of housing is a good one. But the reality is that the elderly and the ill are all crammed together in a close space without proper beds or enough food... It makes a man realize how much he's taken for granted."

Speechless, Ella Mae stared at the impassioned young man before her. "Why don't you want me to tell anyone?"

"It would ruin my reputation," he grinned, trying to reclaim his former persona.

But it was too late. The ruse was exposed. Ella Mae smiled approvingly. "I don't know as much about politics as you do, of course, but I did learn that George Washington became president to serve our country, not to be served. It is that spirit of selflessness which makes a man a great leader."

Daniel straightened in his chair, leaning toward her he whispered, "I'm also planning to reinstate the tradition of keeping harems, but that won't be until my second term." He winked.

"You are a scoundrel," she said to satisfy him.

The conversation moved on to other things, such as the way Morris pined for Penelope and what a hopeless cause it was. Although Ella Mae enjoyed the evening alone with him, he never broached the topic of his intentions toward her.

"It was good to see you," he said with his hat in his hand as he paused by the open door, the cold air gusting in behind him and tousling his dark hair.

Ella Mae offered a smile in reply. The oil lamp on the hall stand flickered.

"Good night," Daniel said, placing the hat on his head and closing the door behind him.

Turning slowly, Ella Mae saw her reflection in the mirror. She looked lovely in her new red dress, but she may as well have been wearing a waistcoat and trousers. He had not spoken of intentions toward her because he had none. She and Morris were both pining away for someone who wanted only friendship.

Returning to the chair she had vacated in front of the fireplace, Ella Mae covered her mouth and sobbed quietly into her hands. She could never be sophisticated enough to be the First Lady. She was qualified only as a housekeeper.

Chapter Three

January 1888
Centreville, Maryland

Ruth rubbed her back gently as Ella Mae sobbed into a handkerchief. She'd pasted a smile on her face from the moment the train arrived in Centreville, wearing it throughout the meal with the Turners and giving a cheerful report of how her holidays had passed at home.

Sensing that there was something she held back, Ruth had invited Ella Mae into her bedroom after supper. The two young women sat together on Ruth's bed, the shadows from the glow of the oil lamp dancing on the wallpaper. They shared a woolen coverlet, tossed over their full skirts for extra warmth against the cold which crept through the plaster walls and window panes.

"There, there," Ruth said, as if Ella Mae were a child. "He must not realize the way you feel for him. Perhaps you should say something."

Ella May shook her head with certainty. "Daniel is anything but shy. If he had affections for me, he would say so. I would just make a fool of myself."

"You've met my brother. Francis can be an absolute imbecile sometimes. Completely oblivious of not only everyone else's feelings, but his own. Men can be like that. Daniel just may not realize his affection toward you, but if you say something…"

"I can't," Ella Mae sobbed, her shoulders shaking violently. "It would be too humiliating."

"Oh, Ella... I'm so sorry," Ruth said, pulling her friend close and letting her weep into her neck. "What you need is a distraction," she decided. "Remember that young man you met at the dinner party before you went home? Albert Nichols seemed quite taken by you. Perhaps you should allow him to call. It wouldn't hurt to get to know him."

"I suppose not," Ella Mae replied reluctantly.

Albert's sister, Fannie Nichols, attended the seminary with Ruth and Ella Mae. Albert was two years older than Ella Mae and employed as a clerk at the courthouse. Life would go on with or without Daniel in it, and she decided she should make room for someone else to fill the role she had hoped for him.

Over the next few months Ella Mae genuinely tried to give Albert a chance to win her heart, but it was no use. There was nothing he did wrong, no fault she could find with him. He just never developed into anything more than a distraction. There was no excitement or eagerness to be in his company again, no racing of her heart when he smiled at her.

Unfortunately for Ella Mae—though fortunately for Ruth— Albert introduced them to his best friend, Wallace Reynolds. And it felt as though in the span of a few weeks Ella Mae had lost her best friend. Although they continued to attend the seminary and study exams together, Wallace came to call several evenings a week and on the weekends. When he was present, he was the full center of Ruth's attention.

Ella Mae retreated into a world of literature, reading everything she could get her hands on. When the weather was pleasant, she took a book with her on a walk down the path that cut through the fields to a creek called Gravel Run. She would find a fallen log to sit upon while she read or sat in quiet contemplation, the tinkling of the shallow water as it gurgled over the stones and the song of the birds in the trees making a pleasant background for her thoughts. The smells of the fresh growth in the spring awakened her senses, soothing her loneliness and feeding her soul.

She read everything from Nietzsche and Tolstoy to Mark Twain and Louisa May Alcott. Dickens, Jules Vern, and Thomas Hardy also occupied her time. Her mind came alive with characters such as Josephine March and Ebenezer Scrooge, Huckleberry Finn and Anna Karenina. She contemplated the words of Zarathustra and the choices of Captain Nemo… Her inner world was far from silent, though she often sat alone in the parlor or roamed the fields and forest unaccompanied.

Ella Mae's life was small, but her world was very large.

When she completed her first year at the seminary, she returned home for the summer. She knew she was not the person she had been the year before. She was older and more confident, and yet less certain of so many things.

The farmhouse she had grown up in seemed to have shrank in size and appeared far more run down than she remembered. Whether it was so or was a trick of her memory, she couldn't be sure. But it was still—and always would be—home.

Her father picked her up at the train station and her mother welcomed her with an enveloping hug and freshly baked cake. Rows of green corn stalks standing no taller than a foot marched down the acres of fields. The dogwood tree in the yard looked like an old friend, and the barn cat had given birth to another litter of kittens. Such chores as milking the cow no longer seemed like a burden, and she was eager to volunteer.

The first milking of the morning beneath a twilight sky was a time of contemplation and simplicity. Streaks of pink and gold crept into the dark canvas, pushing back the night and welcoming the light of a new day. The scent of the dew on the grass mingled with the aroma of damp hay and the tang of manure as Ella Mae pressed her forehead into the cow's warm belly, streams of fresh white milk foaming into the pail between her feet.

Her sister Nora was happy to have her in town again and Ella Mae made it a point to visit her often and spend time with her nephews. Nora often seemed tired and flustered, and Ella Mae did what she could to help around the house or to watch the boys so that Nora could take a rare afternoon nap.

Penelope too was delighted to have her home again. Ella Mae enjoyed the time they spent picking berries, picnicking by the river, and talking about the mysteries of life. Of course, they talked about men, too. Penelope recently had a similar experience to the one Ella Mae had with Albert, except that Penelope was not looking for a distraction but for the chemistry and yearning she had yet to experience. Morris remained devoted to her, but she insisted he was only a chum.

"Do you think you'll ever marry?" Ella Mae asked as they walked arm and arm down the lane.

"Of course, I'm just not in any great hurry. What about you? Are you going to waste your whole life waiting for Daniel?"

Penelope's heart was in the right place even if her words might have been softened. Ella Mae considered her answer. "I'm going to wait a while longer."

Daniel wrote to her less frequently, but she still heard from him regularly. He was very busy with his studies and with the social life he had developed in Chestertown. He'd taken a position as a clerk at the mayor's office and would not be returning to Ridgely for summer break, although he promised to pay her a call when he came into town to visit his parents. While he hadn't mentioned having ties to any particular woman, Ella Mae couldn't help but wonder if that wasn't part of what kept him so preoccupied.

Like the farmhouse, the town of Ridgely seemed smaller than Ella Mae remembered. She could understand why Daniel felt he must move on to a bigger pond if he was going to grow into a bigger fish. The town was showing signs of growth, but it was slow and inconsequential by comparison to more established towns like Chestertown or Centreville.

The public school had outgrown its one room building, and construction was underway to add another classroom. Miss Amanda Saulsbury, who had been Ella Mae's teacher when she graduated the year before, was being promoted to principal. Her childhood teacher, Mr. James Swann, was the current Superintendent of Schools.

Reflecting upon her life, she realized that her imagination had first been awakened when she was very young under the tutelage of this now elderly man. He had been the town's first teacher, when the "school" had been just a room over the train station. Several teachers had followed in his wake and Ella Mae had been among the first to experience a female teacher, Miss Wiley, in 1876. After her departure Mr. Swann resumed the position, and he was by nature a kind soul with an innate ability to impart his passion for learning to his students.

They had spent many hours pouring over the American Fifth Reader, reading the poetry of Wordsworth, Milton, and Thomas Gray, and reading the plays of Shakespeare which Daniel even now complained were difficult to understand. She remembered many young boys suffering through the same hour that she found to be one of escape and rapture. Often these lads excelled at the subject she dreaded most—mathematics—eager to work with something as simple and straightforward as numbers, which she found stifling and oppressive.

Now, as a young lady of almost eighteen years, Ella Mae found her appreciation rekindled for the power of words to stir the emotions as well as the imagination. For the last few years she'd felt as though she had lost herself in the fruitless dream of romance and marriage, losing sight of the passion she had once possessed and viewing all schoolwork as a drudgery.

A bird's nest rested in the fork of a tree stirred her memory and the opening lines of Wordsworth's poem rose to the surface. *"Behold, within the leafy shade/ Those bright blue eggs together laid!/ On me the chance-discovered sight/ Gleamed like a vision of delight."*

As a child, to find delight in the most common of sights, a bird's nest, had seemed expected. But as one grew into adulthood the joy found in simple pleasures was often lost in a mindset of survival and practicality. Ella Mae did not want to lose her delight. She did not want to be swept away into the doldrums of daily life as if there was still no pleasure to be found in the beauty of nature or in the workings of the mind.

She'd written poems and stories through the years, viewing them as a form of play rather than a serious undertaking. Now she began to consider if perhaps writing was her destiny. Although it was still a man's world, there were women who had made a name for themselves as novelists: Jane Austen, The Bronte Sisters, Harriet Beecher Stowe, and Louisa May Alcott, to name a few.

Was it possible that one day she could see her own name on the cover of a novel, that there might be men and women who read her words and allowed her thoughts to live within their minds? The idea made her feel heady… and afraid.

She retrieved paper and pen and settled into a wicker chair on the front porch to contemplate what she might write about. There was no way to know if she possessed the necessary talent to succeed unless she tried. As Ella Mae gazed out at the undulating sea of green leaves made by the immature corn stalks, she let her mind drift like a feather on the breeze over the fields, open to whatever path it might take.

But it seemed the feather landed at her feet, having travelled nowhere. After a time, she abandoned the idea and returned the writing materials to her room with a disappointed sigh.

That night, as she lay in her bed attempting to quiet her restless thoughts and fall into the gray oblivion of sleep, the muse of inspiration appeared to her. A story took shape before her mind's eye, the characters acting out the scenes with striking detail. And before they could fade from her memory she sprang from the mattress and lit the lamp on the nightstand, pulling back the chair from her small writing desk and setting pen to paper.

Previously her stories had been of a romantic nature, but now, knowing more about unrequited yearning than about love reciprocated, Ella Mae endeavored to write a novel in the tradition of Charles Dickens. It was set in London and featured a protagonist who was an underdog in society, fighting against the injustice of social class and the natural pride inherent in human nature.

The pen scratched furiously over the pages throughout the night until the light of dawn began to brighten her room. Only then did Ella Mae realize that she was exhausted. She tucked the sheaf of papers into the drawer of her desk for later review, extinguished the lamp, and fell into bed.

When her mother came to awaken her she was certain Ella Mae was ill, feeling her head for signs of fever.

"I'm just tired," Ella muttered, gently pushing the concern aside.

Seeing the ink stains on her daughter's hand, Mrs. Hutchins said, "Ah. I can see why. Get some rest, then. I'll wake you up in a while."

Ella Mae had already fallen back into dreams before her mother left the room.

Mrs. Hutchins awakened her in the late afternoon, having prepared a plate of fried potatoes and eggs in anticipation of her hunger. Gratefully Ella Mae consumed the nourishment, relating between bites the plot of the novel as she had mapped it out thus far.

"That sounds very interesting," her mother commented, smiling indulgently.

After she had cleared her plate, Ella Mae went outside to clear her head and meditate on the next installment of her novel. The summer afternoon was bright and warm, and Ella Mae settled onto the swing her father had made for her when she was young, a wooden seat suspended from a tree branch by two sturdy ropes. As she languidly drifted back and forth, the movement created a breeze which fanned her face. Relishing the relaxation, she almost missed a sound behind her.

Turning, she saw that it was Penelope balanced on a two-wheeled contraption known as a bicycle. Disappointed that her plans for writing had been interrupted, Ella Mae was nonetheless happy to see her friend.

Penelope brought the bicycle to a stop, stepping down and swinging her skirt through the open center. This particular model had been made with women's attire in mind and lacked a bar running from the seat to the handles.

She leaned the bicycle against the tree next to Ella Mae and announced, "I've just met the most interesting man! His name is Albrecht Krause and he's visiting his family in Jumptown—they're German, if you'd hadn't guessed. Anyway, he has dark hair and a thick mustache, and the faintest trace of an accent. He lives in Pennsylvania. And he's invited me on a picnic tomorrow afternoon!"

Ella Mae had never seen Penelope so excited about a man before. She hardly knew how to respond. "How old is he? What does he do for a living?" she queried.

"He's a little older, I'm not sure exactly. And he owns a bakery in Philadelphia..." Penelope expounded upon the man's attributes until finally Ella Mae interrupted her.

"I have news of mine own. I've decided to pursue a career as a novelist."

Penelope raised a pale eyebrow. "Does that mean you're giving up on marriage?"

"I'm not sure," Ella Mae answered honestly. "But I may as well find something else to dedicate myself to while I wait. I only began writing last night, and I've no idea if it's any good or not, but the thrill of writing is something that nothing else in life gives me. I feel certain that it's what I'm meant to do. I think I'll let Mr. Swann read it when I'm finished."

"Well, I always enjoyed reading your stories," Penelope affirmed.

Their conversation was interrupted as an orange tabby kitten cried plaintively from a tree branch above them. The chirping of the baby birds in the nest must have aroused its curiosity, and once it had achieved a certain height, it realized its mistake. It had no idea how to come back down.

"Oh, the poor thing!" Ella Mae exclaimed.

"He'll figure it out," Penelope answered, unconcerned.

The kitten mewed in disagreement. "He's frightened! I have to help him."

"How do you propose to do that?" Penelope demanded wryly.

"If you hoist me up onto that branch, I can stand up and reach him, then hand him down to you."

"You can't be serious," Penelope laughed.

"Hoist me up," Ella Mae insisted.

Penelope complied, cupping her hand to make a step for Ella Mae's heel, then lifting her up to grab onto the branch. Once there,

Penelope slid her shoulder under Ella Mae's rear end until she was sitting on the thick, overhanging limb.

"Now what?" Penelope asked, thoroughly amused.

"I'm going to stand up," Ella Mae answered, her voice quavering. Carefully, she held onto the trunk of the tree and slid her feet underneath her. Then slowly straightening, she gripped the branch above her. "Now, I'm going to hand him down to you," she called, reaching for the kitten's scruff and grabbing hold before he could panic and scratch her.

A male voice behind them chuckled, "Do my eyes deceive me? There can't possibly be a young woman up in that tree. No—wait— there certainly is. What on earth are you doing, Miss Hutchins?" Daniel's voice contained concern   and disbelief.

Mortified, Ella Mae felt her cheeks flame. "I'm rescuing a kitten, obviously."

"Don't they climb?" She heard him ask Penelope.

"He's too little to climb back down," Ella Mae responded defensively. The kitten wriggled in her grip, and with one hand on the trunk for balance, she lowered herself to drop the little one into Penelope's outstretched skirt. The terrified kitten landed, then sprang out and raced back to the barn as if the demons of hell were chasing after him.

Having accomplished her mission, a new challenge faced Ella Mae: getting herself back onto to the ground without suffering further disgrace or injury.

"How exactly do you intend to get down?" Daniel's voice held more laughter now than concern, and Ella Mae began to wish she'd given the kitten more time to figure out its own descent rather than rushing to its rescue.

"Penelope can help me," Ella Mae said, although the perspective from her perch was much higher than it had seemed when she had proposed this plan from the ground.

"Allow me," he said, walking around the tree until he stood just in front of her. His dark brown eyes sparkled, eyebrows drawn together in humor, a smirk shaping his handsome mouth. He wore a gray linen suit and looked every bit the gentleman.

Beads of perspiration born of humiliation sprouted upon Ella Mae's forehead and nose. Her heart pounded against her ribcage as she realized that Daniel intended to take her in his arms, hold against his chest for a brief moment before placing her on the ground. Of the many thousands of times she'd imagined being in his arms, it had never been like this.

She sighed with resignation. There was no other way. She reached for his shoulder with one hand and before she knew it, she was cradled against his chest. Then, almost instantly, her feet were firmly planted on the grass.

"Only you, Ella Mae," he chuckled.

She wished a hole would open in the earth and swallow her up.

"Well, that was more fun than I expected," Penelope grinned. "I must be going. Good to see you, Daniel," she called as she reached for her bicycle.

"I hear that a lot," he grinned. Penelope arched an eyebrow and he clarified, "That it's good to see me."

Shaking her head by way of reply, Penelope placed her feet on the pedals and cycled down the lane.

"She came by to tell me that she'd met someone," Ella Mae blurted, trying to distract Daniel from her embarrassing escapade.

"Is he strange?"

"I don't know. Why do you ask?"

"He'd have to be strange to show interest in Penelope."

Ella Mae crossed her arms. "That's not a very kind thing to say."

"Maybe not, but it's true," he replied with a careless shrug. "So, tell me what made you think it was a good idea to climb a tree, Miss Hutchins?" Daniel steered the conversation back to the incident.

Flustered, Ella Mae stepped over to the swing and sat down. "He was crying," she explained, arranging her skirt around her.

To her surprise, Daniel moved behind her and took hold of the ropes, pushing her forward. "You are pathetic," he pronounced.

Then, as the swing carried her back toward him, he gently pushed the small of her back to sustain the motion. "I'm glad you didn't fall and break your ankle. Or your neck. I would have missed you."

Chapter Four

*E*lla Mae only saw Daniel one more time that summer of 1888. In the fall, she returned to Centreville to complete her second and final year at the Female Seminary.

Once classes resumed, her time for writing was severely limited. She found that it was usually at night when the house was quiet and the distractions minimized that her mind was free to create. The following day always required a nap as soon as she and Ruth returned home.

Ruth and Wallace Reynolds continued their courtship, and Ella Mae found that she was no longer jealous. Writing her novel filled the empty spaces in her life, occupying her mind and satisfying her emotions. When she was bent over the paper at her desk, her pen scratching ink onto the white page, her imagination painting a picture onto a blank canvas, she felt as though she were tapping into the same reserve as all the writers who had preceded her, coexisted with her, and would follow her. It was as if there was one great well of creativity which she had been graciously granted access to, and thus she experienced solidarity with such geniuses as Shakespeare and Dickens.

She thought often of Daniel, cherishing every letter he sent and hoping that somehow a miracle might still bring them together. Until then, her life was busy and full.

Whenever her creativity hit a dry spell Ella Mae looked outside of herself for inspiration. There were a million stories all around her, a million characters who each had a story of their own and who would never know if she borrowed an element of it to weave into her novel.

One such "borrowing" came from the Turner family. Ruth's father hosted a gathering of men he'd known in the war, an eclectic group of former soldiers, to celebrate the birthday of an elderly man who had served as chaplain. Even at the pinnacle of youth Ella Mae was certain Chaplain Davies must have been a small man, but age had shriveled him into a diminutive elf. With a shock of unruly white hair and a face creased with laugh lines, he seemed more like a caricature than a character. Everyone loved him.

"You never thought I'd last this long, did you?" he teased. "Don't you know it's the ornery ones that live the longest?"

"Then you should live forever," Jeremiah Turner retorted with an affectionate grin.

"Well, one-hundred-and-five is pretty close to forever," a large, burly man piped in.

The Chaplain chuckled as he corrected, "I'm seventy-five, Phillips. Don't rush me."

"Is that all? I was going to say you held your age well, but…" the big man shrugged his shoulders, letting his words trail off. The men laughed, Davies among them.

Ella Mae noted the camaraderie these men shared and tried to imagine them as strong and robust soldiers. The Chaplain, offering guidance and encouragement to the younger men, would have been past his prime already. As her own father had chosen to remain outside of the war, not being the fighting sort, this was an entirely new experience for her.

Mrs. Turner seemed to hold Chaplain Davies in high regard, kissing the man's wrinkled cheek with sincere affection and wishing him a wonderful day. "I will always be grateful for the blessing you've been to my family," she added, an odd catch in her voice.

"They say God works in mysterious ways," Jeremiah rested his right hand on the man's emaciated shoulder. "Here's proof of it," he teased.

The old chaplain grinned. "If He could use Balaam's donkey, He can use even me."

"Here, here!" the others agreed with a round of laughter.

After serving the men a lunch of cold sandwiches Mrs. Turner sent them out to the back porch for whiskey and cigars. The weather was perfect for outdoor recreation, the summer heat having yielded to milder fall temperatures. On the trees the colors of autumn were beginning to paint the leaves with hues of orange and crimson. A tang scented the air, a crisp reminder that winter would be upon them all too soon.

"Mother, what role did the Chaplain play in our family?" Ruth wondered. "I don't believe I've heard that story."

Clara Turner motioned for the girls to follow her into the parlor. Once they were seated, Mrs. Turner said, "We don't often talk about the darker stories hidden in our family history. They can be painful to recall and uncomfortable to discuss. But, no matter how we might try to sweep history under the rug, it all remains fixed as part of the past."

The girls exchanged curious glances. "Is the story about Uncle Charlie true?" Ruth asked.

"It is. He fought with the Confederacy when your father chose to fight with the Union. An unfortunate series of events brought both of their regiments to a place called Culp's Hill, in Gettysburg, Pennsylvania. Uncle Charlie had seen the horrors of battle, and when an opportunity presented itself to see his brother removed from the front and sent home, he took it. He shot your father in his left hand, knowing he would then be taken away from the fighting to a place of safety.

"Your father was hardly grateful for this act of kindness," she mused, her eyes growing distant as she gazed backward into the past. "By the time I reached Gettysburg-"

"You went there?" Ruth interrupted, shocked.

"I did. I knew he needed me, though I had no idea what I would find when I arrived. Nor did Uncle Charlie have any way of knowing what the aftermath of that battle would look like. It was worse than anyone could have imagined... It was days before your father's wound was treated. By then, the only option left to the field surgeon was amputation. Jeremiah couldn't understand why his own brother should have hated him so much as to intentionally hurt him. He was bitter and angry. It took many months, a bit of deception on my part, and the intervention of the Chaplain, to reconcile the brothers. You know your father can be a mite stubborn," Clara said to her daughter with a smile. "I'm not sure anyone else could have gotten through his thick head that Charlie had acted with love when he fired that rifle."

"I can understand why that would have been difficult for him to believe," Ruth commented softly.

Ella Mae listened as an observer and outsider, but she filed the details away in her memory. What an interesting story!

"We kept quiet about this because there was, and still is, quite a bit of hard feelings for the 'rebels.' It was better for the sake of all involved to let it remain a family secret. I'm asking you both now to hold your silence on the matter."

"Yes ma'am," Ruth and Ella Mae chorused obediently.

Uncle Charlie had taken a position as overseer at a plantation called Bloomingdale, one of the large estates which had found a way to endure after the War Between the States. He had married the great-niece of the women who owned it in those days, Sallie and Mary Harris. After Sallie's death in 1880, ownership of the property was transferred to her cousin, Severn Teackle Wallis, who left the running of the estate to Charlie while he continued to pursue his career as a lawyer and politician.

"Does Mr. Wallis know about Charlie's affiliation with the Confederacy?" Ruth worried.

"I'm sure he does," her mother said certainly. "Mr. Wallis was a sympathizer himself. In fact, he was serving on the House of Delegates when the vote was to be taken on whether Maryland should secede from the Union. Mr. Wallis was arrested without warrant, along with other legislators and citizens, and held at Fort McHenry before being transferred to other forts. He was imprisoned for over a year without trial, nor was the cause of his arrest ever stated. Of course, the reason was obvious enough. Those in favor of secession were prevented from casting their vote, which was why Maryland remained in the Union during the war."

"Is that really true?" Ella Mae blurted before she could stop herself.

Not appearing the slightest offended, Clara Turner nodded solemnly. "It is all quite true. Remember, my dears, history is always told by the victor. If the truth might paint them in a less than flattering light, they exclude those details from their narrative."

Ella Mae wrote to Daniel that night, relating the story and the details she had learned. She knew, with his interest in politics, he would find the personal anecdote fascinating.

In the weeks leading up to Christmas break she counted down the days until she would see him again. Unfortunately, between his new work position and school demands, he was only able to pay her a brief visit. Ella Mae's disappointment was further compounded by Daniel's mention of a young woman he had escorted to a grand event associated with his job at the mayor's office. He commented that he didn't see a future with said young lady, but it was evident he did not see a future with Ella Mae either.

Penelope was preoccupied with the arrival of Mr. Krause, in town to visit his family, and hardly had time—or thought—for anything else. Morris was the only one with nothing better to do than spend time with Ella Mae, and as he was as dejected as she was, the atmosphere was hardly festive.

When she returned to school in January of 1888, it was almost a relief to be preoccupied with her studies. Ella Mae threw herself into her writing with renewed determination. Her novel was taking on the air of a tragedy, but so was her life. She feared she would end up a spinster, her heart held by someone who had no value for it, living out her years in a state of romantic melancholy not unlike the literary figure Miss Havisham.

Ella Mae was forced to take a brief hiatus from her creative work while she dedicated herself to a new form of torture introduced to her at the seminary, known innocuously as Geometry. If she had thought Algebra was difficult, it was nothing compared to the agony of axioms, points, lines, planes, angles... She began to foster a very personal dislike for Euclid and wondered why he had felt inspired to develop such a method of misery.

Another distraction soon arrived in a letter written by Penelope with much enthusiasm. Albrecht Krause had proposed to her and they planned to wed in July of the same year. She wished Ella Mae to be her Maid of Honor. Hardly able to decline such an invitation, Ella Mae had no choice but to accept. To save money, Penelope's mother was making the dresses. Ella Mae sent her measurements with a special request that the color be one which complimented her complexion.

She had once anticipated her graduation from the Female Seminary as a great accomplishment which would open the door for future opportunities. Now Ella Mae saw it merely as another stepping stone in her life, leading nowhere.

In May, she graduated with as little fanfare as possible. Her parents insisted on having a party to celebrate her accomplishment, with her grandparents and brother coming into town for the occasion. Her sister gave her a new fountain pen with well wishes for her future as a writer, Randall surprised her with a leather satchel for carrying her writing supplies, and her parents gifted her with a portable "desk" that she could balance on her lap if she wished to spend time writing in the out of doors. Penelope and Albrecht were there to congratulate her as well, giving her a special edition copy of Shakespeare's plays with gold-tipped pages. Morris was also in attendance, giving her a quartz paperweight with the face of cat carved into it.

Daniel was once again tied up in Chestertown.

Ella Mae was appreciative of the kind support from her family and friends. She felt a little guilty for the extreme relief she felt at the end of the day as she retreated to her bedroom and sank down upon the bed. However, the silence of solitude was comforting.

The weeks that followed were busy with preparations for Penelope's wedding. Her mother had done a fine job with the dress and Ella Mae only needed two additional fittings before it was completed. To her dismay, Penelope had chosen a shade of lemon yellow that was far from flattering on Ella Mae. It was exactly what she had feared but, as it was Penelope's special day, she could hardly complain. Penelope's younger sister, Adeline, was a bride's maid, and since the color suited her well it wasn't difficult to ascertain why it had been chosen.

Ella Mae assisted Penelope's mother and sister with the baking of cakes, cookies, and pies, and the gathering of orange blossoms and tying of ribbons to be placed on the pews at the Reformed Church on Central Avenue where the ceremony was to be held. They were busy days, but Ella Mae knew better than to wish them away. After the wedding Penelope would be moving to Pennsylvania to live with her husband there.

Gone were the days of their youth. They were moving on to the next season of life, yet rather than embracing these changes, Ella

47

Mae resented them. She wished she could turn back time to picnics on the bank of the Choptank and Christmas parties at her parents' farmhouse. Rather than excitement or anticipation, Ella Mae felt only sentimental longing for the times that were lost forever.

All too quickly the day of the wedding arrived, and Penelope was a lovely bride with her face hidden behind a lacy chiffon veil. Albrecht Krause stood beaming at the altar as he watched her approach in a cloud of white satin and lace, while Ella Mae found herself blinking back tears.

Then there was dancing and celebration, cake, gifts, and more dancing. Ella Mae's cheeks hurt from the false smile she pasted on her face, not wanting to cast a pall over her friend's wedding day. When at last the festivities ended and the guests began to leave the church to find their way home, Ella Mae and Morris shared a moment of silent understanding beneath the shade of a poplar tree. She leaned against his shoulder, lacing her arm through his, and offered her support in his moment of grief. Heartache was something she knew all too well.

The sudden emptiness of the days which followed seemed to swallow Ella Mae up, stretching out aimlessly ahead of her. But, after a few days of moping and napping, Ella Mae found her creative senses reawakened and she resumed work on her novel. The openness of her days then became a blessing and she bent over the pages day and night with feverish intensity.

By the middle of August, she had finally completed her first novel! A thrill of accomplishment raced through her as she gazed at the manuscript on her desk, admiring the thick stack of pages which contained an entire world her imagination had brought to life.

She carefully placed the stack in the leather satchel and took the buggy into town to the cottage where her old teacher, Mr. Swann lived. He grinned broadly as he met her at the door, his white mustache curving into a smile.

"Miss Hutchins!" he said in surprise. "Please do come in. I'll put a kettle on."

Ella Mae followed him down the hallway to a small kitchen, taking a seat at the table where he indicated.

"I hope you don't mind the intrusion, but I wanted to ask your advice about something," she began tentatively, suddenly overcome with a case of nerves.

"Intrusion? I'd hardly call a visit from one of my old students an intrusion. More like a pleasant diversion for an old man. How can I help you, Miss Hutchins?"

"Well, I... You see, I've taken an interest in writing. Novels, that is. And I was wondering—I was hoping—that you wouldn't mind reading over my manuscript and telling me what you think," she finished, her earlier pride now replaced by uncertainty.

"Of course! I would be happy to!" His teeth showed in a big smile. "I was quite proud to hear you graduated from the Seminary, and now to learn that you've taken to writing makes me even more proud."

Ella Mae procured the manuscript from her satchel and placed it on the table, suddenly dreading leaving it behind with him. It was in so many ways an extension of herself. If he deemed her work unworthy, that judgement would also fall on her as the author.

The kettle on the stove hissed, and he pushed back his chair to retrieve it. After pouring her tea, he reached for the precious document, scanning over the first page. "Can I hold onto it for a week or two? I want to give it my proper attention."

"Certainly," Ella Mae answered, though she felt that was an awfully long time.

She stayed another half hour to give him a proper visit before she took her leave. She wanted to tell him to give his honest opinion, but she wasn't sure if she was ready to receive unvarnished criticism.

"When do I get to read it?" her mother queried as she removed her hat and hung it on the peg by the door.

Ella Mae smiled. "When Mr. Swann returns it, I'll be happy to let you have a turn."

"Daniel stopped by while you were out," her mother added. "He said he would come again tomorrow."

"Oh…" Ella Mae was sorely disappointed to learn that she'd missed him. On the other hand, if she anticipated his arrival, she could put more effort into her appearance.

The following morning she donned a pink floral day dress with a triangular shaped overskirt that drew attention to her narrow waist, accented by a wide band of pink fabric. She studied her reflection in the mirror, fluffing the frizzled bangs on her forehead and smoothing the hair which covered her ears. Even if she was only a farmgirl content to sit alone for hours and write novels, at least she could look like a fashionable young woman.

Ella Mae remembered the embarrassing incident last summer when Daniel had found her in a tree. What timing! He couldn't have arrived twenty minutes later? No wonder he didn't believe she could ever be the woman he needed to walk beside him as he pursued his career in politics. She was neither elegant nor sophisticated and preferred to avoid social events and mingling with strangers whenever possible.

She was, however, willing to be whatever he needed, even if it went against her nature. Hadn't he figured that out by now? If he only let her know what was expected of her, she would do all in her power to fit the mold. Although she struggled with an interest in current politics, she could read newspapers and listen to his tirades. If he only loved her, she could be anything he asked.

She sat at her desk and stared through the open window at the dirt lane, watching for his arrival. Her fingers tapped idly on the ink-stained oak, her mind circling without knowing where to land.

For the last year, whenever she had a free moment, she was in the habit of scratching out a few sentences or compiling ideas for the next scene. The completion of her novel left an empty, restless feeling inside her.

Just when she feared he wasn't coming, she heard the clop of horse's hooves as his buggy turned down the lane. Not wanting to appear overly eager, Ella Mae waited until her mother announced his arrival to descend the stairs. Daniel stood in the parlor with his hat in his hand, a broad smile slowly spreading over his face at the sight of her.

"It's good to see you," he said. "It feels like it's been forever."

"It's been a while," Ella Mae replied, her heart hammering against her ribcage. He was as tall, lean, and handsome as she remembered.

"You look like you're finally growing up," he said, his brown eyes sweeping over her with appreciation.

"Thank you. I'll be nineteen in two weeks."

"Is that all?" he mused, rubbing his chin thoughtfully.

"What, you're an old man now?" she teased, gazing up at him through her eyelashes.

"Feels like it some days," he admitted. "Care for a walk?"

"Certainly," she replied. She would have followed him to the ends of the earth.

Tying the ribbon of her straw hat under her chin, Ella Mae allowed him to lead her outside and down the lane. The rounded brim shielded her eyes from the afternoon sun, which was helpful as she had to tilt her chin up to look at Daniel. The top of her head reached only to his shoulder.

"You missed Penelope's wedding," she commented, thinking it was just as well he hadn't seen her in that awful yellow dress.

"I know. I was sorrier to have to miss your graduation party. Congratulations."

"Thank you," Ella Mae said. "I finished my novel and it is currently in the hands of our former teacher, Mr. Swann."

"That's wonderful!" he praised. She had often shared her ideas in her letters to him. He frequently replied with comments or suggestions, some of which she took to heart and incorporated into her story.

"Now what are you going to do with it? Take it to New York and become the next bestselling author?" he asked.

Ella Mae laughed wryly. "I wish... I honestly don't know what to do with it. I'm going to ask Mr. Swann for his advice."

"Well, there's not much opportunity here in Ridgely," Daniel stated, as if he hadn't already hammered that truth home to her.

"What about you? Two years left of school, eh?"

"Yes, ma'am. After that, I'll have to find my own town," he grinned. "I think I'll take over one and declare myself a dictator, and anyone who doesn't obey me will be either banished or beheaded."

"And have you found a woman to rule by your side in this cruel dictatorship?" she queried, hoping Daniel would finally ask her to wait for him.

He sighed woefully. "It's a very hard position to fill, I'm afraid. Not many women possess the necessary qualities."

Swallowing down her feelings, Ella Mae tried to keep her tone light as she continued the playful banter. "You can't find any woman in Chestertown to meet your expectations?"

"There are a few possibilities," he admitted, and Ella Mae felt the small spark of hope she had been nurturing inside her flicker and burn out.

Chapter Five

*I*t has merit," Mr. Swann said kindly, her manuscript resting on the table before him next to a cup of tea. "Just keep working at it."

Ella Mae forced a smile. It was hardly a glowing commendation.

"Do you have any specific suggestions…?" she asked, fearful that he would deliver a complete list of her shortcomings.

"Write from your heart, Miss Hutchins. Don't model your style after someone else's merely because they were successful. Find your own voice," he encouraged gently.

She nodded as if she understood, but she believed she *had* written from her heart. What exactly was it that her writing lacked?

With shoulders sagging, she climbed into the buggy and placed the leather satchel containing her manuscript on the seat beside her. She wished Penelope still lived in Ridgley so that she could cry on her shoulder, but her best friend was happily married and living in another state.

As the horse covered the miles to the farm, Ella Mae made no effort to dam the tears which spilled from her eyes and coursed down her cheeks. She had nothing… Daniel had made it clear that she was not worthy of his romantic interest, and now Mr. Swann had expressed that her writing was mediocre, at best. She was destined to be a spinster, and a failure at love as well in life.

Her eyes were swollen and red-rimmed when she reached home, and it only took her parents a second to guess what had happened.

"What did he say?" her mother worried.

"That I needed to keep working at it," Ella Mae answered, wiping her nose with a handkerchief.

Her father rested his hand on her shoulder. "That's hardly something to cry about. Of course, you need to keep working at it. You're still young and it was your first attempt."

"Don't be discouraged," her mother drew her into a hug. "And don't give up."

Ella Mae nodded, but her heart was too heavy to grasp for any thin threads of hope that might be offered.

"I'm going to my room for a bit," she said, excusing herself and retreating into the solitude.

When she came down for supper, she could see that her mother had something on her mind. "Ella Mae, your father and I have been talking. What would you think about staying with Grandma and Grandpa Greene in Annapolis for a while? Perhaps you could find a position as a private tutor with a family there."

"It's already September," Ella Mae answered dismissively.

"Oh ye of little faith," her father teased. "It can't hurt to write."

Ella Mae shrugged.

To save time, her father sent a telegram. To Ella Mae's surprise, a reply arrived the very next day stating that her grandparents had made some inquiries and learned of a family in need of a personal tutor for two children, a boy and a girl. The woman they had hired decided to run away and get married at the last minute.

"Well, there's no danger that I'll follow suit," Ella Mae sighed dramatically. "What ages are the children?"

"It doesn't say, but does it really matter? This is the perfect opportunity for you," her father stated.

He was right. As marriage did not appear to be in her future, she must find a way to provide for herself and to prove to both her parents and grandparents that the money spent on the Female Seminary was not wasted.

"You may reply that I'm interested. How soon should I leave?"

The next few days were a whirlwind as details were solidified and Ella Mae packed her things to move to her grandparents' house. The family offered to send a buggy to pick her up in the morning and return her in the evening, allowing her to stay with her grandparents. It benefited them in terms of costs, not having to provide for her meals, but it also benefited Ella Mae by guaranteeing her time away from the children.

Grandma and Grandpa Greene lived in a modest cottage on the outskirts of Annapolis. Her grandfather had made his living as a mason, laying brick sidewalks, garden paths, retaining walls, and building some of the houses which lined the streets in the wealthier part of town where Ella Mae's employer lived. A warm-hearted couple, the Greenes were delighted to have their granddaughter stay with them and worked out a more than equitable arrangement to allow her to cover some of her expenses while also saving a portion of her earnings.

Ella Mae was grateful for the kindness her parents and grandparents were showing her, for the love that motivated their actions. Without it, she wasn't sure she would have enough strength to rise and face each new day.

Before leaving Ridgely, her mother had taken her hand and said, "Don't give up, Ella Mae. I know things may seem bleak right now, but as long as there is a tomorrow, there is always hope."

Ella Mae held onto those words and prayed they were true.

She sent a letter to Daniel informing him of her sudden change of circumstances and included the address at her grandparents' house where she could be reached. As she travelled by train, ferry, and coach to her new destination, Ella Mae told herself to view it as an adventure, one from which she could certainly glean new material for another novel.

The children she would be teaching were a girl and boy, ages seven and ten respectively, by the names of Meredith and Lance Perry. Ella Mae hoped that she did not prove a disappointment to their parents as they were paying her handsomely to do something she had never done before. At least there were only two of them.

She was more than a little intimidated when she met Mr. and Mrs. Perry for the first time. Their house was the closest thing to a mansion Ella Mae had ever seen, and every room was impeccably furnished and immaculately clean. There were several maids employed to keep it this way, in addition to a cook and a gardener. If the couple hadn't been so unassuming and kind, Ella Mae would have been absolutely terrified.

Grandma and Grandpa Greene were eager to make her feel at home and Ella Mae wondered what exactly her mother had told them. They were plump and gray, with creases around their eyes and mouths revealing their love of laughter. Garrulous and cheerful, they were very involved in their local church and took every opportunity to minister to those less fortunate.

Staring at her sad reflection in the mirror, Ella Mae knew what her reputation in the community was: the rejected spinster granddaughter of the Greenes, accompanied no doubt by the added indignity of "poor thing."

The first few weeks in Annapolis were spent adjusting to her new home and employment, but Ella Mae was thankful for the distraction from her self-pitying thoughts. The children were well-mannered and polite, even if at times a bit livelier than Ella Mae knew how to manage, especially Lance. He could only sit still for so long before he seemed to explode with energy, and Ella Mae had to build regular breaks and exercise into their daily routine to manage her own frustrations.

Meredith was as sweet as she looked, like a porcelain doll with round rosy cheeks and curly golden hair. Every day she wore a different dress, protected by a starched white pinafore. Despite being rich and spoiled, the girl was a little darling and Ella Mae found her easy to love.

Ella Mae was thankful that, before abandoning her post, the previous governess had prepared the first two week's lesson plans, which Ella Mae was able to use as a template as she moved forward. She kept the children on a set schedule which made it easy for all three of them to know what to expect.

"It's time you met some people your own age," Grandma Greene announced one evening. "We've invited our neighbors, the Hudsons, to dinner this Saturday. They have a daughter about your age, and their niece is staying with them as well. It would do you good to make some friends."

Ella Mae had noticed there were two young women living next door and had hoped for an opportunity to meet them. She was eager to have someone her own age to converse with. The Hudsons' daughter Beatrice proved to be outgoing and friendly while her cousin Deborah was more reserved.

Perhaps it had something to do with her heritage, which Ella Mae could clearly see was more exotic than her own. Deborah's skin was a shade darker than white but not quite brown, like a cup of coffee heavily laced with cream. Her hair was sleek and truest black, although her almond-shaped eyes were brilliant blue. She had broad cheekbones, a strong nose, and full lips. Ella Mae had never seen anyone like her before. She was beautiful and intriguing.

Mr. and Mrs. Hudson owned a fishing business, selling their catch to the local markets. Beatrice told Ella Mae that along with her mother, she and Deborah helped to filet the fish and transport them on ice to the markets. She was almost the same age as Ella Mae and did not seem the slightest bit perturbed that she was still unmarried. Deborah was one year younger than Beatrice and seemed no more concerned about men than her cousin. Their attitude toward matrimony made Ella Mae feel less like a pathetic spinster, although she knew that the feeling was directly related to Daniel's lack of interest. If it hadn't been for him, she probably would have felt the same as her newfound friends.

Daniel had written to her with his surprise at her sudden leap into employment and expressed his shock that she had given up the rural paradise of Ridgely to live in Annapolis. He seemed to entirely miss the fact that she was a single woman who needed to find a means to support herself since the man she loved had failed to reciprocate.

He seemed as oblivious, preoccupied, and self-absorbed as usual, and Ella Mae wished she knew how to get through to him. Despite all his faults and flaws, she would never love anyone the way she loved him. Couldn't he see that? Or did her love mean so little to him?

Ella Mae only had a few hours alone in the evening to apply herself to writing, and she threw herself into it with renewed passion. Mr. Swann had told her to write from her heart, to find her own voice, and so she tried to do just that.

This novel, she was sure, would be one of such epic proportions that it would sweep the reader up and carry them away on a journey of the ebb and flow of human emotions. The protagonist was a man tortured by the rejection of his one true love, struggling to find a reason to live and a means to make it in a world that seemed superfluous to his heartache. The style was slightly reminiscent of Edgar Allen Poe, but it was her story, born of her own tears and longing.

Finally, she would make a name for herself and take her place in the world, and maybe then Daniel would at last see her worth. He would hold her novel in his hands, a heavy leather-bound volume with her name in gilded print, and as he read the story he would recognize the seed of suffering from which it had grown. He would call himself a thousand kinds of fool and come to find her at her grandparent's modest cottage, falling on his knee before her.

It was a lovely fantasy, and one she indulged in far too frequently. But it was all she had to fill the aching emptiness that haunted her in the dark hours of the night.

Ruth Turner wrote to her also. Wallace Reynolds had proposed, and they had set the date for June 1889. She wished Ella Mae to be a bridesmaid, and her older sister Henrietta was to be the Maid of Honor. Ella Mae wrote a reply stating how happy she was for her dear friend and that she would be honored to be in her wedding. Then she lay down upon the bed and cried herself to sleep.

When she awoke, her head aching from the force of the tears she'd spent, the sunlight was streaming through the window and slanting across the patchwork quilt upon her bed. She remembered her mother's words: *"As long as there is a tomorrow, there is hope."* Morning had dawned, it was a new day. She had to keep hoping.

Beatrice and Deborah were her saving grace. They took her all around Annapolis, showing her the State House where many historic moments had occured, the city dock where the ships harbored, and the Naval Academy where future officers were trained. They knew all the best places to buy pastries and coffee, and they showed her the markets where the Hudsons sold their fish and seafood. They were happy and, in their presence, it was hard not to be happy as well. They walked, arms linked, up the hill on Main Street, laughing at nothing but the knowledge that they were young and the weather was fine.

One afternoon they sat on a bench beneath a tree on the campus of St. John's College to rest their feet. Deborah had just sat down when an older man approached, his bushy white brows drawn together in a fury. He stood before Ella Mae and Beatrice, his cheeks turning red as he said, "You can dress her up and you can treat her like one of us, but it doesn't make it so. Send her back to where she belongs."

"I beg your pardon?" Ella Mae was taken aback.

Beatrice, having encountered this sort of attitude before, clenched her fists and stepped forward to confront the heavyset man. Even though he dwarfed her, she tilted her face upward so that he could clearly see the sparks flying from her eyes. "She is not a Negro, sir, but even if she were, I would believe she had every right to be here with us as an equal. I suggest that you move on before I report your harassment to the police."

"She's no white woman," the man insisted as he ambled away.

Beatrice lowered herself onto the bench beside Deborah, wrapping an arm protectively around her shoulder and kissing her cheek. "Pay no attention to him."

"I'm so sorry," Ella Mae took the place on the other side of Deborah. "Why would he say that?"

"I'm not Negro," Deborah insisted. "I'm half-Lakota. You would say Indian."

"Really?" Ella Mae's eyes widened. She'd never met an Indian before, only heard about them from books or from the former soldiers who visited the Turners' house. They would sometimes mention the Indian Wars fought in the West and how they had subdued the savages.

Deborah hardly seemed like a savage—not even a half-savage.

Ella Mae had a thousand questions, and she tried to arrange them in her mind in an order that was logical and showed proper respect. "You are half-Lakota," she repeated. "Mother or father?"

"My mother was Lakota," Deborah explained. "She married my father and we lived in log cabin like the other cattle ranchers." As if anticipating the questions to follow, she continued, "My father did his best to protect us, but it was not always easy to be Lakota.

Just being an 'Indian' made you dangerous to most white people. You may have heard of the Sioux Wars or of General Custer and the Battle of Little Bighorn? I was just a little girl when gold was found in the Black Hills and the treaties the government made became of no effect. Much fighting followed, and many of my people died.

"Then Indian children were taken away from their families and sent to boarding schools where they were treated poorly and forbidden to speak our native language. My parents were afraid for me, so they sent me here to live with people they trusted. Auntie Vivian is not related to me by blood, you see, but by love. My sisters, Elizabeth and Miriam, stayed here for a time but they are both married now. My brother, Frank, chose to stay in the West."

Ella Mae realized that she had never once considered the trials the Indians faced. She was confused by such words as "Lakota" and "Sioux," but she was reluctant to give away her own ignorance by asking for clarification. She decided to ask a safer question: "How did your parents know Mr. and Mrs. Hudson?"

"For a time, they lived in Wyoming. That is where they met and fell in love. But Mr. Hudson did not take to cattle ranching. He missed the Chesapeake Bay, and so he brought his wife back to this place where he had been a boy, so that he could catch fish." She laughed. "There was no water where I grew up except for an occasional lake or pond. Very few trees, as well. It was too open and dry for his liking. He'd rather smell like fish than round up the longhorns.

"Just as well, my mother says. Last year devastated the cattle ranchers out West. A scorching summer left them without enough grain to feed the herds through the winter and heavy snows, followed by a record breaking blizzard, wiped out millions of livestock. When spring finally came, the plains were littered with corpses. My parents thought about leaving, as many did, but they decided to stay it out. This year they will grow more crops, raise less cattle, and keep them fenced in, rather than letting them roam so far away from the homestead."

Ella Mae tried to envisage the world Deborah described, but her imagination failed. There was so much she had yet to learn.

"It sounds like a harsh place to live. I'm sure your parents were glad you were here during that time as well." Remembering the incident which had sparked the conversation, she asked, "Do people treat you like that often?"

"Not very often, but it happens from time to time," Deborah admitted. "I do not look like a Negro, but I do not look white, and some people care more than others. Most see that I associate with a white family and give little thought to what is different about my appearance."

"I'm sorry he was so rude to you," Beatrice said. "But never you mind. You know who you are, and that is my beloved cousin," she winked.

Deborah smiled, and Ella Mae took her hand.

Because of his interest in politics, Ella Mae thought it might behoove her to bring the plight of the Indians to Daniel's attention. He replied that it was much more involved than Ella Mae realized, and that while he didn't consider himself an expert on the subject, the complexity of the problem forestalled a simple solution. She hoped to discuss the subject with him in more depth over the Christmas holiday, assuming he had the time to stop by for a visit.

She'd forgotten how long it took to get from Annapolis back to Ridgely. By the time she reached the train station, she was exhausted and eager to lie down on her own bed at the farmhouse. Her mother and father were both waiting on the platform when she stepped down, eager to welcome her home.

It was already dark as they traveled through town, the December air biting and cold. Inside the farmhouse a fire blazed in the hearth and abundant Christmas decorations gave the small, humble space an atmosphere of cheer.

When morning came, Ella Mae stood by her window, gazing out at the familiar landscape. How she had missed the open expanse of the fields, the distant line of trees, the contour of the barn silhouetted against the sky. A gentle snow began to fall, dusting the ground with powdery white. Ella Mae wrapped her shawl more tightly around her shoulders. There was comfort in the familiar, but pain too as she remembered the Christmases past, spent with Penelope and Morris and, of course, Daniel... Good times that were forever consigned to memory, never again to be repeated.

Not knowing when or if he might stop by, Ella Mae dressed each day with care, hoping he would surprise her. On Christmas Eve, just after breakfast, a knock upon the door startled her as she sat in the parlor curled up in front of the fire with a book. She rose to answer it, expecting it was her sister Nora.

She was pleasantly surprised to see that handsome lopsided grin, a spark igniting in her heart and charging wildly through her veins at the sight of him. "Daniel! I wasn't expecting you!"

"I can't stay long," he said as he entered the house, removing his hat and placing it on the hallstand. "I'm only in town today and tomorrow, but I wanted to come by and say hello." His eyes said how pleased he was to see her.

"Come into the parlor," Ella Mae invited him, grateful he had made the time for her even if it was to be brief. She was also glad she had taken the extra care with her appearance that morning.

The subject of politics was never broached as their time together was so limited. Daniel only stayed for an hour and the conversation revolved around her life in Annapolis and a recent altercation he'd had with his brother. Ella Mae thought it strange that he was like a member of her family while she was a virtual stranger to his.

It was only another element of the mystery which made up their relationship, one she feared she would never be able to understand.

Chapter Six

June 1889

The winter months passed in a dreary succession of long gray days acting as a warden for two energetic children. Ella Mae was so exhausted from trying to keep Lance and Meredith from destroying the schoolroom she had little energy for writing by the time dinner was finished. On the weekends she tried to rekindle the creative spark, but it was difficult without regular input throughout the week.

She found it easier to lose herself in reading or to spend quiet afternoons crocheting with Deborah and Beatrice. Her grandparents were happy to have her company as they delivered meals to those in need or checked in on the ill or elderly. Time alone to create was scarce.

Ella Mae was grateful when spring arrived and the children could be turned out in the afternoons to play. It made their behavior far more manageable and boosted her own spirits as well. But it wasn't until the end of the school year and her return to Ridgely that Ella Mae finally found the freedom she needed to finish her novel.

The fresh country air and the empty days were the perfect catalyst for her to pour herself into writing. Sometimes she wrote during the day and slept through the night, but at other times inspiration seized her after she had gone to bed and she could not sleep until it had run its course. Her mother indulged her, letting her sleep as late in the afternoon as she needed to make up for the hours she'd spent awake during the night. Her meal schedule was correspondingly erratic.

By the beginning of June, she'd finished the rough draft and begun the process of editing. Ella Mae read through it from the first page to the last twice over, making changes and improvements, before declaring that she had reached the end of her abilities. It was time to hand it over to Mr. Swann.

But, with Ruth's wedding looming on the calendar, she decided to postpone that meeting a little longer. She didn't dare risk anything that might make her more susceptible to tears.

At least the dress Ruth had chosen for her was ecru with pastel purple trim, cut in the latest fashion and made by a dressmaker in Centreville. Unlike the yellow dress which had only seen the light of day that one special occasion, it was something Ella Mae would be delighted to wear again.

Rather than a church wedding, Ruth had opted to celebrate her nuptials at Laurel Hill. The ceremony was held in the backyard beneath the shade of a white canopy. Roses and dahlias bloomed in profusion. Hydrangea, zinnias, lavender, and Queen Anne's lace had been gathered into vases and fastened to the chairs along the aisle. It was an extravagant and lovely affair, and Ruth's smile beneath her white chiffon veil was one of perfect happiness.

Chaplain Davies officiated, standing on a stool behind the podium. He looked to Ella Mae like an elfin king, smiling from ear to ear with the wind ruffling his white hair. Uncle Charlie was in attendance with his wife Abigail, and to watch them interacting with Jeremiah and Clara one would never guess the secrets which lay hidden in their past.

Ella Mae wished Ruth and Wallace Reynolds a lifetime of happiness, not begrudging her this much deserved blessing. She kept a smile fixed on her face throughout the day, visiting with old friends from the seminary and answering questions about her current affairs with optimism. She indulged in the delicious fare that was offered and helped herself to a second piece of wedding cake.

By evening, when the newly married couple rode away amid a flurry of rice and well wishes, Ella Mae was spent. No more so than the rest of the Turner family, who had been in a whirlwind of activity for days in advance. Ella Mae joined Mrs. Turner and her oldest daughter, Henrietta, as they collected plates and cleared away food, gathering vases to be brought indoors, and sweeping up crumbs from the floor. She had spent the night before the wedding at Laurel Hill, and would sleep there again the night after, leaving on the morning train.

Ruth and her new husband were on their way to Europe for their honeymoon.

Ella Mae returned to Ridgely and went to straight to her room, crying herself to sleep from exhaustion and envy.

The following day, her sister came to visit. Understanding that the sisters needed time alone, Mrs. Hutchins took her grandsons into the kitchen to entertain them while the women took a short walk outside.

They paused beneath the old dogwood tree, the summer breeze stirring the tall, green stalks of corn in the fields surrounding them.

"How are you doing?" Nora asked, and Ella Mae knew exactly what she meant.

"I'm tired and sad," she answered honestly. "I've loved Daniel for as long as I can remember and I'm tired of attending other people's weddings with no hope of happiness in my own future."

Nora was four years older than Ella Mae, and everyone said they looked very much alike. Her eyes were dull as she said, "Marriage doesn't always guarantee happiness, Ella dear. You may be just as well to find it on your own."

"How are you doing?" Ella Mae turned the question on her sister, searching her eyes for the truth.

"Tired and sad," Nora replied. "But there's no use talking about it."

"I'm sorry," Ella Mae offered, resting her hand on her sister's, wishing she knew what else to say.

Nora nodded in acceptance of her sister's sympathy. "Sometimes things just aren't what you thought they were going to be."

The boys, James Jr. and Mark, came racing outside, their grandmother huffing after them. "I couldn't contain them any longer!" she laughed.

James Jr., now the age of six, leaped onto the swing and cried, "Push me!"

Mark, four years old, wailed, "No, push me! My turn!"

Nora scooped her youngest son into her arms and said, "Your turn next." With one arm, she gently pushed James Jr. into motion.

Mark squirmed, and his mother set him down. He promptly ran off to dig earthworms from the ground with a sharp stick, watching them wriggle around on his dirty little palm.

Ella Mae considered her sister's advice. Perhaps her happiness wasn't to be found in marriage and children—as these certainly did not appear to guarantee it—but rather in success as a novelist.

That afternoon, after Nora had departed with her offspring, Ella Mae placed her new manuscript into the leather satchel and with renewed determination set off for Mr. Swann's cottage. This was her second full-length novel. Certainly, it had more merit than the first.

Mr. Swann was as delighted to see her as always, and eager to read her latest literary efforts. When she returned in two weeks to retrieve it, he said, "Miss Hutchins, you know I am but a retired teacher in a farming town. If you are serious about your pursuit, perhaps you should be submitting this to an agent or the editor of a publishing company." Beneath the wild rows of his white eyebrows, his clear blue eyes were kind.

Was he implying that she had the potential to be published, or was he kindly directing her to someone who would speak the truth without fear of hurting her feelings?

"Do you think I should?" she asked, hoping for a clue to his motivation.

"Clearly, you have both passion and talent for writing. It would only make sense to share it with a professional who can help you achieve your dreams. All I can do is offer my personal opinions, which along with two cents will buy you a cup of coffee," he said with a self-deprecating smile.

Driving the buggy home, Ella Mae considered Mr. Swann's suggestion. If she was ever to going be published, she would have to do more than share her novels with family and friends. She would have to be brave enough to risk both criticism and rejection.

Her novel, though she would never compare her own feeble work to Tolstoy's genius, ended in a similar fashion to Anna Karenina with the suicide of her main protagonist. While it was drastically different in many ways, her story was similar in that it followed the lives of two men until the one was happily wed and the other despondently broken. Her intention was to illustrate the power of love to transform one's life and infuse it with meaning.

She'd titled it, *The Waning Moon,* but now she began to reconsider. If she mailed it to an agent, the first two details he would see were the title and author. If she gave it a less romantic title and used a male pseudonym, perhaps she would have a better chance of being taken seriously.

To keep the same initials, Ella Mae decided to use the pen name, Edward Hudson. The book she retitled simply, *Walter Rye,* after the character who had met with such a tragic end. The next feat was to copy by hand, page by page, the entirety of the manuscript so that she could retain the original.

By the time she had finished, her fingers were cramped and stained with ink, her eyes were red, her head ached, and she'd gone three days barely eating or sleeping. If determination and perseverance were what it took to be published, she would one day see her work in print. She hated to think it was possible that she had poured so much of herself into this dream only for it to go unfulfilled.

Once the package had been sent, Ella Mae knew it could be months before she received any correspondence. Still, the delivery of the mail had taken on a new allure as she anticipated a reply. One afternoon she was surprised to receive a very elaborate envelope from a stranger. Opening it, she saw that it was a wedding invitation sent from the parents of the bride-to-be of her friend, Morris. She hadn't heard much from him lately, and admittedly had not done her part at keeping in touch. Now she could hardly believe Morris was getting married! She hadn't even known he was courting!

Ella Mae wondered if this was an indication that he had moved on from Penelope, or if it meant he was trying to fill the void left by her marriage to another man. The wedding was set for the middle of November, which meant it was unlikely that she would be able to attend.

The following week, a letter arrived from Daniel expressing his surprise at having received the same invitation. *"Did he ever mention this woman to you? I haven't talked with him in some time, but I admit this came as quite a shock. Do you plan to attend? I would like to be present for this occasion, if you are in need of an escort."*

Unfortunately, Ella Mae knew there wasn't any way she could afford to take the time off to come home in November and then again in December for Christmas. She would have to decline Daniel's offer and forego Morris' wedding, though she was certain that Daniel could easily find another woman willing to attend with him.

Sitting down on the dogwood swing, Ella Mae let a tear slip from the corner of her eye. She remembered another summer afternoon in the same place, the day he had found her in a tree rescuing a kitten. She closed her eyes and felt the pressure of his hand against the small of her back, heard the affection in his voice when he said, *"I'm glad you didn't fall and break your ankle. Or your neck. I would have missed you."*

Should she have taken that as an opportunity and confessed her feelings for him then? What would he have said if she had? Most likely she would have put him in an awkward situation and ruined their friendship. As she had told Ruth Turner, Daniel was hardly shy. If he had wanted a relationship with her, he would have initiated it.

Like Morris, perhaps Ella Mae needed to accept that the one she loved did not—and never would—reciprocate her feelings. Either she must plan to remain unmarried or give up her silly romantic school girl notions and live in the real world where marriage was a societal institution intended to provide for women and create a safe environment for the procreation of the species.

What was love anyway if not a choice to be with someone till parted by death, a commitment to remain faithful to one person in sickness and in health, for better or for worse? All it really required was two like-minded people willing to commit to one another for the good of both parties, and for the sake of the continuation of mankind. Some countries still practiced arranged marriages, where the bride and groom didn't even meet until the day of their wedding. Perhaps the ideal of love as an emotion was just a lot of literary propaganda that ultimately led to pain and disappointment.

In the words of Louisa May Alcott: *"We all have our own life to pursue/ Our own kind of dream to be weaving ... / And we all have the power/ To make wishes come true/ As long as we keep believing.*"

She was on the cusp of turning twenty. It was time to grow up and take a more practical approach to her life. Maybe love and marriage were still possible for her, just not with Daniel, just not the way she had imagined it.

Chapter Seven

September 1889
Annapolis, Maryland

"The last time I checked, God was still on His throne," Grandma Greene responded when Ella Mae poured out her feelings to her. "Have you prayed for His will to be done in your life?"

Ella Mae huffed. "Of course, I have." Nothing had changed. Her grandmother was religious and old-fashioned, and she believed that prayer was the answer to everything.

"Well, my dear girl, sometimes the answers are long in coming. And sometimes they aren't what we want them to be, but He always answers and He's always in control," Grandma said with certainty, placing a plate of steaming hotcakes on the table in front of Ella Mae.

"Here's the syrup."

"Thank you," Ella Mae liberally poured it liberally over her pancakes, wishing the key to improving her life was as simple as prayer.

She quickly fell back into her routine of rising early and waiting for the Perry's carriage to fetch her and take her to their house on Duke of Gloucester Street. From the street, the house and yard were impressive, but the interior was especially so with ornately carved furniture, damask sofas, silver candelabra, Japanese urns, and walls covered with exquisite artwork. It seemed more like a museum than a home to Ella Mae, but the Perry family were quite at ease among the opulence that surrounded them.

The schoolroom was on the second floor, down the hall from her pupils' bedrooms. Ella Mae could hardly believe the luxury that was afforded the children. Meredith's room was outfitted with a massive canopied bed, with matching cherry dresser and vanity table. Porcelain dolls sat daintily on the shelves next to velvet rabbits and plush bears. Lance's room, though more masculine, was no less elaborate. His featured a nautical theme with model ships, ships in glass bottles, anchors, and various seafaring equipment.

Ella Mae spent most of her time in the schoolroom, on which the Perry's had spared no expense. She had her own desk to prepare the day's lessons, and each of the children had their own small oak desk at which to complete their assignments. There were shelves along the walls filled with books, art supplies, and scientific apparatus.

She dressed in black or gray, as suited her position. It was an interesting role in the household, as she was neither a mere employee like the maid or cook, nor was she a member of the family even if she was included in occasional outings or parties.

Ella Mae was thankful that Mr. and Mrs. Perry were kind and generous and went out of their way to be sure she was comfortable and felt appreciated for her work with the children. Ella Mae wasn't exactly sure of the source of Mr. Perry's income, only that he owned several successful businesses and was often out of town to oversee their management. When home, he spent hours in his study pouring over documents or meeting with business associates.

Mrs. Perry oversaw the running of the house, preparing the weekly menu, being sure the employees executed their jobs efficiently, and graciously welcoming everyone who entered her home. She never seemed at a loss for the right thing to say and was always dressed impeccably. She was exactly the sort of woman that

Ella Mae imagined Daniel wanted for a wife. Compared to Mrs. Perry, Ella Mae was awkward, bookish, and rural.

Sometimes she would stare at the books on the shelf, many of which the children wouldn't be ready to read for years to come, and imagined that one day her own work might appear alongside these classics. She would run her finger over the spines, pausing where she could see in her mind's eye the name "Edward Hudson" tucked in among them.

Would Daniel read her books when they were published? Would he be proud of her?

It seemed far more likely that her books would never be published, that she was destined to remain a governess forever, with only the admiration of her young pupils. Sighing, Ella Mae turned away from the bookshelf.

At the end of the day, the Perry's driver took her back across town to where the peasants lived, or so it seemed to Ella Mae. Her grandparents' home seemed more than merely humble compared to the Perry's mansion. It was cramped, ramshackle, and dirty. And it was where she belonged.

The second week of December, before she went home for the Christmas holiday, Mr. and Mrs. Perry hosted a party for an eclectic assortment of associates and acquaintances. Ella Mae was asked to remain late to entertain the children while their parents and other household employees were occupied downstairs.

Dinner was served to the children and their governess in the schoolroom, followed by a delivery of Christmas cookies, pastries, and hot cocoa. Ella Mae tried to make it a party atmosphere for her charges, leading them in song while they decorated the room with strings of popcorn and cranberries. They danced to music on a phonograph, Meredith twirling her skirt while Lance pretended to accidently step on her toes.

Mrs. Perry insisted that, once the children had been put to bed, Ella Mae should come down to the kitchen for a sampling of the cook's delicacies before the driver took her home. After the children had been changed into their pajamas and tucked into their beds, she took the servant staircase in the back of the house to avoid having to encounter what she thought of as the "real people." The smells wafting up from the kitchen were heavenly and even though she'd eaten a generous meal, she found she was hungry again.

The household employees were gathered around a table in the kitchen, enjoying their own small feast. Cook had a glass of wine in hand and looked as if she had exhausted herself in preparation for the event. Ella Mae filled a plate and took a seat next to her. The gardener, who also served as her driver, appeared in no hurry as he filled another plate and settled back at the table. The maids came and went from the kitchen, attending to the needs of the guests.

Mrs. Perry swished into the kitchen in a lovely dress of silver and green satin, with a strand of diamonds sparkling at her throat. "Ah, Miss Hutchins! There you are. I would like for you to come meet one of our guests," she smiled brightly. "Mr. Wescott is a literature professor at St. John's college, and when I mentioned that you were an aspiring novelist, he said he simply had to meet you. Won't you come and say hello?"

Ella Mae would have preferred to walk home, barefoot, in the snow. But what could she say?

"Certainly, Mrs. Perry." She forced a smile, following her employer into the parlor where a fire blazed in the enormous hearth and well-dressed visitors sat or stood around the opulent room with glasses of wine or sherry. Feeling every bit the lowly governess in her plain black dress, Ella Mae reluctantly trailed behind her elegant hostess to meet the gentleman standing in front of the fireplace.

"Mr. Wescott, this is our governess, Miss Hutchins, whom I've told you about," Mrs. Perry introduced her warmly. "And Miss Hutchins, please meet Mr. Wescott."

Ella Mae fervently wished she had never mentioned her attempts at writing to Mrs. Perry. She had only done so to impress the lady, and now she was being punished for her vanity.

"Pleased to meet you," she managed.

Mr. Wescott was younger than Ella Mae had expected. He had honey brown hair, green eyes, and beneath his mustache, a gentle smile. He wore wire-rimmed glasses and his black suit was worn at the collar.

"Mrs. Perry informed me that when you aren't teaching her children, you are writing the next great American novel," he said with a smile. "I would love to hear about it."

Hoping that a brief overview would suffice, she explained its similarities to and differences from Tolstoy's *Anna Karenina*, and the overriding principal she hoping to convey. He looked both intrigued and amused, and Ella Mae was unprepared for the detailed questions he asked and the interest he took in her plot and character development.

What she hoped would be a quick meeting turned into an hour-long conversation. Mr. Wescott was the first person she'd met in quite some time who shared her avid interest in literature. She found herself enjoying the evening far more than she'd expected.

"Are you familiar with the poem *Kubla Khan*, by Samuel Taylor Coleridge? I'm currently discussing it with my students at St. John's."

"I am," Ella Mae answered. "It's also sometimes called *A Vision in A Dream*."

"That's right!" Mr. Wescott said, appearing pleased. "Originally, Coleridge only shared it in private readings with his friends, but in 1816 he published it at the encouragement of Lord Byron."

"*In Xanadu did Kubla Khan/ A stately pleasure-dome decree:/ Where Alph, the sacred river, ran/ Through caverns measureless to man/ Down to a sunless sea,"* she quoted the first stanza of the poem.

Truth be told, they were the only lines she could remember, but it was enough to gain approval from Mr. Wescott.

He smiled broadly, "Very good, Miss Hutchins! Do you know the story of how he came to write the poem?"

Ella Mae didn't, and he preceded to inform her that the poet claimed to have fallen asleep reading *Purchas' Pilgrimes*, wherein was described the land of Xanadu and the stately palace and gardens of the Mongol ruler, Kublai Khan. Just prior to this nap, Coleridge had taken a dose of opium for indigestion prompting a most vivid dream of this land, which he attempted to capture in his poem. Unfortunately, he was interrupted before its completion and when he returned to it, memories of the vision had evaporated into thin air.

"There is nothing worse than a flash of inspiration rudely interrupted by the mundane demands of every-day life," Ella Mae commented, relating to the frustration the poet had certainly felt.

Conversation flowed naturally between she and the professor, and she was surprised when the clock on the mantel—echoed by the grandfather clock in the hall—chimed the hour.

"Oh my! I'm afraid I shall have to excuse myself," Ella Mae said reluctantly. "It was lovely meeting you."

"I would be very interested in reading your novel, Miss Hutchins, if you would like my professional critique," he offered with a half-smile.

"Yes, I'm sure I could use some advice," she replied, flattered that he would take such an interest in her work.

"There's a coffee and pastry shop on North Street, near the college, if you would like to meet me there next Saturday?"

"I know it," Ella Mae replied, having been there with Beatrice and Deborah on more than one occasion. "That would be wonderful."

To have a literature professor take a personal interest in her—a mere governess—was flattering and exciting! She could hardly wait to tell Beatrice and Deborah!

"A word of advice, my dear," Grandma Greene cautioned when Ella Mae related the night's events upon her return home. "It may be more than just your words he's interested in."

"Would that be such a bad thing?" she asked.

"That all depends on what kind of man he is," Grandma answered, kissing Ella Mae's forehead. "Be careful."

"I will," Ella Mae promised.

Her friends were far more positive when she told them about her encounter with the literature professor.

"Why, Ella Mae, that's so exciting!" Beatrice exclaimed, taking Ella Mae's hands in her own enthusiastically. "Maybe he can help you get your novel published."

"I don't know, but at least he might help me to improve my writing," Ella Mae said, afraid to hope for too much.

"What does he look like?" Deborah asked, her dark brows lifting in curiosity.

"He's an average looking fellow," Ella Mae admitted, "but he's not unattractive."

"Well, it's character that counts," Beatrice said. "At least, that's what my mother always says," she added with a giggle.

"Grandma thinks he might be personally interested in me, but it's more likely he's just being kind since I'm an aspiring writer," Ella Mae reminded them.

"It's possible… but I doubt it," Deborah replied with a giggle.

When Saturday arrived, Ella Mae was a bundle of nerves. Not only was she going to be giving her juvenile and amateur writing to a literature professor for evaluation, but there was a possibility he might be interested in her as a woman. While she knew she needed to let go of the dream of being with Daniel, the idea of opening herself up to another man made her feel guilty… and vulnerable.

She wore a blue plaid dress with a high collar and demure bustle when she met Mr. Westcott at the coffee shop. Grandpa Greene drove her there in the buggy, insisting upon meeting the professor before he took his leave and promising that he would be back to pick her up in one hour. While Ella Mae appreciated the protective gesture, it only made her feel more like a little girl.

After the initial greeting and the ordering of the coffee and pastries, the awkwardness began to dissipate as they discussed such nonthreatening subjects as grandparents, the weather, and the divine properties of chocolate.

"Now then, let me see this novel," Mr. Wescott said, once the dessert plates had been removed from the table.

Ella Mae retrieved her satchel from where it rested in the empty chair next to her, carefully removing the thick manuscript and placing it on the table in front of him. "I'm sure that it's full of errors of many kinds, but I hope it has enough redeeming qualities to make it worth the read."

"I'm sure it does," he smiled kindly, his eyes glancing over her face before moving to the page in front of him. Adjusting his glasses, he scanned the title page, then the first page, nodding as he read. "Do you mind if I take it with me to read at my leisure? That way I can take some notes to give you when I return it."

"Yes, of course," Ella Mae answered, wishing it wasn't her only copy.

They discussed her novel for only a few more minutes before the conversation turned personal.

"How did you come to live with your grandfather?" Mr. Westcott asked.

Ella Mae explained how she'd moved in with her grandparents when she had taken the job with the Perry family. "I grew up in a small farming town on the Eastern Shore."

Mr. Westcott asked her about her parents and siblings, about the town of Ridgely, and told her that he had lived in the Annapolis area his entire life. He had attended St. John's college himself, before moving on with his education and finally coming back to teach there.

The time passed quickly, and Ella Mae was surprised when she saw her grandfather's buggy parked outside on the street.

"I see my grandfather has come for me," she said. "Thank you so much for taking the time to meet with me today. When would you like to meet again to discuss your thoughts on my novel?"

"I believe I should be able to make good progress with it this week. Is next Saturday acceptable to you?"

"I'll be going home for Christmas," she answered. "I'll be back after the first of the year."

"Then let's plan for the first Saturday in January. Here's a card with my address, should you need to contact me," Mr. Westcott said.

Ella Mae accepted his card with a smile. "Have a good Christmas."

"And you as well," he answered, his green eyes once again lingering before he looked away.

Ella Mae couldn't help but wait with eager anticipation for their next meeting. She imagined Professor Wescott sitting in his study, the walls lined with bookshelves containing the works of history's greatest scholars, and her own novel resting in front of him. She wondered what he thought about her writing style, about the story she'd concocted, and more specifically, about *her*.

Chapter Eight

*A*lthough she enjoyed spending Christmas with her family, she was disappointed that Daniel didn't make time to visit. Ella Mae felt his absence keenly and wondered if he hadn't made time for her because had brought a female friend home to meet his parents. She was glad she had already made the decision to let go of the foolish hope that he might love her, as any such hope was clearly in vain.

She enjoyed the holiday with her family but was distracted by thoughts of the professor and wondering about his assessment of her writing ability. It was the first time she was eager to get back to Annapolis.

If Ella Mae had been nervous upon their first meeting, she was doubly so now as Mr. Wescott would report if he thought she had any real hope of publication, or if she was wasting her time. She needed him to be honest with her—she only hoped that he could truthfully tell her she had talent and potential. A negative review would likely reduce her to tears.

Once again, her grandfather drove her to the coffee shop and made his protective presence known to the gentleman. Mr. Wescott was gracious and polite, even inviting Mr. Greene to stay and join them.

Grandpa declined, stating he had errands to run and would be back for Ella Mae once they were finished. She was relieved he hadn't chosen to stay. She had been looking forward to another opportunity to visit with Mr. Wescott, and her grandfather's presence would have decidedly changed the dynamic.

Once coffee and pastries had been purchased, Ella Mae and Mr. Wescott took their places across from one another at the small table. He began with polite conversation, asking about her holiday and her family. He had spent the week catching up on grading papers, reading her novel, and visiting with his parents and sister. Once the small talk was out of the way, it was time to dive into the purpose for their visit.

"I enjoyed reading your novel, Miss Hutchins. It gave me a window into your heart and mind. I sensed that there were some underlying emotions which guided the story?" he asked, his green eyes searching hers through the wire-rimmed glasses.

She nodded, not willing to discuss the topic of Daniel with him. "Every author draws on some personal experience," she replied vaguely.

"You have a natural gift for description and your use of dialogue is excellent. There are a few stylistic habits that you should work on correcting, but overall your writing is solid. The only major criticism I might have is that the novel's point of view is supposed to be from a man's perspective while it was clearly written by a woman." He softened this appraisal with a smile and added, "And that is by no means an insult."

"You don't believe it has any hope of publication?" Ella Mae tried to keep the disappointment from her voice and failed.

"I wouldn't go that far, Miss Hutchins. I think it just needs some male influence to improve its sense of realism."

Ella Mae suspected that an invitation was forthcoming, and she wasn't disappointed.

"I'd be happy to go over it with you, if you'd like," Mr. Wescott graciously volunteered.

Grandma Greene's warning echoed in her mind: *"Be careful."*

She stared across the short distance that separated them, noting the earnest expression he wore. Mr. Wescott was a literature professor. His job was to mold young minds, to teach them the wisdom of those who had gone before and to guide them into their own destiny. As long as he didn't suggest she meet him at his own apartment or in some other remote location, she had no reason to believe his intentions were anything but noble.

"That would be very kind of you," she smiled. For the first time, she felt as if there were hope for her—both for her dreams of publication and for love.

"It's probably best to find a less distracting location if we are going to work through your manuscript," Mr. Wescott said thoughtfully. "Perhaps I could meet you at the Perry's house one day a week, after you've completed your duties with the children?"

"I'll ask Mrs. Perry on Monday," Ella Mae promised.

Her employer was more than happy to accommodate her request and expressed pleasure that her meeting with Mr. Wescott had ended so productively. Ella Mae was grateful for Mrs. Perry's kindness and the support of her interests outside of teaching the children.

Beginning that Thursday evening, Mr. Wescott met her in the schoolroom at the Perry's house at quarter after three. They began by discussing elements of the first chapter that might be altered to reflect a more masculine voice, then the conversation once again shifted to a personal nature.

Mr. Wescott leaned forward, his voice gently inquisitive. "It's obvious to me that this story has a very personal meaning to you, that's it an expression of your pain. I would very much like to know what—or who—it is that hurt you so."

His eyes were sincere, his expression patient. Ella Mae hesitated, understanding that once the line had been blurred between a professional and a personal relationship, there was no turning back. But as she met his gaze, his attention fully riveted upon her, she realized that was exactly what she wanted.

She told him about Daniel, about how he had strung her along and broken her heart by never taking that last final step. He was only a friend, yet so much more than a friend, but never willing to commit himself to her in even the smallest of ways. She realized as she rambled on about Daniel what a pathetic little fool she had been.

"I'm so sorry, Miss Hutchins. It sounds like he didn't appreciate you," he said sympathetically.

Ella Mae felt a blush touch her cheeks. "Well, I suppose we weren't right for each other really," she admitted. "He wanted to pursue politics while I'm content to sit alone and read and write."

"Common interests do make a big difference in relationships," he agreed, and Ella Mae sensed that he was talking about more than Daniel.

Not knowing how to respond, she merely nodded in agreement.

"I was in love once," he confessed softly. "Engaged, even. But she died in a train accident just months before our wedding."

"Oh, how horrible!" Ella Mae exclaimed. "I can't imagine what a terrible loss that must have been!"

"It was devastating," Mr. Wescott admitted. "For a time, I wasn't sure I wanted to go on."

"I am so sorry," Ella Mae consoled. "I'm sure it's been very hard for you."

"It's been a little over year now and I've come to terms with it. I wasn't sure if I could ever love again, but I don't want to discount that I might have another chance. Life can be a long, lonely road for an unmarried man. All his accomplishments are nothing if he has no one to share them with."

His eyes were full of sadness and hope as they met hers. Swallowing nervously, Ella Mae knew with certainty that they had crossed over into a more personal relationship.

When they met the following week, it seemed only natural that they should be on a more familiar basis. "Please, call me John," he said. And she encouraged him to call her Ella Mae.

From then on, their time together was spent increasingly less on making alterations to her manuscript and more on getting to know one another. She was hardly surprised when he invited her to a concert performed by the St. John's College Band.

Walking down the brick sidewalk leading to the white-domed brick building of McDowell Hall, her hand tucked into the crook of John's elbow, Ella Mae felt like a different person. No longer the unwanted farmgirl, she was an aspiring novelist who had caught the attention of a literature professor. She had worn one of her nicest gowns, a rich merlot red with a wide skirt and an abundance of material draped across the underskirt and gathered in the back over the bustle. She felt worldly, desirable, and chosen.

She'd never attended a concert like this before and sitting with John's shoulder inches from hers, the music swelling around them—violins, cellos, flutes, and oboes—she felt as if she were being carried away to a new and magical world where dreams could come true. The flickering candlelight from the brass chandelier overhead filled the room with a soft glow, glinting off the musician's instruments.

John was well known, and everyone was quick to express their pleasure at seeing him with a woman on his arm. Ella Mae was introduced to more people, both students and faculty, than she could possibly remember.

"Mr. Wescott is such a dear man. We were all so heartbroken when Leanne died. But now that he's met you, we couldn't be more thrilled!" the wife of another professor told her enthusiastically.

Before the evening was over, Ella Mae must have heard the same sentiment expressed a hundred times over. The more she heard the woman's name spoken, the more Leanne became a person than a part of the past. Not to mention the pressure Ella Mae felt. If she ever changed her mind about her relationship with John, all these people would judge her as cruel for breaking his heart.

Though at this time, she had no reason to halt the budding romance. John was attentive and respectful, and she enjoyed the time they spent together. They had almost completely abandoned the work on her novel, but she found she was too distracted living out her own story to focus on it anyway.

Nothing was said of the nature of their relationship in the first three weeks that that they met weekly at the Perry's, but after the concert it seemed there was an unspoken understanding. Ella Mae did not want to assume anything, as Daniel had spent inordinate amounts of time with her without ever making a commitment. She hoped that John would speak plainly and make his intentions clear.

One evening as he was driving her home in his buggy from the Perry's, a light snow began to fall from the gray February sky. When John halted the horse in front of her grandparents' house, he rested his hand lightly on her arm and said, "Wait."

Reaching behind him on the seat, John retrieved a picture frame. From the faint glow of the street lamp, Ella Mae could see that it contained a poem. Removing his glasses, John looked deeply into her eyes as he said, "This isn't much, but I don't have much to give. I'm a professor of literature and not a wealthy man. I never thought I would be able to love again, but then I met you and everything changed. I want you to know, Ella Mae, for what it's worth, I love you."

The lamplight from the street caught in the honey brown of his hair, thinning in the front. Where he had removed his glasses, there were indentations in his nose at the corners of his eyes. His mustache rested lightly over his full top lip, which he licked nervously as he awaited her reply. Snow fell silently around them, insulating them inside the buggy.

In response to such a romantic gesture, Ella Mae wished she could say something of equal value. But instead of the rush of warmth she would have expected to feel after such a declaration, she felt only a strange desire to flee.

She accepted the framed poem, holding it in her gloved hands and glancing over the words which she couldn't quite make out in the shadows. "Thank you," Ella Mae whispered, unable to say more.

"I'll see you again next week?" John asked nervously, his voice as soft as her own had been.

"Yes, John. Thank you," she said again, sliding across the seat toward the door.

Taking the cue, he climbed down from his side of the buggy and walked around to open her door. The hushed silence as the snow fell, covering the world in a blanket of white, surrounded them as they walked to the house. John tipped his hat and bid her goodnight as she opened the door and slipped inside.

Ella Mae retreated to the parlor, standing in front of the fire to warm herself. By the orange glow of the flames, she read the poem John had given her.

Love and Sorrow, by Tennyson

O maiden, fresher than the first green leaf
With which the fearful springtide flecks the lea,
Weep not, Almeida, that I said to thee
That thou hast half my heart, for bitter grief
Doth hold the other half in sovranty.
Thou art my heart's sun in love's crystalline:
Yet on both sides at once thou canst not shine:
Thine is the bright side of my heart, and thine
My heart's day, but the shadow of my heart,
Issue of its own substance, my heart's night

Thou canst not lighten even with thy light,
All powerful in beauty as thou art.
Almeida, if my heart were substanceless,
Then might thy rays pass thro' to the other side,
So swiftly, that they nowhere would abide,
But lose themselves in utter emptiness.
Half-light, half-shadow, let my spirit sleep
They never learnt to love who never knew to weep.

Ella Mae sank down into the armchair, staring at the reflection of the leaping flames on the glass covering the printed page John had removed from a book. The frame was ornate and gilded, and she wondered if it had previously contained a photograph of his former love, Leanne. She understood the message he was sending through Tennyson's words, that because he had experienced such deep pain, his heart had been carved out to contain deeper love.

Ella Mae felt conflicted. She had longed to be so loved... and yet, she felt an odd niggling of doubt. Did John truly love her as he claimed?

And, just as important, did she truly love him?

The logs in the fireplace popped as the blaze consumed them, sparks flying into the air as they shifted in the red-hot coals. Ella Mae stared into them, searching for answers. Perhaps what she had always dreamed of was no more than a child's dream, unrealistic and unobtainable. She was an adult now, and this was real life. All the romantic notions that had once occupied her fantasies would have to be relinquished, cast out like old toys, now outgrown.

John said he loved her, and she felt great affection for him. They both longed to *be* loved, and have someone *to* love. That was the basis of marriage: a decision to come together and build a life. Once all the frills and dressings were removed, that was it.

Carrying a cup of hot tea, Grandma joined her in the parlor. "Here you go, dear," she said. "It's awfully cold out tonight."

Noticing the frame Ella Mae held in her hands, she asked, "What do you have there, child?"

Ella Mae surrendered the frame in exchange for the steaming tea. It smelled of orange peel and spice, and she inhaled its warm steam gratefully. "Mr. Wescott gave this to me tonight," she said.

After reading the poem, Grandma lifted her eyes to Ella Mae's. "And what do you think about this?"

"I don't know, Grandma," she answered honestly, searching the round, wrinkled face of the woman who had given birth to her mother. "I care for him. We have similar interests and enjoy spending time together. He does have a woman in his past, but even though Daniel and I were never engaged, he had a piece of my heart. I guess life and love are just more complicated than I had once thought."

"That's the truth, my dear," Grandma rose, pressing a kiss to the crown of Ella's head. "Even so, pray for wisdom. Who you have by your side as you walk the path of life can make all the difference in the world."

"Yes, ma'am," Ella Mae answered, suddenly feeling overcome with fatigue.

She finished her tea and excused herself for the night. Once buried beneath the thick quilts with a hot water bottle tucked under her feet, Ella Mae tried to follow her grandmother's advice and pray for discernment to know if John was the man she should marry. He hadn't proposed, but the poem was a means of gauging how she would respond if he did. She needed to know what her answer would be.

Silence, like the hush of falling snow, surrounded her as she listened for some voice from beyond herself.

Chapter Nine

There was only one reason Ella Mae would have chosen not to marry John Wescott. But when Daniel replied to the letter she'd sent, he'd wished her good luck with both her novel and the professor.

Her choices were clear. Either she married the man who claimed to love her or she chose to remain a spinster, languishing into old age, yearning for a man who'd made it clear that he had no such feelings for her. She would be a fool to choose the latter.

And so the next time Ella Mae met John in the schoolroom at the Perry's house, she told him how much the gift had meant to her and that she was sorry she hadn't been able to respond at the time.

"I guess it just took me by surprise, and I didn't realize how afraid I was until that very moment."

"What are you afraid of?" he asked, taking her hand and gazing at her through the lenses of his glasses.

"I suppose it's just the fear of the unknown," she said, unsure herself what exactly the root of her fear was. "Maybe I'm afraid that no man could truly love me…" she finally admitted.

John leaned forward, cupping her jaw in his hand. "My dear, let me put that fear to rest." He closed the distance between them, pressing his lips gently against hers.

His mustache tickled and his breath was warm against her skin. Any ideas of spine-tingling or dizziness were quickly disproven. Nothing magical occurred. It was just his face awkwardly close to hers. But the words he'd spoken and the promise within them warmed her heart. His thumb gently stroked her cheek, and she leaned into his hand.

He had declared his intentions. There was no doubting what the nature of their relationship was. He was courting her.

She wrote to tell her mother, Penelope, and Ruth about this new development. Her mother expressed more concern than enthusiasm. Penelope admitted that marriage was much harder than she had expected, but claimed she was still happy with her choice. Ruth was thrilled for her and confessed that she was already expecting her first child.

Beatrice and Deborah were delighted, nearly swooning when she showed them the framed poem John had given her. Grandma and Grandpa Greene were cautiously approving, inviting the professor over for dinner to formally meet them. Ella Mae felt as if she had finally crossed over the threshold from childhood into adulthood. At last, marriage was in her future.

Ella Mae made Mrs. Perry aware of the new nature of her relationship with John Wescott. Her employer encouraged her to continue meeting with him at the house to provide an appropriate chaperone, but offered to allow them to meet in the parlor rather than the schoolroom. The spacious, elegantly furnished room added a level of both legitimacy and romanticism to their time together.

She had yet to visit Mr. Wescott's abode, although he had admitted that it was quite a bachelor's pad and hardly suited for female company. He was a man of thought and prone to allowing his environment to fade into the background as the inner workings of his mind often took precedence over more practical activities.

Ella Mae translated this to mean that his small apartment was in a state of continual disarray and he was embarrassed to let her see it. Since there was no formal commitment between them, she did not feel it appropriate to force the issue. In passing, he also mentioned that his finances were in a similar condition, but once again Ella Mae did not feel entitled to press for details.

John did, however, take her to meet his parents and sister, who lived in a modest house on the outskirts of town. They were more enthusiastic even than the folks she had met at the college band concert. His mother embraced her warmly, kissing her cheek and exclaiming over how beautiful she was. His father stood back, smiling his approval, while his sister seemed eager to befriend her. Cora was only a year or so older than Ella Mae, sharing the same tall frame, wide shoulders, and honey brown hair as her brother.

After their initial meeting, Sunday dinners with the Wescotts became an institution. The weeks passed, and slowly the wintry days began to warm, promising spring would soon arrive. Ella Mae and John began to meet twice during the week, slipping outside into the Perry's flower garden whenever the weather would allow.

John often read or quoted poetry to her, analyzing its meaning and sharing information about the author. They talked about their favorite novels, and he was a fount of information about plot and character development, grammar and punctuation, and the art of capturing the reader.

They discovered a mutual appreciation for the game of checkers, which Ella Mae brought down from the schoolroom and set up on a small table in the parlor. Hours would pass, one game being followed by a rematch, as they laughed and teased one another like old friends.

Often, something would stir a memory of his fiancée and a reminiscence would follow. Ella Mae began to feel as though she knew Leanne personally. She knew her favorite color, foods, books, and places. She knew where John had met Leanne, where they had shared their first kiss, and when they had agreed to spend the rest of their lives together.

Ella Mae understood that he wanted to talk about Leanne in order to share his life with her and to let go of the past, but sometimes it seemed he shared too much.

"I fear I'm competing with a ghost," she confessed one evening as they sat together in the parlor in front of the fireplace where they had first met.

He rested his hand over hers, his voice gentle as he said, "Of course you're not competing with a ghost, my dear! I am completely yours, heart and soul. Whatever I share of my past is only so that you will know me better."

Ella Mae didn't want to diminish the severity of his loss by making Leanne a taboo subject. She did not wish to be either selfish or insensitive to his grief, but John talked about Leanne so often and in such detail that it felt as if there were three people in their relationship, and Ella Mae wasn't sure which of the two women involved held the key to his heart.

Whenever he launched into what Ella Mae thought of as a "Leanne Story," she tried to communicate that it hurt her by becoming silent and withdrawn. John didn't appear to notice. In the beginning he had shown great interest in knowing *her*, but now it seemed he was fixed on the past and the woman he had loved before her.

Ella Mae told herself that he was coming to terms with Leanne's death and clearing space in his life for her. She had to give him time to do that. Besides, she often thought of Daniel, though she did not openly talk of him. Maybe she had no right to hold it against John that he remembered his former fiancée when she still carried a spark for another man quietly inside her own heart.

In March, John invited her to attend a luncheon at the college where he was to be a key-note speaker. It was an event hosted in honor of a professor who would be retiring at the end of the school year and had been on staff at St. John's for forty years. Mr. Wescott proudly introduced her to all his students and associates, many of whom she had previously met at the concert, although she couldn't recall all their names. She was overwhelmingly welcomed with great affection by all, and Ella Mae was grateful that this time no mention was made of Leanne.

The luncheon was held in a room even larger and more elaborate than where the concert had been hosted. This lovely room, located in the Randall Hall, was known inauspiciously as the Edward T. Higgins Dining Hall. Classic white pillars supported the ceiling, embellished with decorative columns and boasting massive chandeliers. Arching windows allowed natural light to spill into the room and an ornate fireplace dominated the rear wall.

Ella Mae couldn't imagine stepping up to the podium in such an elegant setting and speaking to an audience of well over a hundred people. She felt uncomfortable as a mere guest! She was relieved when the crowd finally dissipated, and she was seated at a table with other professors and their wives.

John Wescott had no such reservations, appearing quite at ease as he stood patiently listening to his introduction by the college president. He smiled casually as he stepped forward, arranging his notes before him, which he only glanced at occasionally during his speech. He easily captured the attention and affection of the crowd, regaling them with thoughtful insights and humorous anecdotes of the retiring professor's years at the college.

Listening to John's tribute to his colleague, Ella Mae could see the compassionate and wise man he was. She smiled affectionately as their eyes met, touched by the sweet spirit she saw in him. She was sure that any perceived insensitivity he demonstrated toward her was only the result of his gentle nature and lingering affection for his former fiancée. And his loyalty to Leanne, she realized, was an attribute worthy of appreciation, not jealousy.

In April, Ella Mae was invited back to the college to attend the annual croquet match between the "Johnnies" and the Naval Academy "Mids" in the afternoon, followed by the Spring Cotillion that evening. Students and faculty in their dress attire waltzed the hours away in the Great Hall. Ella Mae had attended a few small dances in Ridgely, but this was a new experience for her.

She wore the ecru and purple dress Ruth had made for her wedding, carefully curling her hair and adding a touch of color to her cheeks. It was wonderful to feel young, alive, and beautiful on a lovely spring evening scented with the perfume of blooming flowers.

Her partner was hardly graceful on his feet, being far more adept at reciting lines of poetry than at moving his body to the rhythm of the violin. But they had a wonderful time just the same, sipping champagne and laughing every time John stepped on her toes, which was often. His arm around her waist, his smile beaming down at her, and the flickering candlelight giving the room a romantic glow, made Ella Mae feel dizzy with happiness.

At midnight the musicians put down their instruments and dessert was served. Cups of diced strawberries topped with whipped cream were distributed, and Ella Mae was certain it was the sweetest she'd ever tasted. That night she returned home with tired legs and sore feet, but she slept soundly with the warmth of his kiss upon her lips and the hope of a bright future in her heart.

Two weeks later, as they sat together on the damask sofa in the Perry's parlor on a rainy evening, John put his arm around her and drew her close. She nestled into the crook of his shoulder, feeling his warmth through her clothing. They talked of nothing, of the little things that comprise daily life.

Then, seemingly out of the blue, he said, "We should get married, Ella Mae."

Startled by the unexpected pronouncement—not necessarily that she hadn't been anticipating the question, but certainly not now, in this moment—she turned to face him with wide eyes. "*Married?*"

"Yes, married," he replied.

Ella Mae swallowed. This was the deciding moment that would change the course of her future. She should have been excited instead of feeling an odd flutter of panic. But having no reason to decline, and having allowed this courtship, how could she do anything else but accept?

She took a deep breath, met his gaze and said, "Perhaps we should."

"Really?" he asked, as if surprised by her reply.

She nodded. It was hardly the proposal she had hoped for.

John stood, drawing Ella Mae to her feet and pulling her against his chest. "I can't afford a diamond ring or promise you a fine house," he told her, "but if you would have me, I would give you all I have." His mouth descended on hers, and he kissed her passionately.

The following evening, he was waiting in the parlor of the Perry's house when Ella Mae finished teaching Lance and Meredith their lessons. He grinned at the sight of her, his mustache lifting at the corners. "There she is!" he exclaimed. "The future Mrs. Wescott."

He took her in his arms and twirled her around until she burst into embarrassed laughter. "Stop it before someone sees us!"

"I brought you something," John said, extracting something from his jacket pocket. He held it up for her to see.

Ella Mae tried to hide her disappointment. Instead of the ring she had hoped for it, it was a bracelet. She hadn't expected him to purchase anything extravagant and would have honestly been happy with almost anything that would have fit the third finger of her left hand.

"It was my grandmother's," he said as he clasped the silver bracelet on her narrow wrist.

He gave Leanne a ring that belonged to her grandmother, but he couldn't find a ring in his own grandmother's jewelry box to give you? A voice inside her head whispered.

She extended her arm, angling her wrist to study the bracelet. A delicate silver braid with a garnet accented by silver filigree set in its center, it was actually a lovely piece of jewelry. Guilt prodded her conscience. Hadn't she been taught to be thankful for any gift she received?

"Thank you, John!" she tipped her chin up to meet his mouth as it claimed hers.

Over the next few days, the disappointment Ella Mae had felt was only exacerbated every time she shared news of her engagement and someone reached for her hand to admire the ring that was noticeably absent. She would point to the bracelet, explaining that John couldn't afford an engagement ring but had given her the family heirloom as a token of his promise. By the fifth time she repeated the explanation she was on the verge of tears.

It was a small thing, she told herself, a material thing that had no lasting value. Love and commitment were what mattered. Beatrice and Deborah concurred and eagerly volunteered to assist with the wedding planning.

No date would be set until John had met her parents and received her father's blessing. Ella Mae wished he could have met them sooner, but it hadn't been convenient. She felt nervous about taking John to Ridgely to see the farm where she had grown up, and she hoped they didn't encounter Daniel during their visit. Ella Mae wasn't ready for these two particular men to meet.

In late May, at the conclusion of the school year, she brought John home with her. It was strange to see the familiar landscape through his eyes. As the train carried them over the flat terrain, surrounded by acres of fields and pastures on both sides, she felt a twinge of loss. When she married John she would have to remain in

Annapolis with him. The city felt cramped compared to this beautiful, open land.

.

Chapter Ten

*H*e seems like a nice fellow," her father whispered to Ella Mae in the kitchen after John had gone to bed in her brother Randall's old room.

"I do wish he'd waited to propose until he'd met us, though," her mother chided gently.

"I know... It seemed more like a spontaneous thing than something he'd necessarily planned. I think after he lost his fiancée, he was just so excited to have found love again that he didn't want to wait," Ella Mae tried to explain.

"Are you certain about this?" Her mother met her gaze squarely as she challenged her.

Ella Mae understood. Mrs. Hutchins knew her daughter's heart would always belong to Daniel. "Not entirely, I suppose. But can one ever be absolutely sure? I have a man who claims to love me, who sits by the fire with me and plays checkers and reads Tennyson... I have a chance at happiness and I want to take it."

"All we want is your happiness," her father said quietly. Ella Mae could tell from his tone that he had reservations about the professor.

She knew her parents would not withhold their blessing without sound reason and would give him the benefit of the doubt for her sake. Ella Mae only hoped that she was making the right decision.

The second day of his stay, she took John on a tour of the farm. Hand in hand they walked around the perimeter of the fields beneath a brilliantly blue sky. She told him stories about her life there, about how she had read to the barn cats when she was little, and about the time she had climbed a tree as a grown woman to save a kitten.

"I wish I could have seen that!" he laughed.

As they passed a mulberry bush, the tweeting of baby birds caught their attention. Quietly, they tip-toed toward the sound and peered between the leaves at the cup-shaped nest made of twigs, the little fledglings within opening their mouths wide as they cried for worms.

Waiting until they had backed away so as not to disturb them, Ella Mae grinned. "They're so defenseless and sweet!"

John smiled. "You have such a tender heart, you know."

He placed her hand in the crook of his elbow as they continue to walk down the dirt lane. From memory, he began to recite the poem Ella Mae had learned in school with Mr. Swann.

"Behold, within the leafy shade,
Those bright blue eggs together laid!
On me the chance-discovered sight
Gleamed like a vision of delight.
I started--seeming to espy
The home and sheltered bed,
The Sparrow's dwelling, which, hard by
My Father's house, in wet and dry
My sister Emmeline and I
Together visited.

"She looked at it and seemed to fear it;
Dreading, tho' wishing, to be near it:
Such heart was in her, being then
A little Prattler among men.
The Blessing of my later years
Was with me when a boy:
She gave me eyes, she gave me ears;

And humble cares, and delicate fears;
A heart, the fountain of sweet tears;
And love, and thought, and joy."

He grinned, quite proud of himself, and Ella Mae laughed.

"Wordsworth," she named the poet. "I often think of it when I see a bird's nest."

"His sister Emmaline reminds me of you," John replied, looking down at her affectionately.

Ella Mae laughed, seeing a bit of herself in the sensitive sister Wordsworth had described. She leaned into John's arm, feeling content.

"We need to pick a wedding date," John reminded her.

"Next June?" Ella Mae suggested.

He hesitated. "Leanne and I were to be married in June. What if we married this December?"

Ella Mae felt her heart sink. "That's awfully soon," she answered.

"Yes, but it still gives us time to prepare. We'll have the wedding at St. Anne's Church in Annapolis, of course. It will already be decorated with candles, red ribbons, and green boughs. It will be perfect."

Ella Mae considered that St. Anne's was a beautiful historic stone church, and there was nothing like it in Ridgely. Most of the guests who would attend the wedding would be Annapolis natives, and her parents could stay with her grandparents while in town. Regardless of the location, Penelope and Ruth would have to do some traveling to attend. It seemed to make the most sense. As for the date, since they couldn't have a summer wedding, they must either do it this winter or wait a year and a half and do it the following.

"I suppose," she reluctantly agreed.

Before leaving Annapolis, John had finally brought her to his apartment to see where she would be living once she took his name. It was small, but it would suffice until they had children. It was in desperate need of a woman's touch, and Ella Mae had a fair share of work cut out for her to make it feel like a home. They had discussed his salary and agreed that they could live modestly on his income. Ella Mae had intended to work another year at the Perry's before getting married. A December wedding meant she had to resign immediately so that the family had time to find a new governess before the school year began.

John stayed in Ridgely for two weeks before returning to Annapolis to teach a summer course. During his time there Ella Mae's parents had the opportunity to get to know him and she was hopeful that her parents would develop some affection for him as their future son-in-law.

The week after his departure Ella Mae received a letter from Daniel. He was planning to be in Ridgely that weekend and intended to call on her. In May he had graduated from Washington College, although she had not been invited to any celebratory events.

She was sitting on the front porch with a book of poetry when he arrived. Ella Mae wore an airy cotton dress the color of forget-me-nots and tried to pretend she hadn't been anticipating his arrival, her head turning to check the lane with every sound she heard.

At the sight of that tall, lean frame, her heart skipped a beat. He stepped down from his open buggy with a jaunty step, removing his hat to let the breeze ruffle his dark hair. As Daniel approached the porch steps a wide smile split his face. Ella Mae felt her breath grow short.

"Miss Hutchins!" he exclaimed, appearing as though he wished to hug her but taking no initiative.

"Mr. Evans," she replied, every ounce of her being aware of his presence. She knew her smile gave her away, but she was incapable of dimming the joy she felt in his company.

"You haven't grown any taller, I see," he teased.

"And you are full of compliments as always," she laughed. "Care to go for a walk?"

"How about a ride?"

She nodded, not caring what they did or where they went, as long as he was with her. Daniel helped her into the buggy, then slid into the seat beside her. Although they did not touch, she felt a warmth charge through her at his nearness.

"So when will you begin your run for President?" she asked, loving the way that lopsided grin fell immediately into place.

"I have a few other rungs on the ladder I'll need to climb first," he chuckled. "But don't you worry, I'll let you know."

Ella Mae laughed. The lovely summer day was clear and blue and she turned up her face to feel the sunshine kiss her cheeks.

"Did you hear that President Harrison hired the first woman staffer at the Whitehouse? Her name is Alice Sanger and she is making history as his stenographer," Daniel reported.

"I hadn't heard! That's great news! Of course, I'll be more excited when women can vote for which man is in the office of president instead of merely recording his words," Ella Mae retorted, prodding Daniel for a reaction.

He didn't disappoint. "I've already told you that I'm going to be the president to make that happen. You'll just have to wait a few more years."

"Well, you'd better get busy. Someone else might steal your thunder if you don't hurry."

"I doubt it," he replied. "I promise to make that priority one in my first term. You know, I'm such a handsome devil *all* the women will vote for me. In fact, I bet I could get *four* terms if women were given the vote!" He winked. "Maybe I'll even become the first American dictator."

"Ha! You're a devil, all right!" Ella Mae shook her head, unable to hide a smile.

"The two major associations for women's suffrage have merged and are making their voice heard," he said, on a more serious note. "It won't be long now until the voting booths are packed with petticoats."

"Apart from your personal, vested interest in the subject, what do you really think about allowing women to vote?"

"What you're really asking is if I am, in fact, an egotistical male chauvinist? The answer is no, which I hope you had already concluded." He nudged her with his elbow. "The honest truth is that when I look at my parents, I see two intelligent people capable of making decisions which could shape this country, but only one of them is given the voice. My mother is not only intelligent, but wise, compassionate, and well spoken. That she is deprived of this basic right merely because she is a woman is a crime."

"Well, I'm actually relieved to hear you say so. I was afraid you were just supporting it for personal gain, being such a ladies' man." Ella Mae replied in a teasing manner, but she was genuinely pleased by his response.

"Have you ever read the speech Susan B. Anthony, one of the leaders of the women's suffrage movement, gave after she was arrested for voting in the 1872 presidential election?"

Ella Mae hadn't.

"Well, I'll have to copy it and send it to you. I think you'll like it."

"Thank you."

Daniel halted the buggy as they reached the edge of the Choptank River. They didn't move from their seats, though he did shift his position to face her. "So how are your efforts progressing with your novel? Has this literature professor been helpful?"

"Ah. As it turns out, as far as the novel goes, he hasn't been. But he has asked me to marry him," she blurted, curious what Daniel's response would be.

"Already? That was awfully fast. Please tell me he doesn't read you Tennyson by firelight?"

When Ella Mae's face registered surprise that he should know this, Daniel covered his face and groaned. "Ugh. You need a real man, Ella Mae, one who knows how to do more than talk about poetry. What is this fellow's name?"

"John Wescott," Ella Mae replied, hoping that Daniel might finally confess to possessing deeper feelings for her.

Instead he tried out her new name. "Ella Mae Wescott. I suppose that would look nice on the spine of a book. You could always go with 'E. M. Wescott,' to be more mysterious."

"Perhaps I will," she said, though she was beginning to doubt she would ever be published under any name.

"Have you set a date?"

"December."

"Ah, that is fast. Is he afraid someone else will snatch you up?"

"I doubt it," Ella Mae answered, trying to keep the hurt from her voice.

"So, what does this fellow look like?" Daniel wondered.

"I can show you a photograph when we return to the house," Ella Mae answered.

When she presented him with the small, framed photo John had given her to place on her bedside table during their months apart, Daniel lifted his eyebrows dubiously.

"He looks like a literature professor," he observed.

Ella Mae placed a hand on her hip as she demanded, "And what exactly does that mean?"

"He looks like he enjoys eating and reading," Daniel replied, his teeth flashing in a wicked grin.

"You are as incorrigible as ever!" Ella Mae snatched the photo from his hands, which only made Daniel laugh.

After he had taken his leave she went up to her room and placed the photo back in its place next to the bed. Without warning, a flood of emotions welled up inside her and Ella Mae flopped down onto the coverlet, covered her face with her hands, and wept.

True to his word, the following month she received a letter from Daniel wherein he had copied the words of the female suffragist Susan B. Anthony: "*It was we, the people; not we, the white male citizens; nor yet we, the male citizens; but we, the whole people, who formed the Union. And we formed it, not to give the blessings of liberty, but to secure them; not to the half of ourselves and the half of our posterity, but to the whole people - women as well as men. And it is a downright mockery to talk to women of their enjoyment of the blessings of liberty while they are denied the use of the only means of securing them provided by this democratic-republican government - the ballot.*"

Impressed by this woman's ability to articulate so clearly the basic right of every citizen, male or female, to participate in the forming of the government, Ella Mae was also impressed with the man who had taken the time to copy these words and send them to her. Although he loved to play the part of the rake, underneath the facade, Daniel truly was a man of noble character.

He also made a small comment regarding her future marriage, stating how much he had enjoyed their visit and that he hoped she would continue to make time for him in the future. "*There are few people who can keep me pointed true north as you do.*"

Ella Mae didn't wish to be a compass, pointing him in the direction he wished to go. Nor did she wish to be like a puppy, always greeting him with an exuberant smile no matter how long he'd been away. She also did not wish to be like his little sister, always around to tease and pester.

She wanted to be his equal, his helpmate, his love. Why was it that he couldn't view her that way?

She folded his letter and placed it in the hat box at the bottom of her wardrobe where she stored all her correspondence from Daniel. Then she sat on the edge of her bed and gazed at John's photograph. At least someone saw her as a woman, worthy of his love.

Chapter Eleven

*J*t was done. She was officially Mrs. Wescott.

Ella Mae stared at her reflection in the mirror, still trying to accept this new role in her life after a week of being called by her new name. She looked the same, but everything was different.

The apartment John rented near the college had one bedroom, a parlor, and a small kitchen. His clothes, books, and dirty dishes were everywhere when she came over to prepare the house for her arrival in the weeks before the wedding. If they could have afforded to hire a housemaid, Ella Mae would have gladly done so. Her parents might have assisted, but she was too embarrassed to tell anyone about the conditions she was moving into. Once they were married, she would be the housemaid and could keep the place tidy.

A young woman stared back at her in the looking glass with a brave expression, brown eyes resolute to accept a less than ideal situation. Life was always full of struggles and trials, and only a naïve child expected anything else.

Her wedding had been lovely, thanks to the efforts of her mother and grandmother. Her sister Nora had been the Matron of Honor, and Penelope and Ruth were her bride's maids. She would have included Beatrice and Deborah, but four bride's maids were too extravagant for the simple affair her family could afford.

She'd worn a gown with a smooth white satin skirt, the bustle accented by a large bow. Pearls and lace had adorned the bodice, and a sheer waist-length veil sewn into a garland of silk roses had crowned her head. Ella Mae had made a beautiful bride, but only her mother knew how she had lost her breakfast in the bushes outside her grandparent's house as they prepared to leave for the church the morning of the wedding.

"You don't have to do this," Mrs. Hutchins counseled, resting a hand on her daughter's arm, her eyes full of love and concern.

"But I do," Ella Mae had answered. "Everyone is on their way to the church right now."

And so, she had donned the gown and veil and walked down the aisle to take his name.

She may have had less reservations if John had kept his thoughts private during the planning of the wedding. He didn't seem to know the difference between what should be spoken aloud and what should be held quietly inside.

"Leanne was going to wear her mother's wedding dress, with a few alterations," he had told her. "When you choose your gown, you may want to avoid tiered ruffles. They were fashionable in the sixties when her parents married, and the dress was a fountain of lace. I only know because the picture from their wedding was on the piano in their parlor."

When the details of the service were chosen, he vetoed her selection of music on the basis that it was the same choice Leanne had made. "I don't want to be thinking of her when I should be thinking of you."

It was difficult not to feel a heaviness weighing her down as Ella Mae went through the motions of preparing for what should have been the happiest day of her life. If only John would let go of the dreams that had died with Leanne and embrace this time with her, Ella Mae would endeavor love him with her whole heart.

Instead, every detail seemed only to serve as a reminder that the woman he had wished to make his wife was dead and he was marrying Ella Mae instead. She had hoped that as the day of their nuptials drew near she could displace Daniel from the shrine he held in her heart and surrender that sacred space to John. But every time he saw her crestfallen face and continued to speak of Leanne, he made it that much more difficult.

And to make matters worse, Penelope had written to Ella Mae explaining an incident which had happened at the wedding. She had seen her bride's maid emerge from a side room with a pinched expression on her face, and when Ella Mae asked her if everything was all right, she had answered cryptically, "I'll tell you another time."

In her letter, Penelope admitted that she had encountered Daniel in the coat room and he had seemed upset. When pressed, he confessed that he wished he had "been more open," before striding from the room. It was moments later that Ella Mae saw Penelope trying to digest this information.

A single tear trickled down the face of the woman staring back at her in the mirror. Why had it taken Daniel so long to realize what they could have had? Why had it required her to marry another man before he considered his feelings for her? If Daniel had acknowledged his affection for her even one day earlier, she would have canceled the wedding if he had only asked.

Her first Christmas with John was uneventful. They spent the morning sharing breakfast, exchanging a few small gifts, then going to his parents' house for dinner. It was the first year she had celebrated the holiday away from home. She missed her parents, the old farmhouse in Ridgely, and she especially missed Daniel.

A few days later, a report in the newspaper caught her eye. She usually didn't bother with the headlines, but on this particular day the words seemed to jump right off the page at her. There had been a battle in South Dakota near a placed called Wounded Knee, involving the U.S. Army and the Indians there.

Ella Mae immediately put on her coat and went out to catch a taxi to take her across town to the Hudson's house. Beatrice met her at the door, nearly pulling her through the threshold.

"Did you see the paper? Mama and Deborah are both in a state."

The two women were sitting in the parlor reading over the newspaper's account of the battle. Mrs. Hudson's arm was around Deborah, their eyes wide with fear and horror as they read the report.

"Is this near her family?" Ella Mae asked Mr. Hudson.

He stood beside the sofa, his hand resting on his wife's shoulder. He nodded solemnly. "I'm afraid so."

"I'm sure your mother will write with more information as soon as she can," Vivian assured Deborah.

It was several weeks before Mrs. Gibson was able to gather more information and send a letter to her daughter in the east. For years, there had been unrest between the Indians and the white settlers. Land which had always belonged to the native people was seized by the government, the bison herds upon which they lived were slaughtered to make way for the railroad, and treaties protecting "reservation" lands from settlers and gold miners were not honored. It was understandable that the Indians resented these intrusions and broken promises.

A man by the name of Wovoka, a Paiute prophet, had a vision which began a movement among the Indians. In his vision, Jesus Christ returned to earth in the form of an Indian and promised to raise all Indian believers above the earth and to make the white invaders disappear. All the ghosts of the Indian ancestors would return to earth, and they would live in peace, in a place of good hunting.

This time of peace and prosperity would be ushered in by the performing of a specific dance, known as the Ghost Dance. It was a slow shuffle accompanied by a single drumbeat. The dancers wore special shirts as seen by Black Elk in a vision, and Kicking Bear claimed these shirts had the power to repel bullets.

It was a peaceful way that the Indians believed they could change their fate.

However, as the many tribes gathered together in solidarity to perform the Ghost Dance, the white settlers misinterpreted its meaning. Fearing that they were planning an attack, the U.S. officials took some of the chiefs into custody. When an attempt was made to arrest Sitting Bull at the Standing Rock Reservation, a protest arose and shots were fired. Sitting Bull, along with several of his supporters and six policemen, were killed.

In the wake of this incident, two hundred members of Sitting Bull's band escaped the reservation and went to join Big Foot at the Cheyenne River Reservation. They, in turn, joined together and proceeded toward Pine Ridge Reservation to seek shelter with Red Cloud.

It was on this journey that they encountered the 7th Calvary, who escorted them five miles to Wounded Knee Creek. There, they instructed the Indians to make camp. In the morning, they disarmed the band of natives. Five hundred soldiers had surrounded the encampment with rapid-fire mountain guns. There were only two hundred and thirty Indian men and one hundred and twenty women and children.

While confiscating the Indians' guns, a scuffle ensued. Instead of merely bringing them into subjection, the soldiers went berserk and a full-scale massacre followed. By the time it was over more than half of the unarmed Indians had been killed. The white soldiers were ruthlessly determined, pursuing and killing women and children who were fleeing for safety.

A three-day blizzard followed, and the bodies were left frozen on the ground. When finally the snow melted, a mass grave was prepared and the bodies dumped into it like refuse.

Deborah's uncle and auntie and two small cousins were slain there.

"Why would they do such a thing?" Ella Mae could hardly fathom such cruelty.

"There was a battle many years ago at Little Big Horn where an evil white man named George Custer was killed and his men defeated. These were his men," Deborah explained quietly, her face pale. "I guess they considered this their revenge."

Vivian pulled the half-Indian woman into her arms, holding her close. "That is why Deborah's mother sent her here, to ensure her safety."

"I don't understand why skin color or race must separate us! Why can't we all live together in peace?" Beatrice demanded of her mother with tears in her eyes.

"My dear girl, you were raised to respect people for their individual character. Not all people see the world this way," Vivian answered.

"And men are greedy, plain and simple," Rob Hudson added. "Instead of living side-by-side with the Indians who inhabited the land first, the white settlers wanted to take the best land for themselves and push the natives into what was left. Conflict could have been avoided, or at the very least, minimized."

Ella Mae listened, remembering the time Deborah had been harangued for "pretending" to be a white woman by a man who had mistaken her for a Negro. Compared to the butchery of the Indians at Wounded Knee, it was nothing, but it was a symptom of the same vile mindset.

"Is there anything we can do to help the survivors, to help those on the reservations?" Ella Mae wondered, imagining how helpless and despairing these people certainly felt.

"Other than donating clothes and money to the missions on the reservations, I'm not sure there is anything to be done," Vivian said. "You can always pray for all involved to find peace and forgiveness."

"If only there was a way to change the way people think," Deborah sighed, dabbing her eye with a handkerchief. "I can't understand how these soldiers could shoot down in cold blood a woman holding a child. Auntie had no weapon. She was trying to save her children."

That night, as Ella Mae lay in her bed next to the snoring form of her husband, an idea came to her. What if she found a way to change the way people thought about Indians through her writing?

Charles Dickens had advocated for the poor and underprivileged in his novels, a topic otherwise considered taboo. He had used his gift for storytelling to influence people to have compassion for those less fortunate and to break down social barriers. Although Ella Mae had neither the fame nor the gift that Dickens possessed, she would see what good she could do with her own feeble talents.

When she broached the subject to John over breakfast the next morning, he said, "I doubt there would be much interest in a book like that, but you could try."

The next time she visited Deborah, she presented the idea to her.

"Really!" she exclaimed. "You would do that?"

"Well, it may not amount to anything. But I'm willing to try," Ella Mae said.

Deborah's blue eyes were alight with excitement. "How will you write such a story?"

Ella Mae had brought a notebook with her in the leather satchel she received as a graduation present. She removed it as she said, "I don't know, exactly, but the first step is research. The story will come alive from there. I need you to teach me about the Indians. I can't educate others until I understand myself."

Beatrice squeezed Ella Mae's hand as she said, "I'll go put on a pot of coffee. This is a wonderful idea!"

For the next few weeks Ella Mae visited Deborah once a week and took notes on all the information she related. It was far more complicated and confusing than she had expected. The "Indians" did not consider themselves as one people group the way the whites viewed them. In recent years they had learned to work together to protect their land and their way of life, but prior to the invasion of the western territory they had remained largely distinct.

First of all, there were different tribes. Deborah's family was Sioux. Among these, there were smaller bands, such as the Lakota. Further still, there were subgroupings, of which she was Oglala.

Each different tribe, whether Sioux, Apache, Cheyenne, Arapaho, Comanche, Pawnee, or any number of others, had their own lifestyle, culture, religion, and specific enemy tribe. The more Deborah spoke, the more Ella Mae realized how difficult it would be to educate people about "Indians" when there was no such basic group.

She would have to find a creative way to simplify the information and bring to life one representative character. It wasn't the details that mattered as much as the principle: that within every person was the same divine spark of humanity, undiminished by skin color, race, or gender.

Ella Mae asked John if he had any ideas.

"That's going to be a difficult story to sell. You would need to write it very well, and you don't really have the training for it."

He was right of course, but Ella Mae wasn't ready to give up. She asked Deborah to write her mother and see if she had any suggestions, since Sarah Gibson had lived in both the world of the Sioux and the world of the whites.

In the meantime Ella Mae was settling into married life, spending her days cleaning the house, preparing meals, and washing the dishes and the clothes. When she had a few quiet minutes in the afternoon, she read. Ella Mae tried to have dinner ready and waiting for John when he came home in the evening. After they shared a meal and some conversation, they retreated to the parlor where he graded papers or prepared his lessons for the following day and she spent the evening lost in a book.

It surprised her to realize how much she missed teaching and, more specifically, Lance and Meredith. The house was quiet and empty throughout the day, and John was preoccupied and tired at night. Ella Mae had never before considered how lonely married life could be.

Chapter Twelve

*I*n later years, when Ella Mae would look back on this time in her life, there would be several moments which would stand out in her memory—moments which would define the nature of her marriage and the character of the man to whom she had been married.

At the time these events occurred she didn't quite understand how they all fit together, like the pieces of a puzzle, to make one larger picture. It wasn't until years into the marriage that she began to identify patterns and make sense of the pieces.

The first incident which seemed odd to Ella Mae involved a student at the college named Bill, who became deathly ill. When John told her about Bill's condition, Ella Mae was deeply moved. He was a young man, in the prime of his life, stricken down and counting the days remaining to him.

John went to Bill's house to visit him, and upon his return, told Ella Mae about the impact he'd had on the student. Bill had been understandably discouraged, and John had found a way to ease his mind through the parable of the lost sheep. John had opened his Bible and read how the Good Shepherd never rested until all the sheep in his care were securely in the fold, leaving the ninety-nine that were safe to search for the one who was lost.

"Bill seemed to really latch on to this idea that every single sheep mattered to the shepherd. With tears in his eyes, he thanked me for giving him such a sense of comfort," John told her.

Several days passed, and when John didn't mention Bill again, Ella Mae asked how the student was getting along.

"Oh, he passed away on Tuesday," John answered nonchalantly. "The funeral is this weekend."

Ella Mae had felt a sense of loss, even though she had never met the young man. Knowing that Bill had suffered so, that his family now grieved his passing, was enough to touch her heart. When she expressed her sorrow over the news, John had seemed completely unaffected.

Perhaps he wasn't comfortable sharing such emotions in front of her, or maybe he had already made peace with Bill's death before telling her of his passing. Either way, Ella Mae assured herself that even though John hadn't expressed grief over the death of his student he surely felt it. It was only natural.

He often talked about his students in the evenings and Ella Mae knew that he met with them outside of the class to offer academic advice or personal counsel. It wasn't until much later that she reflected on his comments about the students and realized that they had all centered back to him. John had told her about the way the young men admired him, trusted and praised him. When she tried to recall details about the students individually all she could remember John telling her was how the students felt about *him*.

Those who didn't look up to John, who dared to question his authority, were shamed and degraded. John would vent and fume about any student who spoke out against him or acted contrary to his wishes and he would ensure that young man was properly put in his place.

John had ambitions to become the president of the college in a few years and actively worked to place himself in the public eye at every opportunity. He was on every committee that existed and attended every event that was hosted. He either cajoled or demeaned members of the staff and administration, depending on whether they could advance his career or posed a threat to it.

Ella Mae had only his perspective with which to form her opinions of these individuals and initially she accepted his assessments as facts. There was one individual, the college treasurer, for whom John developed a strong dislike. He claimed that Mr. Lane was hassling him about the reimbursement of receipts he turned in to the office. John insisted that Mr. Lane was overstepping his authority, using his personal dislike for John to withhold reimbursement, and he began a full-scale mission to see that Mr. Lane was fired from his position.

About three months later he declined to eat the dinner she had prepared. "Are you unwell?" Ella Mae had worried.

"No, I ate already," he said, lowering himself into an armchair.

"Oh, I thought you were a little behind schedule. Who did you eat with?" she asked, assuming he had met with another professor or student.

"No one," he said dismissively, reaching for the book on the table beside him.

"But, our finances..." she let her words trail off. They were barely getting by. There was no money in the budget for such unnecessary extravagances.

"Don't worry," he glanced up to assure her. "I'll have the college reimburse me."

Ella Mae felt her brows draw together in confusion. "How is that a work expense?"

John's green eyes met hers confidently as he explained, "I was on the way home from work, and I was hungry."

At first, Ella Mae wondered if he were teasing. Surely, he couldn't be serious! But he resumed his reading without further comment and she went into the kitchen and ate dinner alone.

Suddenly, rather than disdain for Mr. Lane, she had immense sympathy. He had been right to question John and, instead of admitting fault or amending his ways, John had simply cleared Mr. Lane from his path.

Because John was involved in so many committees and spent time with so many students, it wasn't uncommon for him to receive gifts from students or their parents. When this happened, Ella Mae was always exceedingly grateful as they couldn't have otherwise afforded these little extras. John acted as if it was his due.

She was beginning to realize the character of the man she had married and that she had made a terrible mistake. But, as the old saying went, she had made her bed and now she had to lie in it.

Although she and Daniel corresponded infrequently after her marriage, they continued to keep in touch. One day he mentioned that he had met a young woman named Sabrina. His wording was stilted, as if he felt awkward telling Ella Mae about her. He mentioned a few of Sabrina's winning qualities, concluding with a final commendation: "She reminds me of you."

If Daniel wanted to be with a woman *like* Ella Mae, why hadn't he wanted to be with *her*? His choosing of a woman who reminded him of Ella Mae was at the same time complimentary and cruel. She stored this admission away in her heart, though all it did was add to the ache of longing she felt.

The only bright spot in what otherwise felt like a cavern of darkness, was her writing. Ella Mae found a sense of purpose in her dedication to her novel, and it also provided a means of escape. It had taken hours of research, contemplation, and suggestions from friends and family, but Ella Mae had finally struck upon an idea she felt would capture the plight of the Indian people and bring awareness to their shared humanity.

A lone infant is found by a wagon train passing through the open plains in South Dakota. The Indian mother lies dead beside the bawling child. One of the white settlers has just lost a baby and takes in the starving newborn to nurture as her own. No one knows which tribe this child belongs to, nor the circumstances surrounding her birth and abandonment.

The heroine of the story, along with her husband, want to raise the little girl as their own but fear that they might be keeping her separated from a loving family. They go in search of her father and other extended family, visiting reservations and learning about the conditions there as well as the various cultural differences among the tribes.

Through the eyes of this white couple, the reader learns to respect the natives as fellow human beings and to sympathize with the injustices inflicted upon them by the Federal Government.

Since Ella Mae could not travel west to experience the land or the people for herself, she had to rely on those who knew it to give her the words. Deborah's mother, Sarah Gibson, supplied the details necessary to bring the setting to life. She wrote to Ella Mae about the openness of the plains, the wind which blows unbroken over it day and night, and the vastness of the sky overhead. Mrs. Gibson taught her about the fauna and wildlife indigenous to the area and supplied specific information about the local reservations and their conditions.

Ella Mae absorbed all this information, and a world took shape in her mind. She could see the long grass on the rolling hills as it swayed in the dry wind, billowing like a green sea that smelled fragrantly sweet. She could see the massive, shaggy forms of the bison as they lumbered through these tall grasses, their bulk leaving a flattened trail in their wake.

When she wrote about the Indian girl she imagined Deborah, describing what she might have looked like as an infant and, later, as a toddler. She learned from Deborah what it was like to have a heritage from which she was separated, and for which she is judged, while being raised exactly like those who judge her. She was a part of this white world and yet not fully accepted in it.

Since John was often preoccupied with his activities at the college it allowed ample time for Ella Mae to spend bent over the page, pen scribbling away. She made sure to keep up with the housework, not that John seemed to notice or made any effort to change his habits to make this job easier for her. When she began to feel discontentment building inside her, she reminded herself that at least she was a married woman and not a spinster all alone in the world.

There were times, however, when she wished she was an independent woman who could manage her finances and her life alone.

One winter was especially harsh and both of their coats were thin and threadbare, hardly sufficient to keep them warm. Ella Mae carefully set aside a few dollars each week until they had enough to replace them.

When John wanted to spend two thirds of the money on an expensive coat for himself, Ella Mae reminded him that she needed a coat as well. He insisted that due to his position within the community it was more important for him to appear well dressed. John reminded Ella Mae that she spent less time out of doors, and certainly less time in the public eye. She could make do with a lesser quality wool-blend.

Ella Mae hadn't known how to respond to such a statement. Her father had always made it clear that a man's priority was to provide for his wife and children and if a sacrifice was to be made, it was his duty to make it. John knew that Ella Mae suffered from the cold more than he did and there were reasonably priced men's coats that would have served just as well for his needs. His decision and its defense wounded her but, instead of arguing with her husband, she quietly chose a garment with the remaining funds.

She wondered if he would have treated Leanne the same way or would he have believed she deserved as nice a coat as he did?

Although he spoke of Leanne less frequently now, Ella Mae could never remember their courtship and engagement without a flash of resentment burning through her. She had tried repeatedly to make John aware of how hurtful his reminiscences were. How could he have been so thoughtless as to continue with them? She understood that he had loved and lost Leanne, but why couldn't an intelligent man apply a level of sensitivity to the situation?

Ella Mae truly wished to have a mutually satisfactory relationship with John. She wanted to love him and dedicate herself to him. She wanted to believe that he loved her. Marriage wasn't an easy road, she had often heard, but one that must be traveled with patience and persistence. So, she made every effort to quell her tongue when a criticism burned on its tip and to be as supportive and submissive as possible.

When Daniel wrote that he had proposed to Sabrina and she had accepted, Ella Mae felt the knife of disappointment twist deeper. Even so, she hoped that Daniel would find the love and companionship which had eluded her.

In the second year of her marriage, Daniel and his fiancée traveled through Annapolis and he arranged for them to meet. Ella Mae dreaded the encounter but knew there was no avoiding it. They had dinner at a restaurant on Main Street. John accompanied her.

Sabrina was refined, well dressed, and polite. In terms of appearance, she had brown hair and was what Ella Mae considered an "average beauty." Ella Mae was curious what Sabrina meant when she smiled sweetly and said, "I've heard so much about you, I feel as though we've already met!"

The two women chatted briefly while the men got to know one another. Sabrina asked if she could write Ella Mae, saying that she thought it would be lovely if they could be friends. Ella Mae smiled and nodded. She was curious exactly what Daniel had said to Sabrina about her, and if she wasn't nurturing a friendship as a precautionary measure. There was an old saying, "*Keep your friends close, and your enemies closer.*"

Ella Mae would have to set Sabrina's mind at ease. There was absolutely no cause for jealousy where she was concerned.

But as the evening wore on, it grew even more awkward than Ella Mae had anticipated. John and Sabrina were complete strangers to one another, and Daniel and Ella Mae were the oldest and dearest of friends. After the preliminary introductions and small talk, it was easy for them to fall back into their old routine of teasing and bantering with one another while their partners sat stiffly beside them. As wonderful as it was to see Daniel, Ella Mae was relieved when the visit ended.

The next time she saw Daniel and Sabrina, it was at their wedding. And if it wasn't painful enough to watch the man she loved give his name to another woman, Sabrina had absolutely *insisted* that Ella Mae participate in the ceremony. She had concocted every excuse she could think of, Sabrina refused to accept any of them.

On a sunny day in May of 1893, Ella Mae stood in front of Daniel and Sabrina's friends and family at a large, brick church in Chestertown with a false smile pasted on her face as she performed the scripture reading. Whether coincidence or intended cruelty, Sabrina had chosen I Corinthians 13, known as "the love chapter," for her selection. Ella Mae held her chin up, spoke succinctly, and made eye contact with Sabrina first, then Daniel, then the audience. If she must be tortured in this fashion, she was determined to do it with as much dignity as possible.

Clearly Sabrina's family had money, and they had spared no expense on their daughter's wedding. Everything from her wedding gown to the decorations, cake, and refreshments were lavish and elegant. Sabrina appeared quite comfortable in a gown which looked as if it cost more than three of Ella Mae's dresses.

Since the bustle had gone completely out of style, and Ella Mae could not afford a new formal gown, she'd had the ecru and purple dress she'd worn to Ruth's wedding remade to suit the latest trends. Puffed sleeves and decorated bodices were now in vogue. Despite the made-over fashion, she felt as much like a mouse as ever.

Prior to the ceremony, Ella Mae had left John in the sanctuary while she slipped down the hall to find a powder room. Coming down the hallway, looking as dashing as ever, had been the groom. His face had lit up at the sight of her and while he had refrained from embracing her, Daniel had rested his hand on her shoulder and given it a gentle squeeze.

"Ella Mae!" he'd exclaimed. "It's so wonderful to see you!"

"And you," she had replied, trying to hide the pain growing in her chest.

They had a brief exchange, Daniel rambling about last minute details he had been ordered to attend to while Ella Mae worked to keep her breezy smile in place. She hoped that Sabrina loved him as much as she did, because today Sabrina was living the moment Ella Mae had spent her whole life longing for.

The crack that already existed in her heart split open a little wider as she watched Daniel kiss his new bride. John seemed as unaware of her feelings that day as he had on any other.

Chapter Thirteen

Ella Mae poured herself into her writing. Since John was seldom home, and often engrossed in his own work when he was, it allowed her ample time to work on her novel. Whenever there were gaps in her knowledge from the information sent to her from Sarah or given to her by Deborah, she went to the library to study. Since John didn't seem to notice or care if the house was clean, Ella Mae let her duties as housewife slip. Completing her novel had become her single focus.

It took her three years to complete, but she finished it. Once she had made all the changes she felt it required, Ella Mae copied a second manuscript to send to Deborah's mother. Sarah Gibson responded with glowing praise. She thought it beautifully achieved the intended goal of revealing the plight of the native peoples and their equality as human beings. She included a list of comments and suggestions to improve its accuracy and realism, which Ella Mae immediately set to work implementing.

When this final draft was completed, Ella Mae looked at the stack of pages on her desk with satisfaction and pride. She had accomplished what she set out to do, and she believed in the work she had accomplished. Not only had the act of writing it brought immense joy, with its completion came the hope that she could launch a writing career and use it to make a positive impact on the world.

Since her husband was a literature professor, it only made sense to ask John to read through her novel and provide his commentary.

"I finished it!" she announced one evening when he returned late from a committee meeting. Since meals were often provided at these late meetings, Ella Mae was in the habit of eating cheese, bread, and an apple for dinner while she wrote.

"Congratulations," he said, glancing at the thick manuscript resting on the table.

"Would you mind helping me polish it before I try to find an agent?" she asked hopefully, her heart and her face full of eager hope.

"Of course, darling," John said, kissing her perfunctorily before plopping into a chair and sighing. "I'm exhausted. It was another long day."

But the days ran into each other until two weeks later her manuscript still sat untouched on the coffee table, gathering dust. Ella Mae had bit her tongue every evening as he reached for a book of poetry, a novel, or his student's papers. She understood that he had a job and needed to attend to it.

Finally, Ella Mae asked, "John dear, when do you think you'll have time to begin reading my novel?"

"Oh," he said, with an odd tone to his voice. John leaned forward, closing the book he had just opened and resting it in his lap. "I suppose I have reservations about putting myself in that position," he explained his intentional procrastination.

"What do you mean?" Ella Mae wondered.

"It's just that I know it's going to hurt your feelings when I have to give an honest assessment of it, Ella Mae."

She heard exactly what he wasn't saying. He had no faith in her to write a novel of any merit, and he was so confident in his opinion of her abilities that he didn't even need to read the first page. He had already concluded, by nature of the author, that this novel was of poor quality.

What could she say in response to such a statement? Should she implore him to just give her a chance to prove him wrong? She knew John could be self-absorbed and insensitive, but how could he crush her ambitions without a hint of remorse?

Ella Mae nodded in acceptance of his position and quietly took up the unread manuscript and returned it to her desk. He made no attempt to follow, nor any effort to soothe her wounded spirits.

After a year of marriage to Sabrina, Daniel's letters still arrived intermittently. Sabrina's correspondence, not surprisingly, had ceased altogether within a few months of their wedding. Ella Mae had alluded in her letters to Daniel that her marriage to John could hardly be categorized as blissful but avoided revealing the full truth of her disappointment. Apparently, his marriage wasn't all he had hoped it would be either.

"With age comes wisdom, or so they say," he wrote. *"I want to apologize to you. Looking back, I realize how I failed to fully appreciate your friendship the way I should have. You were patient and kind to me, even when I was a selfish idiot. I'm sorry I wasn't a better friend to you when I had the opportunity. There are many days now when I wish I could rewind the clock and go back to those times sitting on the sofa with you in your mother's parlor. There are so many things I would do differently."*

Ella Mae could only surmise what Daniel meant by this interesting disclosure. Her heart was warmed by his apology, as well as by the insinuation that he had made a mistake by failing to court her when he had the chance. At the same time, it only worsened the dull ache she already felt in her chest, because no one had the power to rewind the past and relive their life differently.

She knew she had no choice but to make the most of the life she was living, so, she squared her shoulders and tried to find a way to reach her husband.

Ella Mae placed a cup of coffee on the table beside John that evening, initiating a conversation by asking, "What are you reading tonight?"

"Ah, thank you," he said, reaching for the coffee and taking a sip, then wiping the liquid from his mustache. "It's a non-fiction book by Tolstoy, entitled *The Kingdom of God is Within Us*."

"I didn't realize he wrote non-fiction," she commented, taking a seat on the sofa facing him with a steaming mug in her own hands.

"He usually doesn't, but he wrote *A Confession* several years ago, and this one is a continuation of his thought process and journey of faith. You see, when Tolstoy wrote *A Confession*, he was trying to work through the question of whether or not God existed, and if not, does life have any meaning? He went through a spiritual conversion which ultimately resulted in the book, *The Kingdom of God is Within Us*, which outlines his understanding of the Sermon on the Mount."

Ella Mae was pleased that he was engaging with her. When he was at home with her, which wasn't often, he was usually either too preoccupied or tired.

"And what was his conclusion?" she asked to prolong the exchange.

"That a literal interpretation of Christ's words dictates that if one claims to believe in Jesus, he cannot endorse or participate in any type of violence, for any reason. When confronted with evil, one should not retaliate with evil, but with love."

Ella Mae considered the assertion and decided to play the part of student.

"So, if a man were to rob you on the way to work tomorrow, you should peacefully accept his blow to your head and give up your wallet?" she challenged for the sake of the argument.

"It may sound strange," John said, "but I believe Tolstoy has struck upon a great truth here. If we are ever to rid the world of evil, it will be not by participating in further evil, but standing up to it with the only weapon strong enough to defeat it.

"Listen to this," he said, flipping pages until he found the desired quote: "*The history of mankind is crowded with evidences proving that physical coercion is not adapted to moral regeneration, and that the sinful dispositions of men can be subdued only by love; that evil can be exterminated only by good; that it is not safe to rely upon the strength of an arm to preserve us from harm; that there is great security in being gentle, long-suffering, and abundant in mercy; that it is only the meek who shall inherit the earth; for those who take up the sword shall perish by the sword.*"

Her intellect had been stirred and Ella Mae now engaged in the conversation not merely to perpetuate it, but with a personal investment.

"I'm not sure I would agree," she admitted. "*'Evil can be exterminated only by good'* sounds appealing, but it isn't practical. If, for example, vicious and cruel invaders want to kill the inhabitants of a land and take that land for themselves, what benefit is it to allow the innocent to be murdered and the evil to be victorious?"

"But if those who say they are only protecting what is theirs resort to murder, can they still be considered innocent?" the professor countered.

"Murder is the taking of life in cold blood. Self-defense is the practice of fighting against a would-be murderer. They are two different things, and I believe Tolstoy is in error by calling them by the same name."

John's eyebrows shot up. "And now you are wiser than Tolstoy?" he scoffed.

"I'm entitled to my own opinions."

He didn't answer, taking another draught from his coffee instead.

Now Ella Mae was riled. "Let us say that while I am walking the streets tomorrow, I am assaulted by a man who drags me to a secluded place and tries to rape me. What would you have me do?"

He met her squarely in the eyes and said: "Submit."

The philosophical conversation had quickly turned personal, and its outcome was hardly what Ella Mae had hoped to accomplish when she had delivered John his coffee. She stared at him now, processing his reply, watching as he dismissed her and returned to his reading.

There may have been a time when such a lack of husbandly devotion would have moved her to tears. But not now. Not anymore. He had been losing her one day at a time, but with this cold and emotionless dedication to an ideal over the safety of his wife, John had lost forever any chance of holding Ella Mae's heart.

When she paid her grandparents a visit that week, she pasted a smile on her face and tried to pretend all was well. But when she went next door to visit her friends, she poured out her heart to them.

"I don't understand," she confided to Beatrice and Deborah, "how a man can claim to love his wife and yet fail, on a daily basis, to show it. The words mean nothing."

Beatrice had recently met a young man who worked with her father's fishing business and was completely enamored. She rested a hand on Ella Mae's and squeezed gently. "I'm so sorry, my dear friend. You deserve better than what John is giving you."

"I would like to throttle him for making such a remark," Deborah fumed. "How could he *think* that, let alone say it aloud?" Her blue eyes flashed.

"Sometimes I wonder if the problem lies with me. Am I so unloveable?" Ella Mae's voice broke and she blinked back tears. Neither Daniel nor John had found her worthy of their love.

"Of course not!"

"Don't even think such a thing!"

The two women gathered around Ella Mae, offering their support. The fabric of three voluminous skirts pressed together as she allowed them both to enfold her in a hug, her tears falling on their shoulders.

"Sometimes, I just fail to understand how a man with such apparent intelligence can be so stupid when it comes to his wife. He's always said hurtful things, but now it seems worse than before. Either he isn't home, we are together in silence, or we're having some sort of altercation. I don't know how to fix it," she sobbed. "I used to believe he loved me, but now..."

"Poor dear, you are the sweetest soul I've ever met. If he doesn't love you, he's a complete fool!" Deborah declared passionately.

Ella Mae smiled through her tears, thankful that she had them to lean on.

It was on the way home from their house that the accident occurred. She heard her taxi driver shout, then felt the impact of the collision as the two buggies smashed into one another. The wheels of the two carriages became entangled and the rear wheel of the buggy Ella Mae was riding in fractured. The buggy smashed down onto the roadway, tossing Ella Mae out of her seat.

As she flopped down, she felt the hard shell of the carriage against her elbow and rib, while her hip had landed on the cushioned seat. She stared into the wreckage below the other carriage, realizing that she had nearly toppled beneath its moving wheels.

The drivers immediately calmed their horses and Ella Mae was rescued from her undignified position. She was mercifully unhurt, but very shaken. Another taxi came to her rescue and transported her home.

When John came home that evening, she recounted the exciting event to him.

"Hmm," he said, his attention fully riveted to the plate of chicken pot pie in front of him.

"I was only inches from falling under the other carriage and being run over," she repeated, not sure if he had missed that part of her story.

"But you didn't," he commented, as if the entire incident was therefore irrelevant.

"You aren't glad I didn't get hurt? You're not even a little concerned?" she pressed.

He glanced up at her briefly. "Why would I be concerned? You're fine."

Ella Mae nodded as if she understood and picked up her fork. Perhaps she was overreacting. After all, she had only *nearly* gotten hurt.

However, when she shared the incident with her grandmother, Mrs. Greene's eyes grew round, and she exclaimed, "Oh thank God you're all right!"

While she couldn't expect her husband to respond in the same way as her grandmother, Mrs. Greene's reaction did seem more fitting than a nonchalant "Hmm."

Ella Mae knew she was an emotional female, but she couldn't help thinking it would have been appropriate for her husband to express some relief over her wellbeing.

Chapter Fourteen

December 1885

Ella Mae was angry. She was no longer hurt by her husband's indifference and selfishness. She was seething mad.

The second John came home from work the sight of him made her fists clench. When he sat in the armchair with his belly sagging over his waistline she wanted to take the book from his hands and hit him over the head with it. His presence beside her in bed at night, his huge snoring form, made her fume. She wanted to kick him squarely in the back and hear him fall onto the ground in a startled heap.

She was tired of being treated like a non-person. If Leanne had lived, would John have treated her in this fashion or would he have actually loved her? What had Ella Mae ever done to make him treat her as though she were little more than an inconvenience?

It was true that she hadn't attended every event hosted at the college, clinging to his elbow and smiling for everyone to see his pretty little wife. She had disappointed him, she supposed, by not wanting to parade around like a puppy in the wake of his very large shadow.

She had wanted to pursue her own aspirations, to write a novel which would influence people to accept her dear friend Deborah and other Indians like her.

Ella Mae hadn't told John when she sent her novel to an agent and it was rejected. He would have only looked at her as if to say, "I told you so." When she did mention that she hadn't given up on her dream, he reminded her that female novelists were rare and few were successful.

When she told him that she intended to publish under the male *name de plume* of Edward Hudson, John replied skeptically, "You would have to be very convincing."

Clearly, he believed women weren't capable of writing anything worthy of publication. He certainly didn't believe *she* could. While Ella Mae didn't want to abandon her dream, she couldn't quite find the courage to pursue it either.

What if John was right and she simply wasn't good enough?

One evening she found him in the parlor, sitting with his elbows on his knees and his head in his hands.

"What's wrong?" she asked.

John sighed heavily, straightening his bulk and raking a hand through his thinning brown hair. "There's a new administrator at the college, and he's determined not to like me. I'm afraid he's going to make things difficult for me."

Their marriage had been steadily deteriorating and their finances were in a deplorable state, yet he had been completely unperturbed. Why was it that these things didn't matter to him the way the opinion of someone at the college did?

She decided to pose the question directly to him.

Careful to keep any judgment or accusation from her voice, Ella Mae asked him to explain. John didn't answer. Instead, he looked thoughtfully into the fire for a moment, then shrugged and leaned back into the chair, closing his eyes. Thus dismissed, with her question as good as answered, Ella Mae left the room.

Going up to the bedroom, she changed into her nightgown and unpinned her hair. It had become her habit to go to bed before him, hoping to be asleep by the time he slipped under the blanket beside her.

Sitting at the vanity table, Ella Mae took out her frustrations by running the brush through her hair with long, vigorous strokes. The oil lamp on the table burned yellow, the pale light reflecting on the shiny, brown locks. Her white nightgown stood out brightly against the dancing shadows in the mirror behind her.

She couldn't live this way anymore. She didn't *want* to live this way anymore.

Dark and morbid thoughts rose up in her mind, but she thought of her mother and pushed them away. She would have to be strong enough to survive this loveless marriage.

If her mother were here with her, right now in this moment, she knew what her advice would be. The same as what Grandma Greene would say: to pray.

But what was she to pray for? John's heart, for whatever reason, was hardened against her. And his callous treatment of Ella Mae had forced distance between them. There didn't seem to be any hope for the marriage. Just what should she pray for?

Perhaps she simply needed to begin speaking to God and the rest would come. Setting the brush down, Ella Mae lifted her eyes to heaven and invited the Creator of the Universe, the Father, Son, and Holy Spirit, to come into this time and place to be with her. To give her comfort. To give her the wisdom to know what her prayer should be.

To see clearly, the answer came so swiftly that Ella Mae knew she had been heard. Puzzled, Ella Mae wondered what it was that clouded her vision, preventing her from seeing clearly. *Forgive*, the whisper came silently within her.

Earlier that month, they had celebrated their fifth wedding anniversary. It had been the longest, and worst, five years of her life. And if the truth were to be told, she'd been unhappy with John before she ever stood beside him and said, "I do." He had been so cruel through their engagement, always reminding her that Leanne had been the bride he had chosen and Ella Mae had only been her replacement.

Fury burned in her heart as she relived those days in her memory. How was she to forgive him for such treatment when he showed no remorse for it?

Ella Mae breathed in deeply, remembering a sermon she'd heard on the topic of forgiveness. It isn't dependent on an apology and is most needed for those who are least sorry. Forgiveness in many ways isn't for the guilty party, but for the one who was wronged. It lessens the weight and brings freedom.

She meditated on these thoughts, trying to find a way to move beyond the innate desire to hold onto her grievances, to keep the wound John had inflicted from healing over. To forgive him didn't mean that he hadn't committed a wrong, if anything it confirmed that he had, but that she no longer wished to be controlled by the hurt his actions had wrought.

Taking a deep breath, she exhaled, releasing the anger and hatred burning in her heart. She would let go. John would never be sorry, and he would never change who he was. Ella Mae would choose to forgive him anyway.

In that moment, it was as if there were scales on her eyes that had fallen away. Her fixation on John's maltreatment of her in the early days of their relationship had blinded her to the greater scope of wrongs he had perpetrated against her. She had been angry at him for one crime, not recognizing the full extent of his offenses.

There was a saying, "To miss the forest for the trees." Ella Mae had been so concentrated on the row of trees blocking the path directly in front of her she hadn't noticed acres of the same stretched out behind them.

She could see clearly now that John's repeated mention of Leanne hadn't been the result of his inability to realize that it hurt her, but rather because he *knew* it did. It was in this moment that all the individual moments that had seemed strange came together to form a single composite.

Ella Mae tried to think of a time when she had seen John demonstrate true and selfless love *for anyone* during the five years of their marriage. It shocked her to realize that she couldn't.

He acted as though indeed all the world was his stage, and everyone in it were there as his supporting actors. John didn't *love* anyone. He *used* people to serve his own needs. All this time she had thought that it was Leanne he loved, when now she realized that John only loved himself.

It was nearly impossible to imagine that anyone could operate in this way. She didn't want to believe it, but now that her eyes were opened, the evidence all lay there in front of her. The next question was what to do about it.

Her parents came into to town for Christmas, staying with her grandparents in their small cottage. Ella Mae wanted to confide in her mother, to tell her the truth she had uncovered about her husband, but she held silent. She wasn't ready to give voice to the ugly reality of her situation.

Ella Mae enjoyed spending the holidays with her family, and the days flew by all too quickly. When it was time for them to return home, she felt a loneliness so great she feared it would consume her.

She accompanied her parents to the train station, fighting back tears as her mother prepared to board. Mrs. Hutchins pulled Ella Mae into a tight embrace, whispering in her ear, "Sometimes we have to make hard choices, but family is always there for the hard times." As she pulled away she met her daughter's eyes, and Ella Mae understood the cryptic message being conveyed.

Even though she hadn't said anything, her mother saw how great her misery was and what a failure her marriage had turned out to be. If Ella Mae decided to leave John, her mother was communicating that she would have her parents' support.

But that was a decision Ella Mae wasn't ready to make. The fear of incurring God's wrath, the public humiliation, loss of income, and finality of the failure were more than she could look beyond. Plain and simple, she was too afraid.

And yet the truth of who her husband was could no longer be ignored. It had been easier to live with him believing he was oblivious to her feelings, but now that she knew John was intentionally wounding her as a means of control, Ella Mae found him even more repulsive than before. Any anger she had felt previously was nothing compared to the fury that burned in her chest now. She may have forgiven him for dwelling on Leanne, but she wasn't ready to forgive him for the way he was currently treating her.

Not only did she make sure she was in bed pretending to be asleep when he came into the room, Ella Mae slipped out from beneath the covers once she heard his tell-tale snore and went down to the parlor to sleep on the sofa in peace and solitude. She could no more bear his touch than she could let a snake slither around her neck.

As she prepared a sandwich for him in the kitchen on a rainy Saturday afternoon, John commented casually, "I've heard it said that when a woman fails to meet her husband's needs, she is sending him elsewhere to have them met."

Ella Mae didn't look up from her task, pretending he had made a statement about the weather. But her mind reeled. Was this a threat or an admission? Either way, Ella Mae felt her skin crawl when John so much as brushed up against her. There wasn't any way she could give him more.

He had always been a very busy man, involved with the college on a number of levels. When his "meetings" began to run later into the evening, Ella Mae said nothing. She enjoyed his absence far more than his presence. Still, she wondered if he was making good on his threat.

One afternoon when she went to the market to buy groceries, she saw a familiar figure standing on the street corner. He was talking to a young woman, leaning over her and wearing a smile she remembered from many years ago. Ella Mae didn't confront him, instead finishing her business and returning home. But that evening, she mentioned in passing what she had seen.

"Oh, that was Emily Hamilton," John told her breezily. "Her brother is a student in my class and he asked me to take a look at some of her short stories."

It was possible that it was innocent. It was equally possible that his motives were less than innocent, but nothing would come of it. She knew that if anything untoward developed, John would be audacious enough not to cover his tracks.

A few weeks later, she found a note in her husband's coat pocket. It read: *"Looking forward to this weekend."* The handwriting was feminine, but it wasn't signed.

Ella May wasn't surprised when John announced he was going out of town for a conference. All she had were her suspicions and his acknowledgement that he felt justified should he choose to be unfaithful. She couldn't prove with certainty, not even to herself, that he had committed adultery.

That weekend, she slept the night through in her own bed for the first time in months. She stretched out, wiggled her toes, and listened to the beautiful sound of silence. Ella Mae imagined that her husband was with another woman at that very moment. She felt no jealousy. Instead she felt... hope. Perhaps John would leave her for Emily Hamilton and she would be set free from this miserable farce of a marriage.

In the days and weeks that followed, nothing changed. Ella Mae realized that John would never jeopardize his standing at the college by publicly leaving his wife for another woman. It would have interfered with his aspirations to become president of St. John's.

No, he was waiting for her to leave him.

"Sometimes we have to make hard choices. But family is always there for the hard times." Her mother's words rang through her mind. If she left John, her parents would take her in. They would understand and support her decision, even if everyone else judged her. But she would be a divorced woman and live forever with the shame and stigma associated with it.

Every night as Ella Mae curled up with a blanket on the sofa in the parlor to sleep apart from her husband, she asked herself if she was brave enough to make such a choice. The darkness of the room was broken by a single shaft of light that slanted through the window from a streetlamp outside. Staring at that pale beam of light, Ella Mae would pray for wisdom. God had spoken to her before, perhaps He would again.

One afternoon in March of 1896, she found the courage she needed to take her life back. The Bible gave only one exception for divorce, and that was adultery.

She was carrying a load of laundry to the washroom when an article of clothing in the basket caught her attention. Amid the pile was a chemise, one which Ella Mae was almost certain was not her own. The lace that bordered the undergarment was far nicer than she could afford.

Setting the basket down, Ella Mae lifted the garment into the air and studied it from every angle. It was, without a doubt, not her own. She closed her eyes, trying to think how it could have ended up in the bedroom of their home.

It was the sort of chemise a woman wore under a low-cut evening dress. When John went to the overnight "conference" with his female companion, her undergarment must have become confused with his when they packed their bags to return home. Ella Mae could only assume that when John realized it, he placed Emily's undergarment with his wife's things until it could be returned to its rightful owner. And then promptly forgot about it.

It was the only explanation. She rubbed the thin cotton between her fingers and let the reality of her situation sink in. Ella Mae had to choose between two futures—one with a husband who would continue to demean her and cavort with other women, and one with all the consequences of being a woman who had left her husband and chosen to reenter the world with his name still attached to hers, but without the financial provision.

There was only one future in which there was any hope.

With her mind made up, Ella Mae tried to act as though nothing had changed when John came home from another late night "meeting." But her mind was whirling with practical plans while a pervasive sense of impending doom surrounded her. She had no idea what the consequences of her choice would be, only that she was willing to risk them.

As she lay awake upon the sofa that night her mind was restless, even though she forced herself to lie still. When the morning came she would wait for John to take his leave, then she would haul the trunks out of the hallway closet and pack what belongings she could. Her mind began to sort through what she could leave and what she would like to keep.

She couldn't sleep, the hours ticking away with the steady rhythm of the pendulum on the mantle clock. During this long night, Ella Mae prayed. She prayed like she should have before she made the decision to marry John. She asked God to be present, to give her wisdom to know what she should do, and the courage to follow through with it. She prayed with ears that were open, ready to listen.

The black of night slowly faded into the rosy hues of dawn, and she went to the kitchen to prepare breakfast for the husband she was plotting to walk away from. Today, she would go to her grandparents' house. After that, she had no idea what she would do: she couldn't think any further than that.

Chapter Fifteen

March 1896

s soon as John left for the college Ella Mae sprang into action packing her things.

She filled two trunks, one with clothing and the other with items from around the house that she wanted to keep. Her heart pounded within her chest, afraid this would be the one morning he would forget something and come home unexpectedly. She couldn't predict how he might react if he found her packing to leave him.

When the trunks were filled to capacity, she hailed a taxi and had the driver load her luggage and drive her to her grandparents' house.

"Sake's alive! What happened?" her grandmother asked when she arrived at the front door with the trunks in tow.

"If you don't mind, I think I'd like my room back," she said, unwilling to discuss personal matters in front of the taxi driver.

"Certainly!" Grandma said. "I'll show you where to put her things," she gestured to the driver to follow her down the hall.

Once they were alone, Grandma pulled Ella Mae into a bone-crushing hug. "Tell me what happened, honey," she ordered gently.

Ella Mae buried her face into her grandmother's plump shoulder. "John was unfaithful," she whispered.

"There, there," Grandma soothed.

Grandpa Greene's face settled into a scowl, his eyes flashing with anger.

"There's more to it than just that," Ella Mae admitted. "But I..." she suddenly felt very weak, as if the strain of it all was just too much.

"Sit down, and I'll fix you a cup of tea and you can tell us all about it," Grandma said. "If you want Grandpa to pay him a visit with a baseball bat, you just give him the word."

The idea was appealing, but Ella Mae knew it was meant only as an expression of their support. "Thank you," she said, to both of them.

Ella Mae sank into an armchair, staring at the familiar floral pattern on the wallpaper. She had left her husband... Her mind was spinning, her heart still beating erratically. When John returned home that evening and found her belongings missing, he was going to be furious.

Grandpa sat down opposite her on the sofa with his steel gray eyebrows drawn together, and his arms folded tightly across his chest. "I never liked him, you know. I didn't want to say anything, but I never liked him."

"I wish you had told me," she said softly, wondering if it would have changed her mind.

"I'm sorry. I wish I had too," Grandpa huffed, as angry with himself as with her cheating husband.

Grandma bustled into the parlor with a tray. "I thought some soothing chamomile might help all of us," she said as she poured the steaming tea into the cups. When they each had been served, Grandma took the spot beside Grandpa and looked at Ella Mae expectantly.

Ella Mae sighed. She was exhausted, frightened, and heartsick. In stilted, fumbling sentences, she tried to paint a picture of what her life with John had been like and the events leading up to her decision of the previous day.

"That dirty—" Grandpa began, but Grandma slapped his knee and give him a warning look.

Grandma Greene pressed her lips together as if trying to keep certain words from slipping out of her own mouth. She closed her eyes briefly, took a deep breath, and said, "You must stay with us until it's all worked out, at least. Then you can decide whether you want to continue on here or go home. Whatever you think is best is what we want for you. I'm so sorry, my dear girl. So sorry." She retrieved her handkerchief from her sleeve and wid at her eyes.

Ella Mae glanced at the clock on the mantle and saw that three hours had passed. Her body ached as if she had been running for days, and her mind felt as though it were going numb.

"Go and take a rest, dear," Grandma said, watching her eyes grow heavy. "I'll wake you for supper."

Barely able to walk down the hall, Ella Mae collapsed onto her bed, curled into a ball fully clothed, and was immediately asleep. She was awakened to the sound of angry voices in the parlor, and a glance out the window revealed that dusk had fallen.

Tip-toeing to the door, Ella Mae pressed her ear against it and listened.

"This is my house, and I've already told you that you are not welcome in it," Grandpa's voice boomed.

"My wife is here," she heard John's angry response. "And I wish to speak to her."

"She does not wish to speak to you!" Grandma Greene growled protectively.

"You cannot mean that you endorse a woman leaving her husband?" John challenged, as if he could shame her into backing down.

"Only when her husband is a useless, cheating, scumbag!" Grandpa retorted in a voice that barely sounded like his own. *"Now leave!"* he ordered.

"You haven't heard the last from me," John snarled, the slamming of the door punctuating his threat.

Her hands trembled as Ella Mae turned the knob and moved quietly down the hallway, fearing the door would suddenly fly open and she would be forced to face his fury.

"Don't worry," Grandpa said when he saw her white face. "He cannot come into my house without my permission."

Ella Mae was shaken. She remembered how John had treated Mr. Lane, the college treasurer, and any students who disrespected his authority. He could quickly transform from a sly fox into a snapping bear.

Ella Mae sent a telegram to her parents, informing them that she had moved back into the Greene's house. She wasn't about to provide gossip for the telegrapher, especially with a line of patrons standing behind her, listening. Her mother would know exactly what the message meant.

The following day, she received a reply, equally simple. *"Glad to hear it. Come home when you can."*

John sent her a correspondence as well, although his was neither short nor sweet. *"Ella Mae Wescott, you are still my wife and I insist that you give up this foolishness and come home immediately. You know the world can be a harsh and demanding place, and you are not strong enough to face it on your own. If you come home now, we can pretend this whole incident never happened."*

"The nerve!" she exclaimed aloud when she read his letter. "And I'm just to forget the whole incident with Miss Hamilton, I suppose."

Holding the letter in her hands, Ella Mae could hear John's voice in her head as she read over his words one more time. The angry slant of his penmanship paired with the veiled threats and bizarre offer for forgiveness only confirmed that he was clearly not a well-balanced man. She was suddenly thankful that God had closed her womb during the years of her marriage to him. In the beginning she had longed for a child. Now she knew that if there had been one, her husband would have used the babe for leverage to keep her under his thumb.

Ella Mae had no idea what was going to happen now, she only knew she was grateful that she had escaped. Beatrice and Deborah were informed of the situation and were sympathetic, though not surprised.

"He never treated you well enough, if you ask me," Deborah said.

Beatrice's courtship with the fellow she'd met through her father's business was progressing well. She was in that euphoric state that comes with infatuation and dreams. Ella Mae felt a mix of jealousy and pity for her.

Ella Mae was surprised when Mrs. Hudson came to call on her. She brought a bouquet of flowers, offered her condolences, and confessed that the young women had given her all the details.

"I came over to tell you that you are not alone. You are not the first woman to suffer through a marriage with a man like him, and there was nothing you could have done to change the outcome," Vivian stated.

From what she knew of Mr. Hudson, he was nothing like John. Ella Mae raised an eyebrow in question.

"I was married to someone else, before I met Rob," Vivian explained. "He passed away while I was carrying our first child, my oldest daughter, Lily."

"I never knew that," Ella Mae exclaimed.

155

"No. It isn't something we talk about," Mrs. Hudson said quietly. "But I thought you should know, because I think my first husband was very much like yours."

"What do you mean?"

"Ricky believed, and acted as if he were the most important person in this world. The rest of us merely existed to serve him. He had to be the center of attention, receiving praise and affirmation from someone at all times. Ricky always found opportunities to degrade me and wound my spirit. I suppose it made him feel in control. He made his own rules, believing he was justified in whatever action he chose. For example, having an affair with our neighbor's teenage daughter," Vivian told her.

"That sounds exactly like John! I didn't know anyone could think this way, let alone behave this way. I guess that's why I couldn't see it until the very end," Ella Mae admitted.

"Don't blame yourself. Not for his behavior, not for his failure to love you, and not even for being hoodwinked into marrying him in the first place. Men like him prey upon women who are both kind and vulnerable. I've since learned that they have a distorted personality called 'megalomania,' and until you've encountered one, it's hard to imagine that someone could be this way."

Ella Mae was deeply grateful for Mrs. Hudson's confession and the knowledge that she supplied. It helped to know that she was not alone and that there was indeed more to her disastrous marriage than her own personal failures.

However, Mrs. Hudson's first husband had died, simplifying the path to freedom for her. Unless John found a way to procure a divorce, they would be bound together legally even if separated physically. While Ella Mae had every certainty that he had committed adultery, she did not have enough evidence to prove it in a court of law even if she'd had the financial means to pursue a divorce.

She wasn't ignorant of the fact that many women remained in marriages with unkind or unfaithful husbands. Many lived with far worse situations than Ella Mae had left. According to the laws of society, women were meant to be provided for by men and thus any financial income was the husband's property, as well as any residence or other physical items.

Essentially nothing belonged to a woman, not even her body, if she was tied to a man who physically abused her.

Did her choosing to leave make her stronger or weaker than the women who remained? Ella Mae didn't know the answer. She only knew that John had broken his vow to love, protect, and honor her, and to remain faithful only to her. She would rather live alone and in poverty than with a man who could care less if she was trampled by horses.

The institution of marriage was a sacred one, created by God to bless those in it. When all was as it should, such as in her parent's household, that purpose was fulfilled. She still believed that marriage could succeed between any two individuals willing to make the daily choices of commitment and selflessness.

If John had been a man of noble character, a man of integrity capable of genuine love, their marriage could have endured. Ella Mae had wanted her marriage to survive but John's heart had been as hard as stone, and his treatment of her had hardened hers toward him.

Jesus himself had said, *"Moses, because of the hardness of your hearts, permitted you to divorce your wives, but from the beginning it was not so."*

When she shared these thoughts with her grandparents, they affirmed her thinking. "Marriage and parenting are the two most difficult jobs you'll have," her grandmother testified. "They both require patience and forgiveness, in heaping daily doses!"

Her grandfather quoted the Bible: "'*And above all things have fervent love for one another, for love will cover a multitude of sins.*' I Peter 4:8. I know I'm not always as patient as I should be, and your grandmother's not always as quick to forgive as you might think," he tossed his wife a wink. "But we made a decision all those years ago to spend our lives together. It's up to us to both of us to make them good years."

Ella Mae reflected on this wisdom: "*Love will cover a multitude of sins.*"

She remembered the story Mrs. Turner had shared about how Uncle Charlie had fought with the rebels and shot his brother in the hand, leading to its amputation. It hadn't been easy for Jeremiah to forgive Charlie, but because he loved him, because he realized that Charlie had acted with love to remove him from the battlefront, he had chosen to restore the relationship. Love, of any kind, wasn't without trials. It was tested and only remained strong by choice.

Once Ella Mae had believed Louisa May Alcott when she said: "W*e all have the power/ To make wishes come true/ As long as we keep believing.*" Now she realized that one only has power over her own choices. Sometimes it's the choices of others that interfere with making wishes come true.

Vivian Hudson had told her that she was not to blame for John's inability to love her. Ella Mae could see the truth in these words. Mrs. Hudson had said that men like him, megalomaniacs, preyed upon women who were kind and vulnerable.

All she had wanted was someone to love her. Pathetically, desperately so. So much that she hadn't chosen more carefully the man she married.

If she wasn't to blame, then who was? How had her life led her to this place of humiliation and brokenness?

When she paused to reflect on what had caused her to become so vulnerable and desperate for love, she realized exactly whose fault it was.

It was Daniel's.

Part Two

"Suffering has been stronger
than all other teaching...
I have been bent and broken,
but – I hope – into a better shape."

– Charles Dickens, *Great Expectations*

Chapter Sixteen

June 1896
Ridgely, Maryland

*H*er small hometown had changed dramatically from what Ella Mae remembered. The last few years had brought a boom to Ridgely, largely because the area's soil was perfectly suited to growing produce, strawberries in particular, and the train station made it convenient for transporting them to buyers. The strawberries had reached their peak and already been picked, sold, or preserved the month before. May was the busiest month of the year in the town of Ridgely.

Most local farmers had slowly transitioned from cereals to produce, her parents included. A cannery and a preserving company had established their business in Ridgely, as well as a basket making factory. Her parents had kept her up to date on the town's progress but seeing was believing. Even the old train station had been replaced with a brick building.

"Thank you, Papa," she said quietly, as she climbed into the buggy beside him.

Her father offered her a sad smile. "I'm sorry things didn't work out for you, honey."

She had spent a few months in Annapolis trying to make decisions about what she should do next. Since she was technically not a divorced woman but not really married either, she considered looking for another job as a governess. Unfortunately, it was the wrong time of year to begin with a new family, and she suspected that if she had found another position, John would have sabotaged it.

John made several more visits to the house and was turned away by her grandfather every time. Ella Mae never left the house alone, not even to walk across the street. She was afraid John might be lying in wait and whisk her away against her will.

He continued to mail her letters and, after the first few attempts at reasoning with him, Ella Mae abandoned it as a wasted effort. John seemed incapable of admitting any wrong doing and alternated between letters dripping with spiteful accusations against her and letters full of sweet words intended to woo her back.

He was determined to punish her for leaving him, even though she had never publicly announced it or gossiped about his infidelity. She considered contacting Emily Hamilton but decided against it. She actually felt sorry for the girl. Ella Mae had no idea what the right thing was in a situation like this.

She had wanted to return to Ridgely as soon as possible, but had lingered in Annapolis hoping there could be some resolution to her marriage. If John would at least be willing to accept the separation, she was happy to leave him to do whatever he pleased. She only wanted to be as far away from him possible.

He refused. She was his wife, and he was not ready to relinquish her. It was more evident than ever that he not only didn't love her, but never had. Her consequence for leaving him was the intentional destruction of her reputation. When she held her ground and refused to return to him, John began a full-scale attack on her character.

He circulated a rumor that it was *she* who had been unfaithful, even visiting people such as the Hudsons and Perrys to try to solicit support. John played the part of wounded victim at their church, at the college, and to everyone else he could.

She was certain John knew the Hudsons could not be swayed against her, and that it had been a strategic visit intended to make her aware of exactly what he was doing, and to whom.

Ella Mae had no way to combat his lies and, short of a full surrender, there was no making peace with him. It was time to go home.

Sitting beside her father in the buggy as he drove her back to the farm, her shoulders slumped forward. She wanted to appreciate the beauty of nature around her, something she had missed very much, but her reason for returning prevented it. Ella Mae was a disgraced woman, unloved by any man, and now forced to depend upon her parent's kindness once again.

Invariably, gossip would find its way back to Ridgely. The world was much smaller than it appeared. Besides, everyone in town knew she had been married and was now returning alone. Her name had been permanently changed to "Mrs. Wescott." She was ashamed and humiliated, and Ella Mae felt as if every dream she'd ever nurtured had been brutally and irreparably crushed.

Her mother held her against her chest like a child, patting her back, and Ella Mae sank into her neck. All the tears she had been holding in throughout the ferry and train ride home, she allowed to pour out onto her mama's shoulder. Her life was ruined. She felt broken, with no idea what to do next.

"Oh, my girl," Mrs. Hutchins stroked her hair. "It's going to be all right. You're going to find a way to be all right, Ella Mae."

Sobbing, gasping for breath, Ella Mae found that awfully hard to believe.

"Come sit down, dear," her mother took her by the hand and led her into the parlor. Her father followed, not knowing how to help, but wanting to.

Ella Mae took the seat beside her mother on the sofa, leaning her head on her shoulder. "I'm sorry I let you and Papa down," she whispered. She knew that the shame she carried, she had brought upon the entire household.

"You're our daughter, Ella Mae, and we love you," her father said, dismissing her apology.

For the next few weeks, Ella Mae moped about the farm. Although her mother tried to entice her with all manner of goodies and delicacies, she had no appetite. She wanted only to sleep, read, or be left alone in the outdoors.

There was comfort to be found in the familiarity of the place where she had spent so many summers wandering. She walked along the path between the fields green with growth, the berries and melons dotting the landscape with splashes of color and filling the air with a sweet fragrance. A thousand memories walked with her down that path. Memories of different times in her life, with different people walking by her side—Penelope, Daniel, John...

Penelope, having two children underfoot and a third on the way, was busy and wrote infrequently. Ella Mae could only assume that Daniel was happy, as his letters had slowly ceased. Her heart ached with longing for the days of their youth, when they had been carefree and hopeful. Could she have changed the course of her life if she had been either brave enough to speak up, or patient enough to wait?

Certainly, her life would be vastly different if Daniel had figured things out sooner, if he had only realized the place she held in his heart before the wedding. Ella Mae would have called it all off if with John in a heartbeat if Daniel had only asked her. Even as the guests filed into the church, she would have cancelled it, if only...

But he hadn't. She had walked down the aisle and taken John's name. Now she was cursed forever to be Mrs. Wescott, a married woman who was as alone as any spinster.

Even if by some miracle John found a way to secure a divorce, Ella Mae knew she could never marry again. Most clergy would not allow a person who had broken their wedding vows to take them a second time. Besides, her heart was too battered for such a risk. She would never have children. She would live out her days alone.

That evening, as she sat picking at the food on her plate at the dinner table with her parents, she said, "It's a shame we can't peek into the future and see how the story will end, where a particular path will lead us."

Mrs. Hutchins reached across the table to squeeze her hand. "It's just as well that we can't see where each road will lead, my dear. Not only would we miss the heartaches, but we'd miss the lessons too. One road always leads to another, and hope keeps us moving forward."

"Perhaps." Ella Mae would have gladly missed out on the heartache she now felt, the terrible pain that split down the middle of her chest, like a cleaver between her ribcage. If she had known how her marriage to John would have ended she would have never stepped onto the path with him.

"Life isn't easy for anyone," her father reminded her. "Everyone faces suffering in one form or another, at some time or another."

"Often it's the joys we make public, while we carry our sorrows quietly," her mother reflected. "That's why it may appear that everyone around us is better off than we are."

Ella Mae remembered the secrets both Mrs. Turner and Mrs. Hudson had quietly carried and knew her mother spoke the truth.

"We have two choices, daughter," her father said. "Think of the loads of seeds and fertilizer I have to carry in the spring, and the baskets of produce at harvest. When I need to carry something heavy, I can either stand tall and let it strengthen me or I can let it pull me down, stooping my shoulders. We all have burdens to carry. We must choose to be strengthened by them."

Her father was right. She had to find a way to carry her burdens that wouldn't bow her under their weight. She must learn to be strong.

"I will, Papa," she promised. "I will try, anyway."

"I saw an ad this morning that the School Board's decided to hire another teacher and they're currently accepting applications. With your schooling and experience, I thought it might be something you could do," he suggested.

Ella Mae considered the idea. While she may have her resume to recommend her, her marital status might prove problematic. Not only were single women preferred, but as a married-but-separated woman her reputation was tarnished. It was possible that they would turn her away without bothering to find out she'd had additional education beyond the public school.

When she voiced her concerns to her parents, her mother said, "You'll never know unless you try, will you? And if it doesn't work out, they are always looking to hire at the cannery."

"The advertisement said to send your application to Mr. Thomas Jones at the Denton National Bank. He's also the president of the Caroline County School Board. If he's interested, he'll contact you to schedule an interview."

Ella Mae liked the idea of being able to provide for herself, but she wasn't going to get her hopes up. She was surprised when she received a telegram the week after she sent her application inviting her to meet Mr. Jones at the bank on Thursday during his lunch break.

That morning, Ella Mae rose early, anxiety twisting her stomach into knots. Eager to have the question settled, she took her father's buggy and set off for Denton. By the time she arrived, the cool of the morning had given way to the oppressive humidity of a

Maryland summer. Sweat beaded her upper lip, and Ella Mae sighed as she glanced down at the watch pinned to her jacket and saw that she still had two hours before her meeting with Mr. Jones at the bank.

A breeze stirred the damp tendrils of hair resting on the back of Ella Mae's neck. She shifted her position on the bench, beginning to feel drowsiness overtaking her. She wished she hadn't been allowed so much time for contemplation as all it had achieved was making her feel more anxious.

With her stomach full of butterflies, Ella Mae rose from the bench and began to meander down the street in search of the bank. Perhaps this interview would be less intimidating if it weren't held at a financial institution. Although Ella Mae was dressed in a traveling suit and looked every bit the part of a respectable teacher, she feared that John would ruin this opportunity for her without even trying.

The town of Denton was only slightly more developed than Ridgely and had several side streets branching off Market Street, its main avenue. Ella Mae stopped an older woman on the street and asked for directions to the bank.

Overhead, the sun had reached its zenith and the temperature had continued to rise without any decrease in humidity. Her clothing stuck damply to her skin and she could feel a trickle of sweat making its way down her back. She longed for something cool to slake her thirst.

Glancing down at her chatelaine watch, Ella Mae decided she had just enough time—if she hurried—to stop into a diner and get a cold drink before meeting the President of the School Board. Searching around for a suitable establishment, Ella Mae forgot to keep an eye on the dirt street where she walked. A sudden splash of mud and horse manure startled her, and Ella Mae gasped as she stared down at the filth which now stained the hem of her dress and stuck to the bottom of her heeled boots.

With an exasperated sigh, she ducked into an alley between two buildings and wiped at her skirt with a handkerchief. Ella Mae's efforts were futile as the dampness and odor could not be removed from the fabric. Her hopes of making a good impression crushed and her bravado slipping, Ella Mae tucked the soiled handkerchief under a bush with a grimace. It could not be placed back into her sleeve or reticule until it had a good washing. If she remembered, she could retrieve it after her interview.

Ella Mae drew in a deep breath as she straightened, squaring her shoulders. No matter how humiliated or inadequate she felt, she had to go through with this meeting. Having no time now for a drink, she instead hurried on her way to locate the bank.

By the time she arrived, she was out of breath and sweatier than ever. Her pulse throbbed in her neck as she turned the knob and entered the tall brick building. She forced a smile at the young man sitting behind the counter and stated her business.

"Take a seat, ma'am, and Mr. Jones will be with you shortly."

Ella Mae found a chair and lowered herself into it, having just arranged her skirt to hide the stains when a door off to the side opened and a balding, middle-aged man emerged.

"Mrs. Wescott?" he queried, offering a brief smile which lifted the corners of his mustache. In response to her nod, he added, "I'm Mr. Jones. Please step into my office."

The room had an austere air, with a shiny oxblood leather chair situated behind an oversized cherry desk. Ella Mae lowered herself into the straight-backed chair opposite Mr. Jones and pasted a smile on her face.

"Have you completed the teacher's exam?" he began without preamble.

"No sir."

"I'll make arrangements with our new principal, Miss Roberta Hobbs, for you to take the exam at the Ridgely Academy at her earliest convenience. I see on your resume that you worked as a governess for two years. How many children were you responsible for?"

"Two, sir." The faint smell of horse manure drifted from her ankles as she shifted her feet.

"Hmm. Mrs. Wescott... I take it you are married? How does your husband feel about you seeking employment?"

Ella Mae bit her lip. "My husband lives in Annapolis, sir. We are... experiencing some marital discord."

"Ah." One eyebrow lifted, and Mr. Jones studied her quietly. Ella Mae could feel more sweat popping onto her brow, but she held his gaze. She had done nothing wrong.

"I'm trusting you don't expect any trouble out of him? We can't have our school associated with any scandals or scenes."

"I think he will leave me be," she said.

"Very good. Additionally, we expect our teachers to conduct themselves respectably at all times, both in and out of the classroom, and to be good role models of civic responsibility to their students through their interactions with the community. Do you have any questions?"

Embarrassed to discuss money, but feeling it appropriate to the setting, she said, "If I were to get the position, what would my salary be?"

"Oh! Of course," Mr. Jones said with a smile of apology. As he answered, Ella Mae nodded slowly.

"I would suggest taking the teacher's exam. If you do well on it, I'll discuss your unusual marital status with the school board. I can't make you any promises."

"Of course. Thank you for meeting with me." She hoped that neither one of them had wasted the afternoon.

As she turned the buggy in the direction of home, Ella Mae fought back tears. If they refused to consider her because she was legally married, she could interview at one of the canneries. She didn't want to be a financial strain on her parents.

It wasn't until she was back home in her bedroom washing her face with tepid water from the basin that Ella Mae remembered the soiled handkerchief she had left under a shrub in Denton.

With a groan, Ella Mae sank down onto the bed. How was she ever going to teach a classroom full of children if she couldn't even manage to avoid mud puddles and collect her personal items?

Chapter Seventeen

Ella Mae awoke the following morning with renewed determination. Whether or not she was naturally predisposed to be a teacher, she must find a way to mold herself into the role, or at the very least convince the school board that she was capable.

After breakfast Ella Mae took the buggy into town to see the old school building where she had attended as a child, and where she hoped now to teach. The public school was known rather pompously as the "Ridgely Academy." As the town's population had increased, an addition had been made to the schoolhouse to accommodate the increase in students. She wasn't surprised to note that it boasted a tower and cupula, in the fashion of modern Victorian architecture.

It was a fine building, and the shrubs and flower beds surrounding it showed meticulous care. Clearly, the community took great pride in the education of its children. Ella Mae considered the pressure that would be placed on her if she were given the honor of teaching Ridgely's children. She twisted her hands together, her stomach fluttering at the prospect.

"Excuse me. Can I help you?" A female voice asked, breaking into Ella Mae's contemplation.

She spun around to find a woman not much older than herself standing behind her, with dark eyebrows arched in curiosity. "I'm Miss Roberta Hobbs," she introduced herself, "the principal here."

Ella Mae swallowed nervously, extending her hand. "What a timely encounter," she said, exhaling an awkward laugh. "I just came by to see the schoolhouse. I met with Mr. Jones in Denton yesterday about teaching here."

"You must be Mrs. Wescott. I wasn't aware that Mr. Jones had scheduled your teacher's examination for today," Miss Hobbs stated. Her gloved hands folded in front of her navy-blue skirt as she added, "I was planning to contact you to make the arrangements."

"Oh no! I'm not here for the exam," Ella Mae hurried to correct her. "I just came by to see the school's addition. You see, I attended the Ridgely Academy when I was a girl."

"Ah. Well, why don't you come in and I'll give you a tour," Miss Hobbs offered graciously, gesturing toward the walkway which led to the front entrance.

Feeling herself relax ever so slightly, Ella Mae replied, "I would like that. Thank you."

As Miss Hobbs showed her around the schoolhouse, the principal performed an informal interview. Ella Mae found it far less intimidating than the exchange with Mr. Jones across the shiny surface of his desk at the bank. After they had made their rounds to each of the classrooms and returned to the main office, Miss Hobbs asked, "Would you like to take the exam while you're here? It will just take me a moment to locate it."

Ella Mae felt the knots in her stomach reform. Whether it was the way her hand fluttered over her bodice or the expression on her face, Ella Mae must have given away her anxiety.

"I don't think you should have any problems passing it," Miss Hobbs said with a reassuring smile. "It's rather basic compared to the education you've received."

"It's just that I—" Ella Mae paused, embarrassed to admit that she feared failing. "It's been so long since I've studied these subjects... especially the algebra and geometry."

A sympathetic look moved into the principal's eyes. "Ah. Would you like to borrow some textbooks to study? We can always give you the exam next week."

"Thank you," Ella Mae sighed with relief. "I would be very grateful."

Walking home with the books nestled in the crook of her arm, Ella Mae committed to spending every afternoon reviewing the material to ensure that she met with Miss Hobbs and Mr. Jones' expectations.

She spent the week cramming her brain with mathematical equations until she had an almost constant throbbing headache. She couldn't risk failing, especially since, even if she passed, it would take a miracle for the board to hire her.

The day of the test, Ella Mae was directed to sit in one of the students' desks. Beads of sweat glistened on her upper lip. She tugged at the collar of her shirt, aware that her discomfiture was not from the heat of the day even though it was warm within the school building. The pages of grammar, vocabulary, and history questions had been relatively easy. It was the pages of equations she now slowly labored through that made her heart pound with the sick fear of failure and her head ached from the band of tension tightening around her temples.

By the time she completed the exam a ring of sweat soaked through her dress beneath both her arms, and she felt as if her eyes were going to bulge out of their sockets from the pressure in her skull. Ella Mae exhaled slowly, reviewing her answers and praying they were correct. Then she came to her feet and carried the packet to Miss Hobbs's desk at the front of the room.

"I'm finished," she announced.

Roberta smiled at her. "I'm sure you did just fine. Why don't you go enjoy the rest of your day while I mark your exam and you can come by tomorrow for the results."

Ella Mae bit her lip. "Is there any way I could come by this afternoon instead of waiting until tomorrow?"

Miss Hobbs's brown eyes sparkled. "If you insist."

"Thank you," Ella Mae said, taking her leave so that the principal could get started immediately.

She exited the schoolhouse and welcomed the refreshing breeze against her damp skin. Ella Mae hated the way her nerves had gotten the better of her, but she was proud of herself for seeing it through. She had been tempted to leave several of the math problems unanswered, but right or wrong, she had given every one of them a try.

Turning in the direction of Railroad Avenue, Ella Mae headed for the Post Office. She needed to mail a letter to Grandma and Grandpa Greene, after which she would take a leisurely stroll until enough time had passed to return to the school house for her score.

As she walked through town, she observed the many new structures which had only recently been built. Railroad Avenue, Maryland Avenue, and Caroline Street all boasted new residences, some quite impressive. On Central Avenue, she counted several stores, one selling food stuffs, another selling everything from clothing to furniture, and a third one, which specialized in seed and farming implements. There were also three churches—Catholic, Reformed, and Methodist.

Directly opposite the latter, were three newly built homes. The left and middle houses were more traditional, the only real embellishment being the gingerbread trim around their front porches. The house on the right was the largest and most impressive, painted white with blue trim and possessing five bay windows, three gables, a wrap-around porch, and a high, peaked roof with cedar-shake shingles. Despite the many odd angles it boasted, it was a beautiful architectural design.

The house in the middle boasted a sign reading, "John C. Jarrell Boarding House & Hotel." It was a white building with green shutters and a front porch which ran the length of the front façade. Ella Mae decided that if she was hired, she would rent a room there and accept her life as a single woman. She was too old to return home and be dependent on her parents.

Looping her way around town, Ella Mae found herself back on Maryland Avenue and preceded to the schoolhouse. She found Miss Hobbs watering the flowers in the front of the building. When she saw her visitor, Roberta waved and smiled.

"Congratulations!" she called.

Ella Mae felt relief course through her.

"You performed very well on your exam, Mrs. Wescott. Not quite as strong in mathematics, but certainly strong enough to teach our students. I don't know why you were so unsure of yourself, but I hope you'll feel more confident now. I believe you'll make an excellent teacher."

Ella Mae's cheeks flushed beneath the words of praise.

"Thank you, Miss Hobbs," she managed.

"You're most welcome." Roberta smiled kindly, then stepped forward and lowered her voice. "I hope you won't mind me asking a personal question. Does your husband mind that you've applied to teach?"

"I'm afraid my husband and I are estranged, Miss Hobbs. He currently resides in Annapolis."

"Oh. I see. I'm very sorry," Roberta appeared to regret her prying.

Ella Mae rested a hand on her slender arm. "It's quite all right. You had every right to wonder."

Roberta relaxed. "I suppose Mr. Jones already asked you the same question."

"He did. He said it was possible the board would reject my application." Ella Mae sighed. "I'll simply have to wait and hope for the best."

"I don't know if it will make any difference, but I'd be happy to put in a good word for you. I think you and I would get along quite well," Roberta stated with a warm smile.

Thanking her sincerely, Ella Mae took her leave. An idea occurred to her, and she directed her buggy to the cottage where her old teacher Mr. Swann still resided. If he was willing to endorse her with the board, his approval would carry a lot of weight.

He met her at the door, looking no older than when she had last seen him. "Well, who do we have here?" he exclaimed. "Miss Hutchins, what a pleasant surprise!"

Ella Mae was genuinely pleased to see the old man and was sorry she hadn't chosen to visit him earlier.

"Have you written another novel?" he asked as he waved her in.

"Actually, I have. But that isn't why I'm here."

"Oh?" He moved slowly around the kitchen, filling the teapot and placing it on the stove.

"I've applied for a job teaching at the academy."

"Well, you don't need anything from me. You already come well recommended," he said as he lowered himself into a wooden kitchen chair.

"Actually, there is a problem..." Ella Mae took a deep breath. "While I was in Annapolis, I married. But now, my husband and I are... estranged." She used the same word she had given Roberta. Somehow it didn't seem quite strong enough. "I know the board might balk at hiring a married woman. But since my husband has remained in Annapolis, I have no family obligations here to distract me from my work."

"Hmmm. What is your name now?" he added, suddenly realizing he had no idea what to call her.

Ella Mae answered with her new name, wishing there was a way she could take Hutchins back.

"Well, that is sad news indeed," he sighed. "I will see what I can do for you, Mrs. Wescott."

"Thank you," she said. "I did write another novel while I was in Annapolis. Would you like to hear about it?"

His wrinkled face creased into a bright smile. "Yes, I would."

A week later, a letter arrived in the mail from the Board of Education. Ella Mae opened it with trepidation. Her eyes skimmed down the page until she saw what she was looking for.

Whether due to the influence of Mr. Swann and Miss Hobbs, or because of her own merit, they were offering her a position at the Ridgely Academy. She was invited to come the week before school to prepare and to meet the woman who would be teaching the older students.

Ella Mae was relieved to know she could establish a career for herself, remain independent, and know that her parents' and grandparents' investment in her education hadn't been wasted. Her parents were surprised when she informed them of her plans to move into the boarding house in town once she began working.

"You know you don't need to do that," her father assured her.

"I know, Papa. But I don't want to be a burden on you for the rest of my life. It's better for me to learn how be independent. And, it will be much easier when the weather is poor to get to and from the schoolhouse if I live in town."

"I suppose," her mother said, as if disappointed that Ella Mae wouldn't being stay on at the farmhouse.

During the two months before school began, Ella Mae savored living in a place surrounded by nature. She had been hungry for it.

She had tried keeping plants, but found she had a brown thumb. Besides, a houseplant or two were a poor substitute for a farm.

Ella Mae loved watching the seasons come and go as different crops were planted and harvested. She'd missed the strawberry boom in May, which had apparently become a major event in Ridgely. Raspberries, blackberries, and peaches were also in abundance. In the fall, there would be apples in the orchard and pumpkins in the fields.

Knowing she had secured employment and could provide for herself, she found it easier to accept her situation. For this brief time she could enjoy the summer breeze as she read a book, drifting languidly back and forth in the old tree swing. The barn cats had produced another generation of kittens, and she found solace in gathering them into her lap and stroking their soft fur as they purred in contentment.

This was a time to nurture her soul, an interlude of sorts as she prepared for the next season in her life. Her mother's cooking and her father's jokes acted as a balm on her soul. She knew it would take many years to heal completely, if in fact she ever did. But for now, she would find strength in the love and comfort of home.

Ella Mae considered using the time to write but after numerous attempts, all resulting in the same blank page she started with, she abandoned the idea. Perhaps her creativity was a well which had run dry, or the conduit for her inspiration was currently too clogged with raw emotions. Either way, she was unable to produce anything.

In September, school began. Ella Mae had never taught more than two students, and the prospect of a room full of children looking to her for knowledge and wisdom was overwhelming. The first morning, she stood before the rows of young faces and introduced herself, trying to sound more confident than she felt, and to keep the tremor in her hands from showing.

Both the principal, Roberta Hobbs, and Phylicia Bolman who was teaching the other class, told her that presenting herself as a strong authority figure on the first day would go a long way toward maintaining discipline. As the days went on she could relax her demeanor and earn the children's trust. But first impressions tended to linger, which was why she needed to bluff her confidence the first week.

Thanks to their encouragement and support, Ella Mae survived her first day of teaching. As she grew more accustomed to standing in the front of the room with ten pairs of eyes riveted on her, she began to dig back into her memories of the early years of her own education and try to remember what had made Mr. Swann such a phenomenal teacher that even as an adult, she sought him out for advice.

She modeled herself after him in many ways, trying to impart to her students a life-long love of learning, an appreciation of nature, and an understanding of the necessity and the artistry of words strung together to convey meaning. Ella Mae had found her calling, and she was grateful for it.

With her first paycheck, in October, she took out a room at the John Jarrell Boarding House and Hotel. It was a new experience for her to live in a house with the proprietor and his wife, their two children, as well as long-term residents and strangers passing through. Since she lived alone but went by the title of married woman, it was commonly assumed that her husband had died. Ella Mae made no effort to correct this misconception.

Chapter Eighteen

December 1897

*O*nce school started, Ella Mae focused on what was directly in front her. She tried not to think about either John or Daniel. Both made her upset.

Beatrice married in the spring of 1897, but Ella Mae did not attend the wedding. She couldn't bring herself to go back to Annapolis. Beatrice was sympathetic, especially after her mother explained more to her about what Ella Mae might be feeling, and why. Ella Mae was sorry that she couldn't be there to celebrate such a special day and felt like it was one more thing John had taken away from her.

She kept herself busy teaching during the school year, and in the summer, she took jobs picking produce for the preserving company and cannery alongside the many migrant workers that flocked to Ridgely from as far away as Baltimore. The entire atmosphere of her small hometown had been transformed by these businesses.

She seemed to have lost all interest in writing, but Ella Mae read and re-read as many books as she could get her hands on. One day she hoped her creative inspiration would return, but it wasn't something she could manufacture.

December was always the most difficult time of the year. Not only was her wedding anniversary a reminder of the fact that she was still married to John, but the season brought back bittersweet memories of the Christmases she had shared with Daniel.

Ella Mae tried to square her shoulders and carry her burdens with strength. Not everyone was blessed to experience love, which was what made it such a priceless gift for those who received it. While she was not to be counted among these fortunate few, at least she was no longer trapped in a hurtful marriage. She tried to be thankful for that and embrace life.

The boarding house turned out to be the perfect place for her to have her independence while still being part of something bigger. When she wanted company someone was usually about, either in the parlor or on the back patio. When solitude was what she needed she simply went to her room and closed the door.

John and Mary Jarrell, the proprietors, were gracious and kind and made every effort to respect their patron's privacy. Their daughter, Bessie, had just graduated from school and kept herself busy helping her parents with the boarding house. Their son, Clifford, was two years older and made himself useful maintaining the grounds and caring for the horses.

Her life had fallen into a comfortable routine. She worked during the week and visited her parents on Sundays for dinner after attending the church service with them at the Reformed Church. She had developed a camaraderie with Roberta and Phylicia and enjoyed spending time with them outside of school. She was happy enough.

In the back of her mind, Ella Mae knew that sooner or later John would make a reappearance, but it was easier not think about it. Then, on the precise day of their seventh wedding anniversary, she was startled to see the return address on a letter Mrs. Jarrell handed her. It was from John.

Ella Mae retreated to her room to read it in private. Her husband informed her that he had finally persuaded a lawyer friend to call in on a favor from a judge he knew and secure a divorce for them. She never thought she would be grateful for his manipulative ways, but she was eager to be free of him in every possible sense.

He didn't miss the opportunity to remind her that this situation was her fault for being an unloving wife and deserting her husband despite his desire to reconcile. *"Watch your mail for a summons from the court. You are required to be present and to sign the official documents. If you fail to do all that is necessary for us to be divorced, you will be gravely sorry."*

Ella Mae guffawed. No threat was necessary. Why on earth should she wish to be married to him a second longer than she must?

She suspected that he had found another vulnerable woman and wished to remarry. Ella Mae had no such desire. She enjoyed being independent, having no one to answer to but herself. And living at the boarding house, Mrs. Jarrell and her daughter cooked dinner daily and took care of washing the dishes and laundry. It was a perfect arrangement.

"John Wescott, this is the most wonderful anniversary present you've ever given me," she laughed in response to his letter.

In late January the summons arrived. Their hearing was set for March. Ella Mae would have to ask Miss Hobbs to take over her classroom for the week while she went to Annapolis to attend to personal matters.

When March arrived, she was a bundle of nerves. The thought of seeing John again made her feel sick to her stomach. She could still remember the way his angry voice had penetrated the walls of her grandparents' house as he stood on their threshold demanding to see her.

When she arrived at the train station in Annapolis, her grandfather was there to greet her.

"Will you go with me into the courthouse?" she asked him.

He tweaked her nose, as he had when she was a little girl. "I was already planning on it, honey. I'm hardly going to send you in to face the wolves alone."

Ella Mae was grateful for his presence beside her when they reached the courthouse. The imposing brick building was intimidating enough without having to wonder what awaited her inside. Although she felt very overwhelmed by the size and authority of the place, she remembered what she had learned on her first day of teaching at Ridgely Academy. She lifted her chin, assumed an air of confidence, and vowed that she would not let John bully her anymore.

When she first caught sight of her husband, she felt her resolve slip. He looked older than she remembered. His hair had thinned even more, and he had gained additional weight. As if sensing her presence, he turned to glare at her. Hate radiated from his body in waves so powerful that she could feel them. Her stomach churned, but she held his gaze steady and nodded in acknowledgement.

He narrowed his green eyes and looked as if he would as soon murder her as be in the same room. Ella Mae couldn't understand why he should hate her so, when it was he who had violated their wedding vows.

John's companion, the lawyer he had strong-armed into achieving this occasion, approached her with an arrogant swagger. He glanced disdainfully at her grandfather standing beside her in his working-class suit. "Is that your attorney?"

"I—I don't have an attorney," she answered, trying to keep her voice steady.

His eyes reminded her of a wild animal when it realized its prey had been cornered. "Ah, I see. Well, you should know that you are being divorced on grounds of desertion. Do you intend to contest the charge?"

How ironic. John had cheated on her with another woman, but *he* was divorcing *her* on grounds of desertion. Ella Mae weighed her options and decided that she would pay the price necessary for her freedom. "I will not."

John's attorney smirked. "And are you intending to lay claim to any of my client's property or finances?"

She hadn't known that she could. It hardly mattered now. "No, I do not."

His grin widened into a sneer. "Then this shouldn't take very long." He turned on his heel and returned to John's side to report the good news. John gave her a gloating half-smile.

The proceedings themselves went quickly, as had been predicted, and Ella Mae was relieved when she was given the order to step down and return to her place beside her grandfather on the bench. The judge granted John his divorce, and they waited while all the necessary paperwork was prepared, signed, and dated.

John puffed out his chest, looking very self-satisfied as he took up the pen to scratch his name onto the official document. Ella Mae could only feel relief that after this day, she would never have to be in his company again.

She wished there was some way she could reclaim her maiden name. But even if she could, it would be too complicated to return to Miss Hutchins now. She would have to continue to carry the daily reminder of her disastrous mistake in the most personal of ways.

When she returned to Ridgely she took a taxi to her parents' farm to give them the report. Her mother met her on the porch, taking her hands and asking, "How did it go? Is it finished?"

Ella Mae nodded, unable to suppress a grin, even though it seemed contrary to the moment. "I am a divorced woman." She felt as if a weight had been lifted.

Her mother squeezed her hands. "Did you have any trouble with him?"

She explained what had happened and how she had pled guilty to the charge of desertion from her marriage. "It didn't seem important to try to protect my reputation at this point."

"Anyone who really matters knows the truth," her father stated from where he stood behind her mother in the doorway. "Come on in, honey. Your mama made a cake to celebrate the knot being severed."

Ella Mae embraced first her mother, then her father, grateful beyond words for supportive and loving parents.

September 1898

Sitting on the front porch of the John. C. Jarrell Boarding House and Hotel on a Saturday evening after dinner, Ella Mae reclined in a wooden rocking chair with the housecat Molly curled in her lap. The day was pleasant, the heat of summer lifting briefly as if to promise that fall was just around the corner. She had spent the week before cleaning her classroom, counting her supplies, and preparing her lessons in preparation for her third year at the academy. School began on Monday.

Mrs. Jarrell sat in the chair beside her, a pitcher of iced tea on a small table between them. Other residents and visitors joined them, taking advantage of the cool evening. Ella Mae watched as squirrels scampered in the grass and birds pecked for worms in the yard, all the while the cat dozed as she stroked its soft fur.

Suddenly a figure across the street caught her eye, and her heart caught in her throat. It was a tall, lean man with dark hair, whose confident walk had something familiar about it. She squinted, watching as the familiar figured ambled in the direction of the mercantile. It couldn't be!

Ella Mae sighed. *Daniel Evans.* She'd tried and tried to put that man out of her head. Even after all these years, the mere sight of him had sent her heart racing like a runaway horse. She clenched her jaw. He had ruined her entire life. She was torn between the desire to chase after him to throw her arms around him or chasing after him so that she could smack him across his finely chiseled jaw.

She did neither, remaining firmly planted in the rocking chair, which had slowly begun to rock faster and faster until the cat was disturbed and jumped down, mewing in annoyance. Ella Mae took a deep breath and regained control of herself and the rocking chair.

She assumed that Daniel was in town to visit his parents. She hadn't heard from him in years. As far as he knew, she was still married and living in Annapolis.

For the remainder of the weekend, she found her eyes scanning the passersby on the street in search of that face, both beloved and despised. If there had been any chance of him spying her, she would have scurried into the house. She was angry and bitter, as well as ashamed and embarrassed. She preferred that he continued to believe she and John were still together.

Monday arrived, and she put him out of her mind, focused on preparing for the first day of a new school year. After a summer of running wild and free, her students would need her to assert her authority and remind them they would be disciplined and orderly while in her care. It was always the hardest with the young children, whose cheeks were still chubby with baby fat and eyes full of wonder.

Reaching the schoolhouse, she spied her nephews, James Jr. and Mark. She waved at them discreetly, and they nodded their heads in reply. They were now sixteen and fourteen, respectively. James was in his last year of school, and Mark wasn't far behind. They had grown into tall, lanky young men who were far too reserved to wave at their aunt. Ella Mae was glad that she had been assigned the younger students, and never been placed in the position of being their teacher.

The first day of school always had the atmosphere of a festival as the children paraded into the schoolhouse in their new clothes, hair freshly washed and combed, or braided and beribboned. Parents who would usually send their children on their own walked them in to greet the teacher and to help the student transition. Ella Mae put special care into her appearance, wanting to look as professional and austere as possible. She was after all, a career teacher.

She had a list with all the names of the children who were registered to be in her class, and she checked them off as they came in. Those who were returning she greeted by name, having run into them off and on through the summer. Many of the new children were younger siblings who had already got to know her coming and going, but she took the extra time to introduce herself. A few were new to town, and she put special care into matching the name with the face in her mind and making sure they felt welcome.

Overhearing a conversation in the hallway, her ears perked up. Miss Hobbs was saying, "It's quite all right. We can certainly make room for another student. If you'll follow me, I'll introduce you to Danny's teacher."

Ella Mae felt as if all the air in the room had been sucked out and she was left gasping for breath. Daniel stood right in front of her, as handsome as ever, with the added touch of distinguished gray at the temples. She forced herself to inhale slowly, exhale slowly, and regain her composure.

"Mr. Evans," Miss Hobbs was saying, "this is Mrs. Wescott. She's been teaching our younger students for three years now and we couldn't be more pleased with her. I'm sure she'll make Danny feel quite at home."

"Ella Mae?" Daniel looked as shocked as she felt.

"Mr. Evans," she greeted him sedately.

"I thought you were living in Annapolis," he said.

"I moved back to Ridgely a few years ago," she said, emphasizing that *she*, singular, had moved and hoping he would hear the implication not to ask about her husband at this time.

"I see," he said. "I've just returned rather unexpectedly myself."

Now that her heart rate had returned to normal, Ella Mae observed that he had shadows under his eyes and appeared haggard and tired. She sensed that he too did not wish to offer further explanation.

Daniel knelt down before his son, gripping his shoulders gently and saying, "Your new teacher, Mrs. Wescott, is an old friend of mine. You be a good boy for her, and I'll be back to walk you home at the end of the day."

"Yes sir," the child nodded solemnly.

Ella Mae pointed to an empty desk and instructed him to take a seat there. As he walked away, Daniel leaned in and whispered, "Keep an eye on him for me. He's just lost his mother."

"Oh, I'm so—"

He shook his head, silencing her. "Don't draw attention, just be aware." With that, he nodded his gratitude and took his leave.

Suddenly everything that Ella Mae thought was ordered in her life dissolved into chaos. She blinked, trying to reorient herself. This was not going to be an easy year.

Gathering her strength, Ella Mae resumed her persona as Mrs. Wescott, career teacher, and called the class to attention. She was glad that she had two years of experience to draw on as her thoughts were in a jumble and her mind was reeling.

She kept an eye on little Danny throughout the morning. He was quiet, withdrawn, and distracted. Her heart went out to him. The fact that he bore a strong resemblance to his handsome father only made it that much harder. Ella Mae wondered how Sabrina had died, and how recently they had moved to Ridgely as Danny's name hadn't been on her roster.

When she released the class for lunch and recess, she made sure that Danny was introduced to another new student who was the same age. Danny, he had told her, was only five years old. This was his very first day of school ever, in a new town, and without his mother. He held himself together bravely, but Ella Mae could only imagine how he was quaking inside.

At recess, Danny seemed to forget about his heartaches and fears as he and the other little lad played ball in the yard behind the schoolhouse. Ella Mae was pleased to hear his laugh, to watch his little legs pumping as he ran after the runaway ball, dark hair ruffled by the wind. The second half of the day he seemed more comfortable and engaged, and Ella Mae was relieved to be able to give his father a positive report.

"We were undecided if we should send him or hold him back another year," Daniel admitted. "We moved in with my parents," he clarified. "I have another son, Robbie. He's only three. My mother thought it might be good for Danny to make friends, to have something else to think about. I guess she was right."

"Yes, I think she was," Ella Mae agreed. "How long have you been back?"

"Only a few weeks," he said. "My parents came to get the children in January. It was the flu that took her. I had to stay to tie up loose ends before I could join them here."

Ella Mae had heard that there had been an influenza epidemic at the beginning of the year that had begun in Europe and quickly spread to the United States.

"I *am* sorry," she whispered softly.

Daniel accepted her condolences, his eyes fixed on his son who had returned to his game of ball as soon as class was dismissed and had not yet realized that his father had arrived.

"I'm glad you'll be his teacher," Daniel glanced at her as he spoke. "What happened to John?"

"We're divorced."

"Oh Ella Mae," his said, his voice cracking with emotion. "I am so sorry to hear that."

Chapter Nineteen

*E*lla Mae felt as if the solid foundation of her life had been shaken. She wasn't ready to go home to the boarding house and instead walked to her sister Nora's after the schoolroom had been cleaned and prepared for the second day of school. She needed to tell someone that Daniel was back, someone who would understand what that meant for her.

But when she arrived at her sister's house, Nora greeted her with puffy eyes.

"What's wrong?" Ella Mae asked as her sister swung the door open wide in invitation.

"I'm sorry," she dabbed at her eyes. "It's just not been a very good day."

"What happened? Is everything all right?"

"Yes, I just dropped the biscuit dough on the floor and now it's ruined. Dog hair and dirt all over it," Nora forced a laugh.

Ella Mae narrowed her eyebrows. "That's why your crying?"

"No, it just didn't help anything," Nora sighed, leading her sister into the kitchen where the dough still lay in a gooey blob on the wood floor. The family dog whined outside the door, offering to clean it up.

"I'll get it," Ella Mae said, directing her sister to the table. "Now tell me why you're crying."

As Ella Mae cleaned the floor, Nora blew her nose into a handkerchief and said, "I just don't know why he's so angry all the time. It doesn't matter what we do, it's never good enough. Now he's going to be angry that I don't have biscuits to go with the chicken tonight."

Ella Mae straightened, her concern growing. "What does James do when he's angry?"

"He never hits me or the boys!" Nora assured her. "He just yells... sometimes he bangs the cabinet doors or slams his fist on the table... I don't know how to help him. No matter how hard I try, he just seems miserable all the time. The boys avoid him, and I can't blame them. James is just *always angry*." She sighed, a heavy sigh that seemed to come from the deepest part of her being.

Joining her sister at the table, Ella Mae asked, "Nora, why he is so angry? He has a job, a house, a wife and two sons... All blessings many men would love to have. What makes him like this?"

"I'm not really sure. Maybe he's never forgiven God for the death of his parents... I really don't know. It doesn't make any sense. It's almost like he refuses to let himself, or us, be happy." Nora leaned forward, resting her elbows on the table and cupping her face in her hands.

"I'm sorry, Nora. I just didn't realize it was that bad," Ella Mae said, feeling guilty for not having been more attentive to her sister.

"It's not always bad," Nora was quick to add. "Sometimes, he can be very loving and sweet, and happy-go-lucky... It just doesn't happen as often as we'd like."

"Oh Nora. What can I do for you?" Ella Mae leaned across the table to rest a hand on her sister's arm.

Nora pulled away. "You think I should leave him." It was an accusation. "I'm not ready to give up on my marriage. I love James."

"I never said..." Ella Mae let her defense trail off.

She had left her husband, therefore Ella Mae was placed into a different category of wives: the kind who gave up, who didn't love their husbands.

She blinked back hot tears. "I never said that, Nora. I'm only sorry that he's hurting you."

"I'm sorry," Nora wiped her nose again. "I think I'm just having a bad day."

Ella Mae accepted her sister's apology. "Would you like me to cook dinner? Would it be better or worse if I stayed and ate with you?"

"Worse. Don't worry about it. I'll be fine," Nora said, pushing down her sadness as she came to her feet. "I'd better get moving, though, if I'm going to have it ready when he gets home."

"Well, then I'll get out of your way," Ella Mae replied.

As she walked back to the boarding house, Ella Mae mulled over her sister's response. What did Nora really think of her choice to leave John? Did she think Ella Mae had been too quick to give up?

The question worried her. *Had* she been too quick to give up on John because she hadn't loved him the way Nora loved James?

Reaching the boarding house, Ella Mae asked Bessie Jarrell to bring up a dinner tray to her room. She wasn't feeling well.

After she had eaten her meal, she waited for Bessie to retrieve the tray, then Ella Mae undressed and slipped into bed, even though the sun had yet to go down. She lay with her head upon the pillow, her cheeks wet with tears, and reviewed those five pivotal years in her mind. Could she have done something that might have changed the outcome?

Mrs. Hudson had told her that the answer was no, that someone like John was incapable of true and selfless love. But Ella Mae still feared that the problem was with her. Maybe she was just not loveable.

After all, Daniel had never loved her either. He had found her satisfactory as a friend, but nothing more. Seeing him face to face today, after all the time apart, only drove the knife of his rejection in deeper. If he hadn't led her on and broken her heart, she would have never fallen for John's charade and been tricked into marrying him.

She was sorry to hear that Sabrina had died, especially sorry for the two sons she had left behind. But Ella Mae wished Daniel hadn't come back to Ridgely. How was she going to endure teaching his son every day, knowing that if he had married her, Danny might have been theirs?

That night she cried like she hadn't in a long time. She sobbed into a pillow to muffle the noise, curling into a ball and hugging herself tight. Ella Mae thought she had accepted her fate as a single woman and a career teacher. But tonight, the truth was exposed.

When morning came, she cringed at her reflection in the mirror. Washing her face twice over with tepid water in the basin, she was able to bring down a little of the swelling around her eyes. Hopefully by the time she had breakfast and walked to school, she wouldn't look like she had spent the night crying.

She donned a tailored suit of pastel plaid, hoping the pink hues would add color to her cheeks. After she had brushed her hair and twisted it up, she surveyed the result in the mirror. She wondered what Daniel had thought of the way she looked, if he could see that she had aged since their last meeting.

On the second day of school, less parents typically walked their children into the classroom. Ella Mae hoped that Daniel would be one of those who walked him no farther than the entrance, but once again he escorted his son into the classroom and let Danny show him the desk where he had sat to do his work the day before. Danny seemed very excited to be there, and that felt something like an accomplishment to Ella Mae.

"He had a great day yesterday," Daniel reported. "He's been talking about it nonstop."

"Oh, I'm glad to hear that," Ella Mae smiled, then made a show of taking up the chalk and writing the date on the board. She was relieved when he took the cue and bid his son a good day. She certainly hoped he didn't feel the need to walk into her classroom every single morning. It was more than she could bear.

She waited until after church on Sunday, sitting at the table with her parents, to announce that Daniel had come back into town, and why.

Mrs. Hutchins set her fork on the table. "How are you doing?" she asked, understanding immediately how disruptive this could be for Ella Mae.

She shrugged, offered a half-smile. "I thought I had made peace with my life the way it is." She blinked away tears. "But seeing him again... I'm angry, Mama. I'm so angry at him. And I feel guilty for being angry when he's a widower with two sons."

"Oh, my dear girl. Nothing's ever easy, is it?" her mother sighed compassionately.

"*'Trust in the Lord with all your heart, and lean not on your own understanding. In all your ways acknowledge Him, and He shall direct your paths,'*" her father quoted from the Bible.

"You know, Papa, maybe I'm angry at God too," she confessed. "I'm twenty-eight years old, and my life is completely ruined."

"*Trust* in the Lord, Ella Mae. In all your ways *acknowledge* Him," Mr. Hutchins said. "*Then*, He will direct your paths. I think we all like to make our own choices, and then blame God for the consequences. It's never too late, honey. Twenty-eight sounds awfully young from where I'm sitting."

When Ella Mae was a girl, she remembered her father taking her and her siblings to a beach on Kent Island. She asked him why there was so much debris littering the sand. There were tree limbs wrapped in seaweed and dead fish scattered all around.

"Remember the storm we had a few days ago? It churned up the bay and the waves crashed onto the shore. When it passed and the water level went down, it left behind what had been forgotten below the surface."

Daniel's reappearance in her life was like that storm. It had churned up emotions she tried to bury, dredging the bottom of her heart and bringing things to the surface she would rather not have to face.

Ella Mae had known days she'd rather stay in bed on a school morning, but she'd never dreaded going into the academy like she did on Monday morning. She hoped and prayed that since it was the second week of school, Daniel would send Danny into the classroom without him.

Her prayers were answered, and she tried to focus on teaching as if her world hadn't been turned on its axis. She tried not to treat Danny any differently than her other students, but he was both motherless and the son of the man she had loved since as long as she could remember. It was almost impossible not to show some favoritism.

At the end of the school day, Ella Mae was supervising her students as they played in the yard while they waited for their parents to arrive or their older siblings to walk them home. She always kept a keen eye on the youngest children, as they were most likely to get hurt because of someone else's foolishness rather than their own.

"I still can't believe you're Danny's teacher," a familiar voice commented beside her. Her traitorous heart skipped a beat. "I never imagined that happening," Daniel said, sounding wistful.

Ella Mae shifted her feet, wishing someone would suddenly need her so she'd have a reason to walk away. "Life has a strange way of working out," she replied.

"My mother would like to invite you to have dinner with us this Sunday afternoon, if you're available," he said softly. "She thought it might be good to get to know you, since you're Danny's teacher."

Black rage boiled in Ella Mae's veins. All the years they had been the very best of friends he hadn't seen fit to invite her to his house. Now his mother only extended the invitation because she was the teacher of her grandson.

"Please convey my regret. I'm afraid I can't make it," she forced out politely. "Excuse me," she added, as she saw someone she needed to speak to. Usually informing a parent of their child's misbehavior was a dreaded task, but at the moment she was thankful for the interruption it provided.

For the remainder of the week, she kept their exchanges as brief as possible. She was neither ready nor willing to go back to their old friendship. Ella Mae made eye contact, gave him a report of Danny's day, and then excused herself as promptly as possible.

"Ell—Mrs. Wescott," he said, gently taking hold of her elbow as she turned to walk away from him on Friday of that week.

She paused, looking over her shoulder and lifting her eyebrows quizzically.

"Is everything all right?" His brown eyes searched hers.

"I beg your pardon?" She feigned ignorance, looking up at him innocently.

Sadness crept into his expression. He shook his head as if to say, "Never mind," and moved to get Danny's lunch pail from the bench where he had left it.

Beginning the following week, Daniel walked his son as far as the school entrance and let him go the rest of the way on his own. In the afternoon, he arrived late enough so Danny had time to play with his friends and they could leave upon his arrival.

"My daddy's not going to bring me to school anymore," Danny informed Ella Mae a few weeks later. "Nana and Poppy are going to bring me, and sometimes Robbie can come too. He's my baby brother. My daddy had to go to work," Danny explained, looking up at her with thick black eyebrows like his father's.

"Where is he working?" Ella Mae inquired, hoping the child could answer the question. She half-feared, half-hoped that he had taken employment outside of town and left his children to the care of their grandparents.

"The canning factory," he answered promptly. "He's going to sit at a desk and help keep all the papers straight."

"Saulsbury Brothers Canning?"

"Mm-hmm," Danny smiled. "It's near the railroad station. I love to watch the trains. Maybe Poppy will take me to watch the trains today. Nana says it's too loud."

Ella Mae smoothed a strand of dark hair that tumbled into his eyes. She noticed his front tooth was wobbly.

"Well, thank you for letting me know, Danny. Go on and find your seat now, it's time for class to begin," she said.

Daniel had taken a job at the canning factory in Ridgely! She could hardly believe it was true. Last she heard, he'd been elected to an entrée level political position in Talbot County.

Tempted to feel sorry for him for all the losses and changes he'd endured, Ella Mae reminded herself that Daniel was the one responsible for ruining her life. He didn't deserve her pity.

Chapter Twenty

"Mrs. Wescott!"

Ella Mae slowed her steps, hearing someone call her name. Even before she turned, she knew the caller's identity. Her pulse accelerated.

"Mr. Evans." She balanced a basket in the crook of her elbow, filled with items purchased from the Saulsbury Brothers Store. He had caught her just before she ascended the steps to the boarding house and retreated safely inside.

"Do you have a moment?" he asked, appearing almost bashful.

Ella Mae glanced down at the basket she carried. "I'm just returning from the store…"

Instead of sending her on her way, Daniel replied. "I'll wait while you take your things inside."

He was standing off to the side of the house, hand in his pocket, gazing off across the street when she returned. She knew him well enough to see that he was attempting a casual pose, not wanting to appear overly eager.

"Would you care for a walk?" he asked when she joined him.

"I'm sorry, I don't have time," she lied. "But there's a patio in the backyard if you'd like to talk for a few minutes."

Daniel followed her around to the rear of the house to a brick patio surrounded by a well-kept flower garden, which currently boasted marigolds and mums. An iron bench, table, and two chairs were positioned in its center. The Jarrells had purchased a double lot upon which to build their spacious boarding house, offering a sprawling green lawn in the backyard for their guests, as well as a large red barn to keep their horses and carriages.

Ella Mae did not take a seat, fearing that would encourage a longer visit. Instead+- she stood, folded her hands in front of her, and looked up at him expectantly.

He cleared his throat. "I just, I don't have anything in particular to say, I just—I miss you, Ella Mae. I miss our friendship." There was an earnest vulnerability in his eyes that she had never seen before.

Sadly, it came too late.

"I'm sorry, Mr. Evans. But we cannot return to the friendship we once had," Ella Mae informed him, her voice hard. "There's a lot of water that's passed under the bridge since then."

Regret marred his handsome features. "You're right, we can't. I'm sorry I wasn't a better friend to you, Ella Mae. I wasn't the friend you deserved. I was pompous, selfish, and ignorant. If I could go back and relive my life, I promise there are so many decisions I would make differently. But I can't... We're here, now. And right now, I need you," he finished, almost imploring.

Ella Mae could feel a storm brewing inside her. "And at what point does what I need matter? You were every one of those things: pompous, selfish, and ignorant. You hurt me, Daniel Evans. All you thought about was yourself, and you either didn't notice or didn't care that you were hurting me."

He bowed his head. "You're right. I'm sorry."

"You have *no idea* what I've been through," she spat, her fists clenched by her sides.

"I'm sorry," Daniel whispered softly. "You deserved so much more."

"Yes, I did. But none of us can relive our decisions. I married John Wescott, hoping he would love me the way you never did.

Only that turned out to be a monumental catastrophe. So here I am, divorced and alone. It's written in stone now."

Ashamed of herself for saying too much, Ella Mae blinked back tears. "Excuse me," she said, spinning on her heel and rushing through the back door of the boarding house, leaving Daniel standing forlornly on the patio.

Her cheeks flamed. She had spoken the words out loud to Daniel! That she loved him had hardly been a secret, but to admit it now was not only improper, but embarrassing. How would she ever face him again?

He had told her the same thing in a letter he had written to her years before. She didn't doubt his sincerity. It just didn't change anything.

Thursday was Thanksgiving Day. Ella Mae was finding it difficult to feel grateful for anything in her life, but she gave herself the same advice she gave her students: "Whenever you're tempted to feel sorry for yourself, think of someone who has it worse off than you. We all have something to be thankful for."

Not having her own kitchen, she was mercifully exempt from bringing a dish or dessert to the meal. She placed two jars of strawberry jam and a tin of store candy in the basket on the front of her bicycle and pedaled over the dirt roads to her parent's farm. Recent rains had made the roads sticky, though the sun had dried up most of the mud.

She could have walked to Nora's and rode in their buggy, but since learning of her brother-in-law's behavior she had tried to avoid him. She had no tolerance for men who mistreated their wives. Ella Mae was afraid she may not be able to control her tongue.

Once she arrived at the farmhouse she was expected to join her mother and sister in the kitchen to finish preparations for the meal. The men congregated in the parlor and waited for the signal that the table was ready. Her brother Randall had made it into town to visit, something that didn't happen very often. Ella Mae was always pleased to see him, even if sometimes he felt more like a stranger than a family member.

Nora had brought a sweet potato pie, a dish of carrots and parsnips, and a basket of dinner rolls. Ella Mae placed her offerings on the table, prepared for the jibes that would accompany her lack of culinary skill. Their mother had prepared a turkey, greens, mashed potatoes, and a blackberry pie. They would all eat their fill and thank the Lord for His bountiful blessings.

The tension between Nora and her husband was obvious to everyone present from the moment they arrived. James Jr. and Mark were not unaffected, both boys wearing the same strained expression as their mother. Ella Mae presumed something had triggered James either directly before they left, or on the way over. It was probably for the best that she hadn't ridden with them, as she may have only made things worse.

Randall made an effort to lighten the atmosphere, taking advantage of his special guest status. He was able to draw the boys out of their melancholy and get them outside playing baseball. Unfortunately, their father's presence cast a pall over the game. Even from the window, the women could see that he was quick to criticize and slow to praise.

"What happened today?" Ella Mae asked her sister, who was hovering nervously near the window as if her sons were still little boys who couldn't be left unsupervised.

"I put parsnips in with the carrots. James doesn't like parsnips. And then Mark wasn't ready when James wanted to leave, and so he berated us all the entire way here," Nora reported, her voice soul weary.

"He used to like them, didn't he? And there were plenty of other dishes he could eat," Ella Mae observed.

"He says I cooked them too much, and now he's tired of them."

"Oh." Ella Mae noted the way the older son glanced nervously at his dad whenever it was his turn to take the bat. James' anger was hurting more than just his wife.

When she saw their teacher on Monday, Ella Mae asked Phylicia how her nephews appeared to be doing. Miss Bolman met her gaze, then answered, "James Jr. has a quick temper and a bad attitude. And Mark tends to be insecure and anxious. I didn't want to say anything, but since you asked."

Ella Mae nodded in understanding. "Do they ever talk about what their life is like at home?"

"Not to me, directly. But you know teachers overhear things."

"Their father?" Ella Mae prompted, respecting Phylicia's aversion to gossip.

Miss Bolman acknowledged Ella Mae's question with a nod. "I assumed you already knew, but I wasn't sure if I should say something or not."

"It's all right," Ella Mae assured her. "If there's ever anything you think I should know, I'm sure you'll tell me."

Since Daniel's apology for past treatment and confession that he "needed" her, Ella Mae had tried to convince herself that Danny was just another pupil. She needed to keep her distance, for all their sakes. His grandparents had made it a point to introduce themselves once they had taken over the task of delivering Danny to and from school, and she maintained a cordially professional relationship with them.

Ella Mae wondered if they had any awareness of just how close she had once been with their son. They never made any mention of her having a past with him.

Danny's younger brother, Robbie, was three years old and liked to suck his thumb. His hair was a lighter shade of brown and his features bore more resemblance to Sabrina's. Ella Mae's heart broke for the poor little boy who had lost his mother so young.

One afternoon, Ella Mae dismissed the class for lunch. On sunny days, they could eat in the schoolroom or in the yard, as they preferred. This particular day was cold and gray, and they had to take lunch at their desks.

Ella Mae took advantage of this time to eat her own sandwich and apple, and to review her lessons for the afternoon. A whimper, followed by a heartrending wail, brought her head up sharply.

Danny sat at his desk, staring in dismay at the slice of toast he had retrieved from his lunch pail. Tears poured down his cheeks.

"What is it?" Ella Mae ran to his side.

"Nana put boogers on my toast!" he cried, pointing at the offending jam.

It was a golden color, tinged with green. Ella Mae smothered a laugh. "I don't think your Nana would do that. Why don't I taste it?"

"No!" Danny grabbed her hand, terrified that she would consume something disgusting.

"I'm sure it isn't boogers, Danny. I'll prove it to you," she said, swiping some of the jam onto her forefinger. He watched, appalled, as she sniffed it before placing it in her mouth. "It tastes like jam," she announced. "It's sweet."

Torn between his trust of Mrs. Wescott and the dubious shade of slime smeared across his toast, Danny examined the slice of bread more closely. He slowly imitated Ella Mae, taking a bit on his finger and smelling it before touching it to his tongue.

"It isn't boogers!" he announced joyously.

Ella Mae grinned, tousling his hair. What a precious little rascal! Her heart ached as she walked back to her desk.

When she informed his grandmother of the misunderstanding at the end of the day, Mrs. Evans covered her mouth and laughed. "Oh, my goodness!" she gasped. "I always make green tomato jam in the fall with the tomatoes that don't ripen. It never occurred to me that he might have never seen it before."

"Well, he was very relieved to discover that it wasn't what he thought," Ella Mae chuckled. She would never be able to look at green tomato jam the same way again.

That evening, she had a letter waiting for her from Beatrice. She thought Ella Mae would like to know that it was reported in the paper that John had remarried in the beginning of November. Whether or not anyone was scandalized, she had no idea. They had been separated for two years, divorced for eight months, and both the legal system and society were slowly beginning to soften on the subject.

Of course, the same laws which now imprisoned women could easily present a different danger if relaxed. If men could dispose of their wife whenever they grew tired of her, there were likely to be many women homeless on the street. Whether or not these men would choose to take care of the children was an entirely different question. Some would, while others wouldn't. Ella Mae sympathized with those who wanted to liberalize the divorce laws, as she was thankful she had been set free, but at the same time she feared the change it might have on the culture if the value of marriage were diminished.

She wondered if John would love his second wife, if he was capable of loving anyone but himself. She was surprised to realize that she wished him no malice. If anything, she pitied the poor unsuspecting woman who'd walked into his trap.

Contemplating unhappy marriages made her think of Nora, so Ella Mae vowed to pay her a visit on Saturday morning. She knew her sister desperately needed her insight as much as her support.

James Jr. let her in when she knocked. "Hi, Aunt Ella," he said. "Mama's in the kitchen."

"Look how tall you're getting! I swear you've grown since last week!" she exclaimed, tipping her chin to look up her nephew.

He grinned, pleased that she had noticed. Tall and lanky, he was losing the look of a boy as he grew into a man. "I'm growing so fast, I get pain in my legs sometimes."

"I certainly never had that happen," Ella Mae replied, and he laughed. She had stopped growing at an early age, and she had been considered petite then.

"Is that Ella Mae?" her sister called from the kitchen.

"It's me. Is now a good time for a visit? I'm happy to help if you need anything," she called back. "Where's Mark?"

"In the back yard," James Jr. answered.

Nora came into the hallway, wiping her hands on her apron. Ella Mae could hardly mask her shock as she registered Nora's swollen and discolored eye.

"I know, it looks awful," Nora sighed. "I forgot I left the cabinet door open, turned around, and banged my face right into it."

Nora could be clumsy, but knowing what she did, Ella Mae's suspicions were raised. "It looks like it hurts," she said by reply.

"James, go on outside and play with your brother," Nora ordered her oldest son. "I'll call you in for lunch."

He glanced at Ella Mae, then nodded at his mother and ran out the back door.

"Did James hit you?" Ella Mae blurted, taking a step toward her sister as soon as the door banged closed.

"No, I swear he didn't," Nora vowed. "If he ever hit me or the boys, I would leave in a heartbeat. I was just flustered because I knew he was in a bad mood and I was in a hurry to get dinner finished. It was my own fault for not paying better attention."

"Do you promise?"

"I promise," Nora said, and Ella Mae could see she told the truth. "Come in the kitchen with me. I'm making soup."

"Where's James?" Ella Mae suddenly thought to ask, hoping he hadn't overheard their exchange.

"He took the horse to the blacksmith for new shoes. I swear, somebody's always needing something around here," she added.

Ella Mae helped her sister chop carrots, onions, and celery for the soup, listening as Nora told a story about how James Jr. had needed a new pair of pants because he'd outgrown all he owned, and his father had yelled at him, telling him to stop complaining and make do.

"I've already let them down three times," Nora said. "When I made them, I hemmed them up so they could grow with him, but he's just shot up so fast! And here it's winter and his ankles are nearly exposed. It wouldn't hurt to let me buy fabric to make him another pair or two, to get him through till spring. But if I do now, James will say I went against him."

"Nora," Ella Mae asked thoughtfully, "you said that if he ever hit you or the boys, you wouldn't stay?"

"No, of course I wouldn't take that," Nora insisted, her eyebrows shooting up. "I swear, he never has."

"I believe you," Ella Mae said quietly. "But what if the bruises he left on your spirit, on your sons' spirits, were visible to the eye? Would you feel differently then?"

Sadness replaced the bravado Nora hid behind. She looked at her sister with tortured eyes. "I hear what you're saying. I do. I just…"

"Love does no harm," Ella Mae stated firmly. "That's something I learned from living with a man who didn't love me and who actually wanted to harm me. Think about Mama and Papa. He would never, ever hurt her—body, soul, or spirit! That's what love

211

looks like. Love is patient, love is kind. Love is a lot more than just words!" she finished earnestly.

"James doesn't *want* to hurt us," Nora defended her husband. "He's just angry, and he doesn't know how to keep it inside."

"I say this because I love you, Nora. That's no excuse," Ella Mae insisted, feeling fury building within herself.

"What would I do, Ella Mae? I've got two children. Where I would live?" Nora demanded.

"There are two empty rooms at the farmhouse. Your sons could share a room and you could have the other," she answered, then bit her tongue, tempted to say more than she probably should.

Ella Mae held her silence to give Nora time to think.

Finally, Nora answered in a near whisper, "We've been married a long time. I can't just give up now."

Ella Mae pressed her lips together to keep from speaking. She had to let Nora come to her own decision. "This soup smells wonderful," she said to change the subject. "You always were a better cook than I was."

"That's true," Nora teased, happy to discuss anything but her marriage.

Ella Mae stayed until James returned, sensing that her presence was not welcome.

When she returned to the boarding house, Mrs. Jarrell said, "There's a parcel for you in the office. Someone brought it by while you were out. He was a tall, handsome fellow."

Curious, Ella Mae went into the room opposite the parlor. It was the mirror image, complete with two front windows and a fireplace with a soapstone mantle to absorb and radiate the heat. On the desk, she saw a package wrapped in paper, tied with a ribbon that bore her name. Standing next to the fireplace for warmth, she pulled back the paper and grinned. It was a jar of green tomato jam.

WHERE THIS ROAD ENDS

Chapter Twenty-One

Ella Mae sent Daniel a thank you note for the jam. It seemed appropriate as Danny's teacher, especially because of the little imp's connection to the gift. She did her best to avoid Daniel, however, which with the colder temperatures keeping her inside and the hours he kept at the cannery made it easy enough to do during the week. On Saturdays she told Mrs. Jarrell that she was not to be disturbed. Sundays she spent at church and with her family.

Daniel only came by the boarding house once after the jam delivery. When Mrs. Jarrell informed Ella Mae that he had come and been sent away, she looked at Ella Mae curiously. "He seems like a very nice gentleman."

Ella Mae thanked Mrs. Jarrell for the information but said nothing more.

One Saturday afternoon in the middle of December Ella Mae went to the schoolhouse to decorate her room for the holidays. The children always acted as if it were a wondrous miracle to find the walls had been strung with pine swags and red bows, and with a gingerbread cookie left on each desk. She erected a small evergreen tree in the corner, which the children would help her to drape in popcorn and cranberry garlands and decorate with paper ornaments.

A small wood-burning stove was the only source of warmth. She was thankful for the heat it generated, and the stack of logs the boys had brought in for her on Friday afternoon. Phylicia had also come in to decorate her classroom. The two women helped one another hang the items on the wall, taking turns climbing the ladder.

When they exited the school house, the sky was leaden and portended snow. Phylicia bid her good-bye and hurried on her way while Ella Mae locked the door behind them. As she turned back to the street she was startled to see a man's figure looming behind her.

She gasped, then laughed at her own foolishness. Daniel stood in his long black coat, wearing a black bowler hat and gloves. In the gray light his tall frame looming over her had seemed imposing, but upon recognizing him she immediately relaxed.

"I didn't mean to frighten you," he said, flashing her that toothy smile that always made her heart flip-flop. "I saw the smoke from the chimney as I passed by on my way to the post office. I thought you might be here."

"Miss Bolman and I were preparing our classrooms for the holidays," she explained. "I'm sure Danny will tell you all about it when he comes home on Monday."

A shadow moved across Daniel's face. "This will be the boys' first Christmas without their mother."

And Daniel's first without his wife, Ella Mae thought quietly.

"I'm sorry. I know this must be hard on all of you," she said sympathetically.

He closed his eyes briefly, exhaling. "I don't know what I would do without my mother to help with the boys right now. She seems to know what they need, but it is hard on all of us."

Not knowing what more to say, Ella Mae waited for him to explain the purpose of his visit. Silence lengthened between them.

"Christmas always reminds me of you," Daniel finally said, his voice nostalgic. "Whenever I hear '*We Three Kings*,' I remember singing with you in the parlor of your parent's house... Those were good times."

The ache which seemed to live in Ella Mae's chest grew heavier. Memories flooded her. "Remember playing charades with

216

Penelope and Morris? I still think of you whenever anyone references a camel," she admitted.

He chuckled. "I remember that." The skin around his eyes crinkled as he smiled. "I was such a prig, wasn't I?"

"Yes, you were," Ella Mae agreed, unable to hide a twinkle in her eye. What was it about him that still affected her?

"Those were some of the best days of my life," he admitted. "I wish I had appreciated them more at the time. Sometimes, you just don't realize how much something means to you until it's too late." His eyes said more than his words. Daniel was speaking of her, and not just of the simple days of their youth.

As Ella Mae searched her mind for something to say in response, she noticed that lacy flakes of snow had begun to fall around them. "It's snowing," she said, torn between the desire to laugh with joy that he cared for her and an urge to weep because it was too late. "I should head home."

"I'll walk you," Daniel answered.

As they made their way down the dirt streets, frozen over and dusted with white, they remained silent. Upon reaching the intersection of Second Street and Central Avenue, Daniel came to a halt and said, "Ella Mae, I hope one day you can forgive me for the way I hurt you. I didn't deserve your friendship then, and I probably still don't, no matter how much I may want it. I mean no disrespect to Sabrina's memory, but..." he hesitated, his breath a puff of mist in the cold air, "I knew the day you married John Wescott that I had made a terrible mistake. I'm sorry your marriage didn't work out, but I'm sorrier that I ever let it happen."

Speechless, Ella Mae could only stare at him. Never had she believed—though she had many times imagined—he would actually say these words. Biting her lip, she blinked back tears.

"Come on, then," he said. "Let's get you out of this weather."

217

They crossed the street, and he walked beside her as far as the steps of the boarding house. Daniel touched his fingers to the brim of his hat in parting, nodded, and turned on his heel. She stood a moment, watching him disappear into the falling snow, a mantle of white growing on the black wool covering his broad shoulders.

Beneath the covering of the porch Ella Mae brushed the snow from her own coat and wiped her feet before entering. The warmth of the fireplaces on either side of the hallway, in the parlor, and the office, were welcoming. Though she was tempted to step into the parlor, the desire to be alone was greater than the chill which had set deep in her bones.

"Can you send Bessie up with a pot of tea and a hot water bottle when she has a moment?" she asked Mrs. Jarrell, who was always hovering nearby to care for her guests.

"Of course, dear," she said, in her kindly maternal fashion.

The first floor boasted ten-foot ceilings, and the staircase was open, angling up to a wrap-around balcony. Today, it felt as if the stairs were a mountain as she dragged her heavy feet up step after step. Ella Mae felt the weight of her decisions and Daniel's, and all their consequences, crushing down upon her.

Exhausted, she went into her room and closed the door behind her. Without a source of heat of its own, it was cold. Ella Mae hung her coat up then took a thick wool shawl and draped it around her shoulders. Shivering, she went to gaze out the window as she waited for Bessie to arrive with the hot tea and water bottle. The street below was now completely hidden by a fluffy layer of white.

A knock at the door signaled the delivery she had been anticipating. Ella Mae thanked the young woman sincerely as she accepted the tray. Once she had poured herself a cup of tea, Ella Mae settled into an armchair with the hot water bottle under her feet and a blanket across her lap. Slowly the heat from within and without soaked into her bones and chased away the lingering chill.

Reaching for the book she had been reading the previous day, Ella Mae tried to divert her thoughts from the conversation she feared would haunt her forever. The pain in her chest was piercing, as if each beat of her heart drove the sharp edge of grief in deeper.

Searching for a distraction from her own tormented thoughts, Ella Mae opened the pages of a book she had read many times over. *Great Expectations,* by Charles Dickens. It was a familiar story, but today she connected with it in a new way.

Like any novel the plot was full of twists and turns, characters woven in and out of the story, with one main character the reader travels alongside through all of it. His name was Pip and when he was just a boy he fell in love with a girl named Estella. After she cruelly broke his heart, he determined to become worthy of her. But after all the ups and downs that come over time, Pip learns that she is already married.

Estella's husband was unkind to her, however, and it was a mercy when he died in an accident resulting from his mistreatment of a horse. Pip had no idea what happened to her after that, and assumes she may have already remarried.

Just when Pip believes all hope is lost for him and Estella, a chance encounter brings them together again. It is in this final conclusion of the novel, in their unexpected reunion, that Ella Mae found a moment of clarity.

"I have often thought of you," said Estella. "...there was a long hard time when I kept far from me, the remembrance, of what I had thrown away when I was quite ignorant of its worth. But, since my duty has not been incompatible with the admission of that remembrance, I have given it a place in my heart."

"You have always held your place in my heart," I answered.

Estella goes on to explain to Pip that *"suffering has been stronger than all other teaching, and has taught me to understand what your heart used to be. I have been bent and broken, but—I hope—into a better shape. Be as considerate and good to me as you were, and tell me we are friends."*

"We are friends," said I, rising and bending over her, as she rose from the bench.

"And will continue friends apart," said Estella.

I took her hand in mine, and we went out of the ruined place; and, as the morning mists had risen long ago when I first left the forge, so, the evening mists were rising now, and in all the broad expanse of tranquil light they showed to me, I saw no shadow of another parting from her.

Ella Mae closed the book, having reached its end, and found that her cheeks were damp with tears. This time, as she imagined the closing scene, it was not the figures of Pip and Estella she saw in her mind's eye, but her own and Daniel's.

Estella's words rang with a truth that Daniel had tried to convey to her only that afternoon. He had apologized for throwing her heart away when he was ignorant of its worth. And she sensed that suffering had indeed been a strong teacher in his life, that he had been bent and broken into a better shape.

If all of this were true, how could she do less than Pip and say, "We are friends"?

They could never walk hand in hand into the sunset. She was divorced and it was doubtful a clergy would sanction her remarriage. But perhaps they could forge a new friendship even if the old days of innocence were gone. The bond between them remained, though changed by time, as spontaneous and steadfast as ever.

Ella Mae yawned, realizing she had spent hours sitting in the armchair, not wanting to lose any of the warmth she had hoarded in her cocoon. Her legs needed stretching and she stood, crossing the room to look down at the dark street cast in the faint glow of light spilling from the first-floor windows. The snow had continued to fall while she read, and an accumulation of several inches lay upon the ground.

Even as she shivered from the cold seeping through the glass panes, Ella Mae felt a warmth growing in her heart as she embraced Daniel's confession. He loved her, even if the admission had come too late and all they could be now was friends. It would have to be enough.

She could forgive him now, knowing he regretted the ignorance and arrogance of his youth. He was sorry, he had suffered, and he had been changed by it. What more could she ask of him?

Ella Mae contrasted the two men who had played the most important roles in her life. John had never admitted fault for anything nor demonstrated remorse for his wrongdoings. He had not only failed to show regret for having hurt her, he had done it intentionally as a means of controlling her.

Her thoughts drifted to her sister, Nora, and the counsel she had given her. *"Love does no harm... Love is patient, love is kind. Love is a lot more than just words!"*

Ella Mae's marriage to John Wescott had taught her what love *wasn't*. It had shown her the antithesis of what a healthy marriage should be. It grieved her to think that Nora was in her home on this snowy evening with a husband who didn't treat her as he should. Perhaps James loved Nora as John had never loved Ella Mae. She couldn't know what was in his heart. She only knew that James was not *acting* with love, and love in its purist form always manifested in action.

Whatever anger he felt towards God or himself or others, James needed to find a way to let it go in order to save his marriage and his relationship with his sons. He had damaged their spirits, pushing them away with his unpredictability and fits of temper.

Nora needed to confront him, to give him a chance to acknowledge his mistakes and change. If she never held him accountable, he would simply go on as he always had.

Ella Mae hoped that if the mirror were held up before him and James were forced to see the truth, he would recognize the ways he had sinned against his family and repent. John had been incapable, but perhaps it wasn't too late for James. That was Ella Mae's prayer.

Tired and hungry, having declined to take dinner when the bell rang, Ella Mae undressed quickly and slipped into her nightgown. She dove under the layers of blankets and quilts and huddled into a tight ball. As she waited for her numb feet to regain their feeling, slowly thawing out until they tingled, she considered the power of love.

She would rather lie alone in the center of her bed, shivering, then benefit from the warmth of a man lying next to her who said he loved her but treated her with malice. And even though Daniel was not in her presence, she found solace in the knowledge that she had held her place in his heart throughout the years. That awareness warmed her from the inside out.

Chapter Twenty-Two

*I*t wasn't much snow by northern standards, but it was enough to shut down this small Eastern Shore town. Luckily it was Sunday, and all the businesses were closed anyway. Ella Mae took one look out the window and knew there wasn't any point in getting dressed for church. She promptly went back to bed and slept for another hour.

Mrs. Jarrell and Bessie had spent the morning making chicken soup and cornbread for the boarders, while Mr. Jarrell and Clifford shoveled off the steps and the walkway in front of the house. A few adventurous souls were out on horseback, but otherwise the street was silent, muffled in a shroud of snow.

Ella Mae was grateful for the warm lunch, taken with the few boarders who stayed on through the winter. This was the slow season for a town whose economy revolved around planting and harvest. After eating, they all congregated in the parlor, the warmest room in the house. The soapstone mantle had been painted to resemble black marble, and within the fireplace the flames consumed the crackling logs.

Standing with her back to the fire, Ella Mae could see the church across the street through the window. Draped in snow, it was a perfect picture of winter's beauty. The Victorian style building boasted gothic windows, gables, an octagonal turret, and an adjacent tower complete with steeple. Looking at it reminded her that life was ever changing, never staying the same.

The town of Ridgely had been established by the Maryland and Baltimore Land Association during the railroad boom which followed the Civil War. The land was purchased from two locals, Thomas Bell, and the Reverend Greenbury W. Ridgely after whom the town was named.

The Association had great dreams for Ridgely, as the original design for the town indicated. They began construction and completed four buildings, including the railroad station, a hotel, and two residences during the first year. But then the Land Association went bankrupt and it was left little more than a failed dream.

Thanks to the railroad, in the decades that followed it began to see some development. Properties were sold at public auction, encouraged by the real estate tycoons known as the Mancha Brothers. A little at a time, it had grown into what it was now in 1898. Both the boarding house and the church across the street were only a few years old. Ella Mae suspected Ridgely would continue to expand in the years to come.

Like this town, so dear to her heart, life was full of stops and starts. Dreams were followed by disappointment, then surprised by unexpected blessings. One never knew what was coming next. She could only take each day in stride, finding strength for the journey by holding on to her faith and the love of her family.

Her thoughts turned again to her sister Nora. Some might look at Ella Mae, being divorced and living alone, and think she had it worse than her sister who remained married and provided for by her husband. But Ella Mae knew better. She had broken free from the man who had wanted to control her, who found some sick pleasure in hurting her, and who had left invisible bruises on her spirit while Nora remained a prisoner.

Thinking about it in these terms made Ella Mae feel the need to walk across town and check on her sister and nephews. She felt restless anyway. She had spent an hour that morning toasting herself by the fire, and was ready to inhale the crisp December air into her lungs. Donning her coat and galoshes, Ella Mae trudged through the snow despite Mrs. Jarrell's protests.

As much as snow could be a great inconvenience, Ella Mae had to admit that it had a magical way of transforming the ordinary landscape into something beautiful and otherworldly. Trees, which had yesterday looked sad and barren, now had their skeletal limbs dressed in white crystals that sparkled in the weak afternoon sunlight.

By the time she reached Nora's door her cheeks were red with cold and her toes had gone numb.

"What on earth are you doing out on a day like today?" Nora demanded, when she saw Ella Mae standing on the front stoop.

Ella Mae laughed. "It's a lovely day for a walk."

"Get inside, you crazy woman," her sister fussed. "I'll put a pot of coffee on."

Obeying, Ella Mae followed Nora into the kitchen. The woodstove where her sister always seemed to be busy cooking something had warmed the room to a pleasant temperature, and Ella Mae took off her coat and unwound the scarf from around her neck.

"Where are all the men of the household?"

"Little James and Mark are bringing in wood, and their father," she hesitated, "went for a ride."

Ella Mae held her tongue, waiting for Nora to elaborate. Nora busied herself with the coffee, procuring a loaf of fresh bread for Ella Mae to slather with butter while she waited.

Finally she burst out, "I don't understand that man! I never will. He stormed out of here an hour ago saying that none of us respected him, and he wasn't going to stick around to be treated like that. But Ella Mae, no one had disrespected him! Little James asked him a question, and when his father didn't answer, he repeated it a little louder."

She slammed a coffee mug down on the table. "What does he want from us?"

Just then the back door opened, and the two boys came into the kitchen with armfuls of firewood and a gust of cold air.

"Aunt Ella! What are you doing here?" Mark exclaimed.

"I just wanted to take a walk through the snow," she said, preferring to sound eccentric than admit she worried for their welfare.

Nora pressed her lips together, waiting while they arranged the wood in the pile by the stove. "Thank you, now run on upstairs and let me visit with your aunt," she ordered.

After they had gone, Nora poured two cups of coffee and joined Ella Mae at the small table. She closed her eyes and rubbed the bridge of her nose. "Oh, this headache."

"How have you and James been getting along?" Ella Mae asked quietly.

Nora sighed. "Why doesn't he love me?" Her eyes welled with tears and her voice broke. "Is it me? Am I so unlovable?"

Ella Mae clenched her jaw and blinked away her own tears. "Don't take responsibility for his problem, Nora. You are kind and sweet and wonderful. If he doesn't love you, it's on him, not you."

Nora sipped her coffee, her shoulders sagging. "He slept on the couch last night. He said he just wanted to be left alone. We hadn't even fought. I don't know what I did…"

"Have you told James how unhappy you are, how you feel unloved? Does he know how the boys feel about him?" Ella Mae asked.

Sighing, Nora said, "I haven't said so directly. He certainly *should* know."

"If he knows, then he has no reason to continue hurting you," Ella Mae stated plainly. "If he doesn't know—and I would agree that he *certainly* should—then you need to give him the chance to understand how he's hurting his family and choose to change."

"I'm always afraid of saying anything that might upset him when he's in a good mood," Nora admitted. "And when he's already angry, speaking plainly will only make things worse."

"You need to try," Ella Mae insisted, reaching across the table to squeeze her sister's hand. "He needs to hear it from your lips. And you need to see what he will do with the information."

Brushing a wayward tear from her cheek, Nora shrugged. "What do I have to lose?"

"I'll visit you next Saturday, Nora, and you can tell me what happened."

Nora nodded reluctantly.

Monday, Ella Mae was disappointed that the snow had kept several of her students away. It was easier for those who lived in town to make the trip than for those who lived on the surrounding farms. The children who did attend were as delighted as she had hoped they would be by the cookie on their desk and the decorations in the room. The snow on the ground only added to the atmosphere of festivity.

She announced that they would wait to decorate the tree until the following day, when she hoped the remainder of the students would be present. A sigh of disappointment went up, but she appreciated that no one complained. In addition to reading, writing, and arithmetic, Ella Mae hoped to teach her pupils to have compassion for others.

School would be closed the entire week of Christmas, and Ella Mae asked if anyone had special plans to travel to visit grandparents, or aunts, uncles and cousins. She shared how her parents had taken her to Annapolis sometimes to celebrate the holiday with her grandparents there, and what special memories they were.

One child said they were going to New Jersey, and two were traveling to Delaware.

Then Danny raised his hand. "I can't visit my mom," he declared, "because there aren't any trains that go to heaven."

For the first time in all the years she had been teaching, Ella Mae had no idea how to respond. She choked down the lump that had formed in her throat.

"That's true, Danny. But maybe you can say a prayer and ask Jesus to give her a special message for you. And you still have your dad and your brother, and your Nana and Poppy to celebrate Christmas with."

His wide brown eyes, framed in thick lashes, stared back at her bravely. He nodded and said, "Yes ma'am."

Ella Mae couldn't resist the urge to give him a quick squeeze when the children were released for recess. Those who wished to play in the snow were allowed to go outside, and the rest could remain inside. Danny chose to remain inside, asking her to please help him practice reading.

"Nana's teaching me to read '*Twas the Night Before Christmas*' to my daddy for a special gift," he explained.

"I think I might have a copy here on my shelf," Ella Mae replied. She quickly turned away to hide the tears that came to her eyes. What a bizarre twist of fate had placed her this position.

"Ah, here it is." Placing a stool next to her chair, she patted it for Danny to sit down. Then she opened the book to the first page and placed it on his lap.

Ella Mae smiled as Danny began to "read." He had obviously had the poem read to him many times over and was reciting it from memory. She made a mental note to spend a few minutes with him the next day with a primer to test his skill. He was only five, so there was plenty of time for him to learn how to read for real. In the meantime, she was sure Daniel would find his son's recitation as adorable as she did.

He stumbled a bit through some of the more difficult phrases, but his childish gibberish only made it all the more precious. She only giggled once when instead of saying, "so up to the house-top the *coursers* they flew," he said, "so up to the house-top the *corsets* they flew."

By the next day, most of the students were in class and they began work on decorating the tree. She divided the up tasks so that each day they had a new project. One day they popped corn over the wood stove and each child took turns threading it onto the garland. The next day they strung the cranberries, and the following they cut out paper ornaments. On Friday they added the finishing touches and placed them on the tree.

Saturday, she made good on her promise to Nora and walked over to see if she had found the courage to confront her husband. As she made her way through the melting snow mixed with mud, she spotted Daniel walking toward her.

His smile brightened the gray morning. "Mrs. Wescott! Why, if it isn't my favorite teacher."

Ella Mae grinned, her heart warming at his words. "Good morning, Mr. Evans. I hope you received my thank you note for the kind gift of jam. Jam which, it is important to understand, looks precisely like something far less appealing."

His laugh was spontaneous and robust. "Leave it to my boy to say that in school."

"Yes, indeed," she returned.

"Where are you headed on such a day?" Daniel asked. "I'd expect you to be hiding in your room with a book."

"I usually would be," she admitted. "But I'm on my way to visit my sister."

"How is she these days?"

"Well enough," she answered vaguely, not wishing to gossip.

"Is her husband the same as he used to be?" Daniel asked, as if reading her mind.

Her face registered her surprise. "How did you know?"

He laughed. "I've acquired new skills, such as clairvoyance," he teased. "You used to talk about your concerns with me."

"That many years ago? I had no idea it's been going on for so long..." she mused. "Funny how the time can get away from you."

"So, I take it he's never changed," Daniel concluded. "I'm sorry to hear that."

"As am I. I hate seeing her so unhappy."

"Were you as unhappy in your marriage?" he queried, his eyes searching hers.

Ella Mae looked down at her boots, feeling her toes going numb in the mud and snow. "I was. John was both unkind and unfaithful. I don't regret leaving him. Not in the slightest."

"He never hit you?" Daniel worried.

"No. The wounds he inflicted went deeper than flesh."

"I'm sorry... so sorry, Ella Mae," he said, his voice ragged.

Lifting her chin to meet Daniel's gaze, she nodded in acceptance of his sympathy. His eyes were golden brown with a darker ring around them, and his lashes were thick and black. Looking into them, she felt the warmth of his affection as if he had drawn her into an embrace.

"Thank you," she whispered softly.

"I don't know how to say this... I'm sorry that you went through so much, Ella Mae. But I'm glad that you're here in Ridgely now. I'm sorry for what brought us here, but I'm glad we are here again," he finished, struggling to give voice to his feelings, to give due respect to the suffering which had brought them both back to this place.

Ella Mae thought of Pip and Estella and smiled. "Me too."

"I don't want to keep you," Daniel said regretfully. "But perhaps I'll see you again soon."

"Yes, I hope so," she answered.

He tipped his hat, his mouth curving into that crooked smile that never failed to melt her insides. "Take care, Mrs. Wescott," he said in parting.

"Mr. Evans," she replied, her voice raspy with emotion.

Hurrying on her way, Ella Mae tried to clear her head in preparation for her visit with Nora. She had no way of knowing what reception awaited her.

Nora opened the door after the first knock, as if she had been anticipating her arrival. "Come in. I have coffee waiting," she said. One look at her puffy face and pained expression, and Ella Mae knew that the conversation hadn't gone well.

"He isn't home?" Ella Mae asked, just to be certain.

"No, he went to his brother's house." Nora looked as if she had spent the entire night crying. She poured the coffee, offered Ella Mae a biscuit, and sank down wearily into a chair.

"Tell me what happened."

"I tried to talk to him. He wanted to know why the boys never want to be around him, so I told him the truth. It's because he's angry all the time. They can't ever do anything right. We all walk on eggshells around him. Do you want to know what he told me? That our marriage was a mistake. That I should have known better than to marry him. That he never loved me..." Tears coursed down her cheeks.

"Oh Nora," Ella Mae came to her feet and stood beside her sister, wrapping her arms around her neck.

"Why can't he love me? Why am I so unlovable?" Nora sobbed into Ella Mae's shoulder.

Ella Mae stroked her back, wishing she could cure Nora's pain. "Remember what I told you, Nora. His failure to love you is because of his inability, not because of anything lacking in you."

"I just want him to love me, to be kind to me, for us to be a real family! Why is that too much to ask?" Nora wept brokenly.

Ella Mae held her sister like a mother would hold a child, offering what comfort she could with her presence. After a time Nora fell silent and pulled away, wiping her face with a handkerchief.

"I'm sorry," she sniffled.

"No need," Ella Mae assured her softly.

"Maybe I *should* take the boys and move back to the farm," Nora agonized. "James Jr. told me that he wished we would. He hates his father, Ella Mae, and I see the same traits sprouting up in him all the time. He doesn't want to be like James, but that is the man he has learned the most from. He has no patience with Mark, and Mark's such a sensitive soul. He is wounded by every harsh word spoken to him and I'm afraid there are many in this house."

Remembering how long it had taken her to act once the thought had taken root, Ella Mae only nodded in encouragement. Nora would need to make her own decision, in her own time.

Chapter Twenty-Three

Christmas 1898

By December twenty-fifth the snow had melted and the landscape was rendered brown and barren once again. Within the Hutchins' farmhouse, however, an atmosphere of cheer prevailed. Ella Mae had learned her love of Christmas decorating from her mother, who placed pine swags and red bows all throughout the house. In the parlor, on the mantel, one could always count on finding her prized porcelain nativity scene.

Ella Mae was glad to see that Nora was in fine spirits, but Daniel's reminder that her sister's marital discord was nothing new had stayed with her. It was easy to expend so much energy fighting the day's battle that one didn't take full account of the bigger picture, of the patterns and cycles which played out over the weeks, months, or even years.

"He's really been trying to be gentler," Nora whispered in the kitchen as they prepared the dishes for the holiday meal. "I think what he said the other day was just his wounded pride talking. He was upset to know that he'd been hurting us, and he didn't know how to respond. But things have been much better lately."

Nora seemed so genuinely hopeful that Ella Mae didn't have the heart to give an honest response. Besides, it was Christmas. For today, she would try to believe miracles were possible.

The day was spent eating too much, laughing a lot, and enjoying the love of family and the celebration of Messiah: *God with us*. Ella Mae was grateful for the many blessings in her life and in her heart, she thanked God for them. She said a prayer for Daniel, Little Danny, and Robbie on this, their first Christmas without Sabrina.

Although she tried not to think about it, Ella Mae wondered what their marriage had been like. If Daniel and Sabrina had been happy together, if they had loved one another. While she was tempted to reach out to Daniel during what she presumed was a difficult time for him, she knew it was best to keep her distance. He would have to lean on his family and God to get him through this holiday season and through the first anniversary of his wife's death the following month.

It was not appropriate for a divorced woman to be his confidante and comfort. As much as they might wish it, they could never reclaim the friendship of their past.

The days between Christmas and the return to school after the new year were always quiet and lonely for Ella Mae. She could have gone to visit her sister or her parents, but it was just another reminder that she didn't have a family of her own, and never would.

"I will not give in to self-pity," she told herself resolutely. "It could be much worse. I could still be trapped with John."

That awareness gave her renewed gratitude for the life she now lived. She glanced over the books on her shelf, but none of them appealed to her. She had read each one of them many times over. Then an idea struck her.

What if she read her own novel, the one that she'd written after the Wounded Knee Massacre? It had been years since she'd looked at it and she was curious what she would think of it now, a little more than five years later.

The next challenge was finding it. Ella Mae had to rummage through the trunk which held the contents of her former life. Wedding gifts made or given by her friends and family had been kept to honor the giver, not the occasion. A quilt made by Grandma

Greene was folded on top of the items. There were a pair of crystal candle holders, a porcelain vase, and a silver tea tray. All lovely things, but painful reminders of a time in her life she preferred to forget.

At the very bottom, tied with twine, was the manuscript. The pages were yellowed where the dampness had seeped in and in places the ink was smudged. As she felt the weight of it in her hands, Ella Mae felt an unexpected surge of pride in the accomplishment. She remembered how hard she had researched so she could paint a realistic word picture of the windswept plains and the native people who had occupied them for centuries before the white settlers arrived.

Why had she abandoned writing? It had been her driving passion for so many years. She had let John break her spirit. Even though she had known he was what Mrs. Hudson called a "megalomaniac," Ella Mae had still taken his criticism and insults to heart.

She had believed John because his voice matched the words of her deepest fears. And that had been his intention.

Anger welled up inside of her. Defiance boiled within her. She would not let John have any more power over her. She had proven herself to be strong and independent the day she left him, but she hadn't realized that he had continued to control her from a distance.

Not anymore! She would not let him take another thing away from her. Taking the manuscript with her, Ella Mae curled up in the armchair where she had read so many other novels. As she began reading the story she had written, the words she had so meticulously penned, she was swept away by a myriad of emotions.

In part, revisiting the story brought her back to the years of her life when she had written it, but at the same time, she found herself caught up in the drama of the story. It was the tale of a woman whose infant had died along the wagon trail, and even as she grieved this loss, an orphaned babe was discovered wailing in the tall prairie grass. She lifted the child to her bosom and held it there. Indian or white, it didn't matter. From that moment on, this baby was hers.

The story progressed to the relationship between husband and wife as they agree together to care for the babe. As they learn to love little Alice as their own, they realize the possibility that the girl might have a biological father or grandparents who wondered of her fate.

Ella Mae had forgotten much of the story and found herself turning the pages with anticipation, wondering what would happen next as they traveled from one reservation to another in search of the baby's blood family.

She was startled to realize that the light in her room grew dim. The hours had passed like seconds. Giving her eyes a break, she went down and took dinner with the others, then returned to her room and lit the oil lamp. Ella Mae stayed up reading late into the night until her eyes gave out and she was forced to sleep.

The following day she resumed reading through the handwritten manuscript. There were so many details she had forgotten. The different reservations, tribes, cultures, people. She had to admit, even if it was her own work, that she had done an excellent job of providing information while still bringing the story to life with believable characters and a captivating plot.

It was a good story, but there was an emotional shallowness which reflected who she had been at the time she had written it. What was lacking wasn't in the mechanics of writing, even though she spotted several grammatical mistakes. She had yet to be refined by the fires of suffering, to have her resolve forged in the flames, her heart scarred and strengthened.

She had no idea what she would do with it once completed, but Ella Mae decided that she would take the wisdom and compassion she had gained through her trials and apply them to the novel. Page by page, she would revise and rewrite until it was as good as she could make it in this present time.

Ella Mae lost all track of day and night, dedicating herself wholly to this mission. She felt a wild elation as the familiar surge of inspiration rose up within her, her imagination flooded with pictures and feelings, her mind racing with the words to describe them. She had her meals sent up to her room, assuring Mrs. Jarrell she was quite well, just overtaken by the power of creativity.

By the time the holiday ended and school began, her fingers were ink-stained and her eyes blood-shot, but she had made great progress. She was exhausted, but content. She had forgotten just how fulfilling writing was for her, and she regretted having let John keep her from it for so long.

For the rest of the month of January 1899, Ella Mae worked on her manuscript for several hours every evening and all the weekend long. She was relentlessly dedicated to the story and to the message it conveyed: we are all created equal in God's sight.

She informed Deborah of her renewed purpose and her friend was delighted to hear of it. Deborah even wrote her mother, Sarah Gibson, in Wyoming and told her that the work had once again been taken up. Ella Mae was plagued by a moment of guilt as she realized that she had lost sight of a greater purpose while caught up in the small world of her own suffering.

But she let the guilt go, knowing that everything had its own time and she had done what she must to heal and grow.

Now, she was ready to give it her everything and she wouldn't let anyone stop her.

"Ah, Mrs. Wescott. I was afraid you might have left town, except my son was still coming home from school with your name on his lips."

Ella Mae spun on her heel at the sound of that deep baritone voice. Would her heart always flutter at the sight of him?

"Mr. Evans, you really shouldn't startle people that way," she admonished playfully. "You gave me a fright."

"My apologies, ma'am. I was just overjoyed to see that you are in fact, alive and well. You haven't been out of that boarding house in weeks, apart from going to school."

"Have you been spying?" She arched her eyebrows curiously.

Daniel grinned. "Just observant. Is everything all right?"

"Yes, quite all right. I've been writing again. Actually, I've been working on revising the last novel I wrote."

"Really?" His brown eyes lit up with genuine enthusiasm. "That's wonderful! When do I get to read it?"

"Not yet," she laughed. *Maybe not ever*, she thought. She still heard that voice of fear whispering in her ear that if Daniel read it, he would discover how untalented she really was.

"This is the one about the Indian girl, isn't it?" he pressed.

Ella Mae was stunned that he remembered. Stunned and touched. "Yes. Yes, it is."

"Well, I hope you'll let me read it when you're finished," Daniel told her.

They were standing in the aisle at the mercantile as they held this conversation. Ella Mae nodded, reaching for a bar of lavender scented soap. She placed it in the basket draped over her elbow. "I'll let you know. I still need to transcribe a fresh copy with all of the corrections."

"I'll be looking forward to it," his white teeth flashed in a smile.

"You look to be doing well," she said, to avoid directly asking if he had finished grieving the anniversary of his wife's passing.

"It's been a difficult month," he confessed. "But I believe I am on the upward swing."

"I'm glad," she said, hoping her smile said what her words could not.

"Perhaps in February you would like to come have dinner with my parents and children? I know Danny would love that, and his grandparents appreciate the way you've helped him thrive this year."

Ella Mae felt her cheeks flush beneath his praise. "I would like that," she answered.

"Very good, Mrs. Wescott," he tipped his hat and winked. "I'd better finish fetching what my mother sent me for or I'll find myself in the woodshed."

Covering her mouth, as it wasn't the appropriate setting for her to be giggling like a schoolgirl at Mr. Evan's jokes, Ella Mae nodded a goodbye and tried to remember what else she had come for.

When she returned to her room in the boarding house, Ella Mae stared at the stacks of pages spread out across her dresser. She had no writing desk and had been making due with the surface of the dresser, careful not to leave any ink stains which might anger Mrs. Jarrell. She had carefully organized the pages so she would know where she had left off.

Daniel wanted to read it.

She bit her lip, feeling a combination of excitement and fear at the prospect. Handing this manuscript over to him—this tangible expression of her inward thoughts and feelings—was to give him power over her, to make her vulnerable to him in a way she wasn't sure she wanted to be. Was she brave enough to risk his disappointment in her, his criticisms of her writing skills or understanding of the issues? Ella Mae knew she had done her very best but the question that haunted her was, *is it good enough*?

Chapter Twenty-Four

*I*t was the second week of February before Ella Mae finished the clean copy of her updated manuscript. She'd struggled to choose a title when she wrote the original draft, but now she called it, "*My Daughter, Alice*." She decided to stay with the pen name "Edward Hudson."

She hadn't seen Daniel since they'd run into one another at the mercantile. Ella Mae still had mixed feelings about allowing him to read her novel.

Mrs. Evans had invited her to their home for dinner on Saturday. Ella Mae was more nervous than she could remember being about anything in years. While she knew she was being invited in her official capacity as Danny's teacher, the reality remained that this was the family of the man Ella Mae had loved since she was a girl. She anticipated it with eagerness, but also with regret that it had not come until now, and in this way.

Every time she thought she had accepted the death of her dreams and come to terms with the life she lived, something happened to stir up the buried longings and the grief that accompanied them. But she, like everyone else who grieved, had to lift her chin and soldier on.

During the week it was difficult for Ella Mae to find time to see Nora, but she made it a point to drop in on Saturdays when she could. Nora always seemed grateful for the visit, allowing James Jr. and Mark to stay if all was going well with she and her husband, sending them upstairs if she needed privacy to complain about their father. James Sr. was usually absent if there had been conflict.

Ella Mae loved her sister, but she was growing increasingly frustrated. It seemed that if James demonstrated any kindness toward her, even once a month, it was enough for Nora to keep feeding her obstinate hope. Even if Nora was unable to track the cycle, Ella Mae saw it.

Whenever Nora had reached the end of her patience, James affected a temporary change and wooed his wife back with the smallest tokens of affection. But his change was always short-lived, if not more accurately described as "brief."

Nora had been crying again. "I just don't know what to do. He's been slamming doors and snapping at the boys for every little thing. He says that I undermine his authority when I go behind him to comfort them. He was so mad at me, he slept on the couch last night. What am I supposed to do?" she pleaded.

Ella Mae clenched her jaw, took a deep breath, and said, "You know what I would do."

"I know, but you didn't have any children to consider. I have two boys and they need a father, need a roof over their heads and food on the table," Nora countered.

"You could live with Mama and Papa, like I did. They wouldn't mind."

"I can't expect them to take care of the three of us. That isn't fair."

"I'm sure you could find a way to make money and help out," Ella Mae said, knowing she wasted her breath.

"We've been married almost twenty years. I can't just throw it away."

"I'm going to tell you what I think, and you may do what you will with it," Ella Mae declared. "You stay with James partly from loyalty and the other part from fear. You don't know if you could live without him. And you worry what people will think. But I know you would find a way to be just fine. You just need to believe that for yourself."

Nora twisted her hands in her lap. "You're right. You're right."

"It may sound noble to stay with James for the children's sakes, but sometimes I wonder if their father's ways don't do them more harm than good," Ella Mae continued, too frustrated to hold her tongue any longer. "Little James is sounding more and more like him all the time, and Mark is becoming sullen and withdrawn. Don't you see that?"

"I do…" Nora admitted, tears running down her cheeks.

"I believe marriage is a sacred institution, created by God. But I do not believe that He is honored when we hold ourselves of so little value that we let someone treat us like we are less than the horse in the barn, protected by laws against cruel treatment. Just because James doesn't strike you or the boys with his fists doesn't mean he isn't leaving wounds on your spirit." Ella Mae could feel her heart racing with passion as she spoke. Her own experience thundered in her veins.

Nora reached for a handkerchief.

"You know what else I think? You need to stop being sad and get *angry*. You have every right to be angry at a man who is supposed to love you and instead mistreats you. Let your anger give you the strength to make a change."

Wide-eyed, her sister stared at her as if startled. She bit her lip, wiped her eyes.

"Please think on what I've said," Ella Mae finished softly, reaching across the kitchen table to squeeze her sister's arm. "I love you. I hate seeing you so unhappy."

"I know. I'll think on it," Nora promised.

Walking home, Ella Mae hoped she hadn't said too much, crossed any lines. She never imagined that one day she would advocate for a woman to leave her husband. There were many activists working to liberalize divorce laws, and Ella Mae understood what a tricky business it was for lawmakers to decide. Marriage was a blessed union created by God, and the words spoken in the vows a husband and wife made to one another were also made before God.

She hoped she wasn't wrong in her beliefs. She hoped she hadn't sinned when she left John. But she couldn't believe that remaining in an abusive marriage accomplished anything that honored God. Many men or women might no longer love their spouse, but they could still choose to treat them with respect, to honor the commitment they had made.

Marriage wasn't meant to be a temporary arrangement until one's feelings changed, but a lifetime partnership through all the varied seasons of life, regardless of how sentimental affections waxed and waned. Marriage was a test of endurance, character, and commitment. It wasn't meant to be a cheap fling, disposed of when it failed to provide the necessary excitement. Nor was it meant to be a prison, entrapping one in abuse.

Ella Mae prayed that James would experience a moment of truth, of understanding the blessings which he'd been given and for which he showed no gratitude. That above all was her greatest wish. But if James could not change, as some men couldn't—or wouldn't—then she wished to see her sister and nephews safely removed from the sharp edge of his anger.

Taking a deep breath, Ella Mae pushed such thoughts aside. She needed to hurry back to the boarding house and begin dressing for dinner at the Evans' house, and she had no idea what to wear.

Once in her room, she opened her wardrobe and stared at the garments hanging there. She no longer wanted to play the part of a career teacher, presenting herself as professional and mature. Nor could she dress as a single woman trying to impress a man. She wished she could find a suitable possibility somewhere in between the two, but unfortunately her wardrobe was severely lacking in options.

She decided on a navy-blue suit with lace embellishing the collar, worn with a white blouse and a brooch positioned at her throat. Ella Mae typically wore her hair pulled back in a more austere fashion, but she took the extra time to tease it up into a loose bun on the crown of her head with curls framing her face. A hat with a jaunty ostrich feather finished the look.

Staring back at her in the mirror was a twenty-nine-year-old divorced woman who might still be considered pretty, but had no business trying to gain a man's attention. Ella Mae sighed and turned away.

The Evans lived on Maple Street, a short walk from the boarding house. The February day was cold with a brisk wind blowing, but the sky was clear and blue. Bundled in a coat and scarf, she walked as quickly as she could, knowing her nose would be red by the time she arrived.

The elder Mr. Evans met her at the door. "Come inside, Mrs. Wescott. Warm yourself by the fire."

She let him take her coat and lead her to the parlor where a fire blazed. Ella Mae had passed by this house more than once, but had never been inside. It was certainly nicer than the farmhouse she had grown up in, but since her stay at the Perry's house in Annapolis, she was hard to impress.

Danny came racing around the corner, his eyes lighting up with pure joy at the sight of her. "You came to my house!"

His father followed behind him, carrying the younger son. Robbie looked as though he had just awakened from a nap, leaning his head upon his father's broad shoulder, thumb in his mouth.

"Good evening, Mrs. Wescott. I'm glad you could make it," Daniel said, the warmth in his voice making the polite statement sound personal.

245

"I'm happy to be here," she replied, feeling a nervous flutter in her middle.

He stared at her silently for just a second, his eyes appraising her softer hairstyle. A slight smile indicated his approval. He sat down on the sofa and patted Robbie's back. "Time to wake up, son. Say hello to Mrs. Wescott."

The toddler turned his head and greeted her in a shy, sleepy voice. He reminded Ella Mae of Sabrina, and with thoughts of her came the familiar feeling of inferiority.

She brushed them away. She was Danny's teacher and Daniel's friend, and she was good enough for both of those roles. Still, the ache had settled in her chest once again as this moment reminded her of just how much she had longed to be his first love, his wife, and the mother of his children.

Mr. Evans, Daniel's father, was a tall broad-shouldered man with strong, angular features. Ella Mae imagined that when he was young, he was probably every bit as handsome as his son. Mr. Evans stood by the fire, keeping watch on young Danny, who bounced around excitedly.

"Can I show Mrs. Wescott my room?"

"No, but you can bring one toy from your room to show her," his grandfather answered.

Danny bounded out of the room, reappearing moments later with a wooden train, painted black and gold, with a string affixed to the front of the engine. He placed it on the carpet in front of her and pulled it along, making the accompanying sounds a steam engine would make as it rattled over the tracks. Ella Mae grinned. The simple pleasures of a child were a delight to watch. How easy it was to forget that joy can be found in anything, if only one was open to finding it.

246

Robbie, no longer sleepy, sprang from his father's lap and ran to steal the train away from his older brother. Danny pushed him away. "No! Get your own toy."

Daniel's voice was firm but gentle as he corrected his oldest son. "Danny, try that again. Robbie, you know you shouldn't grab like that."

Danny scooped the toy up and held it protectively against his chest. "Robbie, please get your own toy," he said politely.

Robbie, completely unfazed, turned and darted into the hallway. When he returned, he carried a similar wooden toy pulled by a string. His was a green alligator. He ran back and forth in front of Ella Mae, pulling his alligator and making fearsome growling sounds. He had no idea how adorable he was and how much she wanted to press a kiss onto his round cheek.

Danny, not to be outdone by his brother, ran alongside him, choo-chooing and click-clacking, until Mr. Evans asked if the alligator and train could please take a rest.

"Dinner's ready, anyhow," Mrs. Evans announced as she came into the room, smiling. The boys ran to grab at her apron. She lifted the littlest one onto her hip and said, "Mrs. Wescott, I'm so glad you could join us today. Follow me into the dining room, please."

Daniel's mother was a wiry woman of average height with sharp eyes and a kind smile. And Ella Mae learned that day she was also an excellent cook. The time passed pleasantly as she had already developed a relationship with Danny's grandparents from their regular visits to the schoolhouse. Apparently Daniel had made them aware of their past friendship, because it was mentioned briefly once or twice.

Ella Mae soon forgot both her discomfort and her heartache as Mr. Evans regaled her with tales of Daniel's childhood, with Mrs. Evans chiming in to add or correct the details. Daniel grinned, not appearing embarrassed in the slightest.

After dessert, the boys bid Mrs. Wescott good night and Danny pressed a sticky kiss to her cheek that melted her heart. Robbie, overtired and grumpy, only wanted his grandmother. Mrs. Evans wished Ella Mae a good night before taking the boys upstairs to put them to bed.

"You should walk Mrs. Wescott home, son. It's after dark," Mr. Evans advised Daniel as if he were still a boy.

"Yes sir," Daniel responded, tossing her a wink when his father turned away.

He helped her into her coat, donning his own as she carefully replaced her hat and wrapped her scarf around her neck. Then together they went out into the cold, moonlit night.

"That's the trouble with living at home again. No matter how old you are, your parents will always treat you like a child," Daniel stated.

"I rather enjoyed those stories," Ella Mae giggled. "The only thing that surprised me was that you let your sons hear them."

He chuckled. "I'm sure they'll think of their own mischief."

"Your parents are delightful. Very kind and sweet," she commented.

"I'm sorry I never had you over before, Ella Mae. I was a complete ass, and I'm sorry," Daniel admitted, his big hands knotting together in front of him.

She could see the chagrin in his eyes and was moved. "At least you admit it," she said, trying to keep her voice light.

"I know my regret can't change anything," Daniel replied, his voice husky. "But I am sorry. For everything."

Ella Mae felt the pain in her chest expand. She sighed, wishing it could be released with her breath into the frosty air. "I know," she said softly.

They walked the next few paces in silence, the full white moon above them casting a pale glow onto the houses they passed. Everything seemed transformed from an ordinary town into an otherworldly kingdom. It was haunting and beautiful at the same time.

"Have you finished that novel yet?" Daniel asked, breaking the silence.

Ella Mae bit her lip. "I did. I'm not sure what to do with it now. I guess I'll send it to an agent."

"You'll give it to me, of course. I told you I wanted to read it."

"But I only have the one copy. I'll need to make another."

"So, I shouldn't spill coffee on it or leave it too close to the fire?" he teased.

"You are incorrigible," she laughed, a flood of memories coming with the use of the old phrase.

They had reached the steps of the boarding house. They paused, turning to face one another.

"I'll wait while you fetch it," Daniel said, giving her that crooked grin that made her insides weak.

"I never said I'd let you read it," Ella Mae retorted.

"It would mean a lot to me if you would," he said, and so sincerely that she couldn't deny him.

"Wait here," she said, moving past him toward the front door.

When she returned, Daniel had taken a seat in one of the chairs lost in the shadows on the front porch. She took one next to him, handing the thick manuscript over with the order: "Take care of it."

"I promise, Mrs. Wescott. I wouldn't dare do otherwise. Besides, I know how precious it is to you."

Why did he have to be so wonderful? Why now, when they could never be together?

"It's cold. I should go in," Ella Mae said, coming to her feet.

"Yes, yes. I'm sorry." Daniel stood, walked her to the door.

"Good night, Mr. Evans," Ella Mae said as she stepped inside.

"Good night, Ella Mae," he replied, his voice tender.

Closing the door, she turned and went up the stairs as quickly as she could, closing herself in her room and sinking down on the edge of her bed.

Chapter Twenty-Five

A week later, Ella Mae had just returned to her room after breakfast when there was a knock upon the door.

Bessie Jarrell stood in the hallway. "Mrs. Wescott, you have a visitor downstairs, ma'am. A gentleman by the name of Mr. Evans."

"Thank you. Please tell him I'll be right down."

Rushing to check her appearance in the mirror, Ella Mae quickly repinned her hair and pinched her cheeks to add a touch of color. Then, taking a deep breath, she tried to calm her racing pulse as she walked in slow and measured steps down the stairs to the parlor.

Daniel stood in front of the fireplace, elbow resting upon the black mantel, his strong profile visible as he stared down into the flames. As she entered the room he straightened and came toward her. His eyes were bright with excitement and his smile made her heart skip a beat.

"It's incredible!" he announced. "Your story! I didn't want to put it down, Ella Mae. You have to get this published."

Ella Mae's jaw dropped. A flush of joy washed over her. "Really? You really think so?"

Taking her by the elbow, Daniel led her to the sofa. Her manuscript rested on the coffee table. "I absolutely think so, Ella Mae. You brought Alice to life! You made me believe that she was just like me, like anyone else. Masterfully done! Where did you learn so much about the Indians?"

Heady from the unexpected praise, she tried to clear her thoughts. She told him about her friend Deborah in Annapolis and about how she had corresponded with her mother, in Wyoming, who was a full-blooded Lakota Sioux.

"After the Wounded Knee Massacre I wanted to do something to change the public opinion about Indians, to find a way to show that they are every bit as human as we are."

"Well, you did it! We need to get this published."

"I'll need to copy another manuscript," Ella Mae replied, still trying to grasp hold of the moment.

"Can you copy two? I'd like one. I know someone who might have some connections. No guarantees, of course. You do what you can, and I'll see what I can do," he promised enthusiastically.

She nodded, fearing it was all a dream from which she would soon wake up.

Daniel rested a hand on her forearm, his brown eyes boring into hers as he said, "I'm proud of you, Ella Mae."

Flustered, she had no idea how to respond. She could feel her cheeks turn crimson.

Daniel came to his feet. "I need to run, I'm afraid. But you have work to do, anyway," he winked.

Ella Mae rose, walked with him to the door. He stepped outside, returned his hat to his head. "I'll see you again soon, Mrs. Wescott."

"Good day," she said, her voice oddly high-pitched.

Ella Mae returned to her room in a trance. She couldn't believe that Daniel had actually read the novel, let alone thought it was worthy of publication! Taking a deep breath, Ella Mae considered the amount of work she had to do in transcribing two more copies. That was hundreds and hundreds of pages!

252

Deciding she would start immediately, Ella Mae accessed her resources and determined she would need to purchase more paper and ink. Donning her coat, she made a trip to the mercantile, hurrying back as quickly as she could. She asked Mrs. Jarrell to send up some tea and set to work copying her novel. For the first time in years, she felt hopeful that at least one of her dreams was within reach.

On Monday, she mailed a letter to Deborah Gibson, informing her that she was finished the revisions and intended to send it to an agent. She was surprised when she received a reply a week later that Deborah wished to come to Ridgely to visit her and to read the latest edition.

"*I would love for you to visit!*" she wrote in reply. "*You can stay with me at the boarding house. I absolutely can't wait to show you my little town and the school where I teach!*" Deborah would have to entertain herself during the days while Ella Mae was working, but they would have the evenings and weekends. She would also have the opportunity to meet Daniel, whom she had listened to Ella Mae talk about for years.

The first weekend in March promised of spring with blue skies and warmer temperatures. "It's a fine day for a stroll," Daniel said, as he stood in the parlor with his hat in his hand.

He had arrived just as Ella Mae had finished taking breakfast in the dining room with the other boarders. Bessie had answered the door, sending him to the parlor to wait while she went to inform Ella Mae with a knowing grin on her face.

"Are you sure a stroll is a good idea?" Ella Mae hated to ask the question, but she didn't want Daniel's reputation tarnished for lack of proper foresight.

"Why? Because you're divorced, and I'm widowed?" he replied candidly. "I don't care what anyone thinks. Come walk with me."

Blushing, Ella Mae was happy to comply. She ran upstairs to fetch a shawl, pausing to pin on a hat and fix her hair before darting back down to where Daniel waited on the front porch. He had never offered his arm when they walked together before, and he did not now. There was no need to add fuel to the fire for those on the prowl for gossip.

"My friend, Deborah Gibson, is coming to stay with me," she told Daniel as they set out down the dirt street. "She's the one who is half-Indian, who I met in Annapolis."

"I remember. I'm looking forward to meeting her."

"She's eager to read the revised novel and, I suspect, she's in need of a change of scenery. I don't know why she's never married. She's a beautiful woman, and as kind and sweet as anyone I've ever met. I don't know if it's her heritage that puts men off or if she just hasn't met anyone worth the risk."

"Men can be quite idiotic, or so I've heard," Daniel replied, tossing her a grin.

"Some more than others," she retorted.

"You know I'm working at the Saulsbury Brother's Cannery now? I'm a manager and accountant, handling the finer details of the business from an office chair. But still, it's not what I had imagined for myself. I suppose God thought I needed humbling," he confessed with a wry chuckle. "And I suppose He was right."

"He usually is," Ella Mae answered, only partially teasing.

"Yes, that's true. It's a shame that wisdom has to come with age and experience, never with youth," he sighed.

"Indeed," she agreed.

"I thought I was so smart," he laughed. "I was such a fool."

"Well, at least you've learned from your trials. Not everyone does."

"That's something," Daniel agreed. "Have you heard anything from John?"

"I heard a while back that he had remarried, otherwise nothing. Which is quite fine with me. I was the greatest of fools when I married him."

Daniel shoved his hands in his pockets, looking ten years younger with the gesture. "I suppose it was easier that you didn't have children," he ventured, glancing at her as if worried he might offend.

Ella Mae felt a familiar stab of grief, but she was thankful for this time to speak openly with an old, dear friend. "It was. I'm not sure how that would have ended. Of course, I'll always regret never being a mother, but I have my students to fill that place in my heart."

"You'll never remarry?" He sounded surprised.

"I'm not sure I could... I'm a divorced woman," she reminded him regretfully.

"Ah," he said, as if he hadn't considered that it could impede her from future matrimony.

"What about you?" she asked, feeling a knot of emotions form in her stomach.

"Me? I don't know. Maybe," he answered vaguely, the sideways glance he cast her sending a shiver of hope and longing through her.

They had turned left when leaving the boarding house, walking south down Central Avenue and then meandering toward the cemetery. As it came into view, Ella Mae asked, "Were you... I mean, was your marriage a happy one?"

"Sometimes," he answered quietly, letting that one word stand alone.

"I am sorry to hear that," Ella Mae replied, unsure what else was appropriate given the circumstances.

The grass was beginning to show signs of new growth and the trees had begun to bud. Birds sang optimistically from above them in the branches. Spring would arrive soon, and with it the age-old hope of rebirth and resurrection.

"We should probably head back," he said. "My boys will miss me. I want to take Danny out in the back yard and teach him how to throw a baseball."

"It's the perfect day for it," she answered, wishing their time together didn't need to end.

"How much more transcribing do you have left?" Daniel reached for her bare hands, which were usually hidden by gloves when he was with her. He examined the ink staining her skin.

She pulled away, laughing in embarrassment. "I still have more work to do."

"You'd better keep your gloves on till you're done," he advised with a crooked grin.

"I'll try to remember that," she said, her skin still tingling from his touch.

They talked of baseball and little boys as they walked along until Ella Mae commented, "I think I'll stop by my sister's house. I haven't check in on her lately."

Speaking of unhappy marriages had reminded her of Nora, and she felt guilty that she'd been so preoccupied with her novel that she hadn't made time for her sister.

Daniel walked alongside her until they reached Nora's house. He tipped his hat and bid her a good day, then continued on his way to his parents' house. Ella Mae said a quick prayer for wisdom before she knocked on her sister's door.

Mark opened the door, exclaiming, "Hello, Aunt Ella! Come on in!"

Ella Mae smiled at her youngest nephew. "Thank you, Mark."

"Mama's upstairs. She should be down in just a minute," he told her. "James and I are going to go with Daddy to lay flooring at Uncle Brice's house."

James Sr.'s brother had been building an addition on his home, so it was no surprise that he was helping. However, that Nora was allowing her sons to accompany him, was.

After they had left, Ella Mae expressed her concern to Nora.

"He'll behave himself well enough if his brother is around," she said in reference to her husband. "He's usually more in control of himself in front of others."

"How has he been at home?" Ella Mae asked, following Nora into the parlor.

Nora eased herself down into an armchair, knotting her hands in her lap and staring down at them for a moment. Finally, she lifted her gaze to Ella Mae. "I try so hard to be a good wife. When he makes a request for meals, I always try to please him. When James says that he needs his coat mended, I'm sure it's taken care of before morning. Even when he chooses to sleep here on the sofa, I still get up early and make his breakfast for him before he leaves for work. And all I ever hear from him is what I'm not doing well enough, or what I should have done differently."

Ella Mae clenched her teeth, took a deep breath, and said, "Nora... Nora, you are not a door mat for him to wipe his feet on. Get up off the floor."

Nora blinked. "I'm trying to be a good wife, Ella Mae."

"You *are* a good wife, Nora. He doesn't appreciate you. I think you are trying to earn your husband's love, and he refuses to give it. Love is a gift, not something you should have to work for, to prove yourself worthy of it. You can't *make* someone love you!"

Her sister's eyes welled with tears.

"I'm sorry, Nora. I'm sorry," Ella Mae rushed to sit beside her, placing her arm around her slender shoulders. "I don't mean to upset you. I love you, and I believe you ought to be treated far better than James has ever treated you. It makes me angry."

Nora retrieved her well-used handkerchief and wiped her nose. "I know. I still love him, though. How do I stop trying when all I want is for him to love me? Am I so hard to love?"

Ella Mae sighed. She didn't have all the answers. She only had her own experiences and what she had learned from them.

"Nora, I'm not sure James loves anyone—not even himself. He is a miserable person. It has nothing to do with you or how loveable you are. I've told you this before. You haven't done anything to warrant his treatment of you. You are loveable—and you are loved! Don't you remember what we were taught as children?

"*'What is the price of two sparrows—one copper coin? But not a single sparrow can fall to the ground without your Father knowing it. And the very hairs on your head are all numbered. So don't be afraid; you are more valuable to God than a whole flock of sparrows.'*"

Sniffling, Nora nodded her head. "I remember learning that verse. But I don't feel valuable."

"That is because you're letting James's behavior determine how you value yourself. You are one of God's creations, made in His image. That is where you find your worth."

"How did you ever find the courage to leave John?"

"I got angry, Nora! Because no one deserves to be treated the way he treated me! Or the way James treats you and your sons. The Bible also teaches *'be angry but do not sin.'* Anger isn't a sin in itself—only if it leads to it. And I don't believe that demanding James treat you with respect, or removing yourself from his reach if he won't, is a sin."

Her sister stared at her thoughtfully, as if turning over Ella Mae's words, evaluating their truthfulness. But in Nora's eyes, Ella Mae didn't see anger. Only fear.

Chapter Twenty-Six

The March winds finally gave way to April showers and the yellow daffodils, purple hyacinths, and pink and yellow tulips began to bloom. Ella Mae always appreciated those first flowers of spring, brightening the dull landscape with their cheerful colors. In the fields the strawberry vines were growing in vast profusion, promising another profitable harvest as their green tendrils sprawled out over the acres surrounding Ridgely.

Deborah arrived in town the first Saturday in April. A fine mist fell from the sky, and Ella Mae stood on the platform with an umbrella as she waited for her friend. Deborah looked relieved to see her as she stepped down from the train, and Ella Mae hurried over to greet her and to take her luggage tickets. Mr. Jarrell had driven her in his buggy and was waiting nearby to load Deborah's trunks.

Once they reached the boarding house, Ella Mae led Deborah up to her room to rest and freshen up. Deborah would share her room, paying half the rate for a double occupancy.

"What a lovely place!" Deborah said as she removed her hat and jacket.

"The boarding house or the town?" Ella Mae asked.

"Both! It's a quaint little town, and I enjoyed the wonderful scenery along the way here. It is a flat, rural place, isn't it? And this boarding house is very nice. I love the wide, front porch and the elegant staircase," Deborah declared.

"I agree on all counts. I'm so glad you're here!" Ella Mae replied.

Deborah grinned. Her exotic features were more beautiful than Ella Mae remembered. She certainly didn't look Indian, not in the way that one would expect. Nor black nor Spanish, either. But there was enough that was different about her to make one suspect she wasn't purely white. Ella Mae observed her almond shaped eyes, high cheekbones, and straight nose.

Why must people be divided by color, when they all shared the same divine spark?

If one had to be categorized, it was easier to be Indian than to be black. Since the thirteenth amendment had been passed and slavery abolished, the Negroes had struggled to find their place in society. There was a general understanding that they were "separate, but equal," although the truth was that they were not treated as equals. Ella Mae hated knowing that there was another school especially for the colored children, taught by colored teachers, as if something horrible would happen if the two races should mix.

"Will you give me a tour of your town when the rain lets up?" Deborah asked.

Ella Mae laughed. "I'm afraid you've already seen most of it. It's a very small town."

"I can't wait to see your schoolhouse."

"I'm eager to show it to you. I really do enjoy teaching there. Perhaps you can come one day during the week to meet my students."

"I'd like that," Deborah said, moving to the basin to wash her face of the grime left from the train ride. "And I'm especially looking forward to meeting this man, Daniel Evans, I've heard so much about."

Blushing, Ella Mae waved the comment aside. "He's only a friend. All he's ever been, or ever will be."

Deborah didn't look convinced.

"And of course, I'm looking forward to reading your novel again. I thought it was perfect before you made your changes to it."

Happy to discuss something other than Daniel, Ella Mae said, "You may not realize the improvements I've made, but I assure you it's much better than it was. Whether or not it's good enough to be published is another matter altogether, and unfortunately a very subjective one. An agent might think it's wonderful, but unless he finds an editor of a publishing house who agrees, who is looking for this type of material, it will never be more than a story I penned with great hopes and dreams."

The rain never let up that day, and the women spent the time catching up on all the small details of life that don't make into letters. Ella Mae was curious if the Jarrells or their guests would treat Deborah differently or make any comments associated with her race. She was relieved when all went smoothly.

Sunday, she took Deborah to church with her, then to her parents' house for dinner. Her mother and father were delighted to spend time with Ella Mae's dear friend, getting to know more about Deborah as well as her heritage, which had inspired their daughter's novel. They stayed at the farmhouse until evening, when Mr. Hutchins gave the women a ride back to the boarding house in his buggy as the roads were still muddy from the recent rain.

While Ella Mae was at school on Monday, Deborah stayed at the boarding house and began reading *My Daughter, Alice*. When Ella Mae returned in the late afternoon, Deborah was still sitting in the armchair reading.

"This is beautiful," she told Ella Mae with tears in her eyes. "It's raw, poignant, touching... It grabs the reader's heart first, and then speaks to his mind. Well done."

"I'm so glad you think so," Ella Mae replied, feeling a bit uncomfortable with the compliments.

"If I didn't need to rest my eyes, I wouldn't put it down until I'd read it all the way through," Deborah insisted.

"Well, let's pray we can find an editor who feels the same way," Ella Mae replied, aware of the obstacles that still stood in the way of publication.

Deborah finished reading the novel the following day, then on Wednesday she came with Ella Mae to school to meet her students. The children noticed right away that she had unique characteristics, but far from being critical, they were curious and enthusiastic.

"Why does your face look different?" one very little girl asked innocently. "You're so pretty!"

When Deborah explained that her mother was an Indian and her father as a white man, they were immediately fascinated. Ella Mae decided to postpone the history lesson she had planned and instead let them ask questions about what Indians were really like and the truth about the Western plains.

"Do Indians really wear buckskins?"

"Do they wear moccasins instead of shoes?"

"Do they ride horses and live in tents?"

"Do they talk funny?"

Deborah patiently answered all their questions, although she did chuckle at the last one. "They are learning English, but that is not their native language, if that's what you mean. There are many different tribes, and they do not all speak the same language."

One boy piped up, "My grandpa told me he killed redskins in the Indian Wars. He made it sound like they were the bad guys. Were they the bad guys?"

Ella Mae glanced at Deborah, who hesitated before answering carefully. "Just because someone has white skin doesn't guarantee he will be a good guy. Some bad guys have white skin too. In the same way, some Indians might be good and others might be bad. All people make choices about whether they want to do what is right, or what is wrong."

The child nodded thoughtfully in response, as if he had never considered this before. Ella Mae was sorry to know that many children—and adults—hadn't come to this very basic realization.

After school, Little Danny thanked Miss Gibson for teaching them about Indians. "I used to want to be a cowboy," he confessed, "but I don't think I want to anymore. Because I don't want to have to shoot Indians. I think I'd like to just be their friends."

Deborah smiled as she told him, "Some cowboys and Indians are friends, you know. We all get to make our own choices."

He appeared pleased with her response. To Ella Mae, he said, "Mrs. Wescott, do you think you can come have dinner at my house again soon? I like having you there."

"I'd like that, Danny," Ella Mae replied, tousling his dark hair affectionately.

"He's...?" Deborah lifted her eyebrows quizzically.

Ella Mae understood the cryptic question. "Yes," she answered. He was Daniel's son.

When the elder Mr. Evans arrived to pick Danny up, he was introduced to Miss Gibson. "It's a pleasure to meet you," he said. "My wife would have been pleased to meet you, as well, but she's home with our youngest grandson. He was having a bit of an outburst. Needed a nap, Mrs. Evans claimed." He winked at Mrs. Wescott, as if he thought the child needed something else.

"We would be pleased if you both would join us for dinner this Saturday evening. We'd like to extend our hospitality while you are visiting our delightful little town," he added to Deborah.

The two women exchanged glances and Ella Mae accepted the invitation for them both. "That would be lovely, thank you."

Danny, overhearing the conversation, jumped up and down. "Yay!" he cried.

After all the children and parents were gone, Deborah leaned over to Ella Mae and whispered, "I cannot wait to meet Danny's father!" When Ella Mae slanted her a warning look, Deborah giggled. "I promise I won't say anything to embarrass you."

Ella Mae tried to hide her eagerness to see Daniel as the two women dressed together in her room Saturday evening. She bit her lip, studying the dresses hanging in the wardrobe. Now that it was spring, she had more flattering options to choose from than the somber colors of winter.

She selected a mauve dress with a high collar, pearl buttons, and puffed sleeves. Then she tried to coerce her hair into the fashion of the day, loosely teased up into a knot on the top of her head.

Deborah put no more effort into her appearance than usual. Ella Mae stared at her reflection in the mirror, recognizing that even without trying, Deborah was far prettier than she. She felt a twinge of envy, worried that Daniel might have his head turned by her young, beautiful friend.

But she reminded herself that Daniel wasn't, and never had been, hers. He was free to turn his head at any woman he chose, no matter how it might affect Ella Mae.

"You look wonderful," Deborah assured her as Ella Mae paused to check her appearance one last time before they left.

Ella Mae grabbed a shawl and her reticule, knowing there was no use in denying that she had been primping.

The evening went well, with Deborah treated as a guest of honor, especially once Daniel explained to Mr. and Mrs. Evans that she was the source of Ella Mae's inspiration for her novel. Ella Mae was surprised to learn that he had boasted of her talents to his parents, who were energetically supportive of her efforts.

Danny and Robbie were as well behaved as two very excited little boys could be, galloping around the parlor on wooden hobby horses, neighing loudly for added effect. Once dinner was served, they immediately put their toys away and ran to the table, eager to fill their bellies with Nana's delicious cooking.

Ella Mae noticed that while Daniel was very interested in what Deborah had to say, his gaze kept straying back to her. She felt her face heat beneath his attention, and he offered her a crooked, guilty grin from across the table. Ella Mae hardly knew what to think.

When the visit came to an end, Daniel told his father, "It's almost dusk. I should probably escort the ladies home."

Mr. Evans gave his son a knowing smile. "Yes, you probably should."

"We'll see you on Monday, Mrs. Wescott," Mrs. Evans squeezed her arm with surprising affection. "And Miss Gibson, I'm so glad you were able to come visit us tonight. We enjoyed it immensely."

"Thank you," Deborah replied.

"Good night, Mrs. Wescott," Danny said, surprising her by holding his arms up for a hug. Kneeling down, Ella Mae wrapped her arms around the boy's small form, feeling an ache of maternal longing.

"I'll be back shortly," Daniel told his sons. "Let Nana put you to bed."

"Yes, Papa," they chorused obediently. But Ella Mae saw the gleam of mischief in Robbie's eyes and suspected he would still be awake when Daniel returned.

Deborah turned the tables on Daniel as they walked back to the boarding house, asking him questions about the cannery and about the economy of Ridgely and its relationship to the land. He had learned much about the art of communication during his years in politics, and he was efficient at promoting the area in its most positive light. Yet Ella Mae sensed that there was genuine affection coloring his perspective. He'd turned into a small-town man, after all.

When they reached the steps of the Jarrells' house, Daniel said, "Miss Gibson, it was a pleasure meeting you, especially in light of the role you played in Mrs. Wescott's novel."

"Thank you, I enjoyed getting to know you and your family," Deborah replied.

"Would you object if I detained Mrs. Wescott for a few moments longer?" he surprised Ella Mae by asking.

Deborah gave Ella Mae a pointed look. "Not at all, Mr. Evans. Good night."

Ella Mae watched as she ascended the steps and disappeared into the house. Dusk had fallen, and the street was draped in lengthening shadows. She turned to Daniel, raised her eyebrows in question.

"I haven't had a minute alone with you in weeks," he said, by way of explanation. At Ella Mae's surprised expression, he grinned broadly. "Don't tell me you haven't missed me?"

She blushed, staring down at her toes.

"Walk with me, just for a minute," he said, offering his arm.

Ella Mae didn't hesitate. She slipped her hand through his elbow. He directed her to the rear of the house, to the flower garden where they had spoken once before.

"You look lovely tonight, Mrs. Wescott," he said quietly. "I couldn't keep my eyes off you, if you hadn't noticed."

Her pulse began to race, and she glanced up at him, confusion and longing clashing inside her. She didn't know what to say for fear of saying the wrong thing and ruining the moment.

They stood on the patio, the light from within the house spilling out onto the quiet night. He indicated for her to sit on the bench, and he sat down beside her, their knees touching as he angled himself toward her.

She felt as if her chest would burst. What was happening?

"I let you go once, Ella Mae, and it was the biggest mistake of my life. I don't ever want to let you go again," his dark eyes, shadowed by thick eyebrows in the pale light, bore into hers with intense feeling. He reached over and grasped her hand.

"*Daniel*," she whispered. She had no idea what to say. She had longed to hear these words for so long, and finally—finally!—he had spoken them.

"I'm... You know, I'm divorced..." she nearly choked on the word. Curse John a thousand times over for all the ways he had hurt her!

Daniel smiled tenderly. "I'm aware, Mrs. Wescott. But if you give me the slightest indication that you return my feelings, I will do everything in my power to find a way around that little detail."

"Do you mean..." Ella Mae was breathless, heady. Did he really want to marry her?

His eyes moved over her face as if caressing it. "I mean exactly that. Should I see what I can do?"

She nodded, her spirit soaring. She laughed, tears of joy springing to her eyes.

Daniel lifted her hand to his lips, brushed a kiss across her knuckles. It was a promise, and Ella Mae grabbed hold of it with her whole heart.

Chapter Twenty-Seven

*D*eborah was sitting on the bed in her nightgown, her black hair hanging in a braid over her shoulder when Ella Mae floated into the room. The flame from the oil lamp burned steadily within the glass hurricane, illuminating the room with a soft glow.

"Just a friend, eh? Tell me what happened!" Deborah exclaimed. "You look positively euphoric!"

Ella Mae felt like she was in a daze as she removed her shawl and slid onto the edge of the bed. "He... He said he wants to marry me," she whispered, still grappling to accept the reality of the moment.

Giggling gleefully, Deborah wrapped her arms around Ella Mae's shoulder. "I knew it! He looked at you like a man sick in love all through the evening. What did you say?"

Trying to shake the spell which held her captive, Ella Mae rose, walked to the dresser and unpinned her hair. "I'm divorced, I don't know if we could find a clergy to marry us."

"Given the circumstances, I think it's certainly possible. What did Mr. Evans say?"

"He seemed determined," Ella Mae replied, the heady feeling returning as she remembered the look of love and resolve in his eyes. Overwhelmed by emotions, she felt as though she would laugh and cry simultaneously.

"Daniel said that letting me go was the biggest mistake of his life," she told her friend, the tears forming. "I feel like I must be dreaming!"

"I'm so happy for you," Deborah said.

"I'm ecstatic... but so frightened. What if now that he finally admits he loves me, we can't find a way to be together?"

"I saw the way that man looked at you. He isn't going to rest until you're together," Deborah promised.

Ella Mae held onto Deborah's words as she undressed and slipped into bed. Within minutes, she could hear the peaceful breathing of her friend as she drifted into sleep, but for Ella Mae, her mind was far too excited for rest to come easily.

The following morning in church, she couldn't focus on a single word the preacher said. It was all she could do to wait until they had reached the privacy of her parents' home to tell them what had transpired. No one in the world, not even Deborah, could understand what it meant to Ella Mae the way her mother did.

Mrs. Hutchins burst into tears, pulling Ella Mae into a crushing embrace. "I knew he would get around to it eventually!"

"He sure took his time," Mr. Hutchins added. "Tell him to come over for lunch next Sunday with his sons. I don't care how old you are, you're my daughter and he must ask for my blessing." His eyes sparkled with joy for his daughter's happiness.

Ella Mae wondered what Daniel's parents thought of their relationship, and if he had even made them aware. She would have to ask him the next time she saw him, because if his parents didn't approve, that was one more obstacle in their path.

On Monday when Ella Mae came home from school, she found Deborah lying in bed with a fever.

"I just feel achy and tired," she said, rolling onto her side and closing her eyes. She wore her nightgown, and at the neckline, Ella Mae noticed a rash.

"I'm getting a doctor," she said, immediately growing concerned.

The town had acquired several doctors, the latest being a young man by the name of Madara. As he was still settling into the practice, Mrs. Jarrell recommended that he might be more readily available than the more established doctors.

Mr. Jarrell offered take the buggy over to the Lucus Hotel on Railroad Avenue where Dr. Madara was staying and bring him back, if possible. Ella Mae took some water up to her room and propped Deborah up in bed, having her sip from the glass.

"I'm all right," Deborah insisted, but her skin was warm to the touch and she moaned whenever she moved as if her joints hurt.

Dr. Madara arrived in short order, and Mrs. Jarrell directed him to the patient's room. Ella Mae rushed to answer his knock upon the door, surprised to discover that he was quite a young man, despite the dark mustache he wore to add the appearance of maturity.

"I heard that there is a young lady in need of doctor?" he said, sounding more professional than he looked.

I must be getting old when even the doctor looks younger than I am, thought Ella Mae.

"Yes, this is Deborah Gibson, visiting from Annapolis. She just took ill today," Ella Mae said, stepping aside so that Dr. Madara could enter the small room.

He carried a medical bag, which he placed on the edge of the bed as he introduced himself to Deborah. "Tell me what's the matter, Miss," he said kindly, listening attentively as Deborah explained her symptoms.

The doctor then performed an examination, taking her temperature, feeling her throat, examining the rash, and finally listening to her heart with a stethoscope. As he continued, Ella Mae watched his expression grow serious and began to have a sinking feeling in her stomach.

"Miss Gibson, isn't it?" She nodded, and he continued, "Have you suffered from a sore throat or similar illness in the last month?"

"Why yes, I did, just a about three weeks ago," Deborah answered in surprise.

"Are you experiencing any chest pain?"

Deborah shifted nervously. "Some."

"I believe that you suffered from streptococcal pharyngitis, which has now caused a secondary condition, known as rheumatic fever," he informed her gravely. "I'm very sorry to say that it has caused an enlargement of your heart. There is no treatment that I know of other than rest. You will need to remain in bed as long as it takes to recover."

"But she *will* recover?" Ella Mae demanded.

The young doctor stood, regarding her with eyes far older than a man his age should possess. "Bed rest and the care of loving friends can be an amazing medicine," he replied vaguely.

Ella Mae felt the color drain from her face, but she quickly drew a deep breath and nodded at the doctor. "I'm sure I'll have her back on her feet in short order," she said, trying to sound cheerful for Deborah's sake.

"I will come by daily to check on her. Certainly, let me know if there is any change in her condition."

"Yes, Doctor. Thank you."

"Thank you, Doctor," Deborah echoed, sagging into her pillow as if it required all her strength to stay awake.

Mrs. Jarrell promised that Deborah would be looked after when Ella Mae returned to school the next day. She hated leaving Deborah, but as there was nothing she could do, and the amount of bed rest she would require was indefinite, Ella Mae knew it was best for her to resume her normal routine. She did send a letter off to the Hudsons immediately informing them of Deborah's condition and assuring them that she was under the care of a physician.

Wednesday evening, as Ella Mae was taking dinner in her room with Deborah, Bessie knocked on the door and informed her that she had a visitor in the parlor. Ella Mae was pleased to see Daniel sitting restlessly on the sofa as she descended the stairs, springing to his feet at the sight of her.

He came toward her and took her hands, squeezing them affectionately. "I heard Miss Gibson is unwell. How is she?"

Ella Mae informed him of Deborah's condition and prognosis.

"How are you doing?" Daniel asked, his brown eyes searching hers lovingly.

"I'm concerned for her," she admitted, basking in the glow of his affection. "We must pray for her to make a full recovery."

"I certainly will," he vowed. "Is there anything else I can do for you?"

Ella Mae smiled. "Your kind visit means so much to me."

He lifted her hand to his mouth and pressed a kiss to it. "I would do more if I could."

The familiar gesture reminded Ella Mae that they were still a taboo couple by most standards. She hated to ask, but she needed to know how Daniel's parents felt about her, and about his interest in her.

"Mrs. Wescott, I assure you that my parents see only the person you are and what you mean to me. They know that John was a—" he bit his tongue, raised his eyebrows to indicate she could fill in the blank. "You don't need to worry, my dear. They approve of you wholeheartedly." His smile was tender as he gazed down at her, and Ella Mae felt its warmth all the way down to her toes.

"And what do Mr. and Mrs. Hutchins think of me?" Daniel asked. "I wouldn't blame them if they thought I was a bumbling idiot. After all—"

"You were," Ella Mae finished his sentence with a coy smile.

"Yes, thank you for that," he chuckled.

"Fortunately, they are forgiving people."

"That's good to know," he said, kissing her hand again.

"My father extended an invitation for you and your boys to come to lunch on Sunday. He said that if you want my hand, you'll have to ask him for it."

"I will be there. And, I have a meeting scheduled with Pastor Reiter on Saturday morning. You've been under his spiritual leadership for years now and he may be willing to perform the ceremony."

Daniel and his family attended St. Benedict's Catholic Church. Father Wolf could not join a divorced woman in matrimony, no matter what his personal feelings might be.

"Will you begin attending the Reformed Church with me?" Ella Mae wondered. "What about the boys?"

"If he will marry us, I will attend, and the boys will adjust to the change," Daniel promised with a grin. "Now, I must be going, but I will come by on Saturday and let you know what Pastor Reiter said."

"I'll see you then," she said, her heart racing nervously at the prospect of the meeting.

After Daniel's departure, Ella Mae returned to her room to finish her dinner, now cold. Deborah smiled weakly as she closed the door behind her.

"Shall I guess who your visitor was?" she teased. "Your face gives it away."

Ella Mae blushed. "Mr. Evans is going to meet with my pastor this Saturday to see if he will consider marrying us. On Sunday he will talk to my father."

Against the white pillowcase, Deborah's black hair contrasted sharply. "It will all work out, you'll see."

A knock at the door indicated the arrival of Dr. Madara, whom Ella Mae admitted gratefully. She felt relieved when each day he said that at least Deborah's condition had not worsened. It would take some time before they began to see improvement.

"Good evening, Mrs. Wescott, Miss Gibson," the young doctor said cheerfully as he squeezed into the room, crowded with three people. Ella Mae stepped aside to allow him access to Deborah, who suddenly appeared slightly flushed.

She greeted the doctor, allowing him to listen to her heart and pronounce that all was the same.

"You cannot truly mean for me to lie here and do absolutely nothing for weeks on end," Deborah said. "Not only is it maddeningly boring, but it isn't fair to Mrs. Wescott to feel that she must keep watch and entertain me."

Dr. Madara offered her a sympathetic smile. "I'm sorry, Miss Gibson, but you absolutely must remain in bed. However, I understand both your boredom and your concern for Mrs. Wescott's welfare. What if I were to relieve her when I can, and read to you or provide some other quiet means of passing the time?" He turned to Ella Mae and said, "We shall keep the door open, of course."

"I think that would be most helpful, doctor. Thank you," Ella Mae replied, sensing that the young man's interest in Deborah was more than merely professional.

Deborah clasped her hands on her lap. "I should hate to keep you from your work, Doctor."

"Not at all, Miss Gibson. In fact, tomorrow I shall come a little earlier, so I can take dinner with you, and Mrs. Wescott can eat in the dining room," he said, indicating the empty plates still sitting on the dresser.

"Thank you, Dr. Madara," Ella Mae was quick to reply before Deborah could offer another protest.

His dark mustache lifted in a smile as he returned his stethoscope to his bag and prepared to take his leave. Ella Mae said nothing of her suspicions, but she observed the way Deborah's eyes followed him from the room.

True to his word, Dr. Madara arrived in time to share dinner with his patient the following day, allowing Ella Mae to join the other boarders in the dining room. She couldn't imagine how restless Deborah must feel trapped in one room day in and day out. But at least the doctor's attention would give her a pleasant diversion.

When she returned to her room after the meal, the kind doctor assured her that Deborah was doing as well as could be expected and that he would check on her again the next day. After seeing him out, Ella Mae asked Deborah how they had passed the hour.

"He is a talker," her friend commented. "His uncle is Dr. Herr, who owns the large brick house with the turret down the street. He intends to take over his practice when Dr. Herr retires. Dr. Madara is from Pennsylvania. I told him about my family in Wyoming, and how I had been staying with the Hudsons. He thought my Indian heritage was fascinating, and I mentioned your novel to him. He said he should like to read it sometime."

Ella Mae hid a smile, certain there was far more on the good doctor's mind than medicine.

Chapter Twenty-Eight

"Try to be patient," Deborah encouraged as Ella Mae glanced out the window for the tenth time that afternoon.

"I can't. I'm too nervous. Oh! There he is!" Ella Mae spotted Daniel across the street, but instead of crossing over to the boarding house, he entered the Methodist Episcopal Church. "Pastor Reiter must have denied us," she said, twisting her hands together worriedly.

Deborah tucked her hands under her cheek, her eyelids drooping. "Don't give up," she whispered, drifting back into sleep.

"I'm going to let you rest," Ella Mae told her dear friend, smoothing her hair back from her forehead.

"All right," Deborah replied without opening her eyes. Ella Mae left the room, closing the door quietly behind her.

She took up residence in a rocking chair on the wide front porch where she could see Daniel the second he emerged from the church. The white steeple stood tall against a sky of cerulean blue, the pink azaleas blooming in profusion around the entrance. In the renewal of nature after a long, bleak winter, Ella Mae found hope that her life too might know a changing of seasons.

The chair rocked back and forth, back and forth, her toes pushing gently to maintain its rhythm. She bit her lip, gripping the wooden armrests, watching the door of the church for the man she loved to appear. When at long last he finally emerged, Daniel's dark eyebrows were drawn together like a thundercloud. Ella Mae sighed, then came to her feet and met him halfway.

"They both said no," she said for him. He offered his arm, and when she slipped her hand into his right elbow, he reached over and squeezed it with his left hand.

"We won't give up," Daniel said firmly.

"There's only four churches in Ridgely. The fourth, The Church of the Brethren, will decline as well. Perhaps we could look in Centreville or Denton?" she suggested.

"Perhaps." They walked together in silence for a moment. "You are the innocent party, and therefore by all biblical precepts, you should be allowed to remarry. Is there any way you can prove that John was unfaithful to you?"

Ella Mae bit her lip, trying to quell the bitterness that rose up inside her. "No. Not without soliciting a confession from the young woman involved. And, even if she did agree, it seems cruel to shame her in that way. John ruined her life, as much as he ruined mine."

Daniel grunted.

"He is remarried now, to a different woman. There is no hope of our reconciliation. That should count for something."

"Yes, it should," he agreed.

"I'm sure his current wife believes I was the unfaithful one," Ella Mae mused. "I understand the pastor's concern. He only wants to do what is right before God, out of respect for the sanctity of the union we call marriage. When all he has is one person's word, how can he know if they are lying as I'm sure John did when convincing his pastor?"

Daniel leaned down to whisper in her ear. "You know, that's one of the things I love about you. You are both kind and wise."

Ella Mae looked up into those brown eyes, so familiar and so dear. "I'm not giving up, mind you. I'm going to think and pray on this."

"I know I've said it before, but I'm sorry for the choices I made when I was young and arrogant. The consequences have been farther reaching than I ever could have imagined," he said thoughtfully.

"I never stopped loving you, Daniel. And I never will," Ella Mae replied softly, thankful there was no one around to overhear their private conversation as they walked arm in arm down the dirt street.

Daniel bent his head toward hers once again to whisper, "I knew the day you married John that I always had and always would love you. If only I hadn't been so slow to see what was right in front of me all along."

Ella Mae knew she had married John only because she believed Daniel would never love her. They had both made mistakes. There was no use staring at the past over their shoulders anymore. It was time to look forward.

"We are together now. And we will find a way to stay together," she said, not wanting to waste another second on fear or regret.

The following afternoon, Daniel brought Little Danny and Robbie to the Hutchins farm for lunch after they finished their church service. Ella Mae was already there, waiting. Seeing Daniel's tall, lean frame step out of his buggy brought a rush of memories, as well as that familiar flip-flop of her heart. He was every bit as handsome as he had been in their youth, perhaps more so as maturity had silvered his temples.

Little Danny sprang from the buggy eagerly when he saw Ella Mae descending the steps to greet him. "Papa says I get to see the house where you grew up and meet your mama and papa!" he exclaimed, as if this were almost too good to be true.

"Yes, you do!" Ella Mae said, feeling a tug on her heartstrings at the joy in his voice.

"Good afternoon," Daniel called, stepping down with Robbie in his arms.

Mr. Hutchins followed on Ella Mae's heels, extending his hand. "It's good to see you again, Mr. Evans," he said in welcome. He knelt down to shake Little Danny's hand as if he were grown, then gave Robbie's chubby fingers a squeeze.

Spying the swing hanging from the limb of the dogwood tree, Little Danny ran toward it. "May I swing, Papa?" he called, even as he leapt onto the wooden seat and began pumping his legs, holding on tightly to the ropes.

Daniel laughed. "Only for a moment, then we're going inside to eat."

Ella Mae walked over to where the boy sailed through the air. "I used to swing on that very swing when I was young," she told him. Little Danny's smile grew even wider.

A thousand memories centered around this place, the farm, the fields, and this swing. Ella Mae looked over at Daniel and felt the tug of his sentimental longing for opportunities lost. She offered him a smile, thankful that even though the road had been long and winding, it had eventually led them back to one another.

When they went into the farmhouse, Mrs. Hutchins was quick to greet Daniel with a hug, as if he were her long-lost son returning home. "I swear you don't look a day older!" she declared. "And look at these precious boys!"

By the end of the afternoon, she had thoroughly spoiled Robbie and Danny and endeared herself forever to them. After lunch, while Ella Mae and her mother helped the boys take turns at the swing, Mr. Hutchins and Daniel took a walk together along the dirt lane. Ella Mae knew what was being asked, and what the answer would be, yet she still wished she could listen in to hear exactly how the conversation went.

Of course, they still needed to find a pastor to perform the ceremony. But more and more Ella Mae felt a peace about it, as if God were asking her to slow down and trust Him this time, as she hadn't the first.

She would always wonder if she had just waited, instead of rushing into marriage with John, would Daniel have eventually come around? There was no way to know, no way to go back and relive the past, for her or for Daniel. They had made their choices then, and they had the opportunity to make new choices now. This time, Ella Mae would trust God and His timing.

In the evening when it was time to leave, Daniel took Ella Mae back into town. As they traveled the dirt roads in the fading light, Ella Mae asked, "I assume the conversation with my father went well?"

Daniel smiled. "It did. Although he did have some questions which I suppose we should have discussed by now. We've been focused on the first step and haven't talked about the second or third. Of course, I'll be purchasing a home. And I'm assuming you would," he hesitated, glancing at his son and speaking in code, "redirect your skills to nurture only certain children."

Ella Mae was still struggling to believe that Daniel was going to marry her. She was going to be his wife—Mrs. Daniel Evans! Of course, she would be happy to quit her job and dedicate herself to raising Danny and Robbie. She hoped in time they would have children of their own to keep her busy. She honestly couldn't care less where they lived, as long as they were all together.

"I'm sure I will be happy with whatever arrangements you make," she replied.

When they reached the boarding house, Little Danny gave her a goodnight hug and said, "That was so fun, Mrs. Wescott! Can I visit there again soon?"

"Yes, you may," she said, cherishing the feel of his little arms around her neck.

Entering the house, Bessie stopped her to say, "I checked on Miss Gibson, ma'am, and she's doing fine. Dr. Madara came by to see her and took dinner with her."

Ella Mae smiled. "Thank you, Bessie."

When she went up to their room, Deborah was propped up in bed reading a book. "How was your day?" she asked, eager to hear Ella Mae's details.

"Wonderful. How was yours?" Ella Mae asked instead of replying. "I heard that you were fortunate not to be left alone to eat tonight. I'm thankful Dr. Madara is so attentive and kind."

"I am grateful for his company—and yours, of course!" Deborah added. "He brought me this book to read, to help pass the time. It's one of his favorites."

"Ah. That will give you something to discuss when you've finished it," she commented.

Deborah nodded, pretending she believed the kind doctor gave the same attention to all his patients. "Now, tell me everything!" she ordered.

Ella Mae complied, sitting down beside her on the bed and reliving the day. "I'm almost afraid to let myself believe this is really happening, to let myself be happy," she admitted. "I've waited so long for this, it doesn't seem real."

"I can pinch you," Deborah offered, teasing.

"If I ever find myself wearing a wedding gown, I may want you to," Ella Mae replied.

On Monday, after school, Ella Mae was surprised to find Daniel waiting on the front porch for her.

"Good afternoon, ma'am," he greeted her with a broad smile. "I was wondering if you would like to sit with me in the garden patio for a while?"

"Of course, I would!" she exclaimed, delighted to have this unexpected time with him.

He offered his arm and escorted her back down the stairs and around the side of the house. Flowers bloomed all around the brick patio, providing their sweet perfume as well as a lovely splash of color. Ella Mae noticed that a pitcher of iced tea and a plate of finger sandwiches were waiting for them on the wrought iron table. She glanced over at him suspiciously, certain there was a twinkle in his eye.

Before she could adjust her skirt and take a seat, Daniel took her hand and said her name. She looked up and saw the gleam in his brown eyes as he dropped to one knee, reaching into his vest pocket and producing a small velvet box. She covered her mouth with her hand as he opened it, revealing a diamond ring nestled within the satin.

"Ella Mae Hutchins Wescott, please accept this ring as a pledge of my undying faithfulness to you alone. There will never be anyone else for me."

"Oh, Daniel," she whispered, her eyes glistening with tears.

He removed it from the box and slid it onto her finger, grinning at her obvious shock and pleasure. She held out her hand and studied the delicate gold filigree and square-cut diamond, shimmering like a prism in the brilliant sunshine.

"I never expected..." she said breathlessly.

Daniel came to his feet and pulled her against his chest, kissing her soundly on the lips. Ella Mae sank into his embrace, her arms winding around his neck to keep her from falling. She clung to him, feeling the softness of his lips and the scratch of stubble on his chin.

Her heart raced, and she felt as though her bones had melted like wax. This was what a kiss should feel like!

When he finally pulled away, she stared up at him in a daze. A slow smile spread across his face, and Ella Mae could see that he had felt the same stirring of desire. "I think we need to find ourselves a preacher as soon as possible," he said, his voice husky.

Ella Mae giggled like a young girl, then looked down at the ring sparkling on the third finger of her left hand and sighed. Joy bubbled up inside her.

Chapter Twenty-Nine

*E*very night before she fell asleep, when she said her prayers, Ella Mae asked God to clear the way for she and Daniel to be joined as husband and wife. She had no idea how He would go about it, but she trusted that He had been at work to bring them together and her job now was to wait and be still.

Friday night, as she lay in bed trying to sleep, Ella Mae found the years of her first marriage replaying in her mind like a ghostly visitation. John had never treated her with respect or compassion, instead manipulating and controlling her, and finally, pushing her away with his cold and selfish ways.

What kind of man would remain unmoved when his wife nearly fell under a carriage? Or would say to her that if she were ever assaulted by a would-be rapist, she should submit?

Long buried anger rose like a spirit from the grave, raging through her veins. The one person who should have loved her the most didn't seem to care if she lived or died, if she was happy or miserable. She had felt trapped, frustrated, frightened. Then, finally, had come the two discoveries which opened a door of escape for her.

The first had been the note she found in John's coat pocket, in decidedly feminine handwriting, which read: "*Looking forward to this weekend.*" Then there had been the chemise.

She remembered finding it mixed in with her own undergarments. Ella Mae had known then that John's weekend away had involved intimacy with another woman. Emily's chemise must have tangled up with his when he was packing to come home, and upon discovering it, he'd tucked it into Ella's drawer. She presumed John had intended to return it to Emily, then forgot all about it. Out of sight, out of mind.

Holding it between her fingers that day in their small apartment, feeling the thin fabric between her fingers, Ella Mae had known she was holding the proof of her husband's infidelity. It wasn't enough evidence to prove to a judge in a court of law that John had committed adultery, but it had been enough to clear her conscience.

That note... Ella Mae could see it clearly in her mind's eye, with delicate, swirling penmanship. She had kept it for future reference, knowing that if John had been careless enough to let her find it, other evidence would later appear. But where had she put it?

In a hatbox with other letters and cards from various family members. Not the one where she kept only Daniel's letters, but in another... One that was pink and white striped, with a border of red flowers... When she left John, had it made it into her trunk?

If it hadn't been so late, Ella Mae would have sprung from the bed, lit the lamp, and immediately begun to unpack the trunk in search of it. But she dared not disturb Deborah, and so she tried to remain still and wait until morning dawned. It was late into the night before she finally succumbed to sleep.

When she awakened, she quietly slid from beneath the quilts. Deborah still lay sleeping, but the gray light of dawn through the curtains promised that daybreak was near. Ella Mae lit the lamp, opened the trunk, and began to remove its contents as silently as possible. She breathed a sigh of relief when she found the hatbox she sought, kneeling on the floor and sorting through the papers in search of the note Emily had given her husband.

It had sifted down to the very bottom, and when she spied it, Ella Mae seized it with a sense of victory. She grabbed hold of it and read it again in the pale, yellow light. It was ironic that this small slip of paper, a risk taken by Emily and an indiscretion on

John's part, had proven the key to her freedom the first time, and now she hoped it would again.

Pastor Reiter was a godly man, as well a man of wisdom and compassion. Ella Mae believed that if she were to present the truth to him, he would believe her. And as Daniel had said, not only was she the innocent party in the dissolution of her first marriage, since John was remarried there was no hope of their reconciliation. She carefully placed the note in her reticule and prayed that Pastor Reiter would be convinced he could perform the nuptials for her and Daniel with God's blessing.

Ella Mae was dressed and pinning her hair into place when Deborah awoke. "Say a prayer for me," she told her friend. "I think I might have found a way to persuade the pastor that he can perform our wedding!"

She had never gone to the Evans' house uninvited, but today Ella Mae knocked upon the door. Mrs. Evans answered, concern immediately springing into her eyes.

"Is everything all right, Mrs. Wescott?"

"Yes, quite. Is Daniel available? I need to speak with him."

"Come in, my dear, and I'll fetch him for you," Mrs. Evans said.

Ella Mae was too anxious to sit. She stood by the window in the parlor, which was open to allow the breeze to move through the room. At the sound of Daniel's footfalls, she spun around and said, "I have an idea!"

His expression quickly moved from relief to curiosity. Ella Mae explained her plan, and Daniel suggested that he accompany her to the church that very moment.

After leaving his mother in charge of the boys, they set off to the Reformed Church in hopes that the pastor would be there, as he often was on Saturday mornings. They were not disappointed, as they found him in his office reviewing his notes for the next day's sermon.

Pastor Reiter looked up from his Bible and came to his feet. "Mr. Evans, Mrs. Wescott, please come in." He gestured to the chairs facing his desk and invited them to have a seat.

"I suspected that I hadn't heard the last from you," he said to Daniel with a hint of a smile.

Ella Mae sat on the edge of her chair, leaning forward as she said, "Pastor, I understand that you only want to do what is right, and I admire that. I realized last night that it might be helpful if I were to meet with you and explain the series of events which led to my divorce."

He nodded in encouragement. "I think that would be helpful, Mrs. Wescott."

Over the course of the next hour and a half, Ella Mae outlined in detail the dynamic of her marriage to John, the character and integrity (or lack thereof) of her former husband and concluded with the two discoveries which had led to her decision to leave him, presenting the pastor with Emily's note so that he might see it for himself. She went on to explain how John had reacted to her choice to leave him, and how he had ultimately divorced her so that he might remarry.

"It sounds as though you have been through quite a lot, Mrs. Wescott," Pastor Reiter said gravely as he perused the only evidence she had to support her accusation against her former husband.

Ella Mae felt emotionally exhausted from reliving those dark and painful years.

"In light of your story, and of the truth I see in your eyes, I feel no compulsion to withhold the blessing of remarriage from you," he announced solemnly, returning Emily's note. "According to Jesus, in Matthew nineteen, the spouse who was sinned against in the case of marital unfaithfulness is free to remarry. In upholding the law of God, I also rejoice in upholding His mercy," he smiled.

"Thank you, Pastor," Daniel said with relief as he came to his feet, reaching across the desk to shake the pastor's hand.

"My pleasure," Pastor Reiter replied.

Offering her gratitude with a weak smile, Ella Mae clung to Daniel's arm as they left the church and went out into the sunny afternoon.

Glancing up at Daniel, she was surprised to see that instead of appearing pleased, his lips were drawn down into a frown.

"Is something wrong?" she asked with concern.

He squeezed her hand and said quietly, "I didn't realize just how much you'd been through, Ella Mae. I am so, so sorry. I know I can't make up for his mistakes, or even my own, for that matter. But I can promise to spend the rest of my life loving you the way you deserve to be loved."

Seeing the sincere commitment in Daniel's eyes, Ella Mae felt the burden of grief fall away and new strength flooded through her. The past was buried once and for all. A new season lay before her.

May 1899

"There must be some mistake!" Ella Mae teased James Jr. when she saw him at school the day of his commencement exercises. "I can't possibly be old enough to have a nephew graduating from school!"

He grinned bashfully, proud to be a young man ready to step out on his own. His father had secured a job for him with his uncle, doing construction. With all the new houses popping up all over town, it was a good business to be in. Of course, his mother worried sick about him falling from heights and breaking an arm or leg, or something worse.

Every year the banquet following the commencement exercises was held at the Jarrells' Boarding House. The dining room was large enough to accommodate an array of goodies, and there was plenty of room for guests to spread out between the dining room, parlor, and outdoor patio.

As a future part of the family Daniel was planning to attend the event with his sons. The Evans and the Hutchins had only just met formally as future in-laws the Sunday before. Daniel's parents had graciously invited Mr. and Mrs. Hutchins to their home for the evening to get to know one another and begin to discuss wedding details.

Ella Mae had suggested an August wedding, which allowed four months for preparations and for the boys to adjust to the idea of a step-mother. Daniel said that four *weeks* would have been quite sufficient, but he agreed out of deference to the will of the women.

He had already purchased a lot on Caroline Street and hired James' brother to begin building a spacious home for his new wife. Ella Mae was so excited by all these changes in her life that she could barely eat or sleep. Little Danny seemed almost as thrilled, although Robbie was too young to understand what was happening.

Nora alternated between well wishes and resentment regarding the upcoming nuptials. She wanted to be happy for her sister, but her own disappointments made it difficult. If Nora believed a happy marriage was possible, she was jealous that she would never know one. However, her own experience had taught her that after the brief honeymoon phase, there were only years of heartache ahead.

Ella Mae tried not to let Nora's bitterness steal her joy. She remembered what she had felt like during the years she was trapped with John, and she didn't wish that misery on anyone. She continued to pray for her brother-in-law to find peace within himself and to become the husband and father he needed to be. Nora was determined to stay it out, to keep fighting, to keep hoping.

It was both admirable and frustrating to watch her struggle. Ella Mae didn't pretend to know the will of God in her sister's life. She only knew that her own conscience was clear for leaving John, and that she was grateful beyond words for the second chance she had been given.

Dr. Madara continued to check in on Deborah daily, staying to take dinner with her several times a week. Her heart had not shown signs of strengthening, but at least it had not weakened. Ella Mae prayed that by August, Deborah would have made a full recovery.

The young doctor, whom she noticed had given Deborah permission to call him Charles, had moved his office from the Lucas Hotel to a fine house on Central Avenue across from Jackson's store. He seemed to be doing quite well for himself, and Ella Mae was pleased that he had taken such an interest in her friend. As a successful and attractive man, Dr. Madara could have had his pick of single young ladies in Ridgely. She was thankful that he saw Deborah's worth.

The evening of the reception, the boarding house was packed tight with parents and family of graduating students. Mrs. Hutchins looked as if she could cry to see her oldest grandson making this transition from boy into man. Nora and James appeared to have called a truce, at least for the evening, although Mark stayed close to his mother's side as if keeping watch over her.

Strawberries abounded, as was always the case in Ridgely in May. There was strawberry shortcake, cookies made with strawberry preserves, and for the adults, strawberry wine. Even though most of the children had earned money picking strawberries with their families every day for weeks, they still enjoyed the sweetness of its bounty. Saulsbury Brothers and the Alliance Preserving Company paid well for the berries, and buyers lined up at the train station every morning to transport fresh strawberries to the north.

Ella Mae held Robbie as she stood beside Daniel in the dining room, the little boy's arms around her neck as they listened to the hubbub of conversation. Reviews were offered of the graduate's essays, praise for the quartet which had performed so beautifully, and a commentary on the Reverend's speech. All the graduates looked as proud as peacocks.

Looking at their fresh, young faces, Ella Mae felt suddenly very old. How long it had been since she was sixteen, dreaming of a bright future which never quite materialized. She prayed for these boys and girls, soon to become men and women, that they would know more joy than heartache, and gain compassion and insight from the trials they faced. Especially, she prayed for her nephew, James, that he would not follow the example his father had set for him but instead be inspired to become a man of patience, kindness, and gentle strength.

She was no longer the young woman she had once been, but Ella Mae still carried dreams inside her battered heart. It might have come late in life, but she would finally be a wife to the man she loved and the mother of his children, whether or not she had given birth to them.

And there was still hope that she might find a publisher for her novel. She'd found an agent to represent her, and he was currently in search of an agreeable editor. There were no guarantees, but for the first time in her life, it was at least possible.

When the banquet concluded, Ella Mae and Daniel sat on the front porch in the fading light, watching the guests take their leave. Robbie slept in his father's lap, while Danny sat on Ella Mae's. It was wonderful to feel like she was part of a family—her own family.

"You look thoughtful," Daniel observed.

"I was thinking how life has turned out so differently than I imagined it would when I was Little James' age, graduating from public school. I'm very thankful for where I am now."

Daniel reached across the short distance between them and took her hand. "We've come a long way, haven't we?"

Chapter Thirty

August 1899

*H*er wedding day dawned hot and humid, and Ella Mae worked to tease her frizzy hair into a fashionable bun, complimented with white rosebuds for the occasion. Her dress was made of loosely woven etamine in pastel blue, with ecru lace accenting the neckline and waist. A strand of pearls graced her slender neck.

"You look beautiful," Deborah smiled, sitting in the armchair by the open window in a dress of pale pink. The breeze stirred her sleek black hair. She was still weak, and needed support when she walked, but she had finally been cleared from bedrest and was beginning to regain her strength.

Dr. Madara was her escort to the wedding that afternoon, and he had made his intentions clear toward her. Once she was well enough, Deborah was going to take a job at Miss Milby's Millinery Shop and remain at the boarding house until their wedding the following summer. Ella Mae couldn't have been happier for her dear friend.

"It's time!" Mrs. Hutchins said, appearing in the doorway in a flutter of excitement.

The event was to be a simple affair as she was divorced, and Daniel widowed. There were no attendants, and the ceremony and reception would be held there at the boarding house. Taking up a small bouquet of white roses, Ella Mae indicated for her mother and

Deborah to precede her, then slowly made her way down the staircase.

A young woman named Elsie Smith stood just inside the parlor with a violin tucked under her chin, her bow drawing out the strains of the wedding march to accompany Ella Mae as she entered the room. Family and friends sat in chairs brought in from the dining room, arranged in rows.

The large bay window had been decorated with floral arrangements of blue hydrangea, white roses, and green ferns. The early morning sunlight filtered through the windows to shine upon them with an ethereal glow. On the mantel, more vases of the same added their fragrance, filling Ella Mae's nostrils as she drifted across the room to join Daniel, standing before the pastor.

Her heart was full, and without reservation. How long she had waited for this day to come! It felt something like a miracle.

Daniel wore a black suit with a white vest, and his dark hair, silvered at the temples, was combed neatly into place. His teeth showing in that crooked grin still managed to make her heart skip a beat. He gazed at her with tenderness and appreciation as she walked toward him, both their eyes glistening with unshed tears.

They faced the pastor and Ella Mae tried to listen as he spoke on the significance of marriage, but her mind kept wandering to the handsome man beside her. He too seemed more interested in staring at her than focusing on the speech being given.

Finally, it was time for them to exchange their vows, the sincerity in their voices bringing new life to the traditional lines they spoke. *Husband and wife, for better or worse, until parted by death.* Ella Mae cherished these words rather than fearing them, because the man she was marrying was one of integrity who would make every effort to love her as Christ had loved the church, with more than mere words—with action and sacrifice.

With absolute certainty, Ella Mae could say that this was the happiest day of her life. As she looked out over the faces of the guests who had come to participate in the celebration of this sacred contract, she knew that her joy was visible on her face for all to see.

She smiled at her new sons, Danny and Robbie, sitting beside their grandparents. Both boys wore grins from ear to ear, and Daniel's parents appeared as overwhelmed with emotion as Ella Mae's. Grandma and Grandpa Greene beamed, rejoicing in this new season with Ella Mae, having walked beside her through the darkest days she had known. Nora, James, and their boys sat next to her brother, Randall.

Ella Mae was delighted that Deborah was well enough to be present, sitting beside her attentive doctor. As her eyes scanned the rows of familiar faces, she saw Beatrice, Ruth, and Penelope, all with husbands and children in tow. Each one of these friends represented a different chapter in Ella Mae's life, each seasoned with laughter and tears, and each moving her story forward to this cherished moment.

When the pastor finally declared Daniel and Ella Mae husband and wife, she tipped her chin up to meet his lips as they descended upon hers, sealing the promise they had made before God and man. Daniel grinned, his eyes failing to hide his anticipation of the moment when they would become one flesh. A blush warmed her cheeks. They were now and forever Mr. and Mrs. Daniel Evans.

A photographer was situated on the garden patio to capture the image of the newly married couple. Several poses were taken, some of them alone, some with the Evans and others with the Hutchins, but Ella Mae's favorite was the one with Danny and Robbie positioned on either side of them.

"Can I call you Mama, now?" Little Danny asked, looking up at her with those big brown eyes.

She felt her heart melt. "If you wish, I would like that very much."

He grinned. "Okay, Mama," he said, trying it out.

Ella Mae kissed his cheek, counting him among her many blessings.

The chairs were returned to the dining room, where Mrs. Jarrell and Bessie had prepared a delicious luncheon. Ella Mae and Daniel floated among their guests, accepting the congratulations and well wishes bestowed upon them. A pile of gifts was stacked in the corner, generously given for them to furnish their new home together.

After the reception, Ella Mae changed into a dark blue traveling suit and she and her new husband stood on the front steps of the boarding house amid a shower of rice and birdseed. They were to catch the afternoon train and spend a honeymoon weekend together at the beach in Rehoboth. When they returned, they would pick up the boys from their grandparents' home and begin settling into the house on Caroline Street as a family.

December 1899

"Mama, can we make a popcorn garland to put on the tree? And a cranberry one too?" Danny asked, staring at the large evergreen tree which his father had just erected. Like the Jarrells' house, their parlor sported a large bay window, which made the perfect spot to place a Christmas tree.

"I think that's a wonderful idea!" Ella Mae said, remembering how much he had enjoyed doing it at school the previous year when she had been his teacher.

Daniel had boxes of ornaments which had belonged to him and Sabrina, bought or given to them through the years of their marriage, which they would hang on the tree once the garlands had been made and draped upon it.

It was a strange position to step into the place previously held by another woman, to become the wife and mother to the husband and children of someone else. But Ella Mae knew that she was loved by Daniel and by the boys, and she held her own place in their hearts which could never be usurped. She honored Sabrina's memory for the children's sake, allowing a picture of her to be among the photos displayed on the table in the main hallway. She was now Mrs. Evans, and this was her home, her husband, and her sons.

The honeymoon weekend she and Daniel had spent together had been a memorable and special time, even if it had flown by too quickly. There had been strolls along the beach at sunset with the reflection of the rosy sky rippling on the waves as they walked together hand in hand, adjusting to the new relationship they shared, which had changed forever from friendship into something far more intimate.

They had both been married before, yet everything was still unique and special. All the years they had been chums or pen pals, and all the history they shared, only made the foundation of their marriage stronger and the bond they shared richer.

When they returned to Ridgely they had adapted to yet another dynamic in their relationship as they shared the responsibility of parenting. It hadn't necessarily been a smooth transition as there had been more than a few misunderstandings and miscommunications, but they had worked together to find a new rhythm as a family.

Now they were preparing for yet another change. Ella Mae rubbed a hand over her protruding belly, inside of which nestled a new life which was the culmination of their union, further cementing Daniel and her together. She expected their child would make his or her appearance in July of 1900, ushering in a new decade, a new century, and a new generation.

Daniel insisted that the babe she carried was a daughter, and he treated Ella Mae as if she were made of glass. She felt cherished, protected, and adored. He didn't always say the right thing or know what it was she needed in her emotional moments, but he loved her with his whole heart and that was all she asked for.

"You sit down," he told her, pointing to the plush armchair by the fire. "I'll get everything we need to pop the corn and string the garlands."

Ella Mae complied with a contented smile, Robbie taking advantage of the moment to crawl into her lap and rub her swollen abdomen. He couldn't quite understand that there was a baby growing inside that large stomach, insisting that it was the result of eating too many cookies and pies.

Having to do her own cooking had been a challenge after so many years of being spoiled, living with her grandparents or at the boarding house. Daniel and the children had suffered through more than one overdone or under-seasoned meal, but she was getting the hang of the cast iron stove as well as the art of cookery. She had successfully made a batch of gingerbread cookies the day before to be enjoyed as they decorated their first Christmas tree together.

The days flew by quickly, and she and Daniel bought and wrapped presents for the boys. Danny was getting his own bicycle and Robbie was to receive a little red wagon. Ella Mae couldn't wait for Christmas Day to arrive, to see the surprise and pleasure on their faces.

For her husband, on this first holiday as man and wife, she had made a special Christmas quilt wall-hanging, featuring three wise men leading their camels. She hoped he would appreciate the time and effort which had gone into it, but even more that he would remember its significance.

When the twenty-fifth of December finally came, she felt as excited as the boys, who woke up early and begged to go down to see if there were presents around the tree. Ella Mae grabbed a robe, tying it above her belly, and carefully went down the stairs in her slippers with her husband at her elbow.

She wondered what Daniel had planned for her. He'd been walking around with a twinkle in his eyes for the last few weeks, and she could tell he was bursting with a secret.

Danny jumped up and down for joy when he saw the bicycle, begging to take it for a spin through the house. Robbie was just as excited about his wagon, and after all the smaller gifts had been opened, he loaded them up and pulled them up and down the hall.

"I have something for you, and I hope that you like it," Ella Mae said nervously as she presented Daniel with a large package.

He arched one thick, dark eyebrow curiously as he opened the paper. When he pulled out the quilt, Ella Mae ordered him to drape it over the sofa. Once it had been spread out and its picture revealed, Daniel laughed and wrapped his arms around her thick waist, pressing a kiss onto her cheek.

"*We three kings of orient are...*" he belted out.

"*Bearing gifts, we've traveled so far...*" Ella Mae joined, giggling like a girl.

"*Field and fountain, moor and mountain, following yonder star...*" they sang together.

Daniel held her against him, as close as he could with her belly between them, and said, "I love you, Ella Mae. This is the best Christmas I've ever had."

Ella Mae smiled, her heart content.

"Now, I have a special present for you," he said. His grin reminded her of a little boy as he led her to the chair and indicated for her to sit down. From beneath the tree, he pulled a box wrapped in colored paper and placed it on her lap, kneeling down beside her as she opened it.

As she lifted the lid of the box, Ella Mae saw that it was a book. Time to read was scarce these days, thought perhaps she could find a few quiet moments at the end of the day.

But as she lifted it out and spotted the title, her heart caught in her throat. *"My Daughter, Alice,"* was the name of the book. Her eyes raced to see the author's name and she covered her mouth as a cry escaped it.

Ella Mae Evans.

Tears gathered in her eyes, pooled over and ran down her cheeks. "Oh, Daniel! When...? How...?" She could hardly comprehend that her novel was in her hands, printed and bound in a hard cover with her own name embossed upon it.

Daniel's eyes sparkled as he laughed at her response. "I've been dying to tell you, but I wanted to wait for Christmas! My friend has a friend in publishing, and he loved your book. I've been working with the publishing company on the contract for some time, making sure they gave you a good deal and that they printed it with the correct name—your name."

Her fingers traced the letters of her name printed on the cover of the book. She brushed the tears from her cheek and laughed. "Thank you, Daniel," she said, sniffling. "I don't know how in the world you convinced them to put a woman's name on it, but thank you!"

Pride shown in his eyes as he kissed her forehead. "The author of the book deserves to have her name on it. He liked it. You wrote it. I refused to waver from those key details."

Ella Mae laughed through the tears that spilled over and couldn't be dammed. Little Danny, still riding his bike back and forth in the hallway, saw that she was crying and ran to her.

"What's wrong, Mama?" he asked, resting his little hand on her shoulder.

"Nothing's wrong. I'm just so happy," she sobbed.

Danny turned to his father in confusion.

Daniel chuckled. "Sometimes women cry when they're happy, son."

"She must be very happy then," Danny decided with a smile. He took her face in both his small hands and kissed her forehead, as he had seen his father do many times before. "Merry Christmas, Mama," he said.

Author's Note

As with all historical fiction, great effort is made to be as factually accurate as possible, however the plot is the primary focus and some of the details may be shifted to accomplish the goals of the story.

In this novel, I have taken liberties with the following:

- The Female Seminary in Centreville was not a "college for women" but a public school exclusively for girls between 1876 and 1907, when they resumed teaching males and females in the same school. This information was not readily available, and at the time I began writing, I believed it was a college. Once I discovered that it had been a school, I decided to stick with it in order to tie in the Turner family from the series My Brother's Flag, as well as providing Ella Mae with a suitable background for a career as a teacher.

- Dr. Madara was an actual person who lived in Ridgely and provided medical care for its residents. He was twenty-six when he moved from Pennsylvania to the Eastern Shore of Maryland, and his first office was in the Lucas Hotel on Railroad Ave. It was later moved to a house on Central Ave. opposite Jackson's store. He was married twice, neither of which were to the fictional character of Deborah Gibson. His first wife was Grace Stambaugh, and she gave him a son named Frederick. When she died, he married his second wife, Bertha Barry.

A great resource for me in writing about the early years of Ridgely, Maryland were the volumes of Caroline Sun Newspaper and seniors' memories compiled by Tom Rampmeyer. I spent many hours collecting information to make the background setting for Ella Mae's story as true to the past as I could.

- Of particular interest to me is the John C. Jarrell Boarding House & Hotel. My husband and I bought this house in

2015 and are slowly—very slowly—working on making improvements to it. I was very excited to be able to write a novel which included my own home!

- As this novel concludes, Ridgely was moving into its heyday as the "Strawberry Capital of the World." To this day, Ridgely holds an annual Strawberry Festival every May.

- Historical persons and fictional characters all walk the streets together in my mind. While most of the characters are products of my imagination, some, like Mr. James Swann, Mr. Thomas Jones, and of course John, Mary, and Bessie Jarrell, were based on real people.

- The idea for Deborah's illness, rheumatic fever, was inspired by the reminiscence of a lady by the name of Helena Hand in Volume 3 of Rampmeyer's collection. She recounted a story in which she was treated by Dr. Fifer, who served Ridgely in the 1930s. She was restricted to bedrest for six months, during which time the doctor made daily visits.

- The churches and names of pastors mentioned are accurate.

- Divorces were not easy to obtain, nor was it easy to remarry if one was granted. In the Caroline Sun dated July 1905, there is an announcement under the title of *"A Good One,"* stating that *"All ministers of Berlin [Maryland] have signed a declaration that hereafter they will refuse to marry any person who has been divorced."*

Thank you for taking the time to read *WHERE THIS ROAD ENDS*. I hope you found as much enjoyment reading it as I found writing it! Stay tuned for the next two books in the *Ridgely Rails Legacy Series*, following Ella Mae's daughter and granddaughter, and the town of Ridgely, through the First and Second World Wars.

Sincerely,

WHERE THIS ROAD ENDS

Rebekah Colburn

Ridgely Rails Legacy

Follow three generations of women through the most dynamic and rapidly changing times in American history.

Ella Mae is raised on the Eastern Shore of Maryland in a small farming town experiencing the boom of railroad expansion in the wake of the Civil War.

Her daughter, Sophie, comes of age during the Great War. As the young men go overseas to fight for democracy, women are fighting their own battle at home for the right to vote.

Gloria must face the uncertainty of the Second World War, stepping out of the conventional roles women previously held to make a new place for themselves in an era of poverty and chaos.

Each woman must find her own way through the struggles of her generation, holding onto faith, family, and the men they love.

REBEKAH COLBURN is the author of the following

Historical Fiction/ Romance Series: *"Ridgely Rails Legacy," "My Brother's Flag,"* and *"Of Wind and Sky."*

Her desire is to bring history to life with rich stories, compelling characters, and inspirational themes which will both entertain and encourage her readers.

In 2001 she obtained a B.A. in Biblical Studies from Washington Bible College. Rebekah loves being outdoors and enjoys mountain biking, cycling, and cruising the local waterways with her husband.

She lives on the Eastern Shore of Maryland with her husband, teen-aged daughter, two sweet dogs, five spoiled cats, and a whole lot of chaos.

You can contact Rebekah Colburn via:

Email: rebekahlynncolburn@gmail.com
Website: http://rebekahcolburn.weebly.com/
Facebook: https://www.facebook.com/ColburnRebekah
Twitter: https://twitter.com/RebekahColburn

95826965R00188

Made in the USA
Columbia, SC
24 May 2018

...t something more than logic is needed if we are to understand
... nature of religious statements was highlighted by the Danish
...losopher Søren Kierkegaard (1813–55). He argued that a 'leap
...aith' was necessary, and that it was not so much the content of
...elief that made it religious, but the way in which it is believed –
...h subjectivity and inwardness.

PASCAL'S WAGER

...ise Pascal (1623–62) put forward what must count as one of
... saddest pieces of logic ever employed within the philosophy
...religion. His *Pensées* were published posthumously in 1670.
...them, Pascal battles (as did his contemporary Descartes) with the
...plications of **scepticism** – the systematic challenging of the ability
...know anything for certain. Pascal was a committed Catholic
...d wanted to produce an argument that would both justify and
...mmend belief.

... appreciate the force of his argument, you need to be
...are that his view of human nature was rather bleak: without
...od's help, people were inherently selfish, and would only
... what seemed to be in their own self-interest. He also believed
...at non-believers would see the life of religion as one which
...uld limit their freedom, and would therefore appear to go
...ainst their self-interest. His famous 'wager' is an attempt to
...unter this view.

...s starting point is that reason alone cannot prove that God
...ists; to believe or not believe therefore involves an element
... choice. Which choice is in line with enlightened self-interest,
...d therefore likely to appeal to the non-believer? His argument
...ns like this:

▶ IF I *believe in God and he does indeed exist, I stand to gain*
  eternal blessings and life with God after my death.
▶ IF I *believe in God and he does not exist, all I lose is*
  any inconvenience of having followed the religious life –
  inconvenience that he considers negligible.

The philosophy of religion

In this chapter you will learn:
- *about religious experience and how it may be described*
- *about the arguments for the existence of God*
- *about miracles, the problem of evil and other key issues.*

In Western thought, the philosophy of religion is concerned with:

▶ *Religious language: what it means, what it does and whether*
  it can be shown to be true or false.
▶ *Metaphysical claims (e.g. that God exists): the nature of the*
  arguments by which such claims are defended, and the basis
  upon which those claims can be shown to be true or false.

In addition to these basic areas of study, there are many other
questions concerning religious beliefs and practices which philosophy
can examine:

▶ *What is faith? How does it relate to reason? Is it ever*
  reasonable to be a religious 'fundamentalist'?
▶ *What is 'religious experience' and what sort of knowledge*
  can it yield?
▶ *Is the universe such as to suggest that it has an intelligent*
  creator and designer?

- *Are miracles possible? If so, could we ever have sufficient evidence to prove that?*
- *Is belief in a loving God compatible with the existence of suffering and evil in the world?*
- *Can psychology explain the phenomenon of religion?*
- *Is life after death possible? If so, what difference does it make to our view of life?*

Faith, reason and belief

Is religious belief based on reason? If it were, it would be open to change, if the logic of an argument went against it. However, experience tells us that most religious people hold beliefs that, while they may be open to reasonable scrutiny, depend on a prior commitment or wish to believe, and therefore belief may persist in the face of reasonable criticism.

Within Christianity, there is a tradition – associated particularly with the Protestant Reformation and Calvin – that human nature is fallen and sinful, and that human reason is equally limited and unable to yield knowledge of God. Belief in God is therefore a matter of faith, and any logical arguments to back that belief are secondary.

Note

The last sentence speaks of belief 'in God' and not just belief 'that God exists'. That is a crucial difference, and we shall return to it on p. 171. Belief 'in' something implies an added element of commitment and valuation. One might, after all, believe 'that' God exists, but think that such belief is quite trivial and of no personal significance, which is not what believing 'in' something is about.

Insight

Hence the frustration of some debates between athe[ists] and believers. The one expects that reason and evid[ence] will settle the matter; the other has deep emotional [and] intuitive 'reasons' for believing. But the key questio[n is] can you believe 'in' something, if you do not also ha[ve] reasons to believe 'that' it exists? Is spiritual intuitio[n] enough?

The quest for certainty is sometimes termed **foundatio**[nalism,] the attempt to find statements that are so obviously tru[e that] they cannot be challenged. We have already seen that D[escartes] came to his incontrovertible statement 'I think, therefo[re I am'.] Some modern philosophers of religion, notably Alvin P[lantinga,] argue for a 'Reformed Epistemology'. That is, a theory [of] knowledge that, like the theologians of the Reformatio[n, is] based on basic beliefs that are self-evident to the perso[n who] holds them, even if they are not open to reasoned argu[ment.] An example of this would be the belief that the univers[e is] designed by God, based on a sense of wonder and beau[ty. We] shall look at the 'design argument' on p. 163; what is c[lear] here is that Plantinga thinks that such belief is not a lo[gical] conclusion to an argument, but is held *prior to* engagin[g with] that argument.

A related idea is **fundamentalism**. Originally used as a [term for] those who wished to set aside the superficialities of reli[gion and] return to its fundamental principles, it is now more co[mmonly] used for those who take beliefs, as they are found in th[e Bible or] the Qur'an for example, in a very literal and straightfo[rward way] and apply them without allowing them to be challenge[d.] A basic problem with this is that the scriptures were w[ritten in a] particular language and in a particular context, and if [they] are taken literally and out of context, the original inten[tion of] the writers may be lost. Of course, the fundamentalist [will not] accept this, believing that the words of scripture are gi[ven] by God and are therefore not open to any form of liter[ary or] contextual analysis.

However:

- ▶ **IF** *I do not believe in God and he does indeed exist, I stand to suffer eternal punishment in hell, banished for ever from his presence.*
- ▶ **IF** *I do not believe in God and he does not exist, I have lost nothing, but gained some benefit from not having had to lead a religious life.*

On balance, therefore, Pascal claims that self-interest suggests that it is best to believe in God and follow the religious life!

Insight

Many philosophers would challenge the idea that one can choose to believe; one either does or one does not, anything else is pretence.

I called this the saddest piece of logic because it takes a rather grim view of God (as one who will punish or reward according to a person's belief), and a less-than-attractive view of the religious life (regarding it as a mild inconvenience, rather than something of value and enjoyable in itself). Fear of hell may drive people to believe; but that is hardly wholehearted belief in God.

Comment

Pascal saw people as caught between dogmatism and doubt, and hoped that he had found a way to overcome the latter without imposing the former. My personal view is that he ended up with the worst of both worlds – self-deception motivated by self-interest!

For the rest of this chapter we shall be looking at reasoned argument concerning religious ideas. However, both in terms of the religious experience and religious language, we shall need to recognize that faith and the religious beliefs associated with it are often rather more complex than the intellectual assent to propositions.

Religious language

If you describe a religious event or organization, the language you use need not be especially religious. Consider the following:

The Pope is the Bishop of Rome.
The Jewish religion forbids the eating of pork.

The first of these is true by definition, since 'Pope' is a title used for the Bishop of Rome. The second can be shown to be true by looking at the Jewish scriptures. (It would not be made invalid by evidence that a non-practising Jew had been seen eating a bacon sandwich, for the moral and religious rules remain true, even if they are broken.)

Provided that the terms are understood, such descriptive language presents few problems.

Religious people themselves use language in a variety of ways. They may pray, give thanks, hold moral discussions and – most importantly – make statements about what they believe. The problem is that these belief statements sometimes make claims about things that go beyond what can be known of the ordinary world that we can experience and examine scientifically. We have already seen that some philosophers want to dismiss all metaphysics as meaningless, and along with it they would therefore discard most statements of religious belief.

But here's the problem. Religious statements are not (or should not be taken as) bad science, so, if we are to take religion seriously, it should not be equated with superstition. Hence, in order to understand religious beliefs, we need to examine the character of religious language and the function that it performs.

HOW? AND WHY?

One way of expressing a distinctive flavour of religious language is to highlight the difference between 'how?' questions and 'why?' questions. Science answers 'how?' questions by explaining how individual parts of the world relate to one another. But religion asks 'why?'; not 'how does the world work?' but 'why is there a world at all?'

A 'why?' question asks about meaning and purpose. It cannot be answered in terms of empirical facts alone. This is illustrated by a story by John Wisdom (1904–93), a professor of philosophy at Cambridge from 1952 to 1968, and also at Virginia and Oregon.

Two explorers come across a clearing in the jungle. It contains a mixture of weeds and flowers. One claims that it is a garden and that there must be a gardener who comes to tend it; the other disagrees. They sit and wait, but no gardener appears, they set up various means of detecting him, but still nothing.

One explorer continues to deny that there is a gardener. The other still claims that there is a gardener, but one who is invisible and undetectable. But – and this is the central point of the argument – how do you distinguish an undetectable gardener whose activity is open to question, from an imaginary gardener or no gardener at all?

Insight

Of course, there is another relevant question: What difference does it make to you if you choose to see the clearing as a garden? In other words, how might your view of life be changed by seeing the world as controlled by a loving God (whether or not such a God exists)?

As originally presented, this story was used to show that a good idea could die the death of a thousand qualifications. In other words, when all obvious qualities that the gardener might have are eliminated, nothing of any significance remains. But the story also illustrates the idea of a **blik** – a particular 'view' of things. In the story, the same evidence is available to the two explorers, but they choose to interpret it differently. We have our own particular blik and interpret everything in the light of it. It can be argued that religious belief is just one such blik; one way of organizing our experience of the world. As such it is no more or less true than anyone else's blik, and every argument ends with someone saying: 'Well, if that's the way you want to see it …'

Insight

That's fine, until you want to argue that your blik is right and another person's is wrong. Then – with no factual evidence to decide between them – you have a problem.

THE PERSONAL ASPECTS OF LANGUAGE

In *Religious Language* (1957), the British theologian I.T. Ramsey pointed out that there were elements of both discernment and commitment in religious statements. They were not simply detached, speculative comments. Although they include facts, they are far more complex than that. He makes the essential point that the word 'God' is used to describe a reality about which the believer feels strongly and wishes to communicate.

We should therefore distinguish between the philosopher who examines arguments for the existence of God in an objective and disinterested way, and the religious believer who uses 'God' to express a sense of direction, purpose and meaning which comes through religious and moral experience.

Arguments for the existence of God can be seen as:

▶ *discussions about something which may or may not exist*
▶ *indications of what it is a religious believer is talking about when he or she speaks of 'God'.*

Ramsey uses the terms *models* and *qualifiers* to explain the way in which religious language differs from ordinary empirical language. A 'model' is like an analogy – an image that helps a person to articulate that which is rather different from anything else. For example, if God is called a 'designer', it does not imply that the religious believer has some personal knowledge of a process of design carried out by God, simply that the image of someone who designs is close to his or her experience of God. Contrariwise, having offered the 'model', it is then important for the religious believer to offer a 'qualifier' – God is an 'infinite' this or a 'perfect' that – the model is therefore qualified, so that it is not mistakenly taken in a literal way.

In other words

▶ Religious language is sometimes simply descriptive (e.g. of religious activities).
▶ When it expresses beliefs it may be:
  ▷ a particular way of looking at the world (a 'blik')
  ▷ based on personal commitment (not simply a matter of speculation).
▶ Since it is not simply a statement of fact, to be checked against evidence, such religious language is 'meaningless' from the point of view of logical positivism (see p. 71)

Religious experience

If nobody had religious experiences, there would be no basis for the idea of a 'god', nor would there have been any reason for religions to have developed. So what is it that makes an experience religious?

The nineteenth-century religious writer and philosopher Schleiermacher described religious awareness in terms of a 'feeling of dependence' and of seeing finite things in and through the infinite. This was rather like mystical experience – a sudden awareness of a wider dimension, which throws new light on the ordinary world around us. What Schleiermacher was trying to express was that religion was not a matter of dogma or logic, but was based on a direct experience of oneself as being small and limited, against the background of the eternal. It was also an identification of the self with the whole: a sense of belonging to the whole world. Feelings like that are destroyed by logic; they are not the result of reasoning but of intuition.

Rudolph Otto, in *The Idea of the Holy* (1917), argued that the religious experience was essentially about the *mysterium tremendum*, something totally other, unknowable; something that is awesome in its dimensions and power; something which is also attractive and fascinating. He outlined a whole range of feelings ('creeping flesh'; the fear of ghosts; the sense of something that is uncanny, weird or eerie) to illustrate that this encounter is with something that is quite other than the self; threatening, but at the same time attractive and of supreme value.

However unusual and special such an encounter with the 'holy' might be, it can only be described by using words that have a rational, everyday meaning – language which, if taken literally, does not do justice to the special quality of the experience. Many words seemed to describe the feelings and express ideas that were close to this experience of the 'holy' (goodness, wonder, purity, etc.) but none of them was actually about the holy itself. This set of words that attempts to describe the holy are (to use Otto's term) its **schema**. The process of finding words by means of which to convey the implications of the holy is **schematization**. Religious language is just such a schema, whereas the 'holy' itself is an a priori category; in other words, the holy cannot be completely described or defined in terms of the particular experiences through which we encounter it. It is conveyed by means of these terms but is always elusively beyond them and cannot be contained by them.

Insight
The holy cannot be fully explained, only experienced, and its 'religious' interpretation is optional.

Examples

1 *You feel overwhelmed at the sight of a range of snow-capped mountains looming above you. Their sheer size and bulk, contrasting with your own minuscule body, give you a 'tingle', a sense of wonder, a sense that, faced with this scene of absolute and almost terrifying beauty, your life cannot ever be quite the same again. You then try to describe the experience to a cynical friend. You cast around for suitable words. You cannot convey that 'tingle', unless, as a result of your description, he or she too can start to sense 'the holy'.*

2 *You watch a horror movie on television. You know that the parts are played by actors, that there is artificially constructed scenery. Yet, for all that, you feel the hairs bristle on the back of your neck, you may even feel a shudder, your heart may beat faster. Because of what you are seeing on the screen, and in spite of all the rational explanations, you are sensing something that is 'beyond' that immediate experience.*

Otto's idea of schematization is important for understanding the nature of the philosophy of religion, and suggests that it is always a secondary activity. Philosophy examines the rational concept by means of which the prime experience is schematized. The proofs of the existence of God are, following this way of thinking, not proofs of the actual existence of a being which is known and defined as 'God', but are rational ways of expressing the intuition about 'God' that comes as a result of religious experience.

Thus, the idea of God as the designer of the universe is not open to logical proof but is a schema, i.e. think what it would be like if this whole world had been designed for a particular purpose, with everything working together as it should: that (according to this schema) is something akin to what it means to believe in God.

Notice that this also applies to language. Following the idea of models and qualifiers, the model is the result of the schema (God is like this or that) but that it is then qualified to show that it is not simply a literal description (e.g. the all-perfect ... or the absolute ...).

We can see, therefore, that the pattern of religious language and the analysis of religious experience point in the same direction – that of an experience and a level of reality which transcends, but springs out of the literal, the empirical or the rational. All of these things can suggest the object of religious devotion, but none can define or describe it literally.

TRANSCENDENCE

One way of describing religious experience is in terms of 'transcendence' – that an experience goes beyond ordinary perception to give some sense of what is 'beyond' or 'absolute' even if that cannot be described in itself. Clearly, great works of art, or a beautiful landscape, or simply the awesome power of nature (whether benign or threatening) can give rise to a sense of transcendence. But there is a fundamental question with which the philosophy of religion needs to deal. Just because an experience is transcendent – just because it gives that sense of awe, or wonder, or a new view of oneself – does that imply that there has to be a transcendent *object* of which we become aware? If not, it might be possible to have the same transcendent experience that inspires the believer, but to have it entirely within a secular context. This is explored in a chapter entitled 'Transcendence without God' by Anthony Simon Laden in *Philosophers without Gods* (ed Louise Anthony, 2007).

Does God exist?

We shall look at some traditional arguments for the existence of God, and the problems they raise. But first we need to have some working idea of what is meant by the word 'God'.

Since we are concerned with Western philosophy, the relevant concepts have come from the Western theistic religions – Judaism,

Christianity and Islam. For these, God may be said to be a supreme being, infinite, spiritual and personal, creator of the world. He is generally described as all-powerful (having created the world out of nothing, he can do anything he wishes) and all-loving (in a personal caring relationship with individual believers). Although pictured in human form, he is believed to be beyond literal description (and is thus not strictly male, although 'he' is generally depicted as such).

Some terms

▶ Belief in the existence of such a god is **theism**.
▶ The conviction that no such being exists is **atheism**.
▶ The view that there is no conclusive evidence to decide whether God exists or not is **agnosticism**.
▶ An identification of God with the physical universe is **pantheism**.
▶ The belief that God is within everything and everything within God (but God and the physical universe are not simply identified) is **panentheism**. (Although this term is used by some theologians, most interpretations of theism include the idea of everything being 'within' God; indeed, if he is infinite, there is nothing which is external to him.)
▶ The idea of an external designer God who created the world, but is not immanent within it, is **deism**.

There is a problem with taking the idea of the existence of God too literally. Thomas Aquinas (whose arguments we shall be examining) described God as being *supra ordinem omnium entium* – beyond the order of all beings. In other words, God is not a being who might or might not exist somewhere; indeed, he is not *a* being at all. So we should not be tempted (as are some evangelical atheists) to assume a crude idea of God and then show that there is no evidence for his existence. On those terms, Aquinas and most serious religious thinkers down through the centuries would certainly have qualified as atheists. The meaning of God is far more subtle than that.

In his *Critique of Pure Reason* (section A, 590–91), Kant argued that there could be only three types of argument for the existence of God:

1 *based on reason alone*
2 *based on the general fact of the existence of the world*
3 *based on particular features of the world.*

They are called the **ontological**, **cosmological** and **teleological** arguments. He offered a critique of all three, and introduced a fourth one: the moral argument.

Insight

Before getting into these arguments, one thing needs to be absolutely clear. God does not and cannot exist in the sense that anything else can be said to exist. God is neither part of the universe nor somehow 'outside' the universe. The question is: what (if anything) is God if he does not exist in that sense?

THE ONTOLOGICAL ARGUMENT

The ontological argument for the existence of God is not based on observation of the world, or on any form of external evidence, but simply on a particular definition of the meaning of 'God'. In other words, it offers a definition of God that implies that he must exist.

This argument is of particular interest to philosophers because it raises questions about language and metaphysics which apply to issues other than religious belief.

The argument was set out by Anselm (1033–1109), Archbishop of Canterbury, in the opening chapters of his *Proslogion*. He makes it clear that he is not putting forward this argument in order to be able to believe in God, but that his belief leads him to understand God's existence in this particular way, a way which leads him to the conclusion that God must exist.

Religious experience leads him to speak of God as *aliquid quo nihil maius cogitari possit* – that which nothing greater can be thought. This does not mean something that just happens to be physically bigger, or better, than anything else – it is the idea of 'perfection', or 'the absolute', the most real thing (*ens reallissimum*).

In the second chapter of *Proslogion*, the argument is presented in this way:

> *Now we believe that thou art a being than which none greater can be thought. Or can it be that there is no such being, since 'the fool hath said in his heart, "There is no God"'? [Psalm 14:1; 53:1] But when this same fool hears what I am saying – 'A being than which none greater can be thought' – he understands what he hears, and what he understands is in his understanding, even if he does not understand that it exists. For it is one thing for an object to be in the understanding, and another thing to understand that it exists ... But clearly that than which a greater cannot be thought cannot exist in the understanding alone. For if it is actually in the understanding alone, it can be thought of as existing also in reality, and this is greater. Therefore, if that than which a greater cannot be thought is in the understanding alone, this same thing than which a greater cannot be thought is that than which a greater can be thought. But obviously this is impossible. Without doubt, therefore, there exists, both in the understanding and in reality, something than which a greater cannot be thought.*

(translation: as in *The Existence of God*, John Hick, Macmillan, 1964)

In other words

Something is greater if it exists than if it doesn't. If God is the greatest thing imaginable, he must exist. I may paint an imaginary masterpiece, but that only means I imagine that I paint a masterpiece. In fact, since it does not exist, it is no better than my actually existing 'inferior' paintings. A real masterpiece must always be better than an imaginary one!

One of the clearest criticisms of this argument was made by Kant (in his *Critique of Pure Reason*) in response to Descartes, who had maintained, in his version of the argument, that it was impossible to have a triangle without its having three sides and angles, and in the same way it was impossible to have God without having necessary existence. Kant's argument may be set out like this:

- ▶ **If** *you have a triangle*
- ▶ **Then** *it must have three angles (i.e. to have a triangle without three angles is a contradiction)*
- ▶ **But** *if you do not have the triangle, you do not have its three angles or sides either.*

In the same way, Kant argued:

- ▶ **If** *you accept God, it is therefore logical to accept his necessary existence*
- ▶ **But** *you do not have to accept God.*

To appreciate the force of Kant's argument, it is important to remember that he divided all statements into two categories – analytic and synthetic (see Introduction):

- ▶ **Analytic statements** *are true by definition.*
- ▶ **Synthetic statements** *can only be proved true or false with reference to experience.*

For Kant, statements about existence are synthetic; definitions are analytic. Therefore, the angles and sides of a triangle are necessary because they are part of the definition of a triangle. But that says nothing about the actual existence of a triangle – necessity (for Kant) is not a feature of the world, but only of logic and definition.

Kant gives another way of expressing the same idea. He says that *existence is not a predicate*. In other words, if you describe something completely, you add nothing to that description by then saying 'and it has existence'. Existence is not an extra quality, it is just a way of saying that there is the thing itself, with all the qualities already given.

Norman Malcolm (in *Philosophical Review*, January 1960) pointed out that Kant's criticism failed in an important respect. You can either have a triangle or not, but (on Anselm's definition) you simply cannot have no God, so the two situations are not exactly parallel.

For Anselm, then, 'God' is a unique concept. This was something that he had to clarify early on, in the light of criticism from Gaunilo, a fellow monk, who raised the idea of the perfect island, claiming that, if Anselm's argument were true, then the perfect island would also have to exist. Anselm rejected this. An island is a limited thing, and you can always imagine better and better islands. But he holds that 'a being than which a greater cannot be thought' is unique. If it could be thought of as non-existent, it could also be thought of as having a beginning and an end, but then it would not be the greatest that can be thought.

This is another version of the argument that he had already introduced in Chapter 3 of the *Proslogion*:

> *Something which cannot be thought of as not existing ... is greater than that which can be thought of as not existing. Thus, if that than which a greater cannot be thought can be thought of as not existing, this very thing than which a greater cannot be thought is not that than which a greater cannot be thought. But this is contradictory. So, then, there truly is a being than which a greater cannot be thought – so truly that it cannot even be thought of as not existing.*

In other words, Anselm claims that necessary existence is implied by the idea of God. But he goes one step further. In Chapter 4 of *Proslogion*, he asks how the fool can still claim that God does not exist, and concludes:

> *For we think of a thing, in one sense, when we think of the word that signifies it, and in another sense, when we understand*

the very thing itself. Thus in the first sense God can be thought of as non-existent, but in the second sense this is quite impossible. For no one who understands what God is can think that God does not exist ... For God is that than which a greater cannot be thought, and whoever understands this rightly must understand that he exists in a way that he cannot be non-existent even in thought.

So what did Anselm mean by speaking of God as 'that than which none greater can be thought'?

In another work, *Monologion*, he spoke of degrees of goodness and perfection in the world, and that there must be something that constitutes perfect goodness, which he calls 'God', which causes goodness in all else. This idea of the degrees of perfection was not new. Aristotle had used this idea in *De Philosophia*, and it is also closely related to Plato's idea of forms. Anselm's idea of God comes close to Plato's 'Form of the Good'.

There are several philosophical points to be explored here (which is why this argument has been set out at greater length than others in this book).

A silly example

You have a classroom full of pupils, and are told that it is 'Class 1A'. Where is the 'class'?

▶ *You ask each of the pupils in turn, but each gives only his or her name.*
▶ *You conclude that 'Class 1A' does not exist.*

This is what is called a **category mistake**. Class 1A is real, and comprises the pupils – but there does not exist anything that is 'Class 1A', which is not also something else, namely a particular pupil (see also p. 105 for the category mistake expounded in Ryle's *The Concept of Mind*).

This suggests that different categories of things can be equally real, but cannot be set alongside one another. Similar problems arise when we try to set an ideal alongside the particular examples of which it is the ideal. So, to continue our example, you may have in your mind the idea of 'the perfect pupil'. However good a particular pupil might be, you could always imagine one that was just a little better. But 'the perfect pupil' exists in a different category from individual pupils and therefore does not appear in the class. But if you had no idea of what a perfect pupil might be like, there would be no way of judging between one pupil and another. 'The perfect pupil' can be seen as a necessary concept in order to make any sense of putting the pupils in some sort of rank order.

Similarly, for Anselm, if there were no idea of perfection, there would be no criterion for judging between one thing and another. Even if our judgements are entirely subjective, we need to have some concept of perfection in order to make them.

Some might see putting pupils in order of merit as politically incorrect, arguing that 'the perfect pupil' is a dangerous idea, since all are equally good, each in his or her own way! But if you remove ideals, how do you assess anything? Perhaps 'that than which a greater cannot be thought' is an absolute which enables us to compare and give value to things.

The class of pupils can illustrate a second point: a comparative or superlative term is not a quality, but simply shows a relationship.

To say that a pupil is the tallest in the class is not a fixed quality that a particular pupil has, but is simply a way of comparing sizes. You do not eliminate the idea of 'the tallest pupil' by amputation – the amputee might be demoted, but immediately there would be some other pupil who qualified as 'the tallest'. What is more, that pupil would not have grown at all since he or she was second tallest! There is no additional height, just a new relationship. So:

▶ *'the perfect ... ' is in a different category from individual things*
▶ *'the perfect ... ' is not simply the top of a series of individual things.*

So God, for Anselm, is not an object, and therefore does not 'exist' in the way that other objects exist. Anselm's idea of God springs from his awareness of degrees of goodness in the world, as a necessary, ultimate point of reference for all values.

This is like the idea of Plato's 'cave', which we considered in Chapter 1. What was taken for reality by those in the cave was, in fact, only a set of shadows, cast because of light coming from behind them. The wise man, although not able to see the source of the light directly, yet knows that it is there beyond the entrance to the cave – the 'Form of the Good'. Something of the same can be said of this argument. The 'greatest thing' for Anselm is an intuition, necessitated by seeing lesser values as merely shadows or copies of something greater.

This approach to the ontological argument was taken by Iris Murdoch, the well-known novelist and Oxford philosopher, in her book *Metaphysics as a Guide to Morals* (1992). She held that an argument about necessary existence can only be taken in the context of this Platonic view of degrees of reality. She pointed out that what the proof offers is more than a simple logical argument, for it points to a spiritual reality that transcends any limited idea of God. It is also something that goes beyond individual religions:

> *An ultimate religious 'belief' must be that even if all 'religions' were to blow away like mist, the necessity of virtue and the reality of the good would remain. This is what the Ontological Proof tries to 'prove' in terms of a unique formulation.*

p. 427

And this, she claimed, is a necessary part of our understanding of life:

> *What is perfect must exist, that is, what we think of as goodness and perfection, the 'object' of our best thoughts, must be something real, indeed especially and most real, not as contingent accidental reality but as something fundamental, essential and necessary. What is experienced as most real in*

*our lives is connected with a value which points further on.
Our consciousness of failure is a source of knowledge. We are
constantly in process of recognizing the falseness of our 'goods',
and the unimportance of what we deem important. Great art
teaches a sense of reality, so does ordinary living and loving.*

p. 430

In other words

▶ *If we simply think of the ontological argument in terms of 'existence
is a predicate' then Kant was probably right, and Anselm wrong – for
to say that something 'exists' is quite different from anything else that
can be said about it.*

▶ *Anselm's argument also shows that some idea of 'the greatest that
can be thought' is a necessary part of the way we think, since, every
time we ascribe value to something, we do so on the basis of an
intuition of that which has supreme value.*

▶ *At its heart, the ontological argument is about how we relate the
ordinary conditioned and limited things we experience to the idea of
the perfect, the absolute and the unconditioned – and that is a key
question for philosophy.*

THE COSMOLOGICAL ARGUMENTS

Thomas Aquinas (1225–74) was probably the most important
philosopher of the mediaeval period, and has certainly been the
most influential in terms of the philosophy of religion. He sought
to reconcile the Christian faith with the philosophy of Aristotle,
which in the thirteenth century had been 'rediscovered' and was
being taught in the secular universities of Europe.

Aquinas presented five ways in which he believed the existence of
God could be shown. They are:

1 *The argument from an unmoved mover.*
2 *The argument from an uncaused cause.*
3 *The argument from possibility and necessity.*

4 *The argument from degrees of quality.*
5 *The argument from design.*

The fourth of these has already been considered, for a version of it came in Anselm's *Monologion*. The last will be examined in the next section. For now, therefore, we need to look at the first three, which are generally termed 'cosmological arguments'.

These arguments are based on the observation of the world, and originate in the thinking of Aristotle, whom Aquinas regarded as *the* philosopher. The first may be presented like this:

▶ *Everything that moves is moved by something.*
▶ *That mover is in turn moved by something else again.*
▶ **But** *this chain of movers cannot be infinite, or movement would not have started in the first place.*
▶ **Therefore,** *there must be an unmoved mover, causing movement in everything, without itself actually being moved.*
▶ *This unmoved mover is what people understand by 'God'.*

The second argument has the same structure:

▶ *Everything has a cause.*
▶ *Every cause itself has a cause.*
▶ **But** *you cannot have an infinite number of causes.*
▶ **Therefore,** *there must be an uncaused cause, which causes everything to happen without itself being caused by anything else.*
▶ *Such an uncaused cause is what people understand by 'God'.*

The third argument follows from the first two:

▶ *Individual things come into existence and later cease to exist.*
▶ **Therefore,** *at one time none of them was in existence.*
▶ **But** *something comes into existence only as a result of something else that already exists.*
▶ **Therefore,** *there must be a being whose existence is necessary – 'God'.*

One possible objection to these arguments is to say that you might indeed have an infinite number of causes or movers. Instead of stretching back into the past in a straight line, the series of causes could be circular, or looped in a figure of eight, so that you never get to a first cause, and everything is quite adequately explained by its immediate causes. This image of circularity does not really help us to understand the force of Aquinas' argument, for it is unlikely that he was thinking of a series of causes (or movers) stretching into the past. His argument actually suggests a hierarchy of causes here and now. Every individual thing has its cause: Why should the whole world not have a cause beyond itself? You could therefore argue that within a circular series of causes, each individual cause would be caused by its neighbour, but what then is the cause of the whole circle of causes? If the world itself had such a cause, that cause too would require a cause, for it would have become part of the known world. The philosopher Kant argued that causality is one of the ways in which our minds sort out the world – we impose causality upon our experience. If Kant is right, then an uncaused cause is a mental impossibility.

A rather different objection came from Hume. He based all knowledge on the observation of the world. Something is said to be a cause because it is seen to occur just before the thing that is called its effect. That depends on the observation of cause and effect as two separate things. *But*, in the case of the world as a whole, you have a unique effect, and therefore cannot observe its cause. You cannot get 'outside' the world to see both the world and its cause, and thus establish the relationship between them. If, with Hume, you consider sense impressions as the basis of all knowledge, then the cosmological proofs cannot be accepted as giving proof of the existence of a God outside the world of observation.

Perhaps this gives a clue to a different way of approaching these cosmological arguments. If we follow them in a literal and logical way, they do not prove that there is an uncaused cause or unmoved mover. But they show how a religious person may use the idea of movement or cause to point to the way in which he or she sees God – as a being that in some way stands behind yet causes or moves everything; something beyond and yet involved with everything.

Note

Although Aquinas' is the best-known version of the cosmological argument, it was not the first. An argument from the existence of the universe to its first cause, known as the *Kalam Argument*, was put forward by the Muslim scholars al-Kindi (ninth century) and al-Ghazali (1058–1111).

THE ARGUMENT FROM DESIGN

Although Aquinas has a form of this argument, the clearest example of it is that of William Paley (1743–1805). He argued that, if he were to find a watch lying on the ground, he would assume that it was the product of a designer, for, unlike a stone, he would see at once that it was made up of many different parts worked together in order to produce movement, and that, if any one part were ordered differently, the whole thing would not work. In the same way he argued that the world is like a machine, each part of it designed so that it takes its place within the whole. If the world is so designed, it must have a designer whose purpose is expressed through it.

Insight

Purpose is acting with a particular intention. Aristotle saw purpose in everything – the striving to fulfil its proper nature. Descartes saw purpose as limited to intelligent human beings, with the material universe following impersonal laws of nature. Both Aquinas and Kant saw elements of purpose and design within the universe, suggesting that nature itself was capable of revealing to us some overall explanation in terms of design.

This argument, reflecting the sense of wonder at nature, was most seriously challenged by the theory of evolution. Darwin's 'natural selection' provided an alternative explanation for design, and one that did not require the aid of any external designer. At once, it became possible to see the world not as a machine, but as a process of struggle and death in which those best adapted to their environment were able to breed and pass their genes on to the next generation, thus influencing the very gradual development of the species. Adaptation in order to survive became the key to the development of the most elaborate forms, which previously would have been described as an almost miraculous work of a designer God.

Actually, the challenge of natural selection was anticipated in the work of Hume, who set out a criticism of the design argument some 23 years before Paley published his version of it. He argued that, in a finite world and given infinite time, any combination of things can occur. Those combinations that work together harmoniously can continue and thrive, those that do not will fail. Therefore, when we come to observe the world as it is now, we are observing only those that *do* work, for those that don't are no longer there to be observed. The implication of this is that we observe a world populated by survivors, but that does not mean that it is so ordered by an external designer; it is merely the result of a long period of time and endless failures.

Insight

Notice that the most this argument can claim is that the world shows features of design. Whether that is a natural phenomenon, or one caused by some external agency is a secondary matter. And even if you accept the latter possibility, you then have to ask if such an external 'deist' idea of God is adequate for religion. On the other hand, the sense of awe at the 'design' of the world is a source of 'religious' experience.

THE MORAL ARGUMENT

Kant believed that the traditional arguments could never prove the existence of God, and therefore hoped to go beyond them by presenting an understanding of God based on faith rather than reason. He did this by examining the idea of moral experience, and in particular the relationship between virtue and happiness. In an ideal world they should follow one another – that, if there is a 'highest good' to which a person may aspire morally, doing what is right (virtue) should ultimately lead to happiness. But clearly, there is no evidence that virtue automatically leads to happiness. Why then should anyone be moral?

Kant started from the fact that people do have a sense of moral obligation: a feeling that something is right and must be done, no matter what the consequences. He called this sense of moral obligation the **categorical imperative**, to distinguish it from a 'hypothetical imperative' (which says: 'If you want to achieve this, then you must do that').

In *The Critique of Practical Reason,* Kant explores the presuppositions of the categorical imperative. What do I actually believe about life if I respond to the absolute moral demand? (Not what must I rationally accept before I agree with a moral proposal, but what do I actually feel to be true, rationally or otherwise, in the moment when I respond to the moral imperative?) He argued that three things – God, freedom and immortality – were **postulates** of the practical reason. In other words, that the experience of morality implied that you were free to act (even if someone observing you claimed that you were not), that you would eventually achieve the result you wanted (even if you would not do so in this life, as when someone sacrificed his or her own life), and that, for any of this to be possible, there had to be some overall ordering principle, which might be called 'God'.

Insight

In effect, Kant turned the old arguments on their head. If all we know are the phenomena of our experience, speculative metaphysics cannot give us evidence that God exists. On the other hand, our minds need the idea of God in order to make sense of our moral experience.

The way in which Kant saw the world obliged him to go beyond the traditional arguments for the existence of God. After all, if the idea of causality is imposed on external reality by our own minds, how can it become the basis for a proof for the existence of God? We can only know things as they appear to us, not as they are in themselves:

- If *we contribute space, time and causality to our understanding of the world*
- Then *to argue from these to something outside the world is impossible*
- *God, freedom and immortality are therefore not* in *the world that we experience, but have to do with* the way in which *we experience the world*
- *In other words,* God is a 'regulative' concept (part of our way of understanding) not a 'constitutive' concept (one of the things out there to be discovered).

In other words

- *The cosmological and design arguments suggest that there are features of the world which lead the mind to that which goes beyond experience: What is the cause of everything? Why is the world as it is?*
- *The moral argument suggests that we all have an intuition of God (along with freedom and immortality) every time we experience a sense of absolute moral obligation.*
- *Even if these arguments are not conclusive, they do indicate the sort of thing a religious person is thinking about when he or she uses the word 'God'.*

THE MEANING OF 'GOD'

In considering all the arguments about the existence of God, it might be worth keeping the whole exercise in perspective by reminding ourselves that the sort of 'god' whose existence might or might not be the case is not what many people term 'God' anyway. Of course, this was the basis of the ontological argument, but it is relevant to consider it in the context of the modern American theologian, Paul Tillich. In his *Systematic Theology* (Vol. I, p. 262), he says:

> *The question of the existence of God can be neither asked nor answered. If asked, it is a question about that which by its very nature is above existence, and therefore the answer – whether negative or affirmative – implicitly denies the nature of God. It is as atheistic to affirm the existence of God as to deny it. God is being itself, not a being.*

This reinforces what has been implied throughout the ontological and cosmological arguments: that what is being claimed is not the existence of one entity alongside others, but a fundamental way of regarding the whole universe. It is about the structures of 'being itself' (to use Tillich's term) not the possible existence of a being.

The arguments explored so far in this chapter presuppose a generally accepted idea of what 'God' means. Earlier we looked at a basic idea of 'God', but let us now take it a little further.

Insight

The problem is that, in popular devotion and a literal reading of scriptures, God appears not just as a separate entity, external to the world and the individual, but as one that has human characteristics – a being who might or might not exist. For many people, it is difficult to switch from this image to an understanding of 'God' as a word used to describe reality itself as we experience it.

The most stringent test of the meaning of a statement is that given by logical positivism (see p. 71). Under this set of rules, a statement has a meaning if it pictures something that can be verified by sense experience. If no evidence is relevant to its truth, a statement is meaningless.

When we turn to language about God, such verification is not possible. Most definitions of 'God' are such as to preclude any explanation in terms of what can be directly experienced. This would lead a strict logical positivist to say that statements about God are meaningless.

The broader perspective – as illustrated by Wittgenstein's view of language as a 'form of life' (see p. 79) – seeks to understand language in terms of its function. Religious language finds its meaning in terms of what it does. So, for example, 'God' (for a religious believer) is not simply the name of some external object, about whose existence there could be a debate. Such a 'god' would not be adequate religiously, and to prove his existence would not significantly contribute to religious debate.

In other words

▶ **If** *you prove that God 'exists' in a way that would satisfy a logical positivist (i.e. testable by empirical evidence)*
▶ **Then** *'God' becomes part of the world*
▶ **So** *he is no longer 'God'.*

So you might call yourself a theist, but a religious person would be more likely to say that your belief was no more than idolatry. It is also worth remembering that idolatry is not simply a matter of worshipping a physical image. A person may claim to believe in 'God' when in fact he or she actually believes in a particular idea of God, not the source of reality itself. That is a very common form of idolatry. Indeed, many religious wars come about when conflicting ideas are elevated to divine status, and people feel the need to defend them as though they were defending 'God' himself, which – in the broader perspective – does seem a particularly silly thing to try to do!

This is an important thing to keep in mind, because it might be possible to see the arguments for the existence of God as either succeeding or failing to give definitive proof of the objective existence of an entity to which the name 'God' can be given.

This is simplistic, and is only part of the issue. More important is to ask what part such arguments play in the religious perception of the believer.

Generally speaking, the arguments show the sort of place the idea of God has in terms of the perception of the world – to say that he is uncaused cause, or the designer of the world, is to locate God in the realm of overall meaning and purpose. Such convictions are a 'blik' that is unlikely to be changed (but could be strengthened) by the traditional arguments.

'BEING ITSELF' AND 'ULTIMATE CONCERN'

Let us return for a moment to the theologian Paul Tillich, whose idea of 'being itself' was mentioned earlier. Tillich insisted that religious ideas could only be expressed by way of symbols. A symbol is something that conveys the power and meaning of the thing it symbolizes, in contrast to a sign, which is merely conventional. He argued that the religious experience has two elements: the material basis (the actual thing seen, which could be analyzed by science) and the sense of ultimate value and power that it conveys, which makes it 'religious'.

For him there were two essential features to the God that appears through religious experience or a religious symbol:

1 *That God is 'being itself' rather than a being. In other words, an experience of God is not an experience of something that just happens to be there, an object among others, but is an experience of life itself, of being itself, an experience which then gives meaning to everything else.*
2 *That God is 'ultimate concern'. This implied that 'God' could not be thought of in a detached and impartial way. For the religious believer, God demands total attention and commitment, covering all partial concerns, all other aspects of life. This sense of God as the most important thing in life is seen in the nature of religious experience.*

Language about 'God' need not be religious. You can have a statement about the structure of the universe which includes the idea of God, but that does not make it religious, only cosmological. In order for something to be religious, it has to use religious language in a way that reflects religious experience and/or religious practice. There are two other distinctive features of religious language:

1 *Martin Buber, the Jewish philosopher (1876–1965), introduced the important distinction between 'I–Thou' and 'I–It' language. 'I–Thou' language is personal, while 'I–It' is impersonal. Religious language is about an I addressing a Thou, not speculating about an It.*

2 *The distinction is often made between 'believing that' and 'believing in'. You believe **that** something is the case if you rationally hold it to be so. At the same time, it may be of no personal interest to you at all. You believe **in** something if you are personally committed to it. The essential limitation of the arguments for the existence of God is that they attempt to show that it is reasonable to believe that God exists, rather than to show why people believe in God.*

Insight

Take Wittgenstein's advice – don't just ask about a word's meaning, look at how it is used.

To sum up ...

We have looked at the nature of religious language and religious experience, the traditional arguments for the existence of God, and have therefore started to examine what the word 'God' can mean. The essential points are:

▶ *the inadequacy of literal, empirically based language to express 'God'*
▶ *the limitations of logical argument to encompass religious intuition.*

We have seen that religious language:

▶ *is a 'schema' by which a person may seek to convey the inexpressible*
▶ *is symbolic, not literal.*

Furthermore, religious experience may involve:

▶ *a sense of the unity of everything, and of oneself being at one with everything (mysticism)*
▶ *a sense of a presence of something quite extraordinary – terrifying, uncanny, fascinating, mysterious*
▶ *a sense of the absolute rightness of something (Kant's categorical imperative)*
▶ *a general sense of the wonder of nature*
▶ *a personal experience, resulting in a sense of value and commitment.*

We now turn to some key issues in the philosophy of religion: whether the world is created and designed by God; miracles; the problem of evil; and whether life after death is possible. We shall also look briefly at explanations of religion offered by sociology and psychology. In all these topics it is important to recognize that philosophy uses rational arguments in order to assess the truth of beliefs that people may hold for deeply personal reasons. This is not to negate the value of beliefs that are held for non-rational reasons, but simply to assess whether or not it is appropriate to try to justify such beliefs rationally.

The origin and design of the universe: religion or science?

Clearly, the origin and the nature of the universe are topics to be examined by science. There is broad agreement that, as far as we can judge at present, some form of 'big bang', whereby the known universe has expanded out of a space-time singularity, is the most likely theory for the origin of the world as we know it, and that – on Earth – there has been an evolution of species along the general principles of natural selection. Naturally, because these are scientific theories, they are open to be revised and perhaps eventually could even be replaced although, given the weight of evidence, that seems unlikely.

But from what we have seen from an outline of religious experience, and also from our brief look at the cosmological arguments (p. 161) and the argument from design (p. 163), it is clear that a sense of the wonder at the nature of the universe is a very common feature of religious awareness, and has given rise to the arguments for the existence of a creator and designer god.

The problem is that, once God is given a role in the origin and design of the universe, any alternative scientific theories that explain the same things without requiring any supernatural agency, may be seen as threats to religious belief. Hence, at a superficial level, religion would seem to have a vested interest in the failure of science to give a complete explanation of the universe. On the other hand, it is clear that many scientists – in the past and also today – do hold religious beliefs and certainly do not see their scientific work as in any sense incompatible with them.

So we need to ask: Are the religious and scientific approaches to these topics compatible?

In *The Blind Watchmaker*, Richard Dawkins makes the point that the argument for the world being made by an intelligent designer is based on the assumption that complexity cannot arise spontaneously. How then can an organized and complex designer exist without further explanation and cause? Surely, it is just as easy to accept that the complex organization of the world can appear spontaneously as it is to accept that a complex designer can appear spontaneously. But his central theme is that the process of natural selection gives us a mechanism which explains how complexity can arise from original simplicity. Once you accept that, there is no need to look for an external cause for design. Dawkins' point is not that belief in a creator can be disproved; rather, he shows that the idea is superfluous. This has been the principal threat to religious belief in a designer-god, ever since Charles Darwin put forward the theory of natural selection – for that theory put forward the first genuinely independent explanation of the appearance of design.

But this argument does not deny the sense of wonder at the beauty and complexity of the world. Indeed, Dawkins himself (in *Unweaving the Rainbow*) expresses amazement at what can arise from what is basically a mathematical sequence. Light and colour is no less impressive for being susceptible to scientific analysis.

Insight

The difference is that the religious person is likely to ascribe its origin to an external deity, whereas the atheist (whether scientist or not) accepts it as beautiful in itself, without seeking any external cause.

The fundamental question therefore is:

▶ *Can the world (in theory, if not in practice) provide us with an explanation of itself?*
▶ *If it can, this aspect of religion appears superfluous.*

If it cannot, is that because:

▶ *Our minds are incapable of understanding any overall cause for that within which we are immersed?*

Or

▶ *The explanation can only come through religious intuition (or the direct revelation of God) rather than through human reason and science.*

But this assumes that, for both scientist and religious believer, the world is such as to display design and intelligence. That can be challenged. One of the key nineteenth-century criticisms of the 'argument from design' came from J. S. Mill. He argued that the world was not a particularly benign place, and that evolution (for he was writing after Darwin's theory had been published) progressed only at the price of immense suffering.

It is clear that any objective assessment of nature is going to reveal the scale of suffering, as species prey on one another in the struggle to survive. If design were the product of an intelligent and loving God, why all this suffering? This leads into two related issues that may be addressed in the philosophy of religion – whether God, if he exists, can and does intervene selectively in the operating of the world through miracles, and whether a rational argument can show the compatibility of a omnipotent and loving God with the fact of suffering and evil.

Insight

Even Kant, who saw logical problems with the argument from design, nevertheless said that it deserved to be treated with great respect, saying that it gave life to the study of nature. In other words, it suggested that the world was a fascinating and wonderful place, worthy of our attention. And that is an inspiration for science, as much as for a this-worldly theology.

Miracles

The cosmological arguments for the existence of God were an attempt to lead the mind from an understanding of the physical world to a reality that lay behind it and was responsible for it. The arguments led from ordinary movement and causes to the idea of an unmoved mover or uncaused cause. But Western theistic religions have tended to go beyond this, and have claimed that the action of God can be seen in particular events, which may be called miracles.

Initially, we will be looking at miracles in terms of events for which it is claimed that there is no rational or scientific explanation. This is not the only type of miracle, and it raises some religious questions, but it will suffice as a starting point.

If you want to find an argument against this idea of a miracle, the logical place to look is among those philosophers who take an empiricist position, for an empiricist will want to relate everything to the objects of sense experience, and this is precisely what is not possible if an event is to be a miracle in the particular sense that we are considering. A critique along these lines is given by Hume.

Hume examines the idea of miracles in the tenth book of his *Enquiry Concerning Human Understanding*. His argument runs like this:

▶ *A wise man proportions his belief to the evidence; the more evidence there is for something, the more likely it is to have been the case.*
▶ *Equally, the evidence of other people is assessed according to their reliability as witnesses.*

He then turns to the idea of miracles and offers a definition.

▶ *A miracle is the violation of a law of nature.*
▶ **But** *a law of nature is the result of a very large number of observations.*

He therefore argues:

A miracle is a violation of the laws of nature; and as a firm and unalterable experience has established these laws, the proof

against a miracle, from the very nature of the fact, is as entire as any argument from experience can possibly be imagined. Why is it more probably that all men must die; that lead cannot, of itself, remain suspended in the air; that fire consumes wood, and is extinguished by water; unless it be, that these events are found agreeable to the laws of nature, and there is required a violation of these laws, or in other words, a miracle to prevent them? Nothing is esteemed a miracle if it ever happen in the common course of nature ... The plain consequence is ... That no testimony is sufficient to establish a miracle, unless the testimony be of such a kind, that its falsehood would be more miraculous, than the fact, which it endeavours to establish.

In other words, it is always more likely that the report of a miracle is mistaken, than that a law of nature was actually broken, for the evidence against the miracle will always be greater than the evidence for it.

For Hume, the only way in which, on balance, a miracle could be accepted, is if it would be a greater miracle if all the evidence for it were to be proved mistaken, than if a law of nature were broken. In practice, that rules out miracles, although strictly speaking it does not preclude a miracle, it simply says that *there can never be sufficient evidence* for a wise man to accept it as such.

Hume's argument is based on the assumption (which we accepted at the opening of this section) that a miracle is a violation of a law of nature; in other words, that the event is inexplicable in terms of present scientific knowledge. But is that necessarily the case for an event to be a miracle?

Take the example of a 'black hole' in the middle of a galaxy. It is a violation of what are generally called 'laws of nature' (according to Newtonian physics). Yet it is not seen as a miracle, merely an extreme case, which suggests that the existing 'laws' of physics need to be modified to take it into account.

We therefore have to ask a further question: *What distinguishes a miracle from a rare or unique occurrence?*

Generally, in order to be termed a miracle, something needs to be seen as fitting into a scheme which displays positive purpose. If a life is saved, against all expectations, that may be regarded as a miracle by those for whom that life was dear. If a person suddenly drops dead, his or her friends are unlikely to call it a miracle. However, the long-lost relative, who had no emotional connection with the deceased, and who is suddenly saved from financial ruin by an unexpected legacy, may well find it miraculous.

Therefore, a unique occurrence (for instance, a previously unobserved event in a distant galaxy) would not be called a miracle unless it had some personal relevance and apparent sense of purpose. Equally, an ordinary event – in other words, one for which there is a perfectly reasonable explanation – may still be regarded as a miracle if its timing is right, or it has particular significance. Thus the long-lost relative just mentioned might find that the legacy arrives at the same time as a final demand for payment of some impossibly large debt. Not that it has happened, but that it has happened *now*, is the remarkable thing.

Insight

With a miracle, it's not so much what happened, but *why*. If the world is an impersonal mechanism, any sense of purpose suggests the deliberate choice of an agent. The problem, without direct evidence, is proving either purpose or agent.

UNIQUE OR UNIVERSAL?

There is an important sense in which the idea of the miraculous and that of the cosmological and design arguments work against one another. The whole essence of the earlier arguments is that the world is structured in a way that displays an overall purpose. Those arguments only work on the basis of regularity, for only in regularity does the sense of design and purpose appear. Yet the literal idea of a miracle violates that regularity, introducing a sense of arbitrariness and unpredictability into an understanding of the world which therefore undermines the cosmological structures.

In other words

You can't have it both ways. *Either* God is seen to exist because the world is a wonderful, ordered place, *or* his hand is seen in individual events because the world is an unpredictable, miraculous place. It is not reasonable to try to argue for both at once, since the one appears to cancel out the other!

The problem of evil

In its simplest form, the problem can be stated like this:

▶ If *God created the world*
▶ And *if God is all-powerful and all-loving*
▶ Then *why is there evil and suffering in the world?*

Conclusion:

▶ Either *God is not all-powerful*
▶ Or *God is not all-loving*
▶ Or *suffering is either unreal, necessary or a means to a greater good*
▶ Or *the whole idea of an all-loving and all-powerful creator God was a mistake in the first place.*

An important book setting out suggested answers to this problem is *Evil and the God of Love* (1966) by John Hick (b. 1922), a philosopher and theologian notable for his contribution to the problem of evil and also to the issue of religious pluralism. In that book he gives two main lines of approach, the Augustinian and the Irenaean:

1 *The Augustinian approach is named after St Augustine (354–430), and reflects his background in neo-Platonism. In Plato's thought, particular things are imperfect copies of their 'forms'. Imperfection is a feature of the world as we experience it. The Augustinian approach to evil and suffering is to say that evil is not a separate force opposing the good, but is a lack of goodness, a deprivation. The world as we experience it is full of imperfect copies, and suffering and evil are bound up with that imperfection.*

But Augustine had a second line of argument, coming from the Bible and Church teaching, rather than from Plato. The biblical account of the Fall of the Angels and of Adam and Eve in the Garden of Eden led to a 'fallen' state for all creation. Because of human disobedience, the world is a place of suffering rather than innocent bliss. Hence moral suffering (the pain caused by humans) can be seen as a consequence of the sin, and natural evil (earthquakes, tsunami, diseases and the like) can be seen as a just punishment for sin.

2 *The Irenaean approach is named after Bishop Irenaeus of Lyons (c. 130–c. 202). It presents the idea that human life is imperfect, but having been made in the image of God, human beings are intended to grow and develop, aspiring to be what God intended them to be. Through free will and all the sufferings of life, people have an opportunity to grow and learn. Without a world in which there is both good and evil, that would be impossible:*

> **How, if we had no knowledge of the contrary, could we have had instruction in that which is good? ... For just as the tongue receives experiences of sweet and bitter by means of tasting, and the eye discriminates between black and white by means of vision, and the ear recognizes the distinctness of sounds by hearing; so also does the mind,**

receiving through the experience of both the knowledge of what is good, become the more tenacious in its preservation, by acting in obedience to God ... But if any one do shun the knowledge of both kinds of things, and the twofold perception of knowledge, he unaware divests himself of the character of a human being.

Irenaeus, *Against Heresies* iv, xxxix.1, quoted in Hick, Fontana, 1968

In other words, it is only by having a world in which there is both good and evil that we can have moral choice and develop spiritually. In this way, Irenaeus can justify the presence of natural evil, for a world that includes sickness and natural disasters is one in which people grow through facing real challenges.

Hick's own approach to the problem of evil is one that treats evil as something to be tackled and overcome, but with the hope that, ultimately, it will be seen as part of an overall divine plan.

Compensation after death?

The issues concerning immortality, resurrection, reincarnation and the general problems concerning whether survival of any sort is possible or meaningful have been examined briefly in Chapter 4, pp. 103–5.

Notice how the issue of life after death has touched on those of faith, the nature of the universe and the justification of the goodness of God with the suffering of the world. Pascal's wager assumed that there was heaven to gain and hell to avoid, and that the extremes they offered outweighed the consideration of the relative benefits of one's lifestyle on earth. Similarly now, both Augustine and Irenaeus, each in his own way, looks beyond this life for an ultimate justification for suffering. Whether suffering is a just punishment or a means of developing, it only makes sense as the prescription offered by a loving God, if there is some form of compensation beyond death.

The crucial difference between the religious and non-religious evaluation of life, is that – in general – the non-religious approach is that life is of value in itself, not as a preparation for anything beyond this world. The challenge of atheism is the challenge of acceptance of a limited life with an unequally distributed mixture of pleasure and pain.

To say 'Yes' to this life, just as it is, and to be prepared to live this life over and over again, just as it is, is the hallmark of someone radically free from the consolations of religion. Indeed, Nietzsche made such 'Yes-saying' a key feature of his *übermensch* (superman), the higher form to which humankind is challenged to evolve.

Insight

That said, a psychologist might argue that it is exactly the consolations of religion (as opposed to those of philosophy) which explain the continuation of religious belief in the face of rational criticism.

Psychological and sociological explanations of religion

In one of the most quoted passages of all time, Marx said, in his *Contribution to the Critique of Hegel's Philosophy of Right*:

Religion is the sign of the oppressed creature, the heart of the heartless world, just as it is the spirit of the spiritless situation. It is the opium of the people.

The abolition of religion as the illusory happiness of the people is required for their real happiness. The demand to give up the illusions about its condition is the demand to give up a condition which needs illusions. The criticism of religion is therefore in embryo the criticism of the vale of woe, the halo of which is religion.

(as quoted in Paul Helm *Faith and Reason*, OUP, 1999)

In other words, Marx wants people to turn their attention to their present situation and to struggle for real happiness. The assumption he makes is that the sort of happiness associated with life after death is illusory. But at the same time, if such an illusion is believed, the fact of suffering and the longing for a life free from it, is a powerful motivation for continuing to be religious in the face of present adversity.

A parallel explanation for religion is given by sociologists, for example, Emile Durkheim. From the sociological perspective, religion provides a cohesive force within society. If a community is bound together by its religion, then the continuation of that religion does not depend so much on the intellectual acceptance of its articles of belief, but the perceived value it offers society.

Freud's criticism of religion was partly based on the parallels he saw between religious behaviour and obsessional neuroses, like repeated handwashing or tidying routines. In both cases, repeated actions (for example, confessing sins; attending worship) were an attempt to escape from a sense of unworthiness and guilt. But more significant for our argument here are the supposed benefits of religion that he sets out in *The Future of an Illusion* (1927). Just as a child depends on an adult for protection, so he sees religion as offering God to adults as a substitute, heavenly Father – a comfort and protection in the midst of the threatening nature of life and the eventual inevitability of death.

These explanations of religion, mentioned briefly here, but well worth exploring further, are a reminder that the sort of rational arguments examined by the philosophy of religion are far from being the whole story. Religious beliefs may claim to be rational, and may be backed up by rational argument, but religion does not ultimately depend on any of these arguments for its continued existence. As the widespread increase of fundamentalism and literalism in religious circles shows, it is often the rejection of an intellectually sophisticated approach to these issues that appeals.

This is not to suggest that the explanations of religion given by the likes of Marx, Durkheim or Freud necessarily invalidate religious beliefs. Those beliefs (examined rationally) may be true or they may be false. What is clear, however, is that – as a phenomenon – there are many reasons for religion to continue and even to flourish, quite apart from them.

Some general remarks

There are two very different approaches to belief in God, miracles and so on. One (sometimes referred to as 'onto-theology') tends to describe God as a being who exists and interacts with the world, the other ('expressive theology') sees God and religion as a way of exploring and expressing value in this world. The problem – as clearly set out by Simon Blackburn in, for example, *Philosophers Without Gods*, 2007, ed Louise Antony – is that the latter, even if more compatible with secular atheism, is not in line with the sort of impetus that beliefs need to have in order to sustain religion. In other words, if you don't believe that God actually, literally exists, it's difficult to be committed to obeying him.

And underlying the difference between the religious and non-religious viewpoints are also seen in the fundamental way of looking at and valuing the world:

> ▶ *Is the world fundamentally an imperfect copy of something more real? As we look at the world, do we see it as a half-empty glass, forever lacking fullness and perfection? Both the ontological and cosmological arguments look beyond the partial experience of 'greatness' or movement or causality, to something than which none greater can be conceived, an unmoved mover, or an uncaused cause. The mind is led from a present experience of a half-empty glass to the conception of what a full glass would be like – a perfection which underpins this imperfect world.*

▶ *Or is the world still developing, working towards a perfection that lies in the future? Is the structure of the world (along with everything in it, good and bad) the means by which growth can take place? The argument from design and the moral argument have a contribution to make to this point of view. Darwin's evolution through natural selection is based on the facts of suffering and death which allow only the strongest members of a species to survive and breed. Without suffering and death, were is no evolution. In Marxist theory, the class struggle, with all the suffering that it involves, is the means of bringing about a classless society in the future.*

These are practical, moral and political as well as religious questions. But they raise an enormous philosophical problem: *Everything that we experience is in a process of change.* Birth, death, suffering and evil are all part of that process. How do you understand anything so mobile and ambiguous? How can you say 'yes' to it with conviction? How can you love it? That is the challenge posed by Nietzsche, by modern atheism and humanism, and also by Buddhism, which has always seen life as fragile and subject to change, but has nevertheless proposed insight and compassion as a recipe for overcoming human suffering.

Comment

Where do you find reality?

▶ *Is reality to be found in an ideal realm outside, over and above the flux of life? (Line up behind Plato, Augustine, Aquinas and most traditional theists!)*
▶ *Is reality to be found as an end product to be arrived at through this process of change? (Line up behind Irenaeus, Marx and evolutionary religious thinkers such as Teilhard de Chardin!)*
▶ *Is reality to be found within life itself, including all its limitations and changes? (Line up behind Heraclitus, Spinoza and the Buddha!)*

For reflection

An important contribution to philosophy as a whole made by the philosophy of religion is the way it highlights the inadequacy of literal language to encompass the whole of life. Although much of it has been concerned with the idea of 'God', the sort of discussion presented in this chapter could be used equally about issues of aesthetics (what we mean by beauty or by art) or morality. Mystical experience and a religious sense of awe are reflected in many common human experiences: falling in love, looking at a beautiful scene, being moved by music. An essential quality of all such experiences is that they require a great flexibility of language if they are to be described – there is always an elusive 'something more' about them.

10 THINGS TO REMEMBER

1 *Foundationalism is the attempt to arrive at statements which are accepted as obviously true.*

2 *Fundamentalism involves a literal acceptance of beliefs and religious texts, often taken out of context.*

3 *Religious language is essentially personal.*

4 *God cannot exist in the sense that ordinary things exist.*

5 *The traditional arguments show what a believer might mean by 'God'.*

6 *There would be no religion without religious experience.*

7 *Religious experience tends to be personal and gives a new perspective in life.*

8 *A miracle is more than a unique event.*

9 *The problem of evil challenges a literal understanding of a loving God.*

10 *The social sciences offer explanations for religion, irrespective of its truth.*

6

Ethics

In this chapter you will learn:

- *about whether or not we are free to act as we wish*
- *the basis of major ethical theories*
- *the relationship between ethics and the values held by society.*

Facts, values and choices

So far we have been exploring questions of knowledge: What can we know for certain? Can we know anything about the nature of reality as a whole? How are our language and our thought related to the experiences that come to us through our senses? These led on to key questions about the nature of science, of the mind and of religion.

But it is a fundamental feature of all sentient life that awareness of its environment enables a creature to act, to find food, to recognize danger, to mate and thereby to survive. Human beings are no different, except that their intellectual ability presents them with a range of choices. So philosophy is also concerned with questions of a very different kind: What should we do? How should we organize society? What is right? How should we understand the idea of justice? On what basis can we choose between different courses of action? These lead to a study of ethics, and of political philosophy.

These more immediately practical aspects of philosophy have a long history. Although the pre-Socratic philosophers of ancient Greece had probed many questions about the nature of reality – questions to which their answers are still interesting in terms of both epistemology and the natural sciences – with Socrates, Plato and Aristotle, the emphasis shifted towards issues of morality. So, for example, Plato's *Republic* is not based on the question 'What is society?' but 'What is justice?', and it is through that question that many other issues about society and how it should be ruled are explored.

Aristotle (in *Nicomachean Ethics*) asked about the 'good' which was the aim of every action, and about what could constitute a 'final good' – something worthwhile for its own sake, rather than for the sake of something higher. He came to the view that the highest good for man was *eudaimonia*, which literally means 'having a good spirit', but perhaps can be translated as 'happiness'. He saw it as the state in which a person was fulfilling his or her potential and natural function. It expressed a form of human excellence or virtue (*arete*). This tied in with his general view that everything had a 'final cause': a goal and a purpose to which it moves. If you understand the final cause of something, you also understand its fundamental essence, which finds its expression in that goal. If a knife had a soul, Aristotle argued, that soul would be 'cutting' – that is what makes it a knife, that is what it is there to do. What then is the essence of humankind? What is it there to do? What is its goal?

Aristotle linked his ethics to his whole understanding of human life. He refused to accept any simple rule which could cover all situations, and he also considered human beings in relationship to the society within which they lived, recognizing the influence this has on human behaviour. Aristotle saw man as both a 'thinking animal' and a 'political animal'. It is therefore not surprising that ethics becomes the study of rational choice in action, and that it should have a social as well as an individual aspect. In this chapter we shall take a brief look at some of the main philosophical approaches to moral issues and in the following chapter we shall examine issues of a social and political nature. Although, for convenience, morality and politics are separated, it is important to remember that morality is more than the establishing of a set of personal values. It is equally possible to examine morality in terms of the requirements of the state and the place of individuals within society; in ethics the personal and the social cannot be separated.

'IS' AND 'OUGHT'

Once you start to talk about morality, or about the purpose of things, you introduce matters of value as well as those of fact. An important question for philosophy is whether it is possible to derive values from facts, or whether facts must always remain 'neutral'. In other words:

▶ *Facts say what 'is'.*
▶ *Values say what 'ought' to be.*

Which leads to the question:

> *Can we ever derive an 'ought' from an 'is'?*

If the answer to this question is 'no', then how are we to decide issues of morality? If no facts can be used to establish morality, can there be absolute moral rules, or are all moral decisions relative, dependent upon particular circumstances, feelings or desires?

Later in this chapter we shall examine two ways in which philosophers have presented facts that they consider to be relevant to what people 'ought' to do:

1 *An argument based on design and purpose (following Aristotle's comments given earlier).*
2 *An argument based on the expected results of an action.*

We shall also examine other features of ethical language: expressing approval or otherwise, recommending a course of action, or expressing emotion. But first, if ethics is to make any sense, we must ask if people are, in fact, free to decide what to do. If they are not free, if they have no choice, then praise and blame, approval or disapproval are inappropriate.

Insight

It is illogical to tell someone that they **ought** to do something, unless we believe that it is at least **possible** for them to do it.

Freedom and determinism

If (as Kant argued) space, time and causality are categories used by the human mind to interpret experience, it is inevitable that we shall see everything in the world as causally conditioned – things don't just happen, they must have a cause!

This process of looking for causes, which lies at the heart of the scientific quest, has as its logical goal a totally understood world in which each individual thing and action is explained in terms of all that went before it. In theory, given total knowledge of all that had happened in the past, everything that will happen in the future could be predicted. This reflects what we may call the Newtonian world view, that the universe is like a machine, operating by means of fixed rules.

We saw that this created problems in terms of the relationship between mind and body. What is the human mind? Can it make a difference? If everything is causally conditioned, then even the electrical impulses in my brain are part of a closed mechanical system and my freedom is an illusion. I may feel sure that I have made a free choice, but in fact everything that has happened to me since my birth, and everything that has made the world the way it is since the beginning of time, has contributed to that decision.

In other words

'I just knew you'd say that!' One of the annoying things about people who claim to predict our choices is that we like to think we are free, but are forced to recognize that we may not always be the best judge of that.

One of the fundamental issues of philosophy is freedom and determinism. It is also related to reductionism – the reduction of complex entities (like human beings) to the simpler parts of which they are composed. If we are nothing more than the individual cells that comprise our bodies, and if those cells are determined by physical forces and are predictable, then there seems no room for the whole human being to exercise freedom.

For now, dealing with ethics, one distinction is clear:

▶ *If we are free to make a choice, then we can be responsible for what we do. Praise or blame are appropriate. We can act on the basis of values that we hold.*
▶ *If we are totally conditioned, we have no choice in what we do, and it makes no sense to speak of moral action springing from choices and values, or action being worthy of praise or blame.*

By the same token, there are levels of determinism. It is clear that nobody is totally free:

▶ *We have physical limitations. I cannot make an unaided leap 30 metres into the air, even if I feel I have a vocation to do so. Overweight middle-aged men do not make the best ballet dancers. It's not a matter of choice, merely of physical fact.*
▶ *We may be psychologically predisposed to act in certain ways rather than others. If you are shy and depressed, you are unlikely to be the life and soul of a party. But that is not a matter of choice, merely of present disposition.*

- *We may be socially restrained. I may choose to do something really outrageous, but know that I will not get away with it.*
- *We may also be limited by the financial and political structures under which we live. There are many things that I cannot do without money, for example.*

In considering the moral implications of actions, we have to assess the degree of freedom available to the agent.

Examples

Is a soldier who is *ordered* to shoot prisoners or unarmed civilians thereby absolved of moral responsibility? Is he free to choose whether to carry out that act or not? Does the fear of his own death, executed for refusal to obey an order, determine that he must obey?

If a person commits a crime while known to be suffering from a mental illness, or if a psychiatric report indicates that he or she was disturbed at the time, that fact will be taken into account when apportioning blame. But how many people who commit crimes could be described as clear-headed and well balanced? How many have no mitigating circumstances of some sort when family background, education, deprivation and other things are considered?

If we are all obeying orders, even those that have been lodged in our unconscious mind since childhood, or influenced by circumstances, are we ever responsible for our actions? Are paedophilia or kleptomania crimes, or illnesses, or both? Do they require punishment or treatment?

We are all conditioned by many factors, there is no doubt of that. The difference between that and determinism is that determinism leaves no scope for human freedom and choice (we are automata), whereas those who argue against determinism claim that there remains a measure of freedom that is exercised within the prevailing conditions.

Notice how many of the topics studied in philosophy are related to one another. This freedom/determinism issue could be considered in the context of:

▶ *How we understand the world (Kant's idea that we impose causality on all that we experience, so that all phenomena are conditioned).*

▶ *The existence of God. (Can there be an infinite number of causes? If God knows what I will do, am I free and responsible, or is He?)*

▶ *How scientific laws are framed. (Can they claim absolute truth? Can we ever be certain that something has caused something else?)*

▶ *The question of whether or not there is a self over and above the atoms and cells of which a body is made up. (If so, does that self have a life that is independent of the determined life of individual cells?)*

But keep in mind that everything we are, everything we believe, and everything we understand about the world is there in the moment when we make a moral choice; not necessarily consciously, but there in the background, exerting an influence.

Not all philosophers have presented the issues of freedom, determinism and moral choice in quite this way. A notable exception in Western thought is Spinoza. He argued that freedom was in fact an illusion, created because we do not know all the causes of our actions. Things that happen to us produce in us either passive or active emotions. The passive emotions, such as hatred, anger or fear, lead a person into bondage, whereas the active ones, those generated by an understanding of our real circumstances, lead to a positive view of life, and an ability to be ourselves. Spinoza held that the more one understood the world, the more the negative emotions would diminish and be replaced by positive ones. One might perhaps say of this that freedom (and the only freedom that Spinoza will accept) is the ability to see life exactly as it is and say 'yes' to it.

Kinds of ethical language

What does it mean to say that something is 'good' or that an action is 'right'? Do these words refer to a hidden quality in that action, something over and above what is actually observed? What sort of evidence can be given for such a description?

I can show you what I mean by 'red' by pointing to a range of red objects, and relying on your ability to identify their common feature. Can I do the same by pointing to a range of actions that I consider to be morally right? Take for example:

- *a married couple having sexual intercourse*
- *someone helping a blind person across a road*
- *paying for goods in a shop (as opposed to stealing them).*

Considering only the *factual description* of each action, what do they have in common? What quality of the actions make them 'moral'? And if moral language is not the same as physical description, what is it and how is it justified?

DESCRIPTIVE ETHICS

This is the most straightforward form of ethical language. It is simply a description of what happens: what moral choices are made and in which particular circumstances. Rather than making a statement about the rights or wrongs of abortion, for example, descriptive ethics simply gives facts and figures about how many abortions take place, how they are carried out, and what legal restraints are placed on that practice. *Descriptive ethics is about 'is' rather than 'ought'.*

NORMATIVE ETHICS

Normative ethics deals with the norms of action, in terms of whether an action is considered good or bad, right or wrong. It expresses values, and makes a moral judgement based on them. It may relate to facts, but it is not wholly defined by facts. It may be justified in a number of ways that we shall examine shortly. *Normative ethics is about 'ought'; it makes judgements.*

META-ETHICS

When philosophy examines the claims made in normative ethics, a number of questions are raised:

▸ *What does it mean to say that something is right or wrong?*
▸ *Can moral statements be said to be either true or false?*
▸ *Do they express more than the preferences of the person who makes them?*
▸ *What is the meaning of the terms used in ethical discourse?*

These questions are not themselves moral statements; they do not say that any particular thing is right or wrong. Meta-ethics is a branch of philosophy which does to normative ethical statement what philosophy does to language in general. It examines ethical language to find what it means and how it is used.

Insight

Meta-ethics produces theories about the nature of ethical language, rather than discussing right and wrong. At one time, many professional philosophers thought that was all philosophy should do. Nowadays, however (prompted by the work of Peter Singer and others) philosophers are expected to make a direct contribution to moral debates.

INTUITIONISM

In his book *Principia Ethica* (1903), G. E. Moore argued that the term 'good' could not be defined, and that every attempt to do so ended in reducing goodness to some other quality which was not common to all 'good' things. In other words, goodness could involve kindness, altruism, generosity, a sense of social justice – but it is not actually *defined* by any of these. Moore therefore claimed that:

> *Everyone does in fact understand the question 'Is this good?'*
> *When he thinks of it, his state of mind is different from what it*
> *would be, were he asked 'Is this pleasant, or desired, or approved?'*
> *It has a distinct meaning for him, even though he may not*
> *recognize in what respect it is distinct.*
>
> *Principia Ethica*, Chapter 1

He likened it to describing the colour yellow. In the end you just have to point to things and say that they are yellow without being able to define the colour. You know what yellow is by intuition. In the same way, you know what goodness is, even though it cannot be defined. This approach is generally referred to as **intuitionism**.

Insight

Moore himself did not use the term 'intuitionism' for his work. He simply wanted to point out that 'good' was known but could not be further defined, whereas intuitionists generally want to go further and say that all moral claims are based on intuition.

NATURALISM AND METAPHYSICAL ETHICS

G. E. Moore had argued that you could not get an 'ought' from an 'is' – that you could not derive morality from the facts of human behaviour. He made an absolute distinction between facts and values. From Plato and Aristotle onwards, however, there have been philosophers who have argued that moral principles and values should be derived from the examination of human beings, their society, and their place within the world as a whole. This task is termed 'naturalism' or 'metaphysical ethics', and it implies that what you 'ought' to do has some close relation to what 'is', in fact, the case about yourself and the world. In other words, that morality should be more than an expression of personal choice, it should be rooted in an overall understanding of the world.

EMOTIVISM

According to this theory, saying that something is good or bad is really just a way of saying that you approve or disapprove of it. In Chapter 3 we saw that, early in the twentieth century, there developed an approach to language known as logical positivism. In this, statements were called meaningless unless they either corresponded to empirical data, or were true by definition. On this basis, moral statements were seen as meaningless.

One response to this challenge was to argue that moral statements were not factual descriptions, but were simply expressing approval or otherwise. They were therefore not true or false by reference to that which they described, but according to whether or not they correctly reflected the emotions or preferences of the speaker. A J Ayer, who popularized logical positivism in the English-speaking world, took this view.

PRESCRIPTIVISM

This is another response to the challenge of logical positivism. It claims that moral language is actually recommending a course of action. If I say that something is good, I am actually saying that I feel it should be done – in other words, I am prescribing it as a course of action.

In other words

▶ *If you describe someone's actions or decisions, the truth of what you say is known by checking the facts.*
▶ *If you say that something is 'right' or 'wrong', there are no straightforward facts to check in order to verify your claim.*
▶ *Meta-ethics, therefore, looks at these ethical claims and asks what they mean, whether they can be true or false, and, if so, how that truth may be established. If ethics is not about external facts, it may be about intuitions, or emotional responses, or recommendations, or the general structures of life and their implications for individual action.*

The theories mentioned here have been developed within the philosophical debate about the nature of language in general and of the status of moral language in particular. But whatever the status of the language they use, the fact is that people continue to make moral claims. It is therefore important to examine the bases upon which such claims may be made.

Three bases for ethics

If moral language is simply expressing an emotion or a preference, then it does not seem to need further justification, it implies no more than the feelings of the moment. If we want to argue for a moral position, however, we need to find a rational basis for ethics. Within the history of Western philosophy there have been three principal bases offered: **natural law**, **utilitarianism** and the **categorical imperative**. We shall examine each of these in turn.

NATURAL LAW

In Book 1 of *Nicomachean Ethics*, Aristotle says:

> *Every art and every enquiry, and similarly every action and pursuit, is thought to aim at some good; and for this reason the good has rightly been declared to be that at which all things aim.*

p.1094a

Aristotle develops this into the idea of the supreme good for human beings: happiness (*eudaimonia*). If you agree with Aristotle that everything has a final cause or purpose, a 'good' for which it exists, or if you accept with Plato that the 'Forms' (especially the 'Form of the Good') have a permanent reality, independent of our own minds and perceptions, then it should be possible to specify which things are 'good' and which 'bad', which actions are 'right' and which 'wrong' in an independent and objective way.

Natural law is the approach to ethics which claims that something is right if it fulfils its true purpose in life, wrong if it goes against it.

Examples

Sex Natural law, based on the idea of a natural purpose inherent in everything, might seem particularly appropriate for dealing with issues of sex, since it is clear that sex does have a natural purpose that is essential for life. In natural law terms:

▶ *the 'natural' function of sex is the reproduction of the species*
▶ *non-reproductive sexual activity is 'against nature' and therefore wrong (or at least a misuse of the natural function of sex). Masturbation, contraception and homosexuality could all be criticized from this standpoint.*

Abortion and euthanasia It is natural for every creature to seek and preserve its own life. If everything has a natural purpose to fulfil, then abortion and euthanasia can be seen as wrong, since they go against this natural outworking of the processes of life.

▶ *Unless there is something sufficiently wrong for there to be a miscarriage, the newly fertilized embryo will naturally grow into a new, independent human being. The 'final cause' of the embryo (to use Aristotle's term) is the adult human which it will one day become. On a natural law basis, it would therefore be wrong to frustrate that natural process through abortion even if the child is not wanted and its life is likely to be an unhappy one.*

▶ *When the body can no longer sustain the burden of illness, it dies. To anticipate this is to frustrate the natural tendency towards self-preservation. The results of an act of euthanasia may be to lessen a burden of suffering, but it would still be seen as wrong in itself, even if the person making that moral judgement had great sympathy for those involved.*

Notice how this approach to ethics relates to the philosophy of religion. The basis of the natural law approach is that the world is purposeful and that the purpose of any part of it may be understood by human reason. It may be seen as the ethical aspect of the traditional argument from design (see p. 163).

Natural law is not the same as a consideration of what appears as a natural response to a situation – natural in the sense that it reflects the nature that humankind shares with the rest of the animal kingdom. Rather, it is *nature as seen through the eyes of reason*; indeed, for most of those who would use a natural law argument, it is also coloured by religious views, with the world seen as the purposeful creation by God.

A newspaper article on adultery (Anne Applebaum, *The Daily Telegraph*, 29 August 1994, p. 17) was headed, 'We have descended from apes but we don't have to behave like them'. In it the author opposed the fashionable theory that it was 'natural' to commit adultery, arguing that, although people are instinctively 'bad', they are capable of exercising self-restraint. In particular, she opposed the idea that adultery was simply the natural expression of a genetic urge to reproduce in the most favourable way possible, and that men would therefore 'naturally' be attracted to a number of other women. She argued that to say that 'we are all genetic adulterers' sounds similar to the traditional Christian view that 'we are all sinners', but with the fundamental difference that the latter regarded moral codes and practices as existing to control our natural instincts, whereas the former seemed to use those instincts to justify behaviour as well as to explain it.

For reflection

▶ Is it possible for something to be natural but wrong?
▶ Is self-restraint always unnatural?
▶ Is the genetic strengthening of a species (which presumably could be helped by allowing the strongest to breed freely with the most beautiful) itself a final 'good' to be sought?

There are many issues within medical ethics that have a 'natural law' component. For example, a 'naturally' infertile couple may be offered IVF or other treatments to help them to conceive a child, and it is 'natural' that they should want to do so. But what about the nature and purpose of the treatments involved? Should they be approved by natural law, in the sense that they facilitate the 'final purpose' of having the child? Furthermore, may it not be part of a natural mechanism of population limitation that some couples are infertile, and that to introduce an artificial process is therefore against the natural reasons for their infertility?

If such treatment is branded as 'unnatural', what is there to be said about medicine in general? It may be natural to die from an infection, and it is therefore unnatural to be saved by an antibiotic. But, if natural law seeks the fulfilment of each human being, is not the prevention of premature death a decision based on the recognition that an individual might well fulfil his or her potential only by being given a chance to live?

Insight

This illustrates again that Natural Law places its emphasis on 'Law'. It considers a *rational interpretation* of nature and its purposes, not an observation of nature itself, which can all too often be brutal and impersonal.

UTILITARIANISM

Utilitarianism is a moral theory associated particularly with Jeremy Bentham (1748–1832), a philosopher, lawyer and social reformer, involved particularly with the practical issues of prison reform, education and the integrity of public institutions, and further developed by John Stuart Mill (1806–73), a campaigner for individual liberty and for the rights of women. Its roots, however, are found earlier in the basic idea of hedonism.

Hedonism is the term used for a philosophy which makes the achievement of happiness the prime goal in life. Epicurus taught in

Athens at the end of the fourth century BCE. He took an atomistic view of the world (everything is composed of indivisible atoms), regarded the gods as having little influence on life, and generally considered the main purpose of life to be the gaining of pleasure, in the broad sense of well-being. Pain, he held, was of shorter duration than pleasure, and death was nothing but the dissolution of the atoms of which we are made, with no afterlife to fear. He therefore considered that the wise should lead a life free from anxiety, and if morality had any purpose it was to maximize the amount of well-being that life can offer.

To be fair to Epicurus, this crude outline does not do justice to the fact that he distinguished the more intellectual pleasures from the animal ones, and that Epicureans were certainly not 'hedonists' in the popular sense. Nevertheless, Epicurus did establish the maximizing of happiness as the prime purpose of morality.

This was to become the basis of utilitarian theories of ethics: that the right thing to do on any occasion is that which aims to give maximum happiness to all concerned. This may be expressed in the phrase 'the greatest good for the greatest number', and Bentham made the point that everyone should count equally in such an assessment – a radical point of view for him to take at that time. Utilitarianism is therefore a theory *based on the expected results of an action, rather than any inherent sense of right or wrong.*

This is very much a common-sense view of ethics; to do what is right is often associated with doing what will benefit the majority. From a philosophical point of view, however, there are certain problems associated with it:

▶ *You can never be certain what the total effects of an action are going to be. To take a crude example: you may save the life of a drowning child who then grows up to be a mass murderer. In practice, there always has to be a cut-off point beyond which it is not practicable to calculate consequences. Added to this is the fact that we see the result of actions only with hindsight; at the time, we might have expected something quite different. Thus, although utilitarianism seems to offer a straightforward way of assessing moral issues, its assessment must always remain provisional.*

▶ *The definition of what constitutes happiness may not be objective. Other people may not want what you deem to be their happiness or in their best interests. The utilitarian argument appears to make a factual consideration of results the basis of moral choice, but in practice, in selecting the degree or type of happiness to be considered, a person is already making value (and perhaps moral) judgements.*

▶ *How do you judge between pain caused to a single individual and the resulting happiness of many others? Would global benefit actually justify the inflicting of pain on a single innocent person?*

An outrageous example

A perfectly healthy young visitor innocently walks into a hospital in which there are a number of people all waiting for various organ transplants. Might a utilitarian surgeon be tempted?

But more serious examples

In allocating limited healthcare budgets, choices have to be made. Do you spend a large amount of money on an operation which may or may not save the life of a seriously ill child, if the consequence of that choice is that many other people with debilitating (but perhaps not life-threatening) illnesses are unlikely to receive the help they need? How do you assess the relative happiness or benefit of those concerned?

Consider the situation of an unborn child known to be seriously handicapped but capable of survival. Is the potential suffering of both child and parents as a result of the severe handicap such that the child's survival does not add to the total sum of happiness? And who could possibly make such an assessment objectively?

Further difficulties arise in a consideration of the first of the above examples, in that experimental surgical procedures carried out today may benefit many more patients in the future.

Insight

The argument for fundamental research in the sciences is often justified on this utilitarian basis – that without it, the long-term development of new technology will be stifled, with the corresponding loss of its future benefits.

Forms of utilitarianism

So far we have considered only *act utilitarianism*. This makes moral judgements on the basis of the likely consequences of particular acts. There is also *rule utilitarianism*, which considers the overall benefit that will be gained by society if a particular rule is accepted. In other words, breaking a rule may benefit the individual concerned, but allowing that rule to be broken may itself have harmful consequences for society as a whole. This was a form of utilitarianism put forward by Mill. There are two forms of rule utilitarianism: strong and weak. A strong rule utilitarian will argue that it is never right to break a rule if that rule is to the benefit of society as a whole. A weak rule utilitarian will argue that there may be special cases in which breaking the rule is allowed, although the overall benefit to society of not doing so should also be taken into consideration. *Preference utilitarianism* is based on taking the preferences of all those who are involved into account. (In other words, the basis on which the 'good' is to be assessed in a particular situation is not impersonal, but takes into account the views and wishes of all concerned.)

Without doubt, utilitarianism is the most popular ethical theory today – and one that, to many people, is taken as common sense. It can be used to present radical moral challenges, as for example in the many books by Peter Singer (b. 1946), who argues that you should give equal consideration to others as to yourself. Thus, if you are able to prevent something bad from happening to another person, without thereby sacrificing anything morally significant to yourself, you should always do so. This has huge implications for tackling the issue of world poverty. He asks how one can morally justify retaining wealth in a situation where one is aware of the benefits it can offer others. The problem, of course, is that it seems 'natural' to care for yourself and your family and friends more than those who live at a distance and are not known personally; but it is difficult to give a rational justification for the resulting disparity in wealth and chances in life.

Insight

This touches on a huge issue – is reason 'natural'? Should a philosopher, motivated by reason, behave in ways that are noticeably different from people who are primarily motivated by their hormones and appetites? Plato clearly thought so – since he argued that only philosophers should rule. Singer implies it, in presenting a clear challenge to the radical selfishness that inhibits people from wholeheartedly doing what is in the common good.

Both utilitarianism and natural law appear to give rational and objective bases for deciding between right and wrong. Both of them, however, have presuppositions which are not accounted for by the theory itself. One depends on the idea of a rational final cause, the other on the acceptance of well-being of all as the highest good.

THE CATEGORICAL IMPERATIVE

We have already looked at the work of the eighteenth-century German philosopher Kant in connection with the radical distinction he made between things as we perceive them and things as they are in themselves, and the categories of space, time and causality by which we interpret our experience. But Kant also made an important contribution in the field of ethics. He sought to formulate a general and universally applicable principle by which the pure practical reason could distinguish right from wrong.

He started with the fact that people have a sense of moral obligation – what he calls the **categorical imperative**. In other words, we all know that there are things we 'should' do, irrespective of the consequences. He contrasted this with a 'hypothetical' imperative, which says what you need to do in order to achieve some chosen result. Thus:

> ▶ *You should work hard (categorical imperative).*
> ▶ *You should work hard if you want to succeed in this business (hypothetical imperative).*

Insight

Of course, you might want to argue that all categorical imperatives are really hypothetical imperatives in disguise – prompted by the unconscious programming of your childhood and social pressure.

Kant's aim was to express this experience of the categorical imperative in the form of universal principles of morality. These principles are generally referred to as the three forms of Kant's categorical imperative. He expressed them using various forms of words, but they amount to this:

> ▶ *Act only on that maxim (or principle) which you can – at the same time – will that it should become a universal law.*
> ▶ *Act in such a way as to treat people as ends and never as means.*
> ▶ *Act as though you were legislating for a kingdom of ends.*

The first of these expresses the idea that, whatever one wishes to do, one should be prepared for everyone else to act upon that same principle. If you are not prepared for the maxim of your action to become a universal rule, then you should not do it in your individual circumstances.

Here you have the most general of all principles, and one which, on the surface, has a long pedigree. It follows from the golden rule – to do to others only that which you would wish them to do to you.

One problem with this, however, is that there may be circumstances in which a person may want to kill or lie, without wishing for killing or lying to become universal. Suppose, for example, that the life of an innocent person is being threatened, and the only way of saving him or her is by lying, then a person would wish to do so. In this case, following Kant's argument, one would need to argue that you could wish that anyone in an *identical* situation should be free to lie, without thereby willing that anyone in *any* situation should be free to do so – and here we are back to the most general of all moral problems, how you relate a particular action and set of circumstances to the general moral principle.

The second form of the categorical imperative follows from the first. If you want to express your own moral autonomy, you should treat all others on the basis that they would want the same. So you should not treat them as 'means' to your own end, but as 'ends' in themselves. And the third form suggests that you should make your moral judgements as though you had responsibility for legislating in a kingdom in which everyone was an 'end', respected as an autonomous moral being.

An example

An article entitled 'Kant on Welfare' (Canadian Journal of Philosophy, June 1999), by Mark LeBar of the University of Ohio, illustrates the problem of applying Kant's universal principle that people should be treated as ends rather than means. It opens:

> *Contemporary debate over public welfare policy is often cast in Kantian terms. It is argued, for example, that respect for the dignity of the poor requires public aid, or that respect for their autonomy forbids it.*

This is a perfect example of where a general principle is not enough to establish whether the one or the other approach is morally right. We know what we might want in theory, what we do not know is the practical steps that are needed to achieve it; but it is in facing those practical steps that we are confronted with moral dilemmas.

Natural law, the assessment of results, and the sense of moral obligation: these three (sometimes singly, sometimes mixed together) form the basis of ethical argument. Natural law and a sense of moral obligation usually lead to the framing of general moral principles: that this or that sort of action is right or wrong. It is quite another matter whether it is fair to apply any such general rule to each and every situation. By the same token, the utilitarian assessment of results, although apparently more immediately practical, is always open to the ambiguity of fate, for we never really know the long-term consequences of what we do.

Insight

So no one basis for ethics is without its problems; sometimes one may seem more useful, sometimes another. Taken together, however, they do provide a broad range of rational strategies for dealing with moral dilemmas.

Absolute or relative morality?

If moral rules are absolute, then a particular action may be considered wrong no matter what the circumstances. So, for example, theft may be considered to be wrong. But what is theft? In one sense, the definition is straightforward: theft is the action of taking what belongs to another without that person's consent. The problem is that 'theft' is a term that may be used to interpret individual situations. Can we always be sure that it is the right term? If not, then is it right to treat an action as morally equal to 'theft', if that is not the way one or more of the people concerned see the matter.

One example of this dilemma might be 'mercy killing', where someone who is seriously ill and facing the prospect of a painful or lingering death is helped to die by a relative or close friend. If you take a view that there are moral absolutes, you may say: 'Murder is always wrong.' The next question then becomes: 'Is mercy killing the same thing as murder?' In other words, you start with absolute moral principles and then assess each particular situation in terms of which of these moral principles are involved (a process that is generally termed **casuistry**).

If you do not think that there are moral absolutes, you are more likely to start with particular situations and assess the intentions and consequences involved. In making such an assessment you bring to bear your general views about life and of the implications that various actions have on society as a whole.

In 1966, Joseph Fletcher published a book entitled *Situation Ethics*, which reflected a reaction against the perceived narrowness of traditional Christian morality at a time of rapid social change. Rather than simply obeying rules, he argued that one should always do what love required in each and every situation, and claimed that his view represented a fundamental feature of the Christian approach to life, as seen in the emphasis on love in *I Corinthians*, the rejection of Jewish legalism, or St Augustine's view that, if you love, what you want to do will be what is right.

By following the law of love and the demands of each situation, this approach suggested that it would sometimes be right to set aside conventional moral rule or go against the expectations of society. Although critics from a traditional position tended to accuse **situation ethics** of leading to moral anarchy, it was a genuine attempt to combine an overall moral principle (love) with a recognition of the uniqueness of every situation.

An example

To illustrate the complexities of applying general rules to particular situations, let us take one actual example of what is generally known as 'date rape'. This is the term used when a charge of rape is made against a person known to the 'victim' (itself a loaded term, pre-judging the outcome of the enquiry) and carried out in the course of a date. Date rape is a good example of the ambiguities that arise in legal and moral debates, since any straightforward description of the situation (sexual intercourse against the will of one partner or, in the particular case we shall be examining, attempted intercourse) is made more complicated by the circumstances in which it takes place, namely that the two people involved have chosen to be together socially.

A solicitor took a colleague to a ball at a London hotel. Each had assumptions about the nature of the relationship between them that was established by his inviting her to the ball and her accepting that invitation. She made a complaint against him, and he was charged with attempted rape. According to a newspaper report, he committed the offence after a night of dancing reels and drinking whisky and champagne with his 'victim', known throughout the trial as Miss X. She invited him to share a room with her at a friend's flat, undressed in front of him, and fell asleep. She alleged that she awoke to find him on top of her, wearing only his frilly cuffs and a green condom.

A newspaper report presented the argument that Miss X, by undressing down to her knickers in full view of a man with whom she had spent the evening, was behaving foolishly and should therefore accept some responsibility for what followed.

At the trial, the solicitor was found guilty of attempted rape and sentenced to three years in prison, later reduced to two years on appeal. He was released after serving half this sentence, on grounds of good conduct, but (at the time of his release) it was anticipated that he would face a disciplinary hearing before the Solicitors' Complaints Bureau, with a good chance that he would be prevented from continuing his legal career.

There are various matters that need be taken into consideration:

Rape and attempted rape are serious matters, involving violence (physical and/or emotional) towards the victim. That is the general principle; the question here is whether this particular situation should be classified as rape.

▶ *If one person invites another to share a room, is that invitation to be taken as at least implying that the idea of having some sort of sexual relationship is not out of the question (i.e. the invitation to share a room might not be a direct invitation to have sex, but might it not suggest that the matter is at least a possibility?).*

▸ *Does an act of sexual intercourse between two people who have voluntarily shared some time together (i.e. on a 'date') require a specific act of verbal consent?*

▸ *If no specific verbal or written consent is given (i.e. there is no exchange of contracts before clothes are removed – even between solicitors!) does a misinterpretation of the situation by one party constitute rape or attempted rape?*

▸ *Consider another possibility. If a woman were to invite a man back to her room after such an evening, hoping for sex (and under the impression that he was willing), but the man – perhaps because of an excess of whisky – were to fall asleep on the sofa, could she take a civil action against him for breach of implied promise?*

▸ *In such circumstances, is the action 'rape' or simply the result of misunderstanding?*

▸ *Can the act of undressing before another person be considered 'contributory negligence' if a rape or attempted rape ensues?*

Contrariwise, a person bringing the charge of date rape could argue:

▸ *Rape, violence and other forms of abuse often take place between people who know one another. The fact of their previous relationship does not lessen the seriousness of the action that takes place or is threatened.*

▸ *There can be no objective proof of misunderstanding. Claiming that you misunderstood something may be a later rationale of the situation, or an excuse.*

Becoming drunk may render a person incapable of behaving rationally or following previously accepted moral principles. That may *explain* subsequent behaviour, but it does not *excuse it*. Two drunken people together may act foolishly, and may regret their behaviour once sober, but that should not, in itself, mean that legal and moral considerations are suspended while they are under the influence. What is more, giving alcohol or drugs in order to render a person incapable of rational thought or behaviour, with the intention of taking advantage of that fact, is itself an act of abuse against that person.

The problem for ethics is that a unique situation may be understood in many different ways. The words chosen (attempted rape; victim) interpret, rather than describe, the event. Even if it is agreed that rape is *always* morally wrong, there remains the problem of deciding *exactly when that term should be used*. Hence there may need to be flexibility, even within a framework of absolute moral values.

That said, allowing each event to determine its own rules is likely to lead to moral and social chaos. As with so many issues in philosophy, the problem here is to know how the particular is related to the universal.

VALUES AND SOCIETY

There is a broader sense in which we need to be aware of relativity in ethics. Each society has its own particular way of life, along with the values and principles that are expressed in it. What might be considered right in one society may be thought wrong in another. A set of moral rules may be drawn up that are valid for a particular society, but cannot be applied universally.

However, if we live in a multicultural and complex society, we have to face the relativity of moral judgements. To this may be added the general sense in a postmodernist era (see p. 257) that everything depends upon taking, using and mixing the cultural, linguistic and mental ideas that we find around us. In such a situation, it is very difficult to try to impose uniform moral principles. Apart from anything else, the principles may tend to be rejected on the grounds of their origin – in the Catholic Church, in the case of natural law, or in the words of a long-dead, male philosopher, in the case of Kant.

Of the theories we have examined so far, preference utilitarianism gets round this problem most straightforwardly, since individual preferences (and therefore the cultural and social factors that give rise to them) are taken into the utilitarian assessment.

Kantian ethics has the greatest problem with relativism. On the one hand, it wants to establish universal moral principles (which relativism will not allow) and on the other it wants to treat each individual as an autonomous moral agent (of which relativism approves).

> ### Insight
> Kant may perhaps be forgiven for not appreciating the scale of the relativist challenge in a multicultural society, since he spent his whole life in his native Köningsberg.

But the real problem for many ethical thinkers today is with a full-blown relativism which simply refuses to accept any general moral norms. In other words, it becomes increasingly difficult to make any moral judgements that may not be challenged on the basis of the gender, race, religion or social position of the person making that judgement. Sensitivity to social norms or particular circumstances has always been a key feature of ethics – and even the much maligned process of 'casuistry' attempted to apply moral principles to particular situations rather than impose them. But at some point, if moral discussions are to be effective, there needs to be a shared set of values, and that implies that there must be a limit to relativism.

THE VALUES YOU CHOOSE

Is morality something discovered, or something created? Some approaches – natural law for example – clearly see morality as linked to objective facts about the world, moulding human morality to fit an overall sense of purpose. There is another approach, however, which suggests that we are free to choose the basis for our morality.

This approach is illustrated by Nietzsche, the title of one of whose books is *Beyond Good and Evil*. For Nietzsche, humankind has a responsibility to develop towards something higher, to say 'Yes!' to life and affirm the future. He saw both Christianity and democracy as fundamentally a morality for slaves, attempting to protect the weak at the expense of the strong, and thereby weakening the species. Rather, he looks to a master morality, deliberately choosing the *übermensch*, or higher man, as the meaning of the Earth.

Equally, existentialism (which we shall look at briefly in Chapter 8), in emphasizing person authenticity, tends to see morality in terms of the affirmation of the self. I shape my life by the choices I make, and take responsibility for that shaping. But choices have ethical implications; so existentialism gives a particularly self-referential approach to morality.

Virtue ethics

Rather than looking at actions, and asking if they are right or wrong, one could start by asking the basic question 'What does it mean to be a "good" person?', and develop this to explore the qualities and virtues that make up the 'good' life. This approach had been taken first by Aristotle who linked the displaying of certain qualities with the final end or purpose of life.

As it developed in the 1950s, this approach appealed to feminist thinkers, who considered the traditional ethical arguments to have been influenced by particularly male ways of approaching life, based on rights and duties, whereas they sought a more 'feminine' approach and a recognition of the value of relationships and intimacy.

Virtue ethics was also seen as *'naturalistic'*, in that it moved away from the idea of simply obeying rules, to an appreciation of how one might express one's own fundamental nature, and thus fulfil one's potential as a human being.

Virtue ethics raises some basic questions:

▶ *Do we have a fixed* **essence**? *Are there particular masculine or feminine qualities that give rise to virtues appropriate to each sex? Or is our nature the product of our surroundings and upbringing?*

▶ *If our nature has been shaped by factors over which we have no control (e.g. the culture into which we have been born, traumatic experiences in childhood)* **are we responsible for our actions**?

▶ *How should we relate the expression of an individual's virtues to the actual needs of society?*

▶ *How are you able to decide between different ways of expressing the same virtue? For example, a sense of love and compassion might lead one person to help someone who is seriously ill to die, yet another might find that love and compassion lead them to struggle to keep that same person alive. In some way, you need to fall back on other ethical theories if you want to assess the actions that spring from particular virtues.*

Comment

Notice that beneath some of these 'virtue ethics' approaches lie the basic questions raised by Aristotle about the end or purpose of human life. Whereas 'natural law' generally examines an action in terms of its 'final cause', virtue ethics examines human qualities in terms of their overall place within human life, and the appropriate ways in which they may be expressed.

The social contract

Ethics may be based on social contract. In other words, morality may follow agreements to abide by certain rules, made between people to limit what they are able to do, in order to benefit both themselves and society as a whole. Most would accept that there needs to be some compromise between the freedom of the individual and the overall good of society and its need for security.

Social contract theories apportion *responsibilities* to individuals and to the mechanisms of government by which society is organized. In other words, they set out what can reasonably be expected of people in terms of their relationship with others. They also set out the *rights* to which individuals are entitled. Many areas of applied ethics have focused on rights and responsibilities, especially in the area of professional conduct. For example, they might ask what responsibility a doctor has to his patients, to the society within which he or she practises, and to the development of medicine – and from this a code of professional conduct can be drawn up. Equally, it can ask what basic expectations a person should have in terms of the way in which he or she should be treated by other people or by the state. This has led to various declarations of human rights, which provide a touchstone for whether a society is behaving justly.

Comment

Discussion of rights and responsibilities tends to reflect both absolutist views – as, for example, in claiming that people should enjoy basic human rights, irrespective of who they are – and also utilitarian ones, in that the benefits that might come from agreements about people's social responsibilities are often assessed in terms of the overall happiness of society.

Although rights and responsibilities are key features of ethical debate, the actual agreements which form the basis of social contract ethics will be examined in the next chapter, which is concerned with political philosophy, since they follow from questions about justice and the right ordering of society.

Applied ethics

Throughout history, philosophers have sought to apply their ideas, and this has been most obvious in the field of ethics. Applied ethics started to come to the fore again during the last three decades of the twentieth century, after a number of years during which philosophers had been rather preoccupied by linguistic questions about the meaning and nature of ethical statements.

There is no scope in an introductory text of this sort to do more than point to some of the major areas within which ethics is applied today, but those interested in following up this aspect of ethics will find that there are a huge number of books covering the different professions and issues.

Professional ethics has been concerned principally with standards of conduct expected of members of the professions and also with drawing up guidelines for those situations where there are difficult moral choices to be made. The medical, nursing and legal professions most obviously provide a whole range of moral dilemmas that need to be examined.

Sometimes advances in technology raise issues that require ethical examination. The rise of information technology, for example, raises issues about privacy, identity theft, and the limits to what can be done with stored information. Should the state be responsible for, and have control of, whatever data it manages to gather on its citizens? Should I have a right to see what information is held about me? Of course, issues of privacy have been around for a long time, but they are brought into sharper focus by the ability to store and retrieve data in digital form. Equally, genetic manipulation of the food we eat is an old issue presented in a very new form. These are matters that affect everyone, and are therefore not limited to those who work in the relevant industry.

Business ethics is an important and growing area of interest, with the conflict between those who favour a market-led approach and those who want more political and social control. Equally, media ethics is relevant to everyone, since assumptions are made about the veracity of news items, the morality of public humiliation or deception, and whether the media should have social and political responsibilities.

A huge and increasingly important set of applied ethical issues concern the environment. The debates about global warming highlight a clash of interest between the potential harm done to the global environment and the economic benefits of increasing industrialization. It spans the globe, and therefore touches on the broader economic and social issues about sustainable development and the obligations of richer nations to help poorer ones. And that, of course, touches on the absolutely crucial issue of the existence of abject poverty in a world of plenty, an issue highlighted starkly by Peter Singer, along with that of our treatment of other species.

Insight

You will find that most arguments in this area are fundamentally utilitarian, with a clash of interest between the short-term economic benefits to the relative few and the potential long-term benefits to all.

And there is, of course, the huge issue of the morality of warfare, raised again in recent years, particularly by debates over the justice of launching the second Iraq war and over the aims, human cost, and likely outcome of the war in Afghanistan. Traditionally, this application of ethics has been divided into issues over when it is right to go to war, and how wars should be fought, once they have started. Hence morality examines both the right of a nation to defend itself against a real or perceived threat, and the types of weapons that are used in battle.

Note

Ethics is a huge subject, both in terms of the range of ethical theories and the way in which these may be applied to moral and social issues. It has provided the impetus for much work in

(Contd)

philosophy as a whole, and is the single largest area of study within departments of philosophy (judging by the number of papers published). It is particularly valuable as an area of philosophical study, since the benefits of clear thinking, analysis and the clarification of concepts and presuppositions can be seen to have immediate relevance to practical areas of life.

Faced with the dilemma of whether or not to turn off the life-support machine of someone in a deep coma and unable to recover, one starts to ask not just about the ethical status of euthanasia, but also what it means to be a human being, what constitutes human life, and therefore whether the person whose body is being maintained by a machine can be said to be living in any meaningful way.

For further treatment of some of these issues see *Understand Ethics* in this series. Readers wanting to examine the ethical issues in particular professions should move on to the very extensive literature now available in this area.

10 THINGS TO REMEMBER

1 *You cannot derive an 'ought' from an 'is'.*

2 *Moral responsibility implies freedom of action.*

3 *Descriptive ethics simply says what happens.*

4 *Normative ethics argues for what should happen.*

5 *Emotivism and prescriptivism attempt to avoid the positivist claim that ethics is meaningless.*

6 *Natural law is concerned with a rational interpretation of nature, not a description of nature.*

7 *Utilitarianism argues in favour of the greatest benefit for the greatest number.*

8 *Kant attempted to frame universal moral principles based on pure practical reason.*

9 *Ethical values may be relative to social norms and may be created rather than discovered.*

10 *The practical application of ethical principles is the most popular area of philosophy today.*

7

Political philosophy

In this chapter you will learn:
- *about the social contract and other political theories*
- *about how society changes and progresses*
- *about key issues of justice, fairness and human rights.*

From time to time, politicians speak of 'getting back to basics', or of the fundamental principles of democracy, or socialism, or human rights, or international law. They seek to explain and justify particular legislation, or the decision to take some action in terms of the good of society as a whole, or concepts of justice.

But what are the 'basics' to which politicians might choose to return?

▶ *Are they the bases upon which a political system is established? If so, what are they?*
▶ *Does it mean 'back to basic values'? Does that imply, for example, conventional 'family values'? Or might they be the values of capitalism, or socialism? Or might it refer to a return to the conventional attitudes of some ideal, past age?*
▶ *But what are the basic human needs? Does everyone need or expect the same sort of things from a government?*

- *More generally, what is the 'basis' of civilized life?*
- *What basic values, if any, can be agreed on? Is a basis something you start from and then develop, or is it something fixed and unchanging to which you need to return from time to time?*

Starting from the phrase 'back to basics', we enter into some of the issues with which political philosophy is concerned. Set out in more abstract terms these concerns are:

- *the concepts of freedom, justice, liberty and equality*
- *the role of the state*
- *the relationship between the state and the individual*
- *the nature of authority*
- *the status of law*
- *the role of power*
- *human rights.*

Only individuals?

Does the state exist? Is there any such thing as society? If I were suddenly to declare that the USA did not exist, I would be thought insane, but is it that obvious? There are two ways of looking at individuals and society:

1 *Society, or the nation, is a reality over and above its individual citizens. It is 'real' in the sense that it can exert its power over them, forcing them to take part in a war, claiming taxes from them, imposing laws on them. Patriotism depends on the idea that the nation is real, worth fighting for.*
2 *There is no such thing as society. There are just individuals who decide on rules and regulations for their mutual benefit and who band together to do things that are beyond the abilities of any one person or family. In this case, Great Britain or the USA are just names: they have no reality other than the millions of people who happen to live in those parts*

of the world, and the various institutions by which they organize their lives.

If you tend towards the first of these, you might take a further step and claim that individuals can only exist as part of larger social groups. You could argue, for example:

▶ *You are part of a family and circle of friends: you are a mother, father, child or friend by virtue of your relationships. Without other people you would be none of these things.*
▶ *You speak a language that is not of your own devising. You share in a common store of words and thoughts. Without society, there would be no language. You have 'rights' as an individual only because they are given to you by society.*

Therefore, although you would continue to be a human being, you would not really be an 'individual', with a name, rights, a language and a stock of inherited ideas, without society.

In other words

▶ *Confronted by a cat, a mouse cannot argue its case for the right to life, liberty and happiness.*
▶ *Individual rights or social obligations are not discovered in nature, they are devised by society.*
▶ *Without society there would be no rights, no obligations, no laws, no morality.*

The idea of the individual or citizen is closely linked to that of society or the state. Each is defined with reference to the other. A central issue for the philosophy of politics is to find an acceptable balance between these two things. Individualism; democracy; totalitarianism; socialism; cultural imperialism; regionalism; internationalism: these are all about the balance between individuals or groups and the larger social wholes of which they are a part.

▶ *Within the European Union, do you look to the overall benefit of a unified political and monetary system, or do you emphasize the needs of (or threat to) local decision making by individual states?*

▶ *Is the United Nations an emerging global 'state' of the future, within which individual nations subsume their own interests for the sake of a greater good? Or is it simply a group of individual nations banded together for mutual benefit, within which each will seek to gain as much for itself as is compatible with retaining membership?*

▶ *What does it mean to be a good member of a team or a company?*

Insight

Margaret Thatcher, at the Conservative Party Conference in 1987, famously declared 'And, you know, there's no such thing as society. There are individual men and women and there are families. And no government can do anything except through people, and people must look after themselves first.' Such a view minimizes the role of government and puts individuals centre-stage.

The social contract

Self-preservation is a fundamental human need. Born in 1588, Thomas Hobbes knew first hand the traumas of civil war in England and used such a lawless and dangerous state as the starting point for his political theory. In Chapter 13 of *Leviathan*, published in 1651, he considers what life is like when a person can rely only on his own strength for protection:

> In such condition, there is no place for industry, because the fruit thereof is uncertain; and consequently no culture of the earth; no navigation, nor use of the commodities that may be imported by sea; no commodious building, no instruments of moving or

removing such things as require much force; no knowledge of the face of the earth; no account of time; no arts; no letters; no society; and, which is worst of all, continual fear and danger of violent death; and the life of man solitary, poor, nasty, brutish, and short.

Hobbes considered that the need for self-preservation was so basic to human life, that (using a 'natural law' form of argument) reason could show that the basis for political science was the preservation of life. He also showed, in the passage just quoted, that society depends upon personal security, and that without it civilization is impossible.

In this situation, Hobbes argued that people would band together for their mutual protection, and would set up a ruler who would maintain order. The value of the state is seen in its ability to protect and benefit the individuals of which it is comprised. His political theory, the start of what is called the 'social contract' tradition, springs from this need for self-preservation. Hobbes believed, however, that the ruler so appointed should be given absolute power, and that only by doing so could the security of the state be maintained.

John Locke (1632–1704) argued from a similar starting point. He saw the laws imposed by a ruler on individuals as based on the need for the preservation of life and private property within the state, and defence from foreign threats. But he went beyond Hobbes, arguing that the people who entered into their social contract should have the right, if the rulers did not benefit them, to replace them with others. In other words, he argued for a representative democracy, with rulers accountable to those who have put them in power. Thus we have a constitutional government, where rulers have power, but only to the extent that they are given it by the people, and within principles that are set out within a constitution.

Such political systems are based on a social contract; on the agreement between people that they shall act together for their mutual benefit. The problem arises over exactly what is to the benefit of society, and who is to decide it. To what extent can an individual, on the basis of a social contract, act on behalf of all? Do all have to agree before some action is taken? On what basis is there to be arbitration between conflicting interests. Locke is clear that decisions must reflect the wishes of a majority, and any minority must accept that judgement:

> *Every man, by consenting with others to make one body politic under one government, puts himself under an obligation to every one of that society to submit to the determination of the majority, and to be concluded by it; or else this original compact, whereby he with others incorporates into one society, would signify nothing, and be no compact if he be left free and under no other ties than he was in before in the state of Nature.*

The Second Treatise of Government, Chapter 13, section 97

Thus a government can act as long as it has the consent of a majority. But what if a government seeks to act in a way which the rulers consider to be in the interests of the people, even if that is not what people as individuals actually want?

The general will

Jean-Jacques Rousseau (1712–78), was a Swiss philosopher who, in spite of having little formal education and a hard and colourful personal life, produced ideas about democracy that were to be hugely influential, particularly at the time of the French Revolution.

Rousseau, recognizing that all existing states were imperfect, sought to start from first principles and establish the basis of a legitimate political system. Like Hobbes and Locke, he looked back to man in a state of nature but, unlike them, he thought that in such a natural state people's needs would be few and relatively easily satisfied, and would be unlikely to lead to conflict.

By contrast, once society becomes established, people enclose property and deprive others of the use of it. The basic requirements of food and shelter become commodities which people have to get through barter, and many are therefore reduced to misery. With private property, inequality increases and leads to civil strife. Thus, where Hobbes and Locke saw private property as a natural right to be defended, Rousseau saw it as something artificially imposed by society. He saw society as tending to corrupt natural man rather than improve him.

Rousseau presents a form of social contract, but one that differs significantly from that set out by Hobbes or Locke. A central issue for Rousseau is how an individual can retain his or her freedom, while at the same time accepting the terms of a social contract, and the requirement that an individual is bound by the wishes of society as a whole. He does this through the idea of the 'general will'. He argues that an individual must give himself or herself totally, including all rights, to the whole community. The general will is sovereign, and individuals find their own freedom by conforming to it.

For Rousseau, natural freedom is, in fact, a slavery to individual passions. By contrast, to set aside one's individual, personal will, and to accept the general will, is to discover one's higher aspirations and moral freedom. There will be occasions when individuals will oppose the general will, but on those occasions the individual concerned should be forced to accept it, for the good of all.

In any political system, someone has to decide how general laws should be applied to individual situations. Rousseau held that there should be a legislator, someone who would know instinctively what the general will was and be able to apply it.

In general, one might say that, whereas for Hobbes and Locke, individuals are freely able to decide what is in their own best interests (although sometimes required to set these interests aside for the benefit of the majority), for Rousseau, individuals are not able to decide what is best, and therefore are required to accept what is deemed to be best by the general will – in other words, by the state.

Comment

The implications of this aspect of Rousseau's thinking are enormous. A state can carry out the most drastic action (decapitating the aristocracy, eliminating whole classes of people in state purges) on the basis of carrying out the 'general will'. The problem lies in the inability to challenge the 'general will' and therefore the possibility that what is being done is not in fact the will of the people. In the twentieth century, the examples of Stalin's Russia, China under Mao and Cambodia under Pol Pot all illustrate the power of the state to claim to act for the benefit of all, while actually perpetrating state terror.

Marx and materialism

Karl Marx (1818–83) has been an enormously influential thinker. Indeed, one cannot start to describe the history of the twentieth century without reference to Marxism and the communist regimes that sprang from it. Born in Germany, he moved to Paris when the newspaper he was editing was forced to close. Expelled from both Paris and then Brussels, he finally settled in London. His most important book, *Das Kapital* (1867), predicts that capitalism has within it the seeds of its own destruction and will give way to socialism.

Marx argued that religion, morality, political ideas and social structures were fundamentally rooted in economics, particularly the production and distribution of goods. People have basic needs which must be fulfilled in order for them to live, and society becomes more and more sophisticated in order to produce the goods and services to meet those needs. He therefore interpreted history in economic terms, as shaped by the struggle between different social classes. The bourgeoisie confronts the proletariat;

employers facing employees as once landowners faced their peasants. Individual actions are judged by the way in which they contribute to the class struggle, and the actions of a class as a whole is seen in a broader context of the movement of society.

In terms of the history of philosophy, Marx was influenced by Hegel (1770–1831) who saw the lives of individuals as bound up with the tide of history, which itself was unfolding by a rational process. Like Hegel, Marx saw reality as working itself out through a process of change. Hegel had introduced the idea of a 'dialectic': first you have a thesis, then in response to this you have the opposite (an antithesis), and bringing these two together you get a synthesis. But for Hegel, this process was non-material, leading to a harmonious awareness of the Geist, or spirit of the age, in which everyone freely accepts the interest of the whole of society.

For Marx, by contrast, the process of dialectic is material. It is the economic conditions under which the classes live and work that produce the urge to change, as a result of which the existing economic system is overthrown through a revolution and a new system is set up, but that, in turn, leads to further class confrontation, and so on. Marx looked towards the achievement of a classless society, where there would be no more confrontation, but where working people would own the means of production and distribution. This classless society would therefore be characterized by economic justice, in which each benefited from his or her own labour.

This was linked to his view of the fulfilment of the human individual. Marx argued that, in a capitalist system, an individual who works for a wage, producing something from which someone else is going to make a profit, becomes alienated from that working situation. He or she cannot exercise true creativity or humanity, but becomes an impersonal 'thing', a machine whose sole purpose in life is production, a means of making 'capital'. He saw this process leading to more and more wealth being concentrated in the hands of a small number of 'bourgeoisie', with the working proletariat sinking into poverty. This, he believed, would eventually lead to the overthrow of the capitalist system by the workers acting together. He believed that, with the advent of the classless society, each individual would be able to develop to his or her full potential.

Marx has things to say about the nature of history, of work, of the self, of political institutions and of social classes, but he is also a prime example of the way in which a philosopher can influence the course of history. It is difficult to study Marx without being aware of the global impact of Marxist ideology in the twentieth century. The decline of communism in the last decades of the twentieth century, and capitalism's failure to self-destruct in the way he predicted, will obviously be taken into account by anyone who studies his political philosophy. Contrariwise, it is difficult to overestimate the general impact of his thinking, particularly, perhaps, in the view that politics is based on economics.

Insight

Although Marx's main work was *Das Kapital* (1867), it may be easier to approach him first through his earlier works, particularly *The German Ideology* (1846) and *The Communist Manifesto* (1848).

Notice that Marx (following Rousseau and, indeed, Hegel) saw the individual as subsuming his or her interests for the benefit of the wider group. The individual acts as a representative of his or her class or nation, and those actions are judged by whatever is deemed to be right by that larger social group. This is in contrast to the tradition which stems from Hobbes and Locke, where the emphasis is on the individual. We shall see in the next section that this divide is still found in political philosophy, as reflected in the differing views of justice taken by two modern philosophers, Rawls and Nozick.

Comment

Mikhail Gorbachev, leader of the Soviet Union from 1985–1991, writing in 2009 to mark the twentieth anniversary of the fall of the Berlin Wall, commented, 'The real achievement we can

celebrate is the fact that the twentieth century marked the end
of totalitarian ideologies, in particular those that were based
on utopian beliefs.' (*The Guardian*, 31 October 2009, page 35).
Looking back on the terrible suffering that such ideologies caused
throughout the twentieth century, one is reminded of just how
important and relevant political philosophy can be – get it wrong
and swathes of humankind bear the burden.

Justice

The idea of justice is fundamental to political philosophy. If
people are to band together for mutual protection, if they are to
enter into social contracts, if they are to set their own interests
aside, they need to be persuaded that the society within which
they live is based on principles that are just. But what constitutes
political justice?

We shall look at ideas of justice presented by three philosophers,
one ancient and two modern.

PLATO

The question 'What is justice?' dominates one of the greatest
works of philosophy, Plato's *Republic*. In this book (presented as a
dialogue between Socrates and the representatives of contemporary
schools of thought), various answers are proposed and rejected,
as, for example, the popular but rather cynical view that justice
is whatever is in the interest of the stronger! Plato recognizes
that human nature can be deeply selfish, and that – given the
opportunity to act with absolute impunity – people will generally
seek their own benefit rather than that of others, or of society as
a whole, and also explores the idea (later to be developed by the
'social contract' theory) that people need to be restrained for the
good of all. But what is the value of justice in itself?

Socrates considers the various classes of people that make up the city, and argues that each class offers particular virtues, but that justice is found in the fact that each class performs its own task. In the same way, the individual soul is divided into three parts – mind, spirit and appetite – and that justice for the individual consists in the balance, with each part performing its own task for the benefit of that individual.

Justice is seen in the harmony and proper functioning of each part of society, and Plato wanted the rulers of his *Republic* to be philosophers, seeking only the truth rather than their own self-interest. This, he argued, would be necessary if justice was to be established for all rather than in the interests of a particular section of the population.

Every philosophy needs to be seen against the background of its particular time and society, and Plato is no exception. His concept of a state ruled by philosophers, seeking a balance between elements in society and in the self, with priority given to the intellectual faculty, is not easily translatable into a modern political context. What is clear, however, is that justice (for Plato) is seen neither in equality (he never envisaged a society of equals) nor in sectional interest (he rejected the idea that it was the interest of the stronger), but in a balance in which different people and classes, each doing what is appropriate for them, work together for the common good.

RAWLS (JUSTICE AS FAIRNESS)

In *A Theory of Justice* (1972) John Rawls considers (as a thought experiment) a situation in which a group of people come together to decide the principles upon which their political association should operate. In other words, they set about forming a social contract. But he adds one further important criterion: that they should forget everything about themselves as individuals. They do not know if they are poor or wealthy, men or women. They do not know their race or their position within society. They come together simply as individuals, nothing more. He therefore seeks by this means to establish principles that:

> **free and rational persons concerned to further their own interests would accept in an initial position of equality as defining the fundamental terms of their association.**

p. 11

In other words, they are concerned to benefit themselves, but do not know who they are. By this means, Rawls hopes to achieve justice, for people will seek to legislate in a way that will benefit themselves, whoever they eventually turn out to be.

Rawls argues that such a group would require two principles:

1 **Liberty:** *Each person should have equal rights to as extensive a set of basic liberties as possible, as long as that does not prevent others from having a similar set of fundamental liberties.*
2 **Distribution of resources:** *Given that there are social inequalities, Rawls argues that the distribution of resources should be such that the least advantaged in society receive the greatest benefit.*

This is justice based on 'fairness'. Rawls argues that it is fair to grant everyone equal freedom and opportunity, and that, if there is to be inequality at all, it should only be allowed on the grounds that it benefits those who have the least advantages in life. The task of society (in addition to the basic protection of individuals who have come together to form it) is, according to Rawls, that it should organize the fair sharing out of both material and social benefits.

Not all philosophers would agree with Rawls' attempt to reduce inequalities. In the nineteenth century, Nietzsche's view was that the strong should not be restrained because of the needs of the weak. His views were that democracy and Christianity had a negative effect, weakening the human species by seeking special advantage for those who are weak or poor and handicapped in some way. By contrast, he looked towards an *übermensch* – an 'over-man' or 'beyond-man' – expressing the idea of striving to be something more. For Nietzsche, man is something that has to be overcome: a starting point from which we move forward and upward.

Insight

Natural selection suggests that competition, rather than fairness and consideration for others, is the basis of evolutionary advance. Applied to human society this evolutionary perspective has a sad history, from Spencer's 'survival of the fittest' to Eugenics, ideas of *racial* superiority, ethnic cleansing, and – under the Nazis for example – to genocide.

But there is a more general criticism of his approach. A little earlier in this chapter we looked at the basic division between those who would give priority to the individual (and for whom the state should have a minimal role), who may go so far as to argue that the state does not exist, and those who give priority to the state, so that it is only in the context of society that individuals come to their full potential. Let us examine Rawls' theory from this perspective.

By making the people who come together to establish the principles of society forget who they are, they also relinquish all that they might naturally have gained and achieved. The successful person is made to forget all that he or she has gained by hard work, and to opt for an equal share of the pooled resources for fear of finding out that he or she was, in fact, the poorest.

In theory this might establish a society where all are offered fair shares. But could it work like that in the real world? It could be argued that there never was, and never will be, an 'original position' from which to devise the rules of a society. All actual legal systems, and all ideas of justice, are framed within, and grow out of, an historical context.

Another criticism of this approach is made by Ronald Dworkin. He argues that, before you can ask 'What is justice?' you need to ask the prior question 'What kind of life should men and women lead? What counts as excellence in a human being?' He argues that the liberal position, as given by Rawls, does not take this into consideration. Rawls' treatment of individuals does not depend on *anything about them as individuals*.

For reflection

If every inequality is allowed only on the basis that it benefits the least well off (Rawls' view), there is little chance that excellence will be developed, since every facility offered for the development of excellence is likely to increase rather than decrease the gap between the most able and the least able. How can such a theory avoid bland mediocrity?

NOZICK (JUSTICE AS ENTITLEMENT)

If the purpose of society is to protect the life, liberty and property of individuals, then each person should be enabled to retain those things which are rightly theirs. A society which, in the name of establishing equality, redistributes that wealth is in fact depriving an individual of the very protection which led to the formation of society in the first place.

This approach to the question of justice is taken by Robert Nozick. In *Anarchy, State and Utopia* (1974), he argued that it is wrong for the state to take taxes from individuals or force them to contribute to a health service that benefits others. It infringes their liberty to gain wealth and retain it. For Nozick, it is perfectly right to give what you have to another person if you so choose, but not to demand that another person give to you. On this social theory, voluntary contributions are welcomed, but enforced taxes are not. He argues that justice is a matter of the entitlement of individuals to retain their 'holdings' – wealth that they have gained legitimately.

An important feature of Nozick's case is that, at any one time, the actual wealth that a person owns is related to history: that of the individual (through having worked for years, for example) or that of his or her family (through inheritance). In practice, however, it is not always easy to establish that all wealth has been gained legitimately. Land which has been in a family for generations may originally have been gained by the most dubious of means.

Nozick also argues, against those that seek equality, that even if people were made equal, they would immediately start trading, and would quickly establish new inequalities.

In other words

▶ *Private property is theft! (This implies that all property should belong to the state, or ultimately to the global community.) Justice demands redistribution on the basis of need.*

Or

▶ *Redistribution is theft! (This implies that each individual has the right to that which is lawfully gained.) Justice demands that each should develop to his or her potential, unhampered by false notions of equality.*

In the name of liberty, it is tempting to suggest that politics should be morally neutral. In other words, there should be equal scope and equal respect for all views, values and beliefs, and that politicians should keep out of issues of personal choice and morality. The danger with this is that politics may become a mechanism for ensuring that everyone is happy, but does not address the moral questions about what should constitute the good life. But where fundamental values differ, agreement on political ends is very difficult to establish. Politics should therefore remain open to moral discussion and debate. This is argued strongly by, for example, Michael Sandel, who teaches a course on 'Justice' at Harvard, and who is concerned that politics should not lose sight of the fundamental questions about what it means to lead a good life. His argument that political argument today is morally impoverished is set out in his recent book *Justice: What's the Right Thing to Do?*, Allen Lane, 2009.

Freedom and law

Freedom in this context means something rather different from the 'freedom/determinism' debate outlined earlier. In that case, the determinist argument was that everything depends on prior causes and may (in theory) be predicted scientifically. Hence we are never free to choose what we do, even if our lack of understanding of the determining causes means that we retain the illusion of freedom.

Here, the debate is about the degree of freedom that the individual has a right to exercise within society, given the impact that such freedom may have upon the freedom of others: freedom to act within certain parameters set out by the law. Once a person acts outside those parameters, society, through the police and the courts, can step in and impose a penalty on the 'outlaw'.

Taking a utilitarian view of morality (see Chapter 6), J. S. Mill argued that in the case of some private matter, where an action and its consequences affect only the individual concerned, there should be absolute freedom. The law should step in to restrain that freedom only when the consequences of an action affects other people. This is the common-sense basis for much legislation.

An example

If smoking cigarettes were a private activity, with consequences,
however harmful, suffered only by the person who chose to smoke,
there would be no need to legislate against it. The law may step in to
prohibit smoking in public places if:

▶ *it constitutes a fire hazard or*
▶ *non-smokers want to be free to breathe air that is not filled
  with smoke.*

Legislation can be justified on a simple utilitarian basis. The law
protects other people from the effects of an individual's action.

But should society as a whole, through its medical services, be
required to pay the price for an individual's decision to smoke, take
drugs, or practise a dangerous sport? Here the law has to balance a
utilitarian moral position with the preservation of individual human
rights.

The idea of individual liberty has been of fundamental importance
in modern political thinking, responding perhaps to the experience
of horrific excesses of twentieth-century totalitarian systems in
Nazi Germany, the Soviet Union and elsewhere. Karl Popper's
book *The Open Society and its Enemies*, published in the 1940s,
made the issue of freedom central. In the 1960s, much political
debate centred on how to maintain social order and yet allow
maximum freedom. Rawls' theory of justice may be seen as
an attempt to justify liberal views of society, and in which the

redistribution of wealth is a logical choice of free individuals. Rawls took the view that, provided all the essentials of life were met (a presupposition of his theory), people would choose freedom rather than, for example, the chance of getting more wealth. This view has been challenged by Ronald Dworkin and others, who think that some people would rather gamble that they would win, rather than play it safe and follow the liberal and egalitarian views of Rawls.

HUMAN RIGHTS

In an ideal society, the law would always be framed on the basis of the agreement between free individuals, and every person would be equally free to enjoy basic human rights. There is, however, a difference between having a set of rights and being free to exercise those rights. In general, even though rights are given irrespective of age and capacities, it is sometimes necessary for the exercise of those rights to be curtailed:

▶ **On grounds of age.** *Children have rights, and are protected by the law from exploitation by others, but cannot, for example, buy cigarettes or alcohol, drive a car or fly a plane. These limits are imposed because below the relevant age the child is considered unable to take a responsible decision and parents, or society, therefore impose a restriction on the child's freedom.*
▶ **On grounds of insanity.** *Those who are insane and are liable to be a danger to themselves or to others are also restrained.*
▶ **On grounds of lack of skill.** *Flying a plane or driving a car (other than on private property) without a licence is illegal. This can be justified on utilitarian grounds, since others in the air or on the roads could be in danger. Equally, to pose as a surgeon and perform operations without the appropriate qualification is illegal. Without the public acknowledgement that a person has the required skills, many such tasks would endanger the lives or well-being of others.*

Rights are also taken from those who break the law, for example:

▶ *through prison sentences*
▶ *through legal injunctions to stop actions being carried out or to prevent one person from approaching another, or visiting a particular place. This may be taken retrospectively, if a person has already broken a law, or proactively, for example, to stop publication of a potentially damaging story in a newspaper.*

In all these cases, a person retains his or her fundamental rights, but cannot exercise them, on the basis that to do so would be against the interests of society as a whole. This approach is based on the idea of social contract, where the laws of society are made by mutual agreement, and the loss of certain freedoms are exchanged for the gain of a measure of social protection. It may also therefore be justified on utilitarian grounds.

But Dworkin argues that a 'right' is something that an individual can exercise even if it goes against the general welfare. After all, there is no point in my claiming a right to do something, if nobody would ever want to challenge it. A right is something that I can claim in difficult circumstances.

This means that (at least in the immediate context) rights cannot be justified on utilitarian grounds. They do not necessarily offer the greatest good to the greatest number. Rights are claimed by minorities. Rights are established by social contract (for example, within the US Constitution or the United Nations) and represent a basic standard of treatment that an individual can expect to receive by virtue of the social and legal system within which those rights are set down.

In other words

▶ *Individual freedom needs to be balanced against the needs of society as a whole. The morality of exercising individual freedom may be assessed on utilitarian grounds.*

> ▶ *Human rights represent the basic freedoms and opportunities that an individual can expect to receive from society. They may sometimes be withheld if their exercise would pose a threat to the individual or society as a whole.*
> ▶ *The exercise of human rights cannot always be justified on utilitarian grounds. It is important for an individual to be able to claim a right, even if it is not to the benefit of the majority.*

Feminism

It may not have escaped the notice of many readers that almost all the philosophers mentioned so far in this book are male. The agenda, both philosophically and politically, appears to have been set by men, and the rational and legal approaches to many issues seem particularly appropriate to a male intellectual environment, but may be thought to ignore the distinctive contribution of women.

Feminism, therefore, introduces the issue of gender into the concepts of justice, fairness and rights, pointing out those areas where men have sought to exclude or marginalize women. A key work in the campaign on behalf of women was Mary Wollstonecraft's *A Vindication of the Rights of Women* (1792), where she argued for equality on the grounds of intellect. This did not imply that there should be no distinction between men and women, however, and she was quite happy to see women and men play very different roles within society. In fact, she saw women as primarily contributing from within the home.

In the nineteenth century, the key issue for the feminist perspective on British political life was the campaign for women to receive the vote. This was not an issue presented only by women, for it received the support of J. S. Mill, the utilitarian philosopher.

Feminism has generally sought to present an historical critique of the social injustices suffered by women, suggesting that gender bias is not simply a matter of individual prejudice, but is inherent in social and political institutions. On a broader front it has also opened up discussion on the relationship between the sexes, the distinctive role of women, and the ethical implications of gender. Notable here is the contribution of Simone De Beauvoir (1908–86), the existentialist philosopher. Her book *The Second Sex* (1949) opened up a serious consideration of the myths and roles that women were expected to play within society, as mothers, wives, lovers and so on, and of their place in society. Perhaps her most famous quote 'One is not born, but rather becomes a woman' suggested that the roles of womanhood were imposed upon women (by a male-dominated society), rather than being essential to her nature.

Insight

De Beauvoir's key complaint is that, in a society shaped by men, women are seen as 'relative beings', existing only in relationship to men. The male philosopher Immanuel Kant would no doubt agree with her, since he argued that everyone should be treated as an end rather than a means, autonomous and independent.

Some conclusions

The problem with political philosophy (and perhaps with all philosophy) is that it works with abstract and generalized concepts, and seldom does justice to the actual situation within which people find themselves. The world is complex. Wealth in one place is gained at the price of poverty in another. A 'free' market will lead some to success, others to failure. Laws that benefit those who want to retain their wealth are seen by those who are the least privileged as an excuse for continued greed.

What we see in the philosophy of politics is an examination of the principles upon which legal and political systems are founded. Human rights, justice, fairness, social contract, democracy – these are all terms that can be examined by the philosopher in order to clarify exactly what they imply. But such ideas arise as a result of more general concepts about human life, its meaning and its value. Political philosophy is therefore the practical application of a fundamental understanding of the value, meaning and purpose of human life.

Once you get beyond Hobbes' view that society is constructed for mutual protection, once you say that it is right to organize society in a particular way, not just that it is necessary for survival to do so, then you imply ideas of justice, of freedom, of equality, of the valuation of human life, and of the place of human life within an understanding of the world as a whole.

A general point

If we divide philosophy up into sections, each dealing with a limited number of issues, it is sometimes possible to forget the more fundamental questions as we concentrate on particular issues of politics or the law. But philosophy grows and develops as an organic whole:

▶ *How you organize society depends on your basic view of ethics.*
▶ *Ethics in turn depends on your view of the self and of what it means to be an individual human being.*
▶ *'The self' has implications for the more general questions about the meaning and value of life that are explored in the philosophy of religion.*
▶ *Religious issues arise out of the fundamental questions about life – questions such as 'What can I know for certain?', 'Why is there anything rather than nothing?', 'What is life for?', 'What should I do?' – which are the starting point for all philosophy.*

10 THINGS TO REMEMBER

1 *You have to decide which takes priority, the individual or society as a whole.*

2 *Hobbes saw the Social Contract as a basis for mutual security.*

3 *Locke established the principles of representative democracy.*

4 *Rousseau thought that the 'general will' could be imposed.*

5 *Marx saw political change in terms of dialectical materialism.*

6 *Plato saw justice in terms of each part of society taking its appropriate role.*

7 *Rawls sees justice in terms of fairness.*

8 *Nozick argues that one should retain wealth that has been legitimately gained.*

9 *Mill argued for maximum freedom compatible with the freedom of others.*

10 *Feminists reject the imposition of roles upon women by a male-dominated society.*

8

Continental philosophy

In this chapter you will learn:
- *the basic difference between analytic and Continental philosophy*
- *key features of existentialist philosophy*
- *some philosophical aspects of the structuralist and postmodernist movements.*

Within Western philosophy there has been a broad division, relating both to the way of doing philosophy and the sort of subjects covered. Most philosophers may be described as belonging either to the 'Analytic' or the 'Continental' tradition of philosophy.

▶ *Analytic philosophy is a tradition that has flourished particularly in the USA and Britain. It is especially concerned with the meaning of statements and the way in which their truth can be verified, and with using philosophy as an analytic tool to examine and show the presuppositions of our language and thought. Well-known philosophers in this school today would include Quine, Putnam, Searle, Rawls, Hampshire and Strawson. It also includes many philosophers already mentioned, including Russell, Ryle and Ayer. The twentieth-century philosophy described so far in this book has come from this tradition.*

▶ *Continental philosophy is a term which may be used to describe a range of philosophers from mainland Europe whose work is generally considered separately in courses on philosophy, although they do have relevance to the basic issues considered already. They include Husserl (1858–1938), whose phenomenology has influenced many other Continental philosophers, Heidegger and Sartre (existentialism) and, more recently, Lacan, Derrida and others. It is in this 'Continental' school that we meet the terms* **structuralism**, **postmodernism** *and* **hermeneutics** *(the study of interpretation: a term originally used of the study of scriptures, but now used more generally of the way in which any text is examined).*

Insight

Continental philosophy often reflects an intellectual approach to the creative arts in general, rather than the more narrowly defined tasks of the Analytic school. Sartre, for example, explored his ideas through novels, short stories and plays. Foucault was interested in the history and 'archaeology' of ideas and how they are shaped by society.

While there is no space in this book to give an adequate account of the thinkers of the Continental tradition, a brief outline of some of the main themes may serve to set it within the context of philosophy as a whole. This is important, because today there is far more mingling of the concerns of the two schools than would have been the case in the mid-twentieth century. Also, although the approach and content of philosophy as taught in universities in the UK and USA is still very much influenced by the broadly Analytic tradition, the philosophers of the Continental tradition are now more widely studied – with some, like Sartre and Heidegger, being hugely popular. It is also important to recognize that the Continental approach to philosophy, as it developed in the twentieth century, looked back and responded to the work of Nietzsche, Hegel, Kant, Rousseau and other great thinkers, back to Descartes – thinkers that have always been there in the core of philosophical study.

Phenomenology

Edmund Husserl (1859–1938), the founder of **phenomenology**, was a Jewish-German philosopher, who taught at the University of Freiburg. Like Descartes, he wanted to find the basis of knowledge, making philosophy a 'rigorous science' that was founded on necessary truths independent of all presuppositions. His most important work was *Logical Investigations* (published in two volumes in 1900 and 1901). In this he declared that, for certainty, we had to start with our own conscious awareness. What is it that we actually experience? Husserl suggested that every mental act is directed towards an 'intentional object': what the mind is thinking about, whether or not that object actually exists.

Examples

▶ I want to eat a cake. I need a physical cake if I am going to eat; but thinking about a cake requires only an 'intentional object' – indeed, I am especially likely to think about a cake when there is no actual cake to be had!

▶ If I reflect on feeling depressed, depression is an 'intentional object' of my thought, although there is no external object corresponding to it. Someone may say 'depression is nothing, it doesn't exist'; but for me, at that moment, it is real.

Husserl takes the subject matter of philosophy to be these 'objects of consciousness': whatever it is that we experience, quite apart from any questions about whether or not it exists in an objective, external world. Phenomenology also seeks to strip individual objects of all that makes them particular, seeking the pure essence – what they share with other objects of the same sort. These fundamental 'essences', he argues, are known by intuition. As soon as we think about something, it takes on meaning for us because of the various essences by which we understand it. I have a consciousness of 'tree' as a pure essence, and as soon as I see (or think about) an actual tree, that essence is there to give it meaning for me.

Examples

A child is shown a number of red objects. The mother says 'That's red.' The child automatically sorts out the common denominator of the experience, and quickly grasps the pure essence 'red'. When subsequently presented with objects of the same colour, the essence 'red' is already there, and becomes one of a number of essences by

(Contd)

which any new object is understood. More sophisticated, the artist will play with unusual shades of red, testing out the 'horizon', the limits of the essence 'red'. Is it red, or is it really magenta? Add a touch more blue to the paint: now how do we see it?

Husserl argued that consciousness required three things:

1 *a self (what he called the 'transcendental ego')*
2 *a mental act*
3 *an object of that mental act.*

Objects become objects of consciousness only when they have been given meaning and significance. An object is only understood (only really 'seen') once the mind has gone to work on it and given it meaning in terms of its pure essences. Everything is therefore dependent on the 'transcendental ego' for its meaning and significance. Once we encounter the world, we start to give it meaning, we start to interpret it in terms of pure essences; in other words, we start to deal with it in terms of its 'objects of consciousness'.

One reason why Husserl has been so important for Continental philosophy is that he allowed questions of meaning and value, and the whole range of emotions and other experiences, to become a valid subject matter of philosophy.

Insight

Continental philosophy was thus set free to explore many aspects of life that were beyond the concerns of philosophers of the Analytic tradition, who remained primarily concerned with language. They were able to ask not just 'What does this *mean?*' but 'What does this mean *for me?*'

Existentialism

Existentialism is the name given to the branch of philosophy which is concerned with the meaning of human existence – its aims, its significance and overall purpose – and the freedom and creative response to life made by individuals.

Notice how this follows on from phenomenology. If philosophy is free to deal with consciousness and the actions which spring from it, it can explore human self-awareness and self-doubt, and the actions and events that give meaning to life. Two important philosophers for the development of existentialism are Heidegger (1889–1976), a German philosopher controversially associated with the Nazi party, whose *Being and Time* (1927) is a key work of existentialist philosophy, and Sartre (1905–80), the French philosopher, novelist and playwright. His most important work of philosophy is *Being and Nothingness* (1943). Probably his best-known quote is from the end of his play *No Exit* (1945): 'Hell is other people.'

A central feature of existentialism is that it is concerned with the way in which human beings relate to the world. Much philosophy examines external objects and the minds that comprehend them as though the two were separable; the mind just observing the world in a detached way. Existentialism, by contrast, starts from the basis of the self as involved, as engaged with the world. We seek to understand things because we have to deal with them, live among them, find the meaning and significance of our own life among them.

An example

You pick up a hammer and start hammering a nail. You do not first think about the hammer and then decide how to use it; you use it automatically. Your mind is engaged with the activity of hammering. Heidegger sees this as a ready-to-hand way of dealing with things: not as an observer, but as an engaged individual.

Husserl had attempted, by bracketing out any particular features and trying to see only the pure essences of a phenomenon, to get a generally acceptable view of things. Existentialism moved away from that position by emphasizing that there is always an element of personal engagement, a particular point of view. This raises the general philosophical question about whether every view is a view from a particular perspective, carrying with it the values and understanding of the person who has it. The alternative (often sought by science, and by empirical philosophy) is a 'view from nowhere': a view that does not take a personal viewpoint into account. But is that possible?

For Heidegger, we are 'thrown' into the world, and our main experience of *Dasein* ('being there') is 'concern', in the sense that some of the objects we encounter in the world are going to be more important for us than others, and so we become involved with them. Heidegger also argued that we are what we take ourselves to be, we do not have a fixed human nature. You live in an authentic way if you take each situation as it comes and show your true nature through what you do.

Insight

The sad alternative is to try to escape from the anxiety of being true to yourself by conforming to what others expect of you, taking on masks that fit your social roles. Part of the attraction of existentialism was that it encouraged people to dare to throw off such social masks and to take charge of their lives.

For Sartre, particular things take on importance and refuse to be categorized. There is also the sense that a person is radically free. Just as individual things are not totally defined by their essences, so a person need not be defined by his or her duties and responsibilities. Such freedom can be threatening; it produces disorientation and (as in his novel of that title) nausea.

For reflection

Have another look at Chapter 4. We are defined by many things, and by the various roles that we take on. But can we ever be fully defined in this way? Is there a self that refuses to be categorized; that insists on the freedom to be unique?

Sartre described three kinds of being:

1 **Being-in-itself.** *This is the being of non-human objects, things just exist as they are.*
2 **Being-for-itself.** *At the level of consciousness or self-awareness, a being is aware of the world around it, of other things that are not itself. If we are self-aware, we cannot be reduced to a thing-in-itself, e.g. I may work as a postman, but I am not fully described as 'postman' (as a thing-in-itself) because, as a human being, I am always more than any such description. If people treat me simply as 'postman' they dehumanize me, they take from me the distinctive thing that makes me a person.*
3 **Being-for-others.** *As human beings, we form relationships and express our human nature through them. Relating to others, and aware of our own freedom, we are able to live in an 'authentic' way: we are being fully ourselves.*

In other words

▶ *Phenomenology allows human experiences and responses to become a valid object of philosophical study.*
▶ *Existentialism explores the way in which people relate to the world, including issues of value, meaning and purpose; it is about engagement, not detached observation.*
▶ *If I act out a role, I am not engaged with the whole of myself. To be authentic, I act in a way which reflects my self-awareness, and the awareness of my own freedom. this is who I am; this is what I choose to do; this is the real me.*

Insight

Existentialism gave philosophical underpinnings to a view of life that rejected social conformity, promoting self-expression and freedom. Taken up by literature and art, it became a cultural phenomenon, centred on the smoke-filled cafes of Paris in the 1940s and 1950s.

Existentialism can be summed up in Sartre's claim that 'existence precedes essence'. In other words, I do not have a fixed essence and then try to live it out in the world; rather, I give meaning to my life in the course of living it. By my present choices, I can shape my future, taking responsibility for what I become.

Structuralism

The main theme of **structuralism** is that you can only understand something once you relate it to the wider structures within which it operates. Things are defined primarily in terms of their relationships with others. Structuralist approaches were developed in the philosophy of language and in anthropology, but spread into many different cultural areas.

Examples

▶ *To understand a word, consider its meaning in terms of other words and the language as a whole.*

▶ *To understand a political statement, look at the politician, how he or she is to stay in power, what the media expect, what effect he or she needs to make with this statement.*

▶ *A 'soundbite' or a newspaper headline can only really be understood in terms of the significance of the paper or the broadcast within which it is set.*

In Husserl's phenomenology there was an independent self that existed prior to the encounter with the phenomena: the 'transcendental ego'. Existentialism focused on that self, especially in its freedom and choices in its engagement with the world. Structuralism (and particularly its later development, known as post-structuralism) is a reaction against the importance given to this 'self' – structures and relationships now take priority.

Jacques Lacan (1900–80) argued that we do not first become fully formed individuals and then start to express our individuality through language, but we become individuals (we develop our personalities, if you like) through the use of language. And that language, with its ideas and its grammar, predates us. We don't make it up as we go along; we inherit it.

Lacan was primarily a psychoanalyst, and it is interesting to reflect that in psychoanalysis it is through a free flow of ideas that thoughts and feelings buried in the unconscious may appear. The flow of language is not controlled by the ego. Indeed, it is in order to heal and change the ego that the analysis is taking place. The subject emerges through language. For Lacan, it would seem that if there is no speech, then there is no subject, but he goes further; there are no metaphysical entities at all. God, for example, is a function of the 'Other' in language, not something that exists outside language.

Two features of a structuralist/post-structuralist approach:

1 *There is no transcendent self that has some pure idea which it wants to convey, and which is later, imperfectly translated into a medium of communication – spoken, written or visual. Rather, the meaning is just exactly what is spoken or written. It is to be understood in terms of the structures of communication, not with reference to some outside author. A story does not have a meaning; a story is its meaning.*

2 *To understand a piece of writing, one should carry out a process of **deconstruction**, laying bare the presuppositions of the text, and comparing what an author claims to be saying with the actual form of language used and the sometimes contradictory claims that such a written form implies. Deconstruction has been developed particularly by Jacques Derrida (1930–2004), an influential figure in this movement. Deconstruction is the attempt to deal with the end of metaphysics. For Derrida, there is no external or fixed meaning to a text, nor is there a subject who exists prior to language and prior to particular experiences. You cannot get outside or beyond the structure.*

Derrida is concerned with 'actuality', with being in touch with present events. But the information we receive through the media is never neutral, but is the product of the structures by which the media operate. This has practical consequences:

> *Hegel was right to tell the philosophers of his time to read the newspapers. Today the same duty requires us to find out how news is made, and by whom: the daily papers, the weeklies, and the TV news as well. We need to insist on looking at them from the other end: that of the press agencies as well as that of the tele-prompter. And we should never forget what this entails: whenever a journalist or a politician appears to be speaking to us directly, in our homes, and looking us straight in the eye, he or she is actually reading, from a screen, at the dictation of a 'prompter', and reading a text which was produced elsewhere, on a different occasion, possibly by other people, or by a whole network of nameless writers and editors.*

From 'The deconstruction of actuality', an interview with
Derrida published in *Radical Philosophy*, Autumn 1994

But Derrida warns against 'neo-idealism': the idea that nothing really happens, that all is an illusion just because it is set within a structure by the media. Rather, he wants to emphasize that deconstruction is about getting down to an event, to a 'singularity', to what is irreducible and particular in an individual happening.

In other words

▶ *To understand anything, look at its relationships and the structure within which it is set.*
▶ *There is no subject that exists prior to language. I may think of something before I write it down, but even that act of thinking borrows from a whole tradition of language and thought.*
▶ *News comes to us through the media; it is the product of a process by which information is sorted and expressed in particular ways, often for a particular purpose. Real events are unique, reports of them put them into categories and start to colour our interpretation of them.*

Insight
Structuralism makes explicit what any critical reader or viewer knows – that we need to see through what is said

and ask *why* is it said and *in whose interest* it is published or broadcast. Communication cannot be innocent of the complex web of political, financial, cultural and personal influences within which it is set.

Postmodernism

Postmodernism is a rather vague term for a number of approaches to philosophy, literature and the arts, which have in common a rejection of an earlier 'modernist' view. The 'modern' view, against which postmodernism reacts, is one that sees the image as the production of the unique human subject. Existentialism in particular is focused on the self, its freedom, and the choices by which it creates itself and its world. Structuralism disputed this 'modern' belief in the primacy of the humanist imagination as a creative source of meaning.

Postmodernism is a term used beyond the writings of Derrida, Lyotard and others who work in the fields of philosophy and literary criticism, for it can apply to all the arts. Indeed, the ideas were explored in architecture before transferring to philosophy. Previously, an image could be taken to refer to something external, in the 'real' world or in human consciousness. In postmodernism, an image reflects only other images, it has no fixed reference. There is therefore no 'authentic' image – authentic in the sense that an existentialist would use that term.

A message is, for postmodernism, no longer a message sent from a creative author to a receptive reader. Rather, it is bound up with a mass of reduplication. We shuffle and arrange images, but do not have any creative control over them. In a work of art, a novel or a film, a postmodernist approach undermines the modernist belief in the image as the production of an individual consciousness.

A postmodern image displays its own artificial nature. It clearly represents – but without depth. So, for example, in the art world, one might contrast Picasso (who, as a 'modernist' strove for a unique view and form of communication) with Warhol's use of mass-produced public images. An interesting discussion of this is found in R. Kearney's 'The crisis of the postmodernist image' in *Contemporary French Philosophy*, A. Phillips Griffiths (ed.), Cambridge 1987.

For reflection

Modernism: The dilemma and existential agony of the blank sheet of paper, a set of paints and brushes, and the desire to express oneself through a unique image.

Postmodernism: The word-processing package comes to the rescue, for it contains a great variety of pieces of 'clip art' which can instantly be printed out and arranged on the paper.

Postmodernism is encouraged by the developments in technology, particularly mass communication and the ability to reproduce images. The individual subject is no longer considered to be the creator of his or her images. What we appear to create is what is already there around us. We produce consumer items. It is not so much philosophy that is postmodern, but the whole of society. There are many images to be shuffled, but there is no metaphysical insight to be had, and no transcendental reality to represent.

Insight

For postmodernism, you cannot get behind the images, symbols and reproduced goods of a technological age in order to discern individuality, purpose or meaning. It is a view devoid of what was traditionally known as 'metaphysics'.

This is also reflected in the postmodernist view, explored by Jean-Francois Lyotard, that statements about the overall purpose of life or society (for example, society exists for the benefit of its members), sometimes called 'meta-narratives', are losing their credibility. It is no longer realistic to make general statements of a metaphysical nature about life, since they do not reflect the fragmented nature of modern society.

A final example

I am the author of this book: I address you, the reader, directly in order to illustrate some of the issues connected with structuralism and the postmodern outlook.

What do you think of me as an author? You could say: 'He's just stuck together bits of information that others have given him.' That is true. You could go on to say: 'There is absolutely nothing original in it!' This is a more serious charge, but made complicated because there is a certain originality in the way that the ideas of others are selected, analyzed, arranged and presented.

But suppose I claim to have said something original. Can that claim be justified?

▶ *What of the words I use? Their meanings are already given by the society that uses this language (if they weren't, you would not understand them). They do not originate in my mind.*
▶ *What of the climate of opinion within which I write? Does that not shape my views? Am I responsible for it, or shaped by it?*
▶ *And what of comments for which I claim originality? If you knew everything that I had read, everyone who I had spoken to, could you not predict my views? Could you not analyze my views, show influences, categorize the style, place my views within a particular tradition. A literary critic often shows that what seems to be a unique expression of a thinking self is in fact an intellectual patchwork of influences.*
▶ *This book is being written to fit a certain number of printed pages of a particular size, and in a particular style. Its chapters reflect the range of philosophy taught in some university departments; suggestions*
(Contd)

about content have been made by professional readers; various things have been asked for by editors. What is said is determined by the constraints of space, purpose and market.

▶ *Thus the author of this book can vanish!*

Personal note

I may keep within the overall structure of language, but I feel that, from time to time, I am entitled to peer round the side of the structure and address you, the reader, directly. It is this that structuralism denies, and indeed, the idea of an author making a personal appeal to a reader is just another literary device. I disappear again!

10 THINGS TO REMEMBER

1 *In twentieth-century philosophy there are both Analytic and Continental traditions.*

2 *For phenomenology, knowledge starts with our own conscious awareness.*

3 *Every mental act is directed towards an 'intentional object'.*

4 *Existentialism is concerned with the meaning of human life and how people relate to their world.*

5 *We are 'thrown' into the world and always have a particular perspective on it.*

6 *We can either accept social masks, or choose to live in an authentic way.*

7 *For existentialism, existence precedes essence.*

8 *We need to be aware of the structures within which information is communicated.*

9 *We always 'borrow' our ideas from a tradition of language and society.*

10 *Postmodernism rejects metaphysical statements about the nature of life.*

9

....

Some other branches of philosophy

In this chapter you will learn:
- *about some issues concerning the philosophy of art*
- *how we interpret the events of the past as 'history'*
- *what some philosophers have had to say about education.*

This book has, of necessity, been selective. In examining some of the major issues in philosophy, it has not been able to show the full breadth of philosophy as it is practised today. Neither has it been possible to include all the major philosophers of the past. Some, for example Hegel, Nietzsche or Frege, have been very influential, but there has been no room to include them, and they certainly deserve more than a brief mention if their thought is to be taken at all seriously. To understand the work of these great individual thinkers is it probably best to look first at general histories of philosophy, in order to set their work in context, and then turn to books on each individual thinker.

This chapter simply attempts to fill a few of the gaps by offering a sketch of three other areas of philosophy, to illustrate the range of interests found in philosophy today and the way in which philosophy is applied to other areas of human experience.

Aesthetics

Most areas of philosophy spring from a simple but fundamental question: epistemology is the attempt to answer 'What can we know?'; political philosophy answers 'What is justice?'. Aesthetics addresses the questions 'What is beauty?' and 'What is art?'

You can trace these questions through the whole history of philosophy, from Greek ideas of art, through mediaeval and Reformation debates about religious images (whether they pointed beyond themselves, or were in danger of being themselves worshipped in an idolatrous way), through Hume's attempt to get a norm of taste and Kant's analysis of the aesthetic experience, to Marxist critiques of art in terms of its social and political function, and on to existentialist and postmodernist views of art.

However, it is far from straightforward to say exactly what makes something 'art'. One could define art as in some way a 'picturing' of reality; but then one would need to leave out music or architecture, which are arts, but which create something that has no direct external point of reference in the natural world. (Both may, of course, suggest or hint at things in the natural world, but that is another matter.) Another approach is to start from the artist, rather than from the work of art. Hence art is the product of a certain kind of human activity, related to the expression of emotion, or the enhancement of perception.

Think of the range of artistic activities that go to produce an opera, for example. There is the designing and painting of sets, the production of costumes, the libretto, the music and the quality of voices that perform it. A single aesthetic experience results from the very special combination of a whole range of 'arts'. Here, as with the appreciation of a 'person', more is understood by synthesis (seeing how everything works together) rather than by analysis (isolating and trying to define each component separately).

The same could be said of literature. Individual words in a work of fiction may well have a straightforward, literal meaning, and the individual events they describe might well be factual (indeed, this leads on to the debate about how much fact can rightly be incorporated into a work of fiction), yet the overall effect – the synthesis – is to create something which reflects, but does not copy real life.

Modern discussions of how to define art may consider its function; in other words, something is art if it is treated as art, or if it works as art for us, even if the medium is entirely new. Alternatively, it is possible to argue that art is defined by the procedures that *lead* to its production and use; does this particular thing or event follow an established tradition (or writing, drawing, composing and so on) and is it accepted as such within the community of those engaged in the arts?

Insight

In this view, art need not have a distinctive form or come within established categories; art is either what works as art, or what the artworld is prepared to accept as art – even if it is quite unlike anything that has been produced before.

Aesthetics links with other areas of philosophy. For example, writing in the USA in the 1950s both the theologian Paul Tillich and philosopher Susanne Langer spoke of art as symbol, as pointing beyond itself to some other transcendent reality. This links aesthetics with the philosophy of religion. Indeed, Tillich held that all religious ideas and images were symbols, pointing to 'being-itself', and that religious truths could not be conveyed other than by symbols. A work of art could therefore be seen as in some sense 'religious', however secular its context, since it pointed to that which was beyond ordinary experience.

How you see the function of art depends in part on how you understand experience and reality. Plato, for example, saw individual things as poor copies of timeless realities (his 'forms'), and therefore criticized art for taking this a stage further, producing copies of copies. Art therefore, for Plato, is presenting something 'unreal' and therefore further from the truth, whereas for Tillich and Langar it is a necessary way of encountering transcendent reality, and therefore supremely 'real'.

The work of the artist also links with the nature of the self, the nature of language and the nature of perception. A novelist, for example, may use language in a rich and subtle way in order to convey a whole range of emotions and intuitions; and not just to convey them, but to evoke them in the reader. A work of fiction thus invites an emotional and imaginative response. No two readers 'picture' the events described in the novel in exactly the same way.

Insight

Contrast this with the ideal analytic philosophy, which presents an argument with as much clarity as possible, or logical positivism, which insisted that a statement could only have meaning if backed up by evidence. That approach seeks language that is clean, precise and straightforward; while a novel or poem may be rich in meaning, evocative, symbolic and often deliberately ambiguous.

The richness of art has produced a variety of responses from philosophers. Plato feared that art in general, and dramatic poetry in particular, had the power to corrupt people by stirring up their emotions. Nietzsche, by contrast, welcomed this aspect. In *The Birth of Tragedy* (1872) he contrasted the Dionysian and Apollonian spirit within humankind, the former bringing elation, intoxication and a stirring of the emotions, the latter bringing cool rationality. Art has the positive function of holding the two together.

For reflection

Plato was hostile to art and in favour of strict censorship. He saw art as subversive, replacing reality with fantasy, manipulating the emotions. Yet his dialogues are great works of literature; they are art!

(Contd)

For those wanting to follow up on aesthetics, one could also look at Hume on matters of taste, and at Kant's *Critique of Aesthetic Judgement* (1790). In the twentieth century, philosophers of particular importance in this area include R. G. Collingwood, who published *Principles of Art* in 1925, written at a time when philosophy was much concerned with literal description (as in Logical Positivism), and, from the 1960s, E. H. Gombrich's *Art and Illusion* (1960) and N. Goodman's *Languages of Art* (1968).

Insight

Interestingly, much of this is an attempt to understand the place of art and creativity against a background of the obvious success of the literal use of language in science. One might explore the relationship between aesthetics and both the philosophy of science and the philosophy of language.

The range of problems associated with aesthetics may be illustrated by the practical dilemma of whether or not you are able to call something a work of art.

An example

I visit the home of a wealthy friend who tells me that he has just invested in a new work of art. I glance out of the window, and see a pile of bricks and rubble in the middle of his lawn. My friend has noticed me looking towards the lawn, and the glow of pride on his face leaves me in no doubt that the load of bricks and rubble is indeed his new work of art!

▶ *He sees a work of art; I see a pile of rubble. Is there any objective way of deciding between these two views ('seeing as')?*

▶ *If I agree that it is a work of art, where is that 'art' located? Is it in the art object (analyzed as a pile of bricks and rubble)? Is it in the mind of the artist? Is its beauty, as the saying goes, in the eye of the beholder? Is art something that takes place in a triangular relationship: artist, art object, person appreciating it 'as' art?*

▶ *Is it pointing to something beyond itself, some feature of reality that I cannot describe literally, but which I sense by looking at the work of art? Or is it simply being itself, and inviting me to give it my attention? And is the act of giving attention itself an aesthetic experience?*

▶ *Would the pile of bricks remain art, even if nobody appreciated it as such?*

▶ *What emotions does it evoke in me? If only irritation and embarrassment, are these still valid as an aesthetic experience?*

▶ *The pile of bricks on the lawn is part of an artificial social construction: an artist making a living; an investor wanting a new 'piece'; a financial deal. Is art still art if it becomes an investment commodity?*

▶ *What is the nature of artistic imagination?*

▶ *Does the artist create an illusion, trying to make me see something more than that which is actually before my eyes?*

▶ *If the artist thought of it as one thing and I see it as something else, are there two works of art here, or only one?*

Different periods have explored different aspects of art. In the eighteenth century, for example, primacy was given to natural beauty, and a sense of balance between nature and the mind perceiving nature. Kant saw a 'formal purposiveness' in those things that produced an aesthetic experience: art objects creating a sense of harmonious pleasure in the mind. The twentieth century has been more concerned with the nature of artistic production, and the process of artistic creativity has often become its own subject matter.

Art reflects the particular self-understanding of each age: wander through any art gallery and it becomes clear that the concerns and values of each period are clearly reflected in its visual art. It is not just a matter of style, but of the changing sense of what it is appropriate to depict in art. There is also great variety in the self-consciousness of creativity; in one period, the aim appears to be to render such an accurate depiction of external reality that the artist disappears from immediate view, in another period, perceived image is distorted in order to reflect the self-conscious intentions of the artist.

Thus, although aesthetics and the philosophy of art may be studied as a separate branch of philosophy, their real fascination comes from interlocking them with questions about the nature of perception, the self and its creativity, the self-transcending quality of religious experience, the ethics of what is expressed or depicted.

Insight

It could be argued that philosophy and art are two sides of the creative human coin, the one focusing on reflective thought, the other on creative expression.

The philosophy of history

What is history? We might be tempted to say that history is the account of what has happened in the past. But that will not do, for a theoretically infinite number of events have already taken place and, even if they could all be remembered and recorded, it would take an infinite amount of time to construct history out of them. In other words, history would unfold faster than it could be recounted.

History is therefore *selective*; most things are ignored. Without such selection, the sheer number of events in the past would smother any attempt to get an overall view of what happened. And this is a crucial point: history involves an interpretation of events, and that interpretation depends on the ideas and assumptions of the historian. *History cannot be an objective account of facts.* It is an interpretation of the significance of particular things that have taken place in the past.

More than one layer of interpretation may be involved; a modern historian examining ancient texts brings his own views to that study but, equally, the original authors of those texts were also interpreting the events they recorded. Much of the study of history is historiography, the study of historical writing.

This has led some postmodernist thinkers to argue that texts are simply based on other texts (the process called 'intertextuality') rather than on external 'facts'. The truth of a document is therefore related to the authority of those who wrote it, rather than to events it claims to describe. The American philosopher, Hayden White, in his book *Metahistory* (1973) put forward the view that the historian is actually producing a creative literary invention, rather than dealing in facts. *Some of the information which the historian uses may be factual, but it only becomes 'history' once it is part of a story.*

The postmodernist approach raises important issues for historians. If history does not present 'facts' about events that took place in the past, then any interpretation of the past would seem to be as good as any other. While no historian would claim that his or her account of an event is totally objective, there is a professional interest in gathering evidence in order to illustrate past events as clearly as possible.

THE MECHANISMS OF CHANGE

Part of the fascination of history is trying to understand the process by which change comes about. The German idealist philosopher Hegel (1770–1831) thought that it was possible to discern a particular 'spirit', or *Geist,* unfolding in the historical process. The process through which this unfolding took place is described as a 'dialectic': each age has its particular feature (its 'thesis') which then produces a reaction ('antithesis') which is then resolved (in a 'synthesis'). This process then repeats itself, always aiming towards a rational ideal and absolute.

Karl Marx was influenced by Hegel's theory of historical change. But he argued that the basis of society was economic and material. He therefore saw the economic conditions under which people lived, and the conflicts between classes, as the mechanism by which historical change came about. In Marx you therefore have a political philosophy which is also a philosophy of history, and you have a philosopher whose expressed intention is to change things rather than simply understand them.

Note

For further information on Marx, see Chapter 7, pp. 226–8.

One key feature of the philosophy of history is the recognition that as soon as events are described, they are interpreted, and as soon as they are interpreted, they are set within an overall pattern of understanding. The philosophy of history seeks to reveal that process of interpretation, and to relate it, as closely as it may, to the events which it seeks to present.

The philosophy of education

The philosophy of education is concerned both with the nature and purpose of education, and with the content of what is taught. As such it relates to many other areas of philosophy – to the theory of knowledge, to language, to ethics, religious and political philosophy. As a specialist area of philosophy, however, it is generally taught within departments of education rather than those of philosophy.

There are a number of key questions with which the philosophy of education is concerned:

▶ *What is education* for?
▶ *By what* process *do we learn?*
▶ *What should determine the* content *of education?*

In *The Republic*, Plato considers the nature of the state and the qualities of those who are to rule it, but he couches his argument in terms of the sort of education that will be necessary in order to produce leaders fit to rule. For Plato, therefore, education does not appear to be an end in itself, but a tool of social engineering – turning out the sort of people the state is going to need. However, that is not the whole truth, for Plato wants his rulers to be philosophers capable of seeing reality itself, rather than the passing shadows of sense experience. Hence it can equally be argued that Plato's scheme of education is aimed at an appreciation of the 'form of the good' (see p. 10).

His approach raises issues which continue within the world of education today:

▶ *To what extent should education be dependent on selection by ability?*
▶ *To what extent should education be aimed to equip students for particular tasks within society? Should society therefore set the curriculum?*
▶ *Should people of different classes and backgrounds be given different types of education?*
▶ *Should education be judged by its ability to turn out those who will maintain the social status quo?*

Insight

Should education be seen as having value in itself, or is it justified in terms of the need to train people for their roles in society? Your answer to that question will influence your views about funding for university departments, for example, or the giving of grants for research.

The process by which people learn is influenced by the general philosophical approach to knowledge of the world. Thus a philosopher such as John Locke, who sees all knowledge as based on sense experience, wants education to encourage experimentation and a rejection of the uncritical acceptance of tradition. A key feature of Locke's theory of knowledge is that people start with minds like blank sheets of paper (*tabula rasa*) and acquire knowledge though experience. (This contrasts with Plato, who held that we have innate knowledge of the 'forms', which we appear to have forgotten, but which enables us to recognize them as soon as we encounter them.)

John Dewey (1859–1952) was an influential American thinker who contributed widely in philosophy, but who is particularly known for his contribution to the theory of 'pragmatism'. This is the view that knowledge is achieved through practical problem-solving engagement with the world. The meaning of a statement can best be seen in terms of its practical application – the difference that it makes. Based on the scientific method of testing hypotheses, he suggested that education was primarily a process of problem solving, an approach which is generally termed 'instrumentalism'. This view has been enormously influential in terms of both educational theory and practice. Today, it is generally recognized that learning is most effective when it is based on practical, problem-solving methods, and the process of checking and testing out gives a clearer knowledge of the subject than the simple learning of facts.

With the pragmatists' contribution to education we have an interesting example of philosophy recognizing the significance of one sphere of life (the success of the scientific method), developing from it a general theory of meaning (that the truth of a statement is shown by the practical implications that follow from it – i.e. whether or not it works), and then applying it to another sphere of life (education) with overwhelming success. Throughout the world, primary school children learn through doing, examining and testing out, and this is largely due to the influence of pragmatism.

There are many other areas of education with which philosophy is concerned. For example, when it comes to the content of what is taught, there is debate about the appropriateness of religious or political education, about the point at which education descends into indoctrination. Equally, there is concern (often expressed by parents) about the methods and content of education in matters of sex and drugs. Does the teaching of contraception, for example, encourage promiscuity?

Central to many of these issues is the matter of personal autonomy. The essential difference between education and indoctrination is that the former seeks to empower and give autonomy to the individual learner, whereas the latter imposes on him or her an already formulated set of ideas. But how do you transmit culture from one generation to the next without at least some element of indoctrination?

The philosophy of education, therefore, arises naturally from the range of practical issues faced by those engaged in education. Both the process, the content and the purpose of education require to be linked to a broader understanding of life.

10 THINGS TO REMEMBER

1 Aesthetics addresses the question 'What is art?'.

2 Art may be defined as what people accept as art.

3 Art often reflects the philosophy of the period in which it is produced.

4 Kant saw art as that which produced harmonious pleasure in the mind.

5 Art may deliberately reflect the self-consciousness of a artist.

6 Plato thought art subversive and in need of strict censorship.

7 History is always selective in terms of the facts upon which it is based.

8 History is always a matter of interpretation, never simply a factual account of the past.

9 There is a fundamental difference between education for itself alone, and purposeful training.

10 Pragmatism has been influential in terms of the practice of classroom education.

10

The scope of philosophy today

In this chapter you will learn:
- *something of the range of issues considered by philosophy today.*

During the twentieth century there were a number of movements that attempted to reduce philosophy to some other discipline. The positivists wanted philosophy to follow science, throwing out all that did not conform to empirical criteria of meaning. Then the linguistic analysts insisted that the whole task of philosophy was the unpacking of statements to clarify their meaning. Marxists wanted everything reduced to its social and political matrix and postmodernists saw everything in terms of cultural and literary metaphors or signs, strung together. One might imagine that philosophy would be shaken radically by such drastic criticisms and re-interpretations of its task, but this has not been the case.

For anyone coming to philosophy at the end of the 1950s, however, at least in university departments concentrating on the Anglo-American analytic tradition, the task and scope of philosophy was precise but narrow. Still dominated by linguistic analysis, it aimed to examine problematic sentences and, through their elucidation, clarify meaning. It did not aspire to offer any new information on any subject. It saw itself as a necessary aid to all other subjects, rather than having a subject content of its own.

Over the last 50 years, however, philosophy has seen remarkable growth, both in its popularity as a subject and in the range and relevance of the topics it covers. One impetus for change came initially within the area of applied ethics. In the days of linguistic analysis, everything was focused on the meaning or otherwise of ethical propositions, and it was quite reasonable for a philosopher to claim to have nothing to say about moral issues themselves. But it was increasingly recognized that ethical guidance was needed by professionals, particularly in medicine and nursing, in order to develop and implement standards for dealing with the many difficult moral questions raised in their everyday work. Questions about abortion and euthanasia, the use of drugs and the conduct of medical research, all needed to be answered by sound moral arguments based on accepted professional standards.

At the same time, the rise of the cognitive sciences, information technology and artificial intelligence has raised questions about the nature of mind. International politics grapples with concepts – democracy, human rights, self-determination, national sovereignty – to direct and justify its action or inaction in various crises. Political philosophy is therefore utterly relevant to the human agenda. Issues concerning the philosophy of art – censorship, copyright, what distinguishes valid erotic art from pornography, what constitutes 'taste' or blasphemy, the nature of artistic expression – may be relevant when a Turner or other prize is judged, or when artists produce images that some find inspiring and others want banned. Relevant here also are legal debates about the ownership of intellectual property, about who should be paid royalties or claim copyright on ideas and words. Social awareness brings with it issues of feminism and of race, of inequality and the dynamics of free markets.

With the internet comes a whole raft of issues about self-expression, privacy, international controls, exploitation and the nature of communication. In a complex world, something more is needed of philosophy than the mere clarification of meaning. *Even beyond the obvious area of ethics, philosophy is increasingly becoming 'applied'*. And it is therefore also becoming more obviously relevant to everyday life – it is *the* subject for dealing with big questions.

Without doubt, philosophy as an academic discipline is alive and well, but the first decade of the twenty-first century has seen another phenomenon – the explosion of interest in 'popular' philosophy. Books by philosophers on a whole range of subjects, but particularly those related to human self-understanding and self-development, are increasingly produced for the general reader, rather than the academic specialist. The nature of status, or of love, of justice or of commitment, of work or of all the elements that go to make up the art of living, all require thoughtful reflection, and philosophy provides the discipline for doing just that.

Perhaps the last word should come from a traditional metaphysical philosopher, writing early in the twentieth century. In *Modes of Thought* (1938), A. N. Whitehead set down very clearly the value of the whole philosophical enterprise:

> **The sort of ideas we attend to, and the sort of ideas we push into the negligible background, govern our hopes, our fears, our control of behaviour. As we think, we live. This is why the assemblage of philosophical ideas is more than a specialist study. It moulds our type of civilization.**

If that is so, there is nothing more important than developing and maintaining an interest in philosophy.

Taking it further

Suggestions for further reading

The books listed here form a very limited, personal selection of those which should prove useful as a follow-up to issues touched on in this book. They are in addition to the classic texts and other books referred to in the text.

For those wanting to deepen their appreciation of the whole tradition of western philosophy, there are a good number of general histories, for example Bryan Magee's *The Story of Philosophy* (Dorling Kindersley, 1998, paperback, 2001) which offers an illustrated history of Western philosophy – lucid and very readable.

Of the older histories, my personal preference would be Bertrand Russell's *History of Western Philosophy* (1946, available in Routledge Classics, 2004). It is incisive, witty and readable, giving a vast panorama of philosophy, with particular reference to the social and political circumstances of philosophers, from the pre-socratics to the early years of the twentieth century. Don't expect Russell to suffer philosophical fools gladly; but he is always intelligently wicked in his criticism.

For general reference, there is *The Oxford Companion to Philosophy* edited by Ted Honderich (second edition, OUP, 2005), and the *Concise Routledge Encyclopedia of Philosophy* (Routledge, 2000), both of which give detailed information on the whole range of concepts, philosophies and philosophers. For quick reference, and for checking on the meaning of philosophical terms and which thinkers are associated with them, there are many valuable dictionaries of philosophy. See, for example, *The Oxford Dictionary of Philosophy*, by Simon Blackburn (Oxford Paperback Reference, 2008).

For clear expositions of key themes in philosophy, suitable for students and the general reader, there are a number of useful titles from Nigel Warburton, particularly his *Philosophy: the Basics* (Routledge, 2004), with useful extracts from the great texts in *Philosophy: Basic Readings*) (Routledge, 2004).

Some books deal with a particular issue, and yet touch on a whole range of philosophical questions and historical periods. Thus, for example, although Karen Armstrong's *The Case for God* (Bodley Head, 2009) is primarily about God, in the course of giving a historical overview of the way that word has been used, Armstrong draws in a wide range of philosophers.

Older books can also be useful. Iris Murdoch's *Metaphysics as a Guide to Morals* (Chatto & Windus, 1992), is much wider in its scope than the title might at first glance suggest. There are particularly valuable sections here on consciousness, on the traditional arguments for the existence of God, on will and on duty – a solid but stimulating book on a whole range of philosophical and religious issues, but those new to philosophy may find it quite difficult going in places. Two other older books that are well worth reading are transcripts of television interviews with distinguished philosophers – Bryan Magee's *Men of Ideas* (BBC Books, 1978), and *The Great Philosophers* (BBC Books, 1987). Magee's introductions and summaries are a model of clarity. The earlier book gives a good overview of twentieth-century philosophy up to the mid-1970s and is a superb example of lucid philosophical discussion.

This present book has outlined only Western philosophy; for those interested in getting a world perspective there is Ninian Smart's *World Philosophies* (Routledge, 1999), and *World Philosophy: an exploration in words and images* (Vega, 2005), a large-format illustrated book, edited by David Appelbaum and Mel Thompson.

For examples of philosophy applied to issues of everyday life, see recent publications by Alain De Botton or Anthony Grayling, and also *The Art of Living* series, published by Acumen, which takes a philosophical look at aspects of life from *Sex*, *Sport*, *Wellbeing* and *Fashion*, to *Middle Age*, *Hunger*, *Work* and *Death*. The present author's contribution to this series is about personal identity, entitled simply *Me* (Acumen, 2009).

Within the *Teach Yourself* series, the following titles cover particular areas of Western philosophy:

Thompson, Mel, *Understand Ethics* (Hodder Education, 2010)
Thompson, Mel, *Understand Philosophy of Religion*
(Hodder Education, 2010)
Thompson, Mel, *Understand Political Philosophy*
(Hodder Education, 2010)
Rodgers, Nigel and Thompson, Mel, *Understand Existentialism*
(Hodder Education, 2010)
Ward, Glen, *Understand Postmodernism*, (Hodder Education, 2010)

The author will also be republishing titles on *The Philosophy of Science*, *The Philosophy of Mind* and *Eastern Philosophy* in late 2010 see www.philosophyandethics.com for more details.

And finally, for those who assume that philosophers live dull, thoughtful, untroubled lives, there is:

Rodgers, Nigel and Thompson, Mel, *Philosophers Behaving Badly* (Peter Owen, 2004).

MAGAZINES

Unlike academic journals, which tend to be specialist and sometimes quite hard-going for the uninitiated, the following magazines are likely to appeal to the general reader wanting to go further into philosophy:

Think, the journal of the Royal Institute of Philosophy, aims to bridge the gap between academic philosophy and the wider public by offering a jargon-free style. See its website for further information: www.royalinstituteofphilosophy.org/think/index.html

The Philosophers' Magazine offers a wide range of interesting and readable articles. See: www.philosophersnet.com

Philosophy Now is an attractively produced and readable general magazine on philosophy, showing just how broad and relevant the subject can be. Like the other magazines, it has useful book reviews. See: www.philosophynow.org

Websites

Today there are a large number of websites for those wanting to know more about philosophy, some hosted by philosophy magazines, but a majority by university websites. For further information on relevant sites, see the Websites page of www.philosophyandethics.com

For information on books, blogs and websites on Philosophy, for additional material of interest to students and teachers, or to contact the author with your views, suggestions or questions, log on to: www.philosophyandethics.com

Glossary

The following is a selection of terms used in this book, gathered here for quick reference. For more information on each of them, please refer to the relevant index entry.

agnosticism The view that we do not have sufficient evidence or other means of knowing whether a god exists or not.

atheism The view that there is no god. This may be taken in the narrower sense of the rejection of the theistic concept of God, or as a broad rejection of all religious ideas. It should be noted that some forms of Buddhism and Hinduism are atheistic, in that they promote a religious and spiritual path without requiring belief in God.

behaviourism The view that the mind can be understood in terms of observed physical activity.

blik A particular way of seeing something, used especially of religious language.

casuistry The process of applying general rules to specific cases; often used in a pejorative sense of an insensitive rejection of particular circumstances in favour of strictly applied rules.

categorical imperative A sense of unconditional moral obligation; used particularly in Kant's ethics for his general principles of morality.

category mistake (as used by Ryle in *The Concept of Mind*) The attempt to treat a collective term as though it were one of the particulars of which it is made up (e.g. right-hand glove/pair of gloves; university/colleges).

cosmological (arguments) Arguments for the existence of God, based on observation of the world.

deconstruction The process of examining a text in the context of the linguistic and social structures within which it was put together (see also **structuralism**).

deductive argument An argument based on logical principles, rather than on the assessment of evidence.

deism The view that God created the world and exists external to it, but is not (or no longer) involved or active within the world itself.

dualism The view that mind and matter are distinct and separate (of importance for the mind/body problem, but also for epistemology).

empiricism A theory of knowledge based on sense experience.

epiphenomenalism The theory that the mind is a product of complex physical processes.

epistemology The theory of knowledge.

existentialism The branch of philosophy concerned with the experience of meaning or purpose (or lack of it) in human existence; part of the 'Continental' tradition of philosophy.

foundationalism The attempt to find an indubitable fact as the basis, or foundation, for a theory of knowledge.

functionalism (as used in Cognitive Science) The view that the mind has a functional role in examining the input it receives from the senses and giving an appropriate response. Hence, the mind is not so much 'over and above' the brain, but is a way of describing the functions that are being performed by it.

fundamentalism Used in a religious context for the attempt to eliminate the superficial and return to the fundamental features of religious belief. Frequently associated with a radical and literal interpretation of doctrine and scriptures.

hedonism The view that pleasure, or human welfare and happiness, is the goal of life.

hermeneutics The study of the way in which texts are interpreted, used particularly for the examination of religious scriptures.

idealism The claim that the world, as we experience it, is fundamentally mental.

inductive method The process of coming to a conclusion based on the assessment of evidence.

interactionism The general term for theories of the mind in which mind and body are distinct (dualism) but interact.

intuitionism The view that 'good' is a fundamental term that is known intuitively, but cannot be defined in terms of anything else.

intuitive knowledge Direct knowledge which is not the result of conscious reasoning or experience.

materialism Reality is material (for example the 'self' is a way of describing the body and its actions).

metaphysics The study of theories concerning the nature, structure and general characteristics of reality.

modernism A general term for the self-conscious approach to philosophy and the arts, developed particularly in the first half of the twentieth century.

Natural Law The rational interpretation of meaning and purpose in nature, used as a basis for ethics.

natural selection Darwin's theory of evolution, by which only the strongest examples of a species survive to breed.

noumena Used by Kant for 'things in themselves' as opposed to things as we experience them.

numinous The 'holy', beyond rational definition (term used by Rudolph Otto).

ontological (argument) Argument for the existence of God, based simply on a proposed definition of God and independent of evidence.

panentheism Belief that everything exists within God (implied by theism, but not the same as pantheism).

pantheism The idea that God is identical with the material universe.

phenomenology The study of what people actually experience (a theory developed by Husserl).

postmodernism A modern, 'Continental' approach to philosophy and the arts, rejecting the modernist concept of a self-conscious, authentic, creative self in favour of a direct appreciation of symbols and texts in their cultural context (see also **structuralism**).

postulates Those beliefs that are implied by the experience of unconditional moral obligation (as used by Kant).

pragmatism The idea that a theory should be assessed according to its practical use, its implications for other areas of knowledge and its coherence with other beliefs.

rationalism The theory that all knowledge is based on, and shaped by, the process of thinking.

realism The view that scientific theories are capable of giving a direct description of reality.

reductionism The tendency to reduce everything to its component parts; the 'nothing but' view of complex things.

scepticism The view that all beliefs are equally open to critical examination and challenge and that none can claim absolute or permanent truth.

schema A cluster of rational terms by which the 'holy' is understood and described (the process is called 'schematization').

situation ethics The ethical view, as expounded by Joseph Fletcher's *Situation Ethics*, 1966, that the right thing to do is that which is the most loving, and therefore that general moral principles may sometimes be set aside in favour of the needs of particular situations.

solipsism The view that we cannot know other minds directly, but have to infer them from our experience of people's physical bodies, words and actions.

structuralism An approach to philosophy, developed within the 'Continental' school in the second half of the twentieth century, which interprets the meaning of a text, a word or an idea in the context of the structures of thought within which it is found.

syllogism A logical sequence of statements, leading from two premises which have a common term to a conclusion which does not have that term.

teleological Describes a theory or view based on the end or purpose of something, used particularly for the argument for the existence of God based on the idea that the world shows signs of purposeful design.

theism Belief in the existence of God.

utilitarianism The ethical theory that evaluates actions in terms of their predicted results ('the greatest good to the greatest number').

verification Checking the validity of a statement, used especially of logical positivist and other empirical approaches to language.

Index

Credits

Credits